John Wells
'93

GOODBYE TO SOME

GOODBYE

Novels by Gordon Forbes
GOODBYE TO SOME
TOO NEAR THE SUN

TO SOME

A *Novel by* GORDON FORBES

Orion Books/New York

Although it is in part based on historical events and some of its places have familiar names, this book is fiction. There is no attempt to preserve the truth in following the course of the events or their outcomes.

The verses at the beginnings of chapters are taken, with the exceptions of Chapters Eleven and Twelve, from the Japanese military song "*Royei no uta*," or "Bivouac Song," and are literally translated for the sake of their strong contrast.

Copyright © 1961 by Gordon Forbes

Copyright renewed 1989 by Gordon Forbes

Foreword © 1990 by Herbert Mitgang

All rights reserved. No part of this book may be reproduced or transmitted in any form or by any means, electronic or mechanical, including photocopying, recording, or by any information storage and retrieval system, without permission in writing from the publisher.

Published by Orion Books, a division of Crown Publishers, Inc., 201 East 50th Street, New York, New York 10022

Originally published by W. W. Norton and Co. in 1961

ORION and colophon are trademarks of Crown Publishers, Inc.

Manufactured in the United States of America

Library of Congress Cataloging-in-Publication Data

Forbes, Gordon.
    Goodbye to some / Gordon Forbes.
        p.   cm.
    ISBN 0-517-57456-X
    1. World War, 1939–1945—Fiction.   I. Title.
PS3556.0666G6   1990
813'.54—dc20   89-77235
                                                                         CIP

10   9   8   7   6   5   4   3   2   1

First Orion Edition

A few of the people in this story lived and are dead, and this book is dedicated to the memory of one of them,

WILLIAM EMERSON BARTLETT

FORMOSA

PHILIPPINE

LUZON

Lingayen

Manila

Cantanduanes

MINDORO

ISLANDS

SAMAR

LEYTE

Sulu
Sea

MINDINAO

MOROTAI

EQUATOR

(REST
CAMP)
i OWI

CELEBES

NEW
GUINEA

GOODBYE TO SOME

The Scene of Action

♣ The Island   ⊛ Scene of
Ditching

Air Routes
of VPB 400   ⊗ Raids

Scale of Miles

0   100   200   300   400   500   600

Map by Alan McKnight

PERSONNEL

AIR WING

Capt. Rowland Hill — Captain of the Wing
Comdr. John (Swede) Engelson — Executive Officer

VPB 400 (Patrol Bombing Squadron)

Lt. Comdr. Juillerat (Ironhead) Backus — Captain
Lt. Comdr. Kirby Stevens — Executive Officer
Lt. Monty Herbert — ACI Officer
Lt. Fred McCord — Personnel Officer
Lt. (j.g.) Tom Parker — Flight Surgeon

PATROL PLANE COMMANDERS

Lt. Comdr. Frank Ainsworth
Lt. Comdr. Stuart Ashton
Lt. William Emerson Bartlett
Lt. William (Skindome) Dougherty
Lt. Tommy Prime

Lt. (j.g.) Carl Iverson (Ivy)
Lt. (j.g.) Roger Smith (Fatfag)
Lt. (j.g.) Bedford Forrest Tuckerman (Tuck)
Lt. (j.g.) John Yokum (Yoke)

COPILOTS

Lt. (j.g.) Tim Brady
Lt. (j.g.) Bob (Standing Room) Mara
Ens. Jim Arnold
Ens. Nathan Benjamin
Ens. A. R. Beppolini (Beppo)

Ens. Stan Cox
Ens. Jack Excel
Ens. Kenny Flournoy
Ens. Pete Foy
Ens. Art Neely

ENLISTED MEN, COMBAT AIR CREW 13

Andretta, Aviation Radioman, 2nd class
Nick Bondar, Aviation Radioman, 2nd class
Cunningham, Aviation Ordnanceman, 2nd class
Bud Hartstene, Aviation Mechanic's Mate, 2nd class
Whitey Nanos, Seaman, 1st class
Robinson, Aviation Radioman, 1st class
Spurlock, Aviation Mechanic's Mate, 1st class
Zalewski, Aviation Mechanic's Mate, 2nd class

VPB 420 (Patrol Bombing Squadron)

Lt. Comdr. Joe Norton (Captain Ahab) — Captain
Lt. Comdr. Herb Millar — Executive Officer

PATROL PLANE COMMANDERS

Lt. Joe (Gorilla Joe) Donohoe
Lt. Brad Scott

Lt. (j.g.) Lou Tindall

INTRODUCTION

BY HERBERT MITGANG

There is a moment in *Goodbye to Some* when, in the midst of the flying dangers during World War II, a young Navy patrol plane commander suddenly finds his mind wandering to the time when he was a child, walking in the Minnesota woods and listening to his great-grandfather tell him about the dead at Gettysburg. His own war is making him ponder the craziness and casualties of wars in general; he even has developed a grudging admiration for the Japanese pilots firing their tracers at his long-range heavy bomber. For in the months just before the atomic bomb is launched and changes everything, death stalks the skies and seas of the South Pacific. Friend and foe are playing the same game: killing each other with increasing skill, professionally.

And so the young pilot in this novel of aerial combat has reached a point where he is willing to open his heart to the unseen reader, to let it all hang out without holding back. He sounds so different from the gung ho, wild blue yonder boys of black-and-white cinematic memory, yet one has the feeling that he is telling it as it truly was on those bad days in the Furious Forties when not all the planes returned to their jungle base after an unlucky dawn patrol:

"I love the dead more than the living because I feel their fellowship, their staunchness, their valor, even their humor, things they can never again lose by being alive. Great-grandfather had a picture of some of them, men from the Third Minnesota, some of them comrades of his from Freeborn County. They seemed sublimely animated, lying there with their knees up and their faces turned discreetly away from one another. It was as though after a regimental death they were insisting on some final privacy. The old man had been there, and I wished always that he had marched into the mystery and fascination of that picture and I didn't have to see him now with his ruined face, the drain of his memories so plain upon it and listen to his efforts to express himself to a small boy disintegrate into a few feeble gestures and a mumble from an angry old man."

The novel begins calmly, traditionally. We follow the adventures of a Naval air wing, stuck away in an island backwater near a Moro village, scouting and bombing the enemy thousands of miles away. They know the war is winding down; one more kill of a Japanese ship or plane at great personal risk is not going to change the final outcome. As we read of overloaded aircraft, of crews that have to shift their weight to balance the bombs and fuel, the risks seem unnecessary. Although the various officers and enlisted men offer a familiar cross section of the best and worst in any outfit—their minds constantly on sex, drink, promotions, medals, and survival—there is a compelling forward motion in the story. The faces begin to emerge from the group portrait. But, the author tells us in his undisguised realistic novel, the air wing has paid a heavy price for its five hundred Distinguished Flying Crosses: "Of the one hundred and eighty flying members of the squadron who made up the crews when I joined a little over twenty months ago, one hundred and nineteen are dead."

Between missions that range as far away as Borneo in pursuit of Japanese targets, *Goodbye to Some* goes beyond the conventional because the author has something to declare. Without lecturing, sometimes what he has to say comes out bitterly: "War remains war, and warriors warriors, and effective ones have never been attractive types. Jackson was a bigot, Custer a murderous fop hated by his men, Nelson poisoned with conceit, Teddy Roosevelt was so in thrall with his bully-boy mystique he could scarcely wait to shoot a Spaniard with his revolver from the *Maine*—or to say he had. It is from these inversions that they draw the superhuman energies they need for such success."

In the background of the story is the temporary dehumanization of otherwise sane men in combat. Both sides have committed atrocities; kill anything that moves is the order of the day. Suddenly, the next war begins to creep up on the present-day reader as we follow these cumbersome propeller bombers, flying along the Mekong Delta and sighting Saigon. The targets sound eerily familiar. Unwittingly, Vietnam is foreshadowed here. In this respect, the novel offers a prescient look at the future when, replacing the colonial French, America became stuck in the big muddy of an Asian war. By the end, *Goodbye to Some* goes beyond the standard World War II war novel and attains something deeper: the elemental truths of an antiwar novel.

The first thing for a captain is to gain,
Safe victory: the next to be with honor slain.
                                                        —Euripides

CHAPTER ONE

Whenever I hear trumpets sound march,
I feel flags wave behind me.

SPRING is supposed to be the dry time in the Sulu Sea, but on this island almost every afternoon or evening, there is a minute or two of heavy rain that falls from the build-ups over the mountains. When we hear the roar of the rain coming down the slopes and across the trees toward the camp, we run out naked and try to get a wash in the wonderfully soft water. I always set out a bucket or my helmet to catch more of the water where it is shed from the tent, for usually the showers are so short that I am still covered with soap at the end of them. The water runs off the canvas dirty brown at first and smelling of creosote after the day of hot sun, but in a few seconds it turns clear and cold.

The showers settle the dust and douse the reek of urine for a while, but in the morning the smells are back, subtly thickened by more rotting vegetation and mold; the dust is swirling under the wheels of the stake trucks and the drivers on the airfield road have handkerchiefs knotted over their mouths again and look as though they have been dipped in brown flour. More rain would be a nuisance, though. At Leyte it rained so long and so hard our beer-can ash trays floated around inside the tent.

The island is small, only about three miles by road from the ruined Moro village at the south end to the airfield at the north.

The road coils around the base of the mountains and skirts the narrow littered beaches in wide curves, and in the middle of the island it divides a big palm grove. In the grove, sprawled in the usual web of guy wires and laundry lines, are the tents of the two Bombing and Search squadrons which constitute the Air Wing—400 on the cooler water side and 420 on the landward. After the road leaves the camp, going south toward the village, it becomes hopelessly winding and vague, and looks as though it might at any moment run up the trunk of a tree and disappear.

The palm trees go right down to the water, to a tiny beach that is littered with fallen trees. The water is muddy and shallow and unpleasantly warm to swim in because of the reef a quarter mile out which blocks even the gentlest surf, so that the knots of coconuts in the water float in the same places day after day without being disturbed, until they become rotten and sink. Yokum and Smith and I have built a boat of P-38 drop tanks and in it we can go out to swim in the cold deep water beyond the reef. Before that I used to take two sticks and push myself along, floating on my belly and trailing my legs so that I didn't touch any of the starfish that lie piled on one another by the thousands in the shallows.

It is a pleasant camp as camps go, not crowded like Tinian, nor busy and important like Leyte, nor quite as hot as Morotai. There isn't much of the aftermath of invasion, wrecks and debris and bodies and piles of equipment rusting in the open air; nor is there any of the noise, dynamiting caves and flushing Japs out of the woodwork. No one has seen a Jap although John Yokum swears he sat next to one at *Objective Burma* the other night. He says the guy kept saying "Oh sclew you, Error Frynn," which Yoke thinks is a better speech test for Japs than the time honored "lollapalooza."

There was a day here before we came, however. A few hours before the assault the Japs murdered over a hundred American prisoners down at the field. They faked an air raid and got the men to go into some deep pits which were to serve as shelters, and there they drenched them with hundred-octane and burned them alive. Only one man survived. He said that about noon that

day a new Jap major arrived at the field, interrupted the work
and announced that American airplanes were approaching. For
their own good, the major said, the prisoners must take shelter in
the pits, which were, and still are, a series of deep holes and tun-
nels dug into the side of a low cliff. But the survivor said the Japs
seemed suddenly to be taking unusual precautions with them.
They had Nambus all around on the flat ground above and a
heavy machine gun in a cart. The major said they were going to
fire at the airplanes and the Americans didn't pay much attention.
They were whooping like children at the prospect of seeing their
own airplanes again. At the last minute the major came and smiled
down on them like an indulgent parent and the soldiers began a
funny conspiratorial tittering, like small boys who are about to
perpetrate some fantastically funny joke and can't wait for the
relief of open laughter.

They kept the prisoners down in the pits with bayonets while
they squirted gas in on them from a bowser. Then a noncom ran
from hole to hole dropping in bundles of lighted waste. The men
came out, blazing, and ran around until they dropped. The machine guns fired occasionally to herd them away from escape into
the jungle or relief in the sea, and some of the burning men ran
deliberately into the patterns of leaping sand spouts. Afterward
the major walked around firing his pistol into the bundles of
smoking rags that still moved.

The survivor played dead although he had terrible burns and
the major had shot him through the jaw. During the night he
crawled on his hands and knees all the way to the village. He was
a private from West Virginia and the field is named after him.

I suppose the highly sensitized Anglo-Saxon would trip over his
ethics when it came right down to burning people to death like
that, Joan of Arc and the witches of Salem aside. Fortunately for
us there is the airplane and a substance called napalm. The airplane can carry the napalm high above and clear around any
ethic. All you have to be is sophisticated enough to use it. We are,
and we burn people alive every day with it. We just don't do it
so exotically.

When we came, there was a nervous, self-conscious quality about the island because of the massacre. Many people felt they should do something yet there was nothing to do because all the Japs they could find were dead. The natives, all self-styled guerrillas now, with ferocious if ambiguous records behind them, were forever digging them up and dragging them around behind carabaos so that everyone could spit on them. This reaction disgusted us because it seemed even more neurotic than the revanchist Bushido of the Japanese, who at least had been stimulated by the sight of the overwhelming power coming at them over the horizon. But Commander John Engelson, the Air Wing Exec, condoned it and in fact did everything possible to get emotion and verisimilitude into what he called "our new dedication" in his own way. He wrote about "harrying to the death the legless writhing centipede whose poisonous body is at last exposed everywhere," and had posters made showing the centipede and a sailor in helmet and goggles astride it with a spitting blowtorch. The sailor is standing on a tiny green island near the centipede's tail and the island is presumably this one.

It was of course ludicrous to hear Swede Engelson taking on the right to judge and punish. Not merely because he already has enough mortal handicaps, but because, although he is a pilot, he doesn't even fly. His sloganized indignation had very little meaning for us and did not drive anyone I know into anything useless and dangerous.

We are flying about as far and as often as is humanly possible, and have been doing so for eight months. Every third day we go out one of the spokes on the big red wagon wheel the Swede has superimposed on his wall maps, fly from the axle to the rim and along it and back again, twenty-two hundred miles and more—thirteen, fourteen, fifteen hours, with one crew and no relief. Most people never leave their seat, and like the airedale who used to fly with John Honey, when they do get out, piss like a cart horse for as long as two minutes.

It is a life's work to do this eighty, ninety, a hundred times, and reasonably hazardous. We have lost six of our eighteen crews, and

420, in a shorter time, has lost eight. The big majority just disappeared. Perhaps half fell to the enemy. No one knows, because
it isn't just the enemy. They give us our only latitude. After all
they sometimes can be left alone. But there are other things about
which nothing can be done, such as the overload, the siphoning,
the maintenance, and the weather—which in the China Sea is
frequent, tropical, and very often violent—the ocean which is endless, the fatigue which is stunning, the noise, heat, glare, fear.
None of these things can be shown by the colored pins stuck all
over the Swede's Big Game Board. Since the Captain of the Wing,
a debonair alcoholic named Rowland Hill, is never here but always island hopping in his Twin Beech, only a flimsy shadow of
outside authority falls upon Engelson and he does as he pleases,
sending us further and further and pushing airplanes into every
crack and cranny from Singapore to Hainan.

"Thirty-one hundred and fifty gallons," Spurlock says. "Is that
okay, Mr. Ashton?" He squats just outside the circle of stones
ringing the little patch of sand called the "garden" where we are
sprawled in our homemade easy chairs. Spur squats to show us
he is unaffected by traditional relationships inside the United
States Navy, and he stays outside the circle of stones to prove
that he desires no leverage on officers socially. He is the Plane
Captain of Combat Air Crew 13, a big blond boy with hair
sticking straight up from his head like a pompom, and he knows
his job in a way none of the rest of us do.

"Now let's just see now," Ashton says wrinkling his brow.
"Mother's fifty . . . and ten for each kid . . . okay, but have the
crew carry the usual extra gas in their mouths, will you?" Stuart
Ashton is the Patrol Plane Commander and, at twenty-five, the
oldest member of CAC 13. He is forever counting the half-dozen
gray bristles among the black at his temples and telling us how
his reflexes are slowing.

"It's quicker to jettison that way," I say. Spurlock grins slightly
and patiently. There is little new in the way of bandying.

"Well, this will scare you, Mr. Iverson," he says to me. "We got our own airplane back."

I groan feebly. "My God, did you count the engines?"

"No squawks on the yellow sheet after the test hop. I'll bet the tachs still wave and of course it'll still siphon . . . but." Spurlock looks cautiously around. "It won't hardly scare Mr. Brady now, everything working again."

Tim Brady is the other j.g. in the crew beside myself. He hasn't flown for almost a month and before that he made only about a dozen patrols. Brady is afraid. His attempts to avoid flying have become more and more ludicrous and pathetic. For Tom Parker, the Flight Surgeon, they are also very tedious.

Brady is that type of muscular and handsome campus hero who has never had any experience with deficiency in his life before, beyond dropping a football now and then at a crucial moment. In airplanes Brady has run head on into limits with which he can't cope. Of course he can't acknowledge them either. Some coach did his work well. A true football hero can't stand being publicly painted one of the primary colors and Brady is in a real spot.

To make it worse we occasionally see him in the movies—Pete Smith shorts—running powerfully through fields of giants and knocking them down in clusters. There was a feature article about him in the L.A. paper ending on the note that the war would now wind up in a hurry because Tim Brady had his wings and would soon be out there carrying the ball.

Ashton puts his hands behind his neck and looks up through the palm fronds at the dark blue sky. "Well, Mr. Brady just can't quite make it, Spurlock. He's having a nasty little bout of ear fungus, I hear." Ashton slouches lower in his chair. "Ear fungus," he says musingly. "America's number-one killer."

"So who's the unlucky guy this time?" Spurlock says.

"Spur, that is not the spirit that took the old *Guerrière*. While Mr. Brady is temporarily not feeling quite himself, Mr. Tuckerman is only too pleased and honored . . ." Ashton's voice trails off as though he has suddenly fallen asleep. Perhaps he has; he does it in the most unlikely places and at the strangest times.

"Any idea where we're going, Mr. Iverson?" Spurlock says softly to me.

"It's a special," Ashton says, his eyes closed. "We are taking a load of torpex to the palace. In the Navy's new, long-range, four-engine, cruises-at-over-three-hundred, Consolidated patrol bomber. Double flight pay as it's only going to be one way. Iverson will be at the controls as I feel a heavy attack of ear fungus coming on."

"It doesn't make any difference where you are *going,*" says my tentmate Roger Smith coming outside and slumping into a chair. "You don't have to worry with these kiddies. Ivy's wrist watch running slow will turn them around. Or the hot plate will burn out. So wherever it is you are *going,* don't worry about *getting* there." Roger flies with Ironhead Backus, the Captain of 400. He is coeval, friend, brother, if I ever had one. His chair is more elaborate than the others. It has at least seven of the striped Navy pillows tacked to it for padding, a brassiere hung like a hammock under one arm to hold cigarettes, and spoons and fly whisks dangling from little hooks at the back. He spends most of his waking life in the chair, his fat stomach bulging through his unbuttoned shirt like a melon, and the remains of a farmer's straw hat on his head, through which his ginger hair sprouts in all directions. Roger has one of the longest mustaches in the squadron which he tends with soap or shoe polish several times a day.

"As a matter of fact my watch has been gaining. Maybe we shouldn't get out too far," I say. Spurlock still squats there, smiling faintly and trickling sand through his fingers. "Cape St. Jacques," I tell him at last.

"Thank you, *sir!*" Spurlock says with a mock salute.

"Suckin' for brig time, Iverson!" Ashton says. "Boy, you know you can't bandy secret stuff around like that in front of enlisted swine . . . I mean men. Son of a rip, boy! Son of a rip!" Ashton's voice is an exact imitation of Joe Norton's. Norton is the commanding officer of 420. Ashton knows that Spurlock is keeping an elaborate illustrated diary which is absolutely forbidden. The diary is complete with maps showing all the tracks we have flown in colored pencil and on the maps are inked the black bows of ships disappearing in the blue sea to mark our sinkings. There are also three red meatballs, one for the Mavis we got on our first patrol to Formosa, and two for the Vals we shot down thirty seconds apart going around the traffic pattern at Naha. Here and there are little bomb bursts to show where we have beaten up something on the ground, a few blockhouses and radar stations, parked airplanes and trucks, and once in China a whole company of Jap infantry complete with pack horses who seemed to be carrying jars of water. The horses ran around with water jetting out of them and everyone said afterward how they all tried to miss hitting the horses—even Cunningham, our bow gunner, professed to find it disagreeable—and just to shoot the men.

Near Amami, Spurlock has drawn the corvette, not in the least sinking, that killed Nick Bondar, our second radioman, with a forty right in the head. On the way home he swelled up in the heat and we had a hard time getting the harness off of him. In the black square beside the corvette is neatly printed Nick's name and rate and the date of his death, March 22, 1945. The whole thing is very artistic with the red bursts and the black bows half gone in the sea.

Spurlock has made a wonderful model of old 897, our first airplane, and I have painted a naked blonde on her bow for him just the way it was on our ship. The blonde is sliding along on her fanny with nothing on but one black garter, carrying a rose in her hand. The original blonde went up in smoke one night at Morotai, along with 897, when a Sonia sneaked in and caught her with one of those little two-bit bombs they use. Our present airplane, 901, hasn't anything painted on her. Ashton has suggested four white feathers.

Spurlock goes off down to the strip to check on 901 again. Someone may have stolen something off her since he last looked.

Ashton gets wearily up and totters back to his own tent where I know he will sleep the deep sleep of a hibernating bear until three o'clock tomorrow morning when we have to fly. How he does this the day before a patrol is beyond me. He is unaffected by what I call the horror progression, which for me goes something like this.

The night we get home, with our ears ringing from fourteen or fifteen hours of engine noise, is the only time I know no fear. I have my enormous liberty ahead—two whole days—undiminished by even one night's sleep. I sit around, drunk and unwashed, and stall about everything. About taking a shower, about eating, about doing any of the things that start the progression again. I feel as if I have been in a race or a game that has been demanding without being at all fun for the players, and now it is over and I am simply relieved without being happy or satisfied. Sometimes at this point I am wistful, if we have killed anyone. Sometimes I see myself down there, scorched with burning oil, clinging to a plank with fifty-caliber ammo making water spouts all around. We have sunk sixteen ships, most of them plodding little hulks of the Sugar Dog category, and always all the people go with them, and always we see some of them go, for we bomb at a very low level. Fifteen feet.

With the shower it starts again. Alone in the darkness with the duckboards hard and slippery under my feet and the trickling water still warm from the sun, there is the bedrock beginning. Under the boards is a wad of white mush from all the soap that has skitted away from bathers and been lost in the dark. It blocks the drain and soapy water rises around your feet and makes thick mud all around, yet it is surprising how patient and good-humored I am this first night home with the soapy mud and the puny trickle, and how irritated I become and how unwholesome seems the mud, two nights later. After the first shower I feel tough, resourceful, full of fight. After the last sticky-footed, tepid aggravation I am a wreck.

The next morning, in the sincerity of daylight, I see things far less ardently. Every trace of confidence is gone. Anxiety begins its tiresome nagging. As time goes by I begin to feel smaller, my muscles actually seem weaker. The carbine and the Aussie machete and the things hanging on belts and nails around the tent assume shapes of mild repugnance and dread. Imperceptibly I begin to strain. The old piano tuner has arrived and has started tightening strings. For another day and night time pads the vibrations, but by evening on the last day I have trembling antennae out in all directions. I have one frantic eye on the weather, the other on the latest ACI news. I begin to sniff out the sector because it makes a great deal of difference whether we go to a hot one such as Singapore, or to a cool or cold one out over a thousand miles of sea. When I know the sector is hot, I spend the night calculating the definite and certain risks we must run, and the likelihood of further indefinite and uncertain ones. Sometimes I react physically. The second time I went to Iwo my stomach knotted so painfully I couldn't walk erect. Jericho, the corpsman, gave me a bottle of paregoric and the way it works is a miracle. When I have the beginnings of the knot I sip the paregoric. Almost as it goes down I can straighten up. To think I was once afraid I wouldn't be allowed to fly because I had a congenital deformity in my stomach, a muscle that had spasms or something and tightened around my pylorus! I, who am in serious, though silent contention with Tim Brady for the honor of being CAC 13's leading coward!

So at last, in the closing night hours, there is simply fear in me, glandular, monotonous, tiring. I guess it is congenital too.

CHAPTER TWO

So long as I'd given my word
That I should return a hero,
I would never die ere I win fame.

IN VPB 400 the airplanes are Liberators, whose Navy designator is PB4Y-1, known as 4-Y's, B-24's, Libs, and occasionally as Flying Whales. In 420 they fly the newer and faster, now that we don't need them, more heavily armed Privateer or PB4Y-2. The commanding officers of both squadrons are trade school two-and-a-half stripers who for one reason or another have acquired Navy designators too. The captain of 400, Juillerat Backus, is known privately as Ironhead, while Joe Norton of 420 is referred to quite openly, and sometimes even by himself in the third person, as Captain Ahab. "Cap Ahab is gonna get himself a big old Fox Tare Charlie today," Norton will say in a paternal way to his officers. Since he already has about twenty-five ships, they can believe him. He is the wheel horse of his squadron and if he keeps it up and stays alive will probably catch our Tommy Prime and Skindome Dougherty, who at present are neck and neck in the mid-thirties.

Last month all told the Air Wing flew 235 patrols, not counting specials or strikes, out of 239 scheduled. There were 917 ship sightings and 90 aircraft encountered. Out of these, 90 ships were sunk and 10 aircraft shot down. The shipping was estimated at 20,215 tons. In addition 3 locomotives, 22 railroad cars, a sawmill, a shipyard, a bus, seven trucks, two roundhouses, and as-

sorted bridges, buildings and what not were demolished. Four
raftloads of Jap soldiers seeking to escape from the tiny islands
to the south of here were shot to death or drowned.

VPB 400 is old and has been around. England, North Africa,
Tinian, Leyte, Morotai, Mindoro, Lingayen. The Stone-agers of
the squadron have been out almost continuously since the spring
of forty-three and are long overdue to be replaced. Skindome
Dougherty has flown well over a hundred patrols and the others
aren't far behind him. Tommy Prime flew Blenheims in night raids
for the RAF before he came to us. Stuart Ashton and Bill Bartlett
were in the same PBY squadron and flew out of Trinidad, British
Guiana, Newfoundland, and Iceland all during 1942. They have
been partners in a bridge game that has gone on continuously
for three and a half years. In Blooey West One on Greenland they
played for eleven days without stopping and won eighteen hundred dollars from Bullet Bill Snyder and Jerry Glenotre. Bullet
Bill was shot down in the Bay of Biscay and Glenotre went in
off the east coast of Luzon still owing eleven hundred. Ashton
is famous for finding and shadowing seven *Narvik*-class German
cans in the Bay although under JU-88 attack for two hours. He is
the only Patrol Plane Commander ever to shoot down a German
in our squadron. Bill Bartlett ditched off the coast of Spain near
Coruña, was picked up by a fishing boat, wined and dined by
the Spaniards from Madrid to San Sebastian, and returned home
in six weeks to England. Frank Ainsworth sank a U-boat. He
lodged a depth charge on the deck grating. When the boat submerged it obligingly carried the charge with it to the necessary
seventeen feet and blew itself up. Frank was written up in
Collier's and was graciously given the Air Medal by the grateful
Navy Department. He and Ashton made loot comm on last
October's allnav and should have been out of the squadron
months ago. We have four two-and-a-half stripers where there
should be two at the most.

But times have changed and it's no good talking about the old
days around the new B-24 types. The killers have taken over and
to talk about the Bay of Biscay and one's adventures there is
about as futile as an old movie star recounting triumphs from her

silent picture days. Buzz Miller and Company has shown what
the B-24 can be made to do if you can find someone to do it.
They have tackled everything up to battleships, and he at least
has sunk as much tonnage as many submariners. He got the
Congressional, which he well earned, and has set the style for
Cap Ahab and Prime and Dougherty and our local boys.

When we came home from North Africa in the summer, the
senior half of the squadron, both Plane Commanders and their
copilots, were relieved. We had lost three crews. Ten were held
in the squadron and eight new ones added as we passed through
the operational syllabus at Camp Kearney. We were on Tinian in
October. Now besides Glenotre, we have lost John Honey and
Al Swansek of the old hands, and three of the new crews have
gone with them. Only three replacements have come out in eight
months and we are down to fifteen crews. This imbalance has
made the elders who are left terribly watchful of their rights,
and they see to it that no one classed as *new* gets anything—not
so much as an extra can of warm beer—ahead of anyone classed
as *old*.

The trouble is that in the middle, between new and old,
half feathers and half fins, are my tentmates and myself. Roger
Smith, John Yokum, Forrest Tuckerman and I are unique, the
first and the last of our species. We went to England as replacements. Until we arrived in Dunkeswell we had never seen the
inside of a B-24 and they had to train us on the job. Now we are
all Patrol Plane Commanders too, but since there are no crews
for us we still fly most of the time as copilots, either with our old
crews, or at the mercy of Kirby Stevens, the squadron exec, on
what are called washer biters. These are trips with Prime or with
Dougherty and they are called that because of the behavior of
your behind on most of them. It is constantly biting washers out
of the seat cushion.

Prime and Dougherty for one reason or another are often in
need of copilots and third pilots. There are only two members
of Prime's original crew still flying with him. Death or wounds
took four, and four simply quit. Dougherty lost two men when

he stayed too low and too long at Iwo, and he has had a few other Purple Hearts and Reluctant Hearts along the road too. I have flown twice with Dougherty but never with Prime, and I brown-nose Kirby Stevens to keep this record intact. Occasionally I get a patrol of my own with a scratch crew.

Since Kirby has turned regular Navy he is much harder to deal with. Like all of his kind he is constantly listening for the rustle of fitness reports and he would schedule his mother to the moon on a rocket if it got him anywhere. Kirby Stevens is the high-school boy everyone knows who could never do anything well, not as an athlete, not as a scholar, the boy who would have remained unobstrusive for the rest of his life if he hadn't discovered this flying thing. There are a lot of him around; they all have the same single asset and they let it work for them where nothing else they have will. Their health. Or rather more correctly the physical make-up which lets them fly. They can make it where someone who has lost his teeth or torn a cartilage playing football cannot. They can make it where many superior people are stopped by something outside themselves.

The single case of Kirby Stevens is enough to debunk the popular conception that only the cream can fly, and once he is in, a man like Kirby is never threatened with anything like excellence again. It is simply a case of staying in a race where the honor is in being allowed to run. Let the Nortons and the Primes risk their necks and pile up the score, Kirby rides along doing the minimum. It is after all no disgrace to say disparagingly about yourself, "God, I wish I had Prime's guts! I got halfway in that harbor and all hell broke loose and my panel suddenly flashed yellow lights all across . . ." Such a statement does not reveal to the unknowing that Kirby was probably a half mile from where all hell was breaking loose, and that he stayed there, and that halfway into that harbor was no way in at all. It is hazy out here, but when he goes home it can become downright obscure. After the war the Navy will get rid of him and he will settle down in some small town to become a respected voice at Reserve meetings and a marching figure on Armistice Day. The local newspaper will mark his anniversaries with capsules of his war record. "Alderman Stevens is prominent among the ex-servicemen in this area. During the war he was executive officer of a Naval bombing squadron and served with such distinction that he contemplated for a time making the Navy his career. He rose to the rank of Lieutenant Commander. On one occasion while flying near Okinawa, he . . ."

On one occasion while flying off the coast of Portugal, Kirby spent twenty minutes taking evasive action against a star. He went round and round, jinking and turning, convinced that what he saw was the exhaust of a JU-88. The kidding was abnormally intense. "Sirius attacks Naval war plane." "Cosmic intervention announced by pilot." Kirby is famous too for the transpacific itinerary he planned for us while he was still navigation officer, in which he included Wake Island as a refueling stop. He hadn't forgotten that the Japs held it; he had never known.

Kirby has a way of telling us bad news with a special look of tragic purpose on his horsy face that says it is out of his hands, fellahs, and if you don't believe it ask McCord who gave the order. Fred McCord is the personnel officer and there is no need to ask him anything.

They say that Ironhead Backus's career was at stake when he took over 400 and there are two legends about him, both of the kind perpetuated by the Naval community. One is rooted in grievance and the other in degradation, two subsoils that nourish legends.

The first holds that he took off in a TBD with the wings folded, ran off the mat and flipped over in mud and that thereupon Ironhead's life was saved at the expense of the enlisted man riding in the back because there was only one respirator and the e.m. died waiting for officer quality to finish using it.

The second has variations, the most popular of which is that Ironhead's wife once gave him a brand of clap, that she had contracted from a Filipino mess boy, that is incurable. It is an

Asiatic variety that will not yield to the most painful and bizarre
treatments of the B Ward.

Ironhead did have a terrible accident. He spun a TBD in taking
off and landed in mud on his back. He spent more than an hour
with his smashed face jammed up between his knees, and his
nose about an inch above the level of the mud before they got
him out. He could feel the rescuers' weight pushing the airplane
deeper and his little air pocket getting smaller and he nearly
drowned in the blood running into his nose. The man in the rear
was stone dead and there was no question of respirators or par-
tiality or anything saving or not saving him. Ironhead is a big
man with gray hair—said to stem from this crash—who must have
once been extraordinarily handsome. Now he is battered and
scarred and there are ridges of white around his eyes and across
his brows and running up into his hair that give him a vague
Oriental look. He has a plate in his head, and in lower circles
it is stoutly maintained that he is compelled to carry on his person
at all times a paper from the head knee-tapper at St. Elizabeth's,
solemnly notarized to the effect that he is considered temporarily
sane.

Stuart Ashton says Ironhead's wife Eileen could have given
him anything. He knew her because he was down there at Pensacola in those lazy pre-Adamic days when everyone worked only
half a day and sprawled around on Mustin Beach all weekend.
Ironhead was an officer student, newly married to the widow of
another officer student killed in a crash, who in her grief had made
herself notorious. She didn't stop with her remarriage. Ashton
says that one day Ironhead found a copy of the year's *Flight
Jacket* hidden somewhere in his house and that pictures of cadets,
many of whom he had seen at his table Saturday nights, were
circled in green ink. In the margins were dates. There were apparently a great many of the pictures compulsively circled that
way and the thing was a sort of stud book she kept.

A man with a nympho wife must be unlike a man with any
other handicap. After all if you go blind or get cancer, your
men friends will probably rally round, but if you have a wife like

that nobody will comfort you. They simply lay your wife instead. I always wonder if Ironhead keeps that book with him, waiting for the day when one of the circled pictures, Ashton perhaps, will run athwart him in the course of Navy life. Of course there is a special zest about the cuckolding of rank. The colonel who wears horns for the private is the same thing as the earl who wears them for his gardener, or the white man who wears them for a man of any other color.

If his career was at stake when he took 400, quite palpably Ironhead has missed saving it all around. Perhaps he had a chance in Europe where encounters with the enemy were rare enough to be noticed, but he never had the luck of Ashton finding seven *Narvik*-class cans or bagging a JU-88, or of Ainsworth depositing the depth charge on the sub so that it went up like a man holding a grenade to his chest. They got the publicity and the medals that Ironhead needed so badly. Out here things like that go unnoticed. Ironhead has over twenty ships but that isn't enough. Thirty marks the killer level, the single-minded myrmidons who slip into the very dangerous places, like weasels into a hen house, and bag ships three and four at a time. Tommy Prime sank eleven, including Sugar Ables and Fox Tare Charlies, out of a convoy inside Formosa with two fighters making runs on him the whole time. But Ironhead hasn't the temperament although he has the nerve. You have to be born a Badman. Ashton calls Prime a Doc Holliday with a sawed-off Liberator up his sleeve and it's a good metaphor.

Ironhead has tried. He has hoped continually to get back into carrier aviation where reputations are made more easily, but he has, it seems, invariably wound up in slack water. Corry Field instead of some job on a big carrier, a tender instead of a squadron of Helldivers. He can't scheme, or be extroverted, and probably his looks are against him. With his face he must lead like a Nelson, or remain merely grotesque.

I have heard him say that he acquired his drawbacks with his eyes open, and while he undoubtedly also meant his wife which he didn't mention, he did remark that it was significant that his

friends were now missing on one allnav after another. Ironhead
has been passed over once and it seems inevitable he will be
passed over again. But he is less downcast over his career, less
ashamed of his private life, and not self-conscious about his looks
any more, and if there is a better liked captain anywhere he must
own a brewery. We like him because he wants to get us all home
if he can, because he is amiable and fair, and takes no short cuts
to popularity. We like him because he knows the working rules
of the game and never encourages their violation, and because he
writes bitter and antithetical letters to the Fleet, to the Frontier,
and to the Bureau, about the lack of relief crews, the lack of
awards, the lack of Australian leaves, the lack of new airplanes,
while Joe Norton writes captions for the photos he has taken of
himself with every hero of the day, pictures showing him pointing
at a new meatball being painted on someone's airplane, or with
his head stuck into a spectacular flak hole. Not that the letters
help, but it proves that Ironhead leads from his conscience and
not with his eye on the bubble reputation. He needs a Navy Cross
and another half stripe—and a new wife and face—but he isn't
going to gamble our necks for his redemption, and probably not
even his own any more. As Ashton says, he would have to go in
on a *Mogami*-class alone, sink it in front of thirty Green Bowlers,
and report to Admiral King and Harry Truman on the White
House steps with the captain's cocked hat. The only other way is
to be "seen and photographed with Hollywood stars."

There are a lot of other reasons to like Ironhead Backus, even
for those who don't sympathize with him. He stands humanely
between us and Swede Engelson and deflects what he can of the
Swede's madness from us. He checks the nuisance value of officers
like Fred McCord and Kirby Stevens and Monty Herbert, our
Air Combat Intelligence officer. He has never stolen an opportunity or usurped a credit the way Norton has. Norton waits until
he hears about a convoy someplace and then flies every day to
it until he has finished it off. But not Ironhead. He goes out in
rotation like everyone else from captain to cabin boy.

I have always had the feeling that someone has deliberately

left Ironhead behind, that he is serving an interest that would be in jeopardy if he advanced. I don't know if this is true, I simply feel it. He is being sacrificed. Like Roland and his horn.

Ironhead still blows, but the echoes of *his* horn are getting mighty faint back at the Bureau.

I have to go to the dispensary because of an infection in the fingers of one hand. I had a scuffle with a fish and he pinked me with his spines and the result is what Tom Parker calls an erysipeloid infection. One finger looks like a bread stick and may have to be cut open. In the meantime I am supposed to soak them all in hot water. Roger Smith decides to walk along with me and we go by way of the well to watch Beppo at work.

The well is an old grievance between the squadrons. It has the only pleasant-tasting water on the island and used to lie in the center of camp. When we heard that 420 was arriving we quickly moved all our tents to the ocean side of the road, occupying every good location and all the sites where the breeze blows. We had to leave the well behind and 420, knowing what we had done, took it over and promptly put up a sign that said the water from the well was reserved for them. The well now lay in the middle of their camp. We kept helping ourselves to it until at last a j.g. named Lou Tindall, who is big and wears Natal boots and a belt with a steerhead buckle, came over and told us he would personally knock the God out of the next mother that dipped in the well.

Beppo Beppolini, who is small, an ensign, and seldom wears anything other than carpet slippers and a towel, grabbed a bucket. Tindall knocked the God out of him. That night the well got the first treatment for "purity." Dye marker, cigarette butts, garbage, and soap. Since then we have all had a hand in treating the well and last night Beppo was caught in the act. Beppo denies it but his face is cut and his lips puffed and it looks as though he was nabbed *flagrante delicto* all right. Ironhead gave him the job of bailing the well out by hand.

"Say," Roger says as we arrive at the well. "Here's a cute little pond to pee in. Let's do number onesy right in here."

Beppo is sitting with his feet in the bottom of the well which is nearly dry, smoking a cigarette and talking to John Yokum, another tentmate of Roger's and mine. We peer in over the edge. Water is seeping slowly back into the hole. It has obviously been a labor of Hercules to bail the well out this dry and Beppo has been at since early morning.

Yokum spits. "It checked out at just over ten million units of cholera to the cubic millimeter. That's roughly the same as a septic tank accommodating a family of seventeen."

"Next time I'll take a general," Beppo says. "I ain't ever bailing this mother out again, I'll clue you."

"Tell us the truth, Beppo. Did you really slant in the well?"

"Hell no! But I'm going to now. Every goddam night."

I wander on alone and there sure enough in the dispensary tent is Tim Brady. He has a syringe and a kidney-shaped dish and he is flushing out his ears with some solution or other. Brady's efforts to portray suffering are famous and part of the daily picture to Parker and Jericho, but I have not seen the act and watch fascinated as I soak my fingers. First there is the premonitory grimace of pain as the nozzle of the syringe touches the ear, then a mighty quiver with each squilch, followed by a violent shaking of the head to clear "the dizziness." Squirting warm water in his ear, Brady looks like he is passing a kidney stone.

Brady has gone through an entire cycle of feigned afflictions since he came to the Pacific, and Tom Parker has met him, parry and thrust, from sinus to ptomaine, patiently and systematically routing each invisible deceit. Brady has retreated slowly, now into the inner ear, a dangerous blind alley where Parker will catch him quickly. There isn't much left after this. Brady will have to fly or quit. He must know he can't beat the game on trumped-up medical grounds. Anyone can quit in this squadron. There are none of the proverbial clichés about being a yellow son of a bitch and no "stinging slaps across the face" kind of nonsense. All you have to do is admit that you are too afraid to take your

place in an airplane. All you have to do is get along with the idea
that someone else will have to take it for you. You can't leave
and the island is only a couple of miles long. You can quit but
you can't hide.

After Parker has looked at my fingers he pulls up a chair to
Brady's suffering side. "Let's have a look," Parker says adjusting
the funnel on an otoscope. Brady puts up one hand as though to
ward off the instrument, holds it there protectingly.

"It looks fine," Parker says after a short inspection. In his tone
there is no room for doubt.

"It feels dull," Brady says. "That's the one they did the para-
centesis on in Norfolk."

"I know. The scar has healed nicely." Parker is unmoved by
Brady's fund of professional terms. "Let's see the other one."
Brady stares at the floor like a doomed man. "Clean as a whistle."
Parker drops the funnel in a basin of methyl prope with a final
air. "Put you back on the schedule. When does your crew fly?"
He gets out a small pad.

Brady stares at the pad. Parker looks over his head and smiles
faintly at me. "I don't know," Brady says in a puzzled voice. "I'd
have to figure it out."

"We're up tonight," I say.

"Yea, but I heard Kirby say he wanted that new guy to go out
with you. He said he wanted him to have a famil hop in a fairly
live sector."

"Arnold? He's assigned to Prime, poor guy. I saw it on the pain
sheet. That'll be lively enough." Brady is being absurd.

"Maybe *you* could go out with Tommy Prime," Parker says.
Prime is a madman. No one goes with him willingly. Brady makes
a flapping motion with one hand. He pretends he hasn't heard
Parker. "Oh, well, in that case, fine, I'll stick with the crew. I just
didn't want to screw things up, that's all."

The preposterous suggestion that returning Brady to duty will
disrupt anything provokes only a sort of low-grade amazement
these days. But Parker has got him quickly back on sides with
the Prime threat. Neely, who is Prime's third copilot, was hurt

last week when a forty burst in the waist where he was taking pictures. The first was killed, the second quit.

"Okay, put me back on for tomorrow," Brady says. "We won't have to shake up the pain sheet." Parker nods and writes on the pad. It means nothing. By midnight Brady can work up cancer.

"One doc told me I had naturally weak tympani," Brady says putting on his shirt. "Tympanitis."

"Tympanitis is a distention of the abdomen caused by air in the intestines," Parker says.

"Well, I meant the eardrums. He said I should have gone into something else. Subs, maybe." He gazes down halfheartedly at his shirt tails. "I never should have eaten that spun-in pelican at noon chow." He shakes his head and smiles at me. The food is common suffering. Perhaps he isn't laying a foundation for any further malingering.

"It was pretty bad," I say.

When Glenotre and Segrave were killed up at Catanduanes the week we first came to Leyte, Brady threw a fit. He decided that Segrave had been his best friend and that Ironhead Backus had served him up to the ambition of the Wing. He cursed the Captain and God and rolled on the ground stuffing dirt in his mouth. He looked very good flinging sedatives into the jungle and wound up the performance by punching Jericho on the jaw. It was strange no one had noticed such a warm bond between Brady and Segrave, and it was significant that when Brady really began to rave, it was about himself, and not the dead. No one was going to sacrifice *him*. *He* wasn't going to be the next sucker. It got him six days rest at Owi. Since Segrave *was* my best friend, and Ironhead never offered up a fly to anyone in his life, Brady didn't convince me and I told him so. He doesn't like me and he told *me* so. I am really sorry because he is a likable guy and we were good friends.

Brady leaves expressing the hope that he won't wake up again tonight with his fingers digging in his ears like claws, and Parker and I go over to Kirby Steven's tent where the daily can of beer is doled out at five o'clock. With Stevens, sitting in their new canvas chairs that they have been given by the Wing, are the Captain and Monty Herbert.

Kirby reaches in a carton beside his chair, hands each of us a can and the opener and checks our names in a book. Today he doesn't make an effort, thank God. Usually he leads us through his absurd ritual—English salutes, swiping up of mustaches, and very bad Royal Navy dialogue, done in one of the worst imitations I have ever heard. " 'Ere naow, fice the ensine and drink yer bleedin' tot, the King, Gor bless 'im," and so on. Kirby still has a hangover from our ten months in England, where he first became impressed with his ability to reproduce the local sounds.

We sit down on two ammo boxes. The beer isn't cold enough but it tastes all right. Anyway, I am not one of the ones who pay violent obeisance to things like beer, who grunt with pleasure, and groan with satisfaction at each sip.

"What have you been doing, Tom?" Ironhead asks Parker wearily.

"Looking in Brady's ears, Captain."

"How are Brady's ears?"

"He can hear about as well as the rest of us."

"How about it, Captain?" Kirby says in his Regular Navy voice. He's dying to put Brady in with Prime to make him take "a brace," as Kirby calls it. Ironhead looks at Tom Parker.

"He's okay, of course," Parker says. "He isn't exactly raring to go. He thinks he's flying tonight, as a matter of fact. But you better get him soon. He's home studying. He came up with McBurney's point the other day. This boy is no amateur."

"What's that, a place on Long Island?" Monty Herbert says.

"A place where you find tenderness in appendicitis . . . just below the right anterior iliac spine, if you ever get in an argument with Brady. I hope to God he never discovers the Brady series. He'll be set for a year. Bradycardia, Bradypepsia, Bradydiastole . . . He'll be able to pass the exam for California when he gets home."

"Inlays . . . and circumcisions," Ironhead says. "California is famous for them. Every dentist in the Navy marvels at my California inlays, and when I turn my head and cough there are always admiring glances."

"I say don't let him dick off any longer," Kirby says persistently. "Pretty soon his relief will come and he'll go home a big hero . . . with about ten patrols in his book."

"You have to take it easy with people like Tim," Ironhead says gently. "I don't want to humiliate him. We'll have another scene like we had in Dunkeswell with Samson . . . throwing his wings at me and calling me a son of a bitch just because he couldn't think of any other way to quit. Tim has had one attack of that."

"Just the same, it isn't fair to the other guys," Stevens says doggedly. "What do you say, Ivy? You know him better than we do."

I shrug. "I think he ought to fly or quit. The whole crew laugh about him. I get kind of sick of the joke."

"He's very frightened," Ironhead says.

"Captain, we all are!"

"All right. Try it. Schedule him with Prime. But let him know. No last-minute stuff."

"Don't worry! I'll let him know. Tell Tuck he's to go with you tonight," Kirby says to me.

"He's counting on it anyway."

Bill Bartlett and Stan Cox come for their beer, both wearing the greasiest flying suits in the squadron. They say the grease comes from Standing Room Mara, the third officer in their crew, who has never been known to bathe. Bartlett clutches his throat and whispers hoarsely to Kirby, "Beer, for the love of heaven! Oh, the sights we've seen!" Kirby scrabbles in the carton, clutching cans and dropping them again.

" 'Ere you be, guv'nor."

"What did you see?" Monty Herbert says. He is always interested.

"You can scratch the Mogami," Bartlett says, gasping after a long swig. It is fun to watch Kirby worry and to see his face sag with relief when Bartlett finally stops kidding and admits the flight was negative. Kirby has one of the worst records in the squadron and he is nervous now because of the rumor that crews tied in seniority will be replaced on the basis of their records in numbers and tonnage of ships sunk.

I have finished the beer and am bored with the conversation, but there is no place to go. We sit there like coffee planters thrown together in the wilderness and talk about the same old things. Airplanes. Replacements. The movies that are coming.

"What is it tonight?"

"A thriller of some kind, I think."

"Like *Stowage of Fire Fighting Equipment to Conserve Hangar Space?*"

"The Bureau of Ordance's fine company of players presents the epic story of the development of the mark four maud three, twelve-pound, water-filled . . ."

I go to look for Tuckerman. Tuck was once in the Captain's crew, along with Roger Smith, but he seldom flies copilot any more. He has no crew but usually takes patrols of his own with a scratch crew. Roger and Yokum and I are in the same boat although Roger and I don't get as many hops as Tuck and Yokum. I have flown only four patrols and sunk two Sugar Dogs of my own. Tuck has done far better. His first time out alone he shot down a Topsy, the Jap DC-3, and the Jap radio declared him a murderer. The Topsy was full of nuns, they said, being evacuated from Malaya, and they referred to the "murder of the peaceful sisters." In the kidding the peaceful sisters became, by stages, crippled, blind, and pregnant. Tuck's full name is Bedford Forrest Tuckerman and he comes from Waycross, Georgia. He is one of those shy smiling southerners and I'm sure he was lost until he found airplanes.

Evening chow looks particularly bad and after one whiff I tell Tuck I'll see him at breakfast. I go home and get out the Coleman and cook flight ration bacon and cocoa. I also write a short and indignant letter to my wife, Corinne, because I haven't heard from her in eleven days. Then I lay out everything so I can dress easily in the dark. I hang my long wool socks and flying suit on the barrel of my carbine and pile the canteen belt, pistol, sur-

vival kits, earphones, life jacket, chute harness, and so on beside
my bed. Last of all I slip on my dog tags and get into the rickety
cot. Under the net it is unbearably hot, but since I don't take
atabrine, I'm afraid not to use the net.

The night begins. I can't sleep but I lie there with my eyes
closed and try to perform the relaxing rituals which they teach
in pre-flight now. You are supposed to think of your muscles and
parts one by one and put them to sleep progressively, starting
with your toes. I have trouble with my chest. I am too aware of
my breast bone when I breathe.

A late patrol comes in, the people laughing and talking, feeling
their enormous liberty. A bit later there is a burst of conversation
in the road. An obscene voice and against it the counterpoint of
a serious and clean, though obviously insincere one. Beppo talking
about his girl to Yokum on the way home from the picture. Beppo
likes to insist that his girl is faithful to him, at the same time
accentuating the fact that she is a real love goddess and wild
for "it" at practically any hour of the day or night. Yokum being
Yokum makes it a point to get Beppo alone once a week and drive
him crazy. "I've been thinking," Yoke says, stopping outside. "Now
let's be fair, Beppo. I don't think for a minute that you have
too much woman there for you, but after all, ten months even
for a woman who isn't much woman . . . let alone for a girl like
that . . ." Beppo curses, with mother prefixes, the girl, the war,
and his luck, and says in his bereaved way that everything is
just shit.

When Tuck comes in he goes to bed silently, trying not to wake
me up, but when Yoke and Roger arrive they talk aloud interminably. They argue about how many corks each has coming for
certain violations of their private rules, like wearing Yoke's
shower clogs, stealing cigarettes from Roger's brassiere, farting,
and so on. When Yokum is finally in bed and safely under the net,
Roger lets a giant one and is promised extreme punishment in the
morning. In five minutes they are snoring.

"Three o'clock," somebody whispers close to my ear. It is
Passage, one of the yeomen. He has his fingers over the lens of

a flashlight and they glow a ghostly shrimp pink in the dark. I hear
the rustle of a slicker.

"Is it raining?"

"It was . . . some . . . not hard." The beam drops to the floor
and goes toward Tuck's corner. I can hear Tuck's polite acknowledgment and the prompt squeak of the dowls as he pulls them
from the pinholes and takes down his netting. I lie and wait until
Tuck is dressed and gone. Three in the morning is the most
hateful time of the clock. I have a theory that when you begin
to sleep at night you begin to die and that you only recover
when your body senses daylight again. And just in time. That's
why you feel sick and your eyes oscillate and your body tingles
and your mouth is foul when they wake you before daylight.
You are dying and have been interrupted in the middle of it.

After a few minutes I stretch. I feel cold for the first time all
night. Then I kick down my mosquito rig and get up. I refuse to
worry about the rain although I used to. I used to jump up and
dash outside half a dozen times a night. I always asked the duty
yeoman what was on the metro chart he had just posted. But
Passage was sure to tell me about some typhoon or cold front
that was a thousand miles from the island and couldn't possibly
affect us, and Barker, the other yeoman and enemy of all officers,
would give me his poisoned version of the weather which you
could be sure was fifty per cent lies. The truth is there is always
something going on in the China Sea and you are always certain
to encounter it sooner or later and since you have to go anyway,
go in ignorance, brother. If it be now it is not to come.

I dress in the sequence I have arranged on the barrel of the
carbine. I am especially careful to brush all the dirt and sand
from the soles of my thick wool socks before I put on my shoes.
The socks are from my old man and so is the advice to take care
of my feet. My father was in the infantry in the first war and I'm
sure never fought a lick, but is full of clichés from the time when
Kaiser Bill went up the hill and Mademoiselle parlez-voused. Take
care of your feet and they'll take care of you, sort of things.

I pick up my gear and tiptoe out and head for the only light in the darkness, the single bulb at the door of the mess shack. There is a smell of Lysol and grease and cooking long before I get there. Outside the door three caldrons are bubbling like witches' vats. In them the enlisted men wash their mess trays, beginning in one where a scum of dirty white froth dances eternally on the surface, and ending in a third where the water is reasonably clean.

Inside the shack a single sleepy cook is beating some viscous looking batter in a bowl. Tuck is sitting alone at a table with a gallon can of bitter grapefruit juice and a white mug. No one else has arrived. I slump down on a bench at Tuck's table and light the first cigarette. Outside the gasoline generator hums.

CAC 13 arrive. They drop their gear by the door and wander around waving their arms and yawning. We are the only crew taking off at this time; most of the routine patrols go out between one and two.

Cunningham, our bow gunner and ordnanceman, takes the trouble to put his finger to his lip and give me a Hitler salute. He is a suck ass and has already gotten two bottles of whisky out of me with one touching little gesture or another. For a friend whose wife just lost her mother or some damn thing. By the time you pin point Cunningham's validity on anything, it is too late, he has the whisky.

We fetch trays and hold them out to the cook who forks enormous hot cakes on to them. There is a running barrage of abuse directed against the hot cakes. Andretta, a radioman second, pretends to try to lift one of the hot cakes on a fork and is borne down on his knees.

"You have to roll 'em to the table," Zalewski says. "Like you was handlin' manhole covers."

"When it's smokin' it's cookin', when it's burned it's done," Andretta says. "From the Mess Cook's Handbook."

"Keep tryin'," the cook says wearily. "Pot holders, saddle blankets, stove lids, manhole covers . . . keep tryin'."

"Listen, cookie, I wrote a song for you. It's called 'I found a stool in the pastafazool.' "

"The Dead End Kids," the cook says disparagingly. "And I know which end is dead. Right here." He taps his head with the big fork.

Andretta grabs his crotch in both hands and shakes it obscenely. "This end ain't dead, mate. Here's ten pounds of swingin' free lunch for some lucky mess cook."

The cook points the fork sternly. "Cut that out. They'll grow together on you."

"He'd die happy," Cunningham says. Robinson, the new radioman who took Nick Bondar's place, looks appalled. He is a skinny, little nonentity I scarcely ever notice.

I try to eat the hot cakes with the watery syrup and the chewy tropical butter on them, but suddenly between one bite and the next there is an abrupt, almost chemical, change in the taste. The piece of hot cake becomes an oily sponge in my mouth.

There is nothing else to eat except some cold toast. It lies in rows on a huge tin tray and there are dark, target-shaped rings on each piece where the toast has soaked up water or steam. Whitey Nanos, the tail gunner, has several pieces of it strung on a fork. He spins the toast on the fork and flies the fork around like an airplane. "Fresh last November," he says, dumping the sodden toast on the table in front of Spurlock, the only one seriously eating.

I drink some of the metallic-tasting coffee, smoke, and reminisce about England and North Africa with Tuck. The theme is always the same. "Only two eggs and crisp bacon," I say. "It was rough when I got there."

"And all those lousy cement runways and lousy radar beacons."

"And that funny thing . . . what did they call it? Maintenance."

In North Africa we flew every fifth day and the hops were never more than ten hours. The maintenance was good, the runways were paved and miles long. Down in Mehdia on beach we had a villa where we "rested up," with jeeps galore, plenty of colonial daughters of France, plenty of good whisky from Gibraltar. The battle of the Wadi Sbu.

Then they weaned us. In the Pacific Fleet there are no toys

for the kiddies. Ours is the only squadron to serve in both theaters and we have never recovered from the shock of the transition from one to the other.

"I wonder what that cig-mooching little Russian babe is doing down there in Casa right now," Tuck says trying his hardest to be worldly.

"Now Tuck, she's got to make a living." But Tuck doesn't smile, and I remember that despite his rough reference to the girl, they had quite a thing together. To make him feel better I tell him that she was easily the best-looking of all the sand crabs that came to the villa. Only I don't say sand crabs.

Ashton comes in and for a moment is caught up in the shenanigans going on with the hot cakes. Hartstene, an aviation machinist's mate, third class, and waist gunner, is pretending to throw the discus. Hot cakes begin flying through the air in all directions. Ashton shakes his head as he sits down with us and stirs a cup of coffee. "A taut crew," he says. "That's our secret, Tuck. Tautness and teamwork. Did I ever tell you how we bagged our JU-88?" Tuck has of course heard the story often, but since it is never told twice the same way, Ashton tells it again. "Nanos, that's that white-haired moron over there playing with the toast, he reports five Beaufighters coming up behind. No one else can see them, only the guy in the tail, but Nanos *knows* they're Beaufighters because he can see the dihedral and we don't have to worry because they can't *possibly* be JU's. Anyway, the Beaufighters line up like good guys, they're out in the sun and we can't see them well, but they wiggle wings and we damn near tongue each other we feel so friendly. All I remember as the load hit the fan was Nanos saying, 'Gee, Mr. Ashton, them Beaufighters ain't got no dihedral any more!' "

Tuck laughs. We do have the only German. One of the five "Beaufighters" mysteriously fell into the sea during the action which was so one-sided that it was impossible to believe that we had hit it. Ashton took us into one of the hairiest cold fronts I have ever seen, trying to escape, but every time we came to a clear spot, there was a JU waiting for us with a fork. They came right into the stuff after us, and if the Japanese played like that out here, where the skies are clear, there wouldn't be many of us left around.

After breakfast we go down the road to the ACI tent. The mechs and ordnanceman board a truck for the field and the officers and radiomen go inside the tent and sit on some benches facing the traditional map rolls on a rack. Monty Herbert is there, fussing with his packets of code books, registered flags and Asian money, and looking as always his pristine, Quonset Point best. His shirt and pants are clean and pressed, his low shoes polished, his expensive-looking socks neatly gartered. But his overseas cap has that particular dilapidated contour to it that only forty-year-old lawyers turned ACI officer seem able to achieve.

Herbert's entire association with the Navy spans about six weeks he spent at Quonset and about six months he has spent with us. Like most of his sort, work is still for him, if not a passion, at least an expression, certainly a nervous habit. But there is not enough for him to do, despite the classifying, revising, destroying and so on he must do among the bales of paper matter that come in. Herbert is a good and intelligent intelligence officer in a place where none is needed. And since he is not a satisfied man, he is a nuisance to us, always trying to touch up the trips with little ideas and extras of his own—a peek in some harbor, a propaganda drop over some insignificant town.

"Well, what have the bloody brass hats at GHQ thought up for us this morning?" Ashton says slumping dispiritedly on a bench.

"I have a surprise for you," Herbert says picking up a sheet of paper.

"No! No! Home! Mother!" Ashton mutters.

"A small convoy sighted off Poulo Condore at seven last night. Four twenty-one worked it over but there should be half a dozen Sugar Dogs and Sugar Charlies left, plus the escort. Just a patrol boat of some kind."

"Sure. Just a fuzzy little old patrol boat . . . with ten-inch quadruple-mounted . . ."

"Of course they could be in Saigon but you may find them holed up somewhere . . . up in the Mekong Delta, maybe. They will have had fifteen hours at, say, five knots. They couldn't be north of Cape St. Jacques. If you have a little extra gas you might take a really good look up in the delta and maybe down there south of Bac Lieu, if they went . . ."

"How about if we just fly home by way of Tokyo and bomb the palace instead?" Ashton says.

Herbert smiles and sucks on his unlit pipe. "Okay, but you might just find them up in there."

"That," Ashton says, "is exactly what we are afraid of."

Herbert natters for a while about recognition signals and shows us the current weather and prognosis. The rain has moved on. Finally he doles out the packets, handling them as if they were bar gold, and watching closely to see that I sign chits for everything.

"Let's get out of here before Donald Crisp, here, thinks up some new insanity," Ashton says.

"I wouldn't give *you* trouble," Herbert says grinning evilly.

"You better not. I'm playing nothing but Richard Cromwell yellow belly parts, and don't you forget it."

Outside a stake truck is waiting. We throw our stuff into the back and climb in after it and the truck lurches off, rattling over the bumps and shuddering in the sandy hollows of the road. Despite the rain, dust swirls up into the dim shafts of light. I can feel it mixed with the smoke of my cigarette.

Long ago this swaying ride in the truck used to stir in me a feeling of resolve, however faint. But not any more. It only reminds me that I wish to hell I had elected to fight this war on the ground, if I had to do it at all. It is that extra dimension that does it. Space. None of my enemies would be so awesome without it. Not the darkness, nor the turbulence, not engine failure, not fire or water or weight. As my dead tentmate Segrave used to sing, "I can't erase, the idea of space, before me." And for me that has been it. Because of space all my enemies have steadily gained ground. Fear of space has routed all enthusiasm, has triumphed completely over adventurous conceit. I suppose a killer, like our one and only Tommy Prime, has nightmares about the lack of space. He has spotted an Irving flying at three hundred feet and hasn't enough air to roll over on his back, pick up three hundred knots, and overtake it. But my dreams are of falling, and they're getting worse.

We begin to pass the first ugly bug shapes of B-24's in the revetments. The gear noises of the truck take on a lost and searching sound, as the driver hunts down our airplane. The groans of the truck go eagerly up, up, and then disappointedly down, down, like some subnormal animal that is trying with its too little intelligence to please us.

Ahead a flashlight shines fixedly on the nose of an airplane. The nose is bare save for the white number, 901. The flashlight makes vigorous crisscross motions, the gears growl lower and lower and their noise finally stops. Now the engine races, panting like a tired thing. Objects thud in the sand. We jump out over the palings. "Goodby-ee, goodby-ee!" the driver calls musically. "So yong-ee," someone calls back. The truck grinds ahead.

We duck under the belly of the airplane and climb in through the open bomb bay, following one another like Alpine climbers. I hang up my gun, canteens, and harness in various places, and sit down in the right seat. I move the seat backward and forward and up and down until I get it to where I have good leverage on the rudder pedals. In the event of an engine failure I can brace my back and stiffen my leg and hold the rudder against the yaw. Not that this will help. We weigh these days seven tons over the maximum specified gross take-off limit. John Honey, our full-blooded Cherokee, died in the most un-Indian fashion at Leyte, mechanically, when his airplane simply went the length of the runway and refused to fly, although everything was apparently working. It was just too heavy. Since with the extra seven tons, the Flying Whale will not fly readily, ever, it is impossible to tell, until too late, whether it will fly at all. Once in the air, weight still so rules the equation that even a simple emergency can be enlarged into a disaster at a speed that no human being can cope with. There is never time for the sober, contemplative actions of the operational syllabus, where in theory you are at five thousand feet on a sunny afternoon, weighing fifty thousand pounds. In the Philippines you are usually at less than a hundred feet on a rainy night, and weigh seventy thousand.

People like Stuart Ashton and John Yokum and Bill Bartlett and some others have developed philosophies that eliminate the struggle for life after, as Ashton says, death has set in. For example, an engine failure on take-off. Ashton wears no shoulder harness, leaves even the belt loose for comfort, sits in a casual posture with no thought of fighting the yaw if an engine quits. Yokum spent hours making a special chamois lining for his headset, with pads to keep the stems of his glasses from chafing his ears, but he has never taken five minutes to practice three-engine procedure for the moment after take-off. There is no such thing at seventy thousand, Yoke believes. Yet anyone who has seen the nightly whirlpool of unhappy confusion down at the field known as Maintenance can guess the shape of things to come. In the midst of rain and darkness, rust and ruin, vital parts are stolen and restolen between squadrons and Wing and Hedron and back again, to the tune of that well-known Naval refrain, "Fuck you sailor, I got mine."

Ashton arrives in his usual fashion, a cup of coffee in one hand, dragging all his gear with the other. As he comes around the base of the crown turret, a strap of the life jacket snags on something, the coffee flies through the air, Ashton curses. In a second he has whipped out the hunting knife from his canteen belt and is about to cut off the offending strap, but Tuck holds up one hand and with the other frees the strap. "It only takes about five seconds to put on," Tuck says mildly.

"Listen, if Nelson had wanted us to wear inner tubes at sea, he would have left some kind of directive!" Ashton says pretending to be very irritated.

Someone whistles outside my window. I crank. Number two is balky and when it finally catches there is a tremendous backfire. Ashton jeers. "Back . . . back . . . going . . . against the fence

. . . it's . . . yes, fans, a fifty-pound Stromberg carburetor all the way into the seats!" I work the toggles for the other starters and switch mags. Ashton handles the throttles and mixtures. We make all the engines backfire before we get them started.

Spurlock hitches himself out through the hatch over the nav compartment and sits there with the Aldis light, squirting it on the wing tips of the airplanes parked around us. It will soon be as crowded as Leyte on this island. Or Lingayen. I push a button on the VHF. "What are we, Tuck?" I shout over my shoulder.

"Two Zebra."

I call. In the tower a soft and eerie green light glows. "Greetings," says a voice in my earphones. "Ee . . . Ta-oo Zebra, Redcoat Tower . . . ee . . . straight ahead and run up on the . . . eee . . . west apron. Your . . . ee . . . wind, north east fiyav . . . and . . . ee . . . your cockrell is not—repeat not—crowing this lovely morning."

"That bastard," Ashton says reaching down and flipping on the IFF, a radar device that sends a signal identifying us as friendly. "That ham. Remember him?" The voice is familiar. Somewhere we had to suffer with it.

"Angaur. That week we spent down there. You said he should be in a *Collier's* airline story."

"That's it." Into the mike Ashton says "Eee . . . how's that, tower? Crowing like a big . . . eee . . . Rhode Island Red?"

"That's okay," the voice says warmly, unconscious of our derision. "And check the boxcar on your left . . . ee . . . excuse us, Navy, on your port. He parked a little close to the taxi strip."

"Did you ever do time around Peleliu by any chance?"

"Ee . . . yes sir! Sho' did."

"I thought so."

"I know *you*?"

"No, but I know you." The voice laughs meaninglessly.

We taxi down the sand connecting-strip to the end of the runway and stop at the edge of the Marsden mat. To our right there is seven thousand feet of it, unlighted except for three tiny red lights at each end. When you roll over it, it sags and gives, but it

is far better than the sand strip the Japs left here and which we
used for the first weeks. It cost 420 a crew the first time they
operated. They hit a pothole with one wheel, tore the strut and
oleo off and went over on their back. The ten hams they raked
out of that one inaugurated the graveyard for aviators who die
locally.

We run up the props, turbos, mags. I run the check list, touching each control briefly with my hand. Wing flaps, cowl flaps,
trim, control lock. "Let her rip," Ashton says. I call. We wait
while they clear us with the night fighters.

This was a moment brimming with mystical forces in the old
days when Tim Brady was along. It was just now that Brady
would take his vizored cap with the bundle of love letters in it,
and place it in a certain niche between coils of the command set,
like a relic on the altar. Andretta, sitting right there, always told
us that Brady's lips moved and that he said, "Please, dear God,
don't take me away from Betty!" This is significant to someone
like me who practices all kinds of rituals and solemnities too, but
in private. I always put it the other way. Don't take Corinne away
from me. I guess I am downright selfish.

We are cleared and waddle out. Ashton adjusts the landing
lights to shine down the runway. The real black cats don't use
them for take-off. Skinhead Dougherty wears red goggles before
he takes off to give him night vision. He even turns the instrument
lights down until they are as dim as watch dials. But not us. We
go off in a blaze.

I hold everything at a thousand rpm's. Ashton gives the airplane
a couple of wiggles to stop the castering in the nose wheel. Spurlock bends in between us. He has a screw driver. If the landing
gear handle sticks he will try to reach through a little hole on the
pedestal and pry something loose with the screw driver. In a
hurry. She won't fly long with the wheels down. Now Ashton
nods, I push, the racket begins. We are slow starting, slow going
by the tower, slower than the proverbial one-armed swimmer in
shit lake. The nose bobs up and down like a little boat in the

waves. Too much weight aft. It makes the airplane trundle. Ashton makes gestures of pushing the throttles ahead. I shake my
head and shout the mournful refrain, "You got it all, buddy!" We
could advance the turbos and get more but you increase the
chances of something going wrong. I watch the fuel flow needles
where you see trouble first. One of the white hands has begun
to semaphor but it shows plenty of pounds per hour and there is
a nice synchronized roar. I strain forward, feeling the slow waddle
become a long undulation on the sagging mat, feeling the overweight in the unrelieved jarring of the wheels over bumps, feeling
the airplane's mighty reluctance to fly. I see the three red lights.
We will never make it. Already we must have gone a mile and the
nose is just up off the ground. We haven't any speed. The wings
of the airplanes projecting out of the revetments on either side
seem to pass in slow motion. But we are committed and can't stop
now if we wanted to. The semaphoring needle begins to fluctuate,
snapping back and forth in wide arcs. Fear takes me completely
and I can do nothing but sit, with my buttocks contracted in a
knot, and lean stupidly forward in an effort to stimulate speed.
We are on top of the lights.

Ashton heaves on the yoke. We lurch and hang a few feet in the
air, the lights blazing dizzily out into black space. I yank the gear
handle and a moment later feel the wheels jar in the uplocks. The
airspeed needles twitter slowly up. Only the rate of climb fails to
move. It is the dangerous time. Sometimes the airplane settles
back because of the false attitude in which it has been placed in
its first struggle to fly, or because the pilot, yielding to contrary
sensations, eases it back. You can see nothing but black and blind-
ing light. The instruments alone must be obeyed.

We seem to wallow. Suddenly the rate of climb drops and
instinctively I look out through the blister. Black water. If I can
see it, it is not more than ten or fifteen feet below us. I yell. Ashton looks as though he is walking a tightrope, leaning this way
and that as he plays the yoke. Then the water recedes until it is
out of sight. In a moment I bring back the throttles and rpm's and

milk up the flaps. I blend the noises into an even, organized sound. Then I deliberately slack myself, the way one does periodically in the dentist's chair.

I am not the only one who has seen the water. There are exclamations from all around on the intercom. Hartstene in the waist swears the tail skag damn near dragged in it. In any case, there it was. The absolute limit on the B-24, given seven thousand feet of Marsden mat, a wind of six miles and hour and a gross weight at take-off of seventy thousand pounds. "A homesick angel!" Ashton screams shrilly. "A scalded cat! A stripe—assed ape! . . . and then, of course, there is the B-24! If we *had* had thirty-three hundred gallons we wouldn't have made it!" Even Tuck shows signs of strain. He grins and shakes his head from the dark depths of the nav compartment, the only signs of fear he ever reveals.

We rise slowly in the pitch blackness. It is a long and painful climb to nine thousand with our weight and it will take nearly an hour. But at least it isn't long till dawn. Not even sparrows in a tree welcome light as enthusiastically as we do. They can see their enemies and we can see ours—or at least some of them. Siphoning, for instance. Now and then I see the flash of the Aldis over the wing. For the first fifteen minutes Spurlock checks the filler caps of the wing tanks to see if we are siphoning. This is a malaise in which gas suddenly begins to suck out through the tiny vent holes in the caps and around the caps themselves. It occurs when the wing tanks are full and "topped off," which they always are, and is some function of the suctioning effect of air over the wing. The gas comes out in a stream like a fire hose and it is possible to lose five hundred gallons in a very few minutes.

This is not the real hazard. Three or four feet below the stream of gas, sparks and chunks of red-hot carbon are flying back from the bucket wheels of the four turbos mounted on the underside of the wing. Together, in a nerve-racking parallel, sparks and gas disappear into the night. Since the most disquieting of the inherent fallibilities of our airplane is its occasional inclination to explode in mid-air, twenty minutes of siphoning on a dark night will make any crew, as they say, bite washers.

There are experts around who invoke the laws of physics and the habits of gasoline in open air and say that siphoning does not cause the explosions. They name the place, somewhere in the convolutions of the Flying Whale's arteries, where a valve stuck or a line burst, fumes gathered, and electricity did the rest. It gives the experts confidence to explain away death in purely mechanical terms, because they believe that there is always, prior to such a death, a sign or augury of approaching disaster, and hence always something for an expert to react to and do, but experts' explanations make the innocent frantic, and the innocent are ninety percent of us. We have forgotten, if we ever knew, all but the most primitive technical secrets about the Flying Whale and its anatomy, and all but the garden variety of checkmate to its moves to kill us.

Al Swansek, our former executive officer, was a technical man. He exploded in the air over Tinian one night in November of forty-four. His tanks were topped off, his airplane was notorious as a siphoner. Yet the Wing went so far as to suggest that he had been shot down by a Jap night intruder, although none was seen or heard, before or after. Other experts worked out a number of likely explanations for Al's death, all of which contained, strangely enough, the same reassurance that "the odds against it ever happening twice are astronomical." Although Al Swansek's last flight was a short one, only about a minute and a half, nobody in his crew was able to finish it alive and consequently there was no one to answer questions, expert or otherwise.

When we are up past a thousand we cut in the auto pilot. It is a sloppy way to fly, the airplane is out of trim and hunts and wallows all over the place. It should be babied up foot by foot instead of ridden with the reins dropped on its neck. But neither Ashton nor I care.

We still worry about losing an engine, because for a while we will be too heavy to fly on three and at the same time too heavy to land safely. In theory you can jettison the overweight. The bombs can go and the bomb bay tanks. But the bombs are only a fraction of the load and the tanks are a bad bet. In tests conducted by the Wing, only one bomb bay tank out of twenty-six released properly and fell clear of the airplane. The others had swelled from moisture and heat and dropped only a few inches, some of them just far enough to prevent the bomb bay doors from closing. Thus it is that sometimes the crew of a B-24 enters a state of limbo. They can't stay up, and on the other hand, they can't come down.

However, practically everyone is confident that the problem of the undroppable drop tanks will soon be solved by the creative agility and characteristic energy always shown by Swede Engelson, the exec of the Air Wing. His record is a series of unbroken successes with this type of difficulty. When for example it was found that there was insufficient horsepower in the performance tables to get the new loads "safely" into the air, Swede revised the graphs in certain ways hitherto unknown to the manufacturers and discovered new "pockets" of power here and there. He obtained by decree what science stubbornly withheld from him. And he has finally put a stop to the theft of spare parts! If a part can not be found down there rusting in the open-air equipment pool, at least it can no longer be stolen from someone's airplane. There are guards with carbines. Maintenance is as poor as ever, but it is honest.

He has often said new bomb bay tanks will be installed. Once a month if necessary. Since it is impossible to get new tanks once a year, and since he will never shorten the patrols or lighten the loads, he will have to "legislate" a liability back into a safety device. And he will have to do better than the subtle nol-pros of the case against siphoning. We are out of the range of Jap night fighters here.

When daylight comes Ashton gives his seat to Tuckerman. Tuck is going to fly the rest of the patrol as P.P.C. at the request of the Captain. It is often done to give more experience to people about to take over their own crew. Like everyone else, Ashton is touchy about night take-offs with overloads, and the take-off is the only thing not included.

When Tuck has everything adjusted around him, he becomes very alert and diligent, sitting up straight in the seat and search-

ing the ocean with glasses, although there is never anything to
see for the first eight or nine hundred miles. It's all out at the
end, in the rind of the watermelon, so to speak. I slouch in my
seat and monitor the auto pilot, keeping course and altitude
within reasonable limits. I smoke and swill coffee and read letters
and even a book I have brought along. The book is called *The
Prodigal Women* and I only read it when I am flying and then
only at random, opening here and there and rereading much of it
over and over. There is some kind of psychic reason for this. I feel
somehow the book has become a talisman of some kind, that the
people in it have shared certain critical moments in my life, and
therefore I don't want to finish it ever, and be alone again. I know
the people in it so well I even feel that some of them are as
anxious about me as I have often been about them. It is as juvenile as juvenile can be, but I am no more worried about that than
I am by the fact that I say Hail Mary and cross myself when I
am scared, although I am not Catholic and, when not frightened,
don't believe in God at all.

After about five hours we sight Poulo Condore, a mountainous
island lying fifty or sixty miles from the coast of Indo-China, with
a neat red-roofed French village on it, and part way up the moun-
tain the governor's ornate mansion, shining like a white fairy
palace in the sun. It is lovely to see and I abandon my pose of
tedium and indifference and look down at it. Tuck is happy because he has wanted to tell me for a long time to stop reading and
start looking. It's a cinch the convoy won't still be here, but Tuck
can't help hoping and he stirs everybody up every few minutes
by asking if anyone sees anything.

"Like what, sir?" Whitey Nanos wants to know.

"Anything . . . except water and land. Are you looking back
there? Or are you crapped out?"

"Not me, sir!" If I know anything Whitey Nanos is not in his
turret yet but stretched out in the waist on a pile of chutes. Of
course he keeps a pair of earphones on his head.

"Well, I guess we better start looking," Tuck says to me shyly.
He wouldn't dream of ordering me to do anything.

"Yup. Getting in there pretty soon," I say. Ashton winks at me as he passes up coffee. Tuck's eagerness is pretty funny, the way he leans quickly back and forth to see past every frame of the windshield and every obstruction with his glasses.

I poke my head in the blister and look down. Now I can see the cavernous holes in the side of the governor's mansion and the gutted black windows. We have been lobbing bombs in there for a long time, just for fun. People who haven't slung bombs through the windows of a palace don't realize that it is *really* fun. It would be as stupid for me to tell deer hunters their sport isn't decent or moral or constructive. I am sure it is fun to shoot and kill a deer, even if I don't think so. It's like that with bombing fairy palaces. Our bombs have spilled stone rubble down on the winding road below this one and there is an oxcart up there this morning, loading stone.

Ashton leans across me to look and makes a face to show his admiration for such industry. I understand him without thinking about it. The noise of the engines becomes such a complete conditioner that we have developed reflexes from it. Talking is an effort and after a time you work out a signal language. It is born of fifteen-hour patrols and no soundproofing. Smiling, shrugging, nodding are standards, but scoffing, for instance, can be done with great art merely by leaning slowly toward the other person, and then rapidly away again in a special manner. Words are lame in comparison to such a gesture.

Soon Tuck sights the mainland through the glasses. He rings the bell and makes the crew call in the "manned and ready" from every station. They even have to test-fire the guns. When Cunningham gets loquacious, as he always does about this time of day, Tuck tells him to belay it.

We approach the flat green land, letting down slowly to four thousand so we can see better. We have a hundred miles of coast to search, including the delta of the Mekong, where there are usually things hidden. They pull the ships up under the banks of the river where there are overhanging trees, and then they cover them with branches and fronds to make doubly sure. It was on one of Tim Brady's few trips with us that we sank two Sugar Dogs over here. There is a tiny panel window in the main windshield and it blew out and hit Brady on the forehead. He was sure he had been shot and began making all the right faces and moaning at the blood on his fingers. On later runs he ducked his head down behind the pedestal until he was almost lying on the floor.

Tuck turns northwest, hand-flying the ship, and in a few minutes we can see far ahead in the haze the lines of trees along the many branches of the Mekong. The trees seem to rise up out of a mirror lake, as though they are detached from the earth at their bases. As we approach, the mirror slowly disappears and we can see the places where the river cuts the shore and the trees now firmly anchored in the green land. Tuck compares the geography with the details on a cloth map he has spread on his knee. On my side there is only the ocean, ruffled with a few whitecaps and stained brown, until far, far out, by the river. I can see nothing on the water.

We circle over the delta, looking hard for the hiding place of Monty's convoy. Tuck goes lower and lower until our shadow becomes plain, flickering over the land, cutting and recutting the ribbons of water. I rest my head in the blister and follow the antics of the shadow. We are banked up steep to my side, turning, the shadow far inland because of the low angle of the sun, when I see another shadow, smaller and blacker, heading obliquely toward us, going in the direction of the sea. I hunt all around but I can't see the airplane. The shadow thing has always confused me and I never know where to look. But I yell at Tuck and make sure I don't lose the flitting shadow.

He banks steeper toward the shadow but it goes beneath us and disappears. We scream and yell at each other and seesaw all over the sky, but we can't find it.

"Are you sure?" Tuck says. He looks mighty desperate for anyone who doesn't believe.

"Goddam right I'm sure." I jerk my thumb like a frenetic hitchhiker. "Turn this way, bring her around fast all the way." In the next moment I see the airplane. It is below us and going out to sea. In the confusion it has gained a couple of miles. I point and

then when Tuck can't see it, I line up a pencil for him. It is hard to
make out against the brown water, and if you didn't know there
was an airplane somewhere there, you would probably never sight
it with an ordinary glance.

Tuck rings the bell and pushes up the throttles to forty inches.
He grabs the mike and begins to tell us just what he plans to do,
although we all know he will have to wait a bit and see what type
of airplane it is before he can plan anything. Tuck talks as if there
isn't a moment to lose, but actually it is a long way down there
and will take several minutes to overhaul the Jap, assuming we
can catch him. If they see us coming they have a good chance to
get away, unless it is something terribly obsolete like a float plane.
But the odds are with us. 400 has shot down about forty airplanes,
including fighters, by chasing them, principally because the latter-
day Japs are addicted to the most useless evasive tactics. They
invariably go down flat on the water and make steep S-turns. This
allows the slower Liberator to fly along just behind and pot at
them with up to six guns. It doesn't occur to the Japs to try to
climb away, which they might do, or head for cloud, or even go
straight and level.

We are going two hundred and thirty knots and the airplane is
jolting like a speedboat on choppy water. Tuck trims it rather
roughly when the nose wants to come up, and we all leave our
seats. One of my bogeymen is the fear that something will fly off
the ship when it is going fast and it is handled too roughly, and
it makes me nervous to see Tuck so savage. Ashton doesn't like it
either. He stands between us and threatens Tuck genially about
what he will do if Tuck tears a wing off. "Listen, Lucky Teeter,"
he says, "I don't mind if I'm a minute late!"

I get the Jap in the glasses. It is a Betty, a medium bomber
that they use for everything. I yell at Tuck. The Japs are low on
the water, but not doing anything extraordinary and probably
don't see us. It flies straight out to sea, thick and stumpy-looking,
except for the cleanly tapered wings.

Tuck grabs the glasses. He wants to look at his prize. I can
smell his breath for a second, like cured ham from the coffee and

cigarettes. I feel a pang of envy. I have discovered it but now it
is his. The chances of my ever finding another for myself are slim.
This one was pure luck. One minute earlier and it would have
still been invisible against the land green, and one minute later it
would have passed too far behind us. It is odd how badly we all
want to kill some men in another airplane merely for the notoriety
it will give us. It certainly won't influence the course of the war
if this Betty lives or dies. It can't even reach the Americans from
here. For a moment I am almost against killing them. Against
Tuck killing them, that is. I begin to admire the crew of the Betty
down there. It takes nerve to fly in an air force that hasn't had a
victory for three years.

"Pictures!" Tuck yells at me. "How about it, Ivy? You take them
so I'm sure I get good ones." I have a small reputation as a pho-
tographer because I once got an unusual shot of a Jap two-man
sub in the harbor at Chichi Jima. It showed the sub, a flak burst,
and all of Futami Ko mysteriously in focus at the same time. I
unbuckle my seat belt and crawl out. Ashton slaps me on the
back, before he sits down in my place, and shakes his head sadly.

"Too bad. It would have been yours if Ironhead hadn't told me
to let Tuck take it."

"The story of my life," I say, smiling bravely, and make my way
aft. On the way I grip one of Spurlock's thick ankles. His legs
hang down into the nav compartment from the crown turret and
for a second I catch a glimpse of his determined face peering
down at me from under his long-billed cap. He is by far the best
turret gunner we have.

In the after station the noise is different and seems far more
urgent. There is a whistling, battering, airstream coming through
the waist hatches and the engine sounds are deafening. Hartstene
and Zalewski are at the single fifties. They squint in the wind and
shout happily at each other. Zalewski shakes my hand like a violent lunatic, congratulating me for having spotted the Betty.
Andretta is also back there with the K-20 camera. He hands it
to me.

"You sure it's loaded?"

"It's loaded. Don't forget to take off the lens cap." I take the cap off and put it in my pocket. Many a man has fired all his film through the lens cap. Then I put on some earphones and talk to Ashton. He says Tuck is going to put the Betty slightly to port and try to fly formation on it. They often don't carry a full crew so far from the enemy, and it may not have anyone in the tail turret.

"For God's sake, get me good pictures," Tuck says breaking in.

"Don't worry about the pictures." I can see the Betty by leaning out a bit through the port waist hatch. Zalewski, who may get a shot now, manhandles his gun and begins looking vicious. But then we change heading slightly and the Betty goes out of sight just ahead of us. For two or three minutes we can't see it, but we can hear the voices on the intercom rising slowly in excitement and we know it must be close. We stand in the battering wind and shrug at one another. Under us the deck vibrates so hard it makes the skin itch. Then the shooting begins. In the crown Spurlock fires in short deliberate bursts but we can hear Cunningham in the bow spraying the whole universe as usual. We crane our necks and scramble about in frustration but can see nothing. Zalewski swears in rage because he can't get a shot.

Suddenly there is a violent wrench. I go backward across the waist and slam my back into Hartstene's gun, nearly dropping the camera out of the hatch. We tilt and I climb back up and grab a hold on the hatch frame. I brace with my knees and shoulders. It takes two hands to operate the K-20. Zalewski is clinging to his gun like a steeplejack but still there is nothing to see. Then without warning, there it is, blotchy brown, not more than fifty feet off the water and turning steeply back toward the land. I can see the meatballs on both upper wing surfaces and another just forward of the huge triangular fin. We are closing slowly as I snap the first picture, but when I have cocked the camera again, the Betty begins to rush up at us. It comes sliding in and it is obvious that Tuck has kept too much speed and will overrun it. The throttles come off with a sickening slack sound, and Tuck yaws back and forth trying to kill his speed. I snap pictures until we go over

the Betty and it disappears beneath us. As I move to the opposite
side, the power comes on again in an unsynchronized yowl and I
nearly go to my knees as Tuck pulls up and does what amounts to
a wingover, in his effort to get around fast. At the top when we
are steeply banked, I lean out the starboard side. I expect to see
the Jap somewhere down below. Instead we nearly ram it! The
Betty has done some wild thing herself and finished up about
thirty feet under us at roughly the same attitude. I stare down at
the intimate features of the enemy, spitting distance away, all
there, the numbers, dents, oil leaks, even the helmeted heads
inside the glass. There is no one in the tail. Nor any guns. But
the crown turret is firing at us and I can see a figure inside the
myriad glass panels the Betty has in her nose.

For a moment there is no direction, no up or down, no out or
in. I can't even tell which way to lean to balance myself against
the changing forces. The airplanes sag in toward each other as
though moving down the blades of a slowly closing scissors. I
cringe and squat down. But there is no comfort in even a reflex
because there is no direction in which to recoil. Then the Betty
is gone. It must have missed us by ten feet.

When it appears again it is a quarter mile away, diving to flat-
ten itself once more upon the sea. Tuck is after it, skidding wildly.
Tracers reach for it but come nowhere near. When the Betty sees
the tracers arcing around it, it begins the inept and fatal maneuvering—S-turns pressed against the sea. We have used up the
speed of our dive; the Betty could probably outrun us going
straight, almost certainly outclimb us. Some people say the Jap
gas detonates if they put on power and it is for this reason they
prefer to dodge. But it is the thing that ensures their destruction.
Because now we catch up to the Betty easily and Tuck has only to
fly along slightly to one side. He doesn't even need to change his
heading.

There is a great deal of shooting and even Zalewski and Hartstene get in a few bursts. Long ropes of tracers go smoking out
toward the Betty where it is turning back and forth on the rumpled water. They seem to go out no faster than driven golf balls

and there is an illusion that the ropes link the two airplanes. As the Betty stops turning one way and begins to turn another, it seems to be towing us by long lines of red balls. The feeble seven-point-seven return fire has stopped.

The Betty weaves gracefully back and forth perhaps three times before the first smoke shows. It jets tentatively from a nacelle, stops, spurts again and then pours back in a thickening stream. Fire twinkles in a wing root and there is a triumphant yell. Some of the yell comes from me. The Betty rises slowly in front of us, flying straight now as though tired of the twisting and turning. It slows perceptibly, fire gushing from the whole wing, and then appears almost to stop in the air. It hangs there against the pale sky above us, tragic and isolated for a moment, then rolls over and drops flat into the sea.

It has been absurdly easy at the end. A half minute of the simplest gunnery, almost no resistance—inevitably Cunningham or someone will say they saw volumes of return fire—and absolutely no skill on the part of the enemy or us.

We circle around the place where the Betty went in. There is a widening ring of burning gas and oil on the water and in the middle of it the tail of the Betty thrusts up through the smoke like a huge shark fin. Cunningham fires a few rounds into the debris. There were at least four of them in there but there is no sign of life, and even before I have finished taking pictures the fin has gone. I cap the camera and go up forward.

There is wild jubilation. Tuck gets out of his seat when he sees me, rubs his knuckles on my head and embraces me. Everyone is howling. It is as though we have just won an important football game. Tuck gets Spurlock out of the crown and hugs him too. Ashton says that Spurlock is the only one who hit anything, from where he sat. What makes Tuck the happiest is the thought of Yokum, who, flying with Kirby Stevens, has yet to be along when an airplane is bagged. This is Tuck's second, and Roger and I have both had at least copilot's shares in "victories," leaving Yoke the only virgin in the tent. "He'll damn near collapse," Tuck says nearly crying with his joy. "He'll break off at the knees!" Flying

with Kirby Stevens you don't see very much, but since Yoke
started out on his own he has caught his old master in shipping.

I test the mass of my own elation. Now it is over I know that
somehow it is different. The first time—the German JU-88—we
were defending ourselves. The second one, the Mavis, fired back
with spirit, if not accuracy. The two Vals at Naha involved some
daring even though they were incredibly stupid. We slipped out
of the overcast and knocked one down a mile off the end of the
runway. We got the second when he flew over and circled to in-
vestigate the first. Yet even then, although I didn't feel badly
about the men in the Vals, the victory antics began to bore me.
But now I have an uncomfortable feeling of irresponsibility, of
having voided human restraints. I don't understand it, and I don't
like it, but apparently everyone else does.

I make out the contact, which we forgot to send, and the action
report, and give them to Robinson, with instructions to send them
three or four minutes apart. I figure a course for home and give it
to Tuck, now happily putting back all the fluorescent lights in
their sockets. When the crown turret fires forward, the muzzles of
the guns are just overhead and the blast is so close that things rain
down from the ceiling. The lights spring out of their sockets and
hang down on their cords.

I sit at the nav table and smoke my umptieth cigarette. Other
than some empty brass and links that have spilled down from the
crown, there is no sign we have been in a fight. But when Ashton
tries to open a can of tuna, and pulls the sharp tin band from the
lid through his fingers, we have plenty of blood. I administer to
him lavishly from the first-aid kit. Ashton points at my own swol-
len fingers.

"War is hell," he says bitterly. "Even the fish turn on us."

"That's a worse wound than Cox's," I say. "You ought to get a
P.H. for it." Cox slid off the roof of a Quonset hut during an air
raid at Tinian and ripped his behind on a projection. He nearly
got the Purple Heart before Tom Parker, who was new then,
wised up.

It takes six hours to get back to the island. I eat again, smoke, and write another letter to Corinne apologizing for the one of yesterday. Yoke is right. That woman has me by the ying-yang. Ashton sleeps and Tuck sits there, beaming at the ocean. When we get home he dives down and buzzes the field before Ashton can stop him. Swede Engelson is hell on his form of celebration. Now Tuck is upset because he knows Ashton will get a chewing out, and for that, or some other reason, he makes a dreadful landing that scares us all half to death.

Once on the ground Tuck is his usual self. While we wait for the truck he even apologizes to Cunningham for "gettin' a little excited and cussin' you out." Cunningham of course professes not to have been aware that he was being cussed out. We all stand around with tuna fish oil glistening on our lips and chins and begin to relate the little intimate parts we have played in the day's drama. This is mere warm-up for the bull shit that will flow when we are no longer restrained by the presence of eyewitnesses. As always, Cunningham takes a quick lead, and by the time the truck has arrived to take us back to the camp it is fairly well established that he will emerge as hero of the day.

In the evening there is a good deal of noise in our tent, other people celebrating Tuck's victory with our whisky. Because he is from Georgia, and because he is so shy and young and amiable, Tuck gets a lot of hard kidding, along with all things southern from generals to Doctor Pepper. Bill Bartlett shows up with a large bottle of grain alcohol and a gallon of grapefruit juice. He is cheered loudly and irrationally and there are more cheers when someone else brings some gaily colored little glasses that came originally filled with cheese. We make room by simply chucking everything out of the tent. Chute harnesses, life jackets, shirts, pants, shoes go sailing out through the flies in all directions.

"We want to welcome the hero back to Valhalla, and to offer him a little mead," Bartlett says pouring out a glass of his bitter concoction and handing it to Tuck. "Now Tuck," Bartlett says to him, "you say you knew you had the slit-eyed bastards when they tried to ram you, because that proved what every American fighting man knows, that they are . . ." Tuck looks blankly at him.

He is already pretty drunk but he doesn't understand intense kidding. "Class!" Bartlett yells. "What did it prove?"

"Dizzy from being carried on their mothers' backs!"

"That they can't make a Chevrolet!"

"They don't have a corner drugstore to fight for!"

There are yells and cheers with each sally of wit. "You say your thoughts were on your pure young sisters as you bored in . . ." Bartlett pauses, hands poised, teeth bared like a gopher.

"There I was flat on my back at thirty thousand," Tuck says his eyes watering with embarrassment.

"When General Lee appeared . . . flying a white Spad!" Bartlett looks ecstatic now. "It was a pure white Spad, like everything else in Georgia, and . . ."

"And it's name was *Traveler*," Ashton says filling Tuck's glass.

"A message in smoke appeared in the sky beside you . . ." Bartlett is writing in the air with his hand. "Eat . . . Marse Robert's . . . Goober . . . Peas!" he says in a measured way.

Frank Ainsworth arrives with the pictures which have just been finished. They are surprisingly good, especially one which I took as we were about to collide. In a freak blend of happy focus and lucky lighting one can see right inside the Betty. The Jap copilot is looking up at us through his side window. Ainsworth produces a magnifying glass and puts it on the picture. "Scared shitless!" he announces after a look.

In another picture the sharp wing of the Liberator slants gracefully down from an upper corner like the pinion of a stooping hawk and points toward the plump pigeon shape of the Betty in one of its frantic turns just off the water. In the last pictures, what looks like a man can be seen swimming in the widening ring of gas and oil. But at the end he has disappeared. The water looks very rough. "Look at the oil leaks around the rocker box covers on that starboard engine. They never would have made it home anyway," Ashton says.

Fred McCord, the personnel officer, comes in and shakes Tuck's hand with a silly ceremonial air. No one likes him. He is pompous and still stupidly persistent about trivial infractions of the rules

that concern his job. He is always after Ainsworth because he is
convinced that he got away with two issue wrist watches while
only signing a chit for one. Besides that McCord is offensive in
another sure-fire way. He is a non-flyer, but he enters "the realm"
as a participant on the strength of the few patrols he has ridden
along on gratuitously. He stresses especially his part in what he
calls "the early days in England," hinting to newer men at some
special qualifications he allegedly had then and recalling the advice or admonishments he gave in the nick of time to pilots bent
on doing something stupid.

Ainsworth gives McCord the close-up picture. "Check that Jap
copilot, McCord. I think the son of a bitch is wearing two
watches." McCord holds up the picture to the light and studies it
professionally.

"Very good. We need it. Norton has just smeared a whole new
bunch of pictures all over the ACI shack of his Frances."

"Who?" Ashton says scowling. "What was the name?"

"Norton. Joe Norton," McCord says innocently. There is a wail
of jeers.

"Oh, you mean ol' Captain Ahab?" Ashton says. "The daring
leader of those hard-shootin', throttle-bustin' Blue Raiders?" There
are groans, cheers, lip noises. To our intense delight Norton has
officially named 420 the Blue Raiders. It is a hard thing for his
squadron to bear but Norton himself blows aside the derision it
has inspired with gusty disdain.

Ashton rises and puts a glass near his mouth like a microphone.
"See . . . The Blue Raiders!" he shouts. "The two-fisted story of
hard-flying Yank hellions in flaming combat with the Mikado's
butcher circus. See . . . captive maidens, brutalized in the savage
holocaust of war! See . . . the iron-nerved leader of a doomed
squadron forced to make the decision that will cost his men their
lives! You'll laugh a mile a minute with the Yank sky jocks . . .
cry with the women they love and leave. It's all there, from
goggles to girls, the thrilling, chilling saga of throttle busters in
action. The BLUE . . . RAIDERS!" There is a long applause. Ashton
and Bartlett have an almost endless act. They satirize every war

hero, book or movie that they can remember and go on for hours with characters flitting in and out of the action, which is sometimes in the Sahara, sometimes on the Western Front, sometimes in a submarine.

Doc Parker leans toward Tuck and me in the noise. "No pregnant nuns this time, I hope, Tuck?" Tuck grins.

"They liked to got even, Doc. I'll tell you." Tuck winks at me. "Right, Ivy?"

"Damn near," I say. "I thought we had it."

"What happened?"

Tuck looks to see if anyone is listening. Then he leans forward, his eyes troubled. "I really fucked up. We were going way too fast and damn near ran into him. Then when I horsed it, he did the same and we liked to hit again. Inches. I mean inches! Did you see how close, Ivy?"

"I had my eyes shut."

"Quiet . . . quiet please! The killers are talking it over." It is Yokum, who has arrived with Roger Smith, and he has overheard us. Yoke, who is slim and dark, wears the affected sulky expression that has become his cachet.

"He's dyin'!" Roger says to us pointing to Yokum.

"Nuns!" Yokum says contemptuously pouring himself a drink.

"That's all right about nuns. For a guy who hasn't shot down a single nun . . ." Roger spits a little when he gets excited. Yokum makes an elaborate thing out of wiping the front of his shirt.

"All I can say, Tuck, is try not to brood. I for one am not going to miss a Bettyload of dirty little blind kids." Yokum starts to drink, sees Tuck's confused face and snorts with laughter.

We have developed a pleasant rhythm, turned in on ourselves and away from what is outside the tent. Everyone is tangled in everyone else's conversation. We are noisy, yelling happily at one another. The torpedo juice makes the rounds of the cheese glasses again and again. We sing. "The Chandler's Wife" is our favorite but since Yoke, Roger, Tuck and I arrived in England as replacements, they invariably tell us after this song that we just aren't and never can be part of its spirit and it would be better if we sang something else. "Sky Anchors Away," for example. The old hands spent about three months longer in England than did the four of us, but they keep up a sort of "those were the good old days" nostalgia and the standard "you should have got there when I did, it was really rough" nonsense, and call us the "new boys." The half of the squadron that joined in San Diego just before coming out here have more status than we do.

Now they begin. "Show me a veteran of the early days in the Bay, and I'll show you a hero," Ashton says.

Yokum makes a noise with his lips. "I'll show you soiled pants," he says. "Now me, I prefer a jumping man. When I was jumping with the old Norfolk . . . oh, I forgot. You never jumped, did you?" Yokum is the only one in the squadron who has. He bailed out of an OS2U that was on fire.

"Well, you can make a story out of any little thing," Bartlett says. "In the Bay we stuck to our ships, Yokum. That's just the kind of heroes we were, that's all. You couldn't have cut it if you were always jumping out like that."

"My old jump sack," Yokum says musing. "I wonder who's got her now. We sure had some exciting times together."

But Roger and I have a distinction, too. We are the only Naval aviators anyone knows of who have traveled by ship. "Now when I served aboard the old *Arthur J. Schofield*, it was really rough," I say. "Those of us here who crossed the sub-infested Atlantic will know what I'm talking about." Roger cheers. "One day I counted fourteen subs in two turns around the deck."

"Of course he was only away from his quadruple forty for a minute . . . what did they give us, Ivy, was it ten minutes off every three weeks, or three minutes every ten days?"

The noise is deafening. Everyone is jeering, shouting or singing. Roger flings himself on the floor, his feet stretched in front of him, his hands under his chin gripping imaginary gun bars. "Feed 'em in!" he shouts. I kneel beside him, heave an imaginary clip of cannon shells into the air over his head. "Foom, foom," Roger says beginning to fire. Each time he says foom he reels with the concussion and revolves around on his buttocks, me after him pushing the unseen shells into the unseen breech, one with each foom. He crashes into a bed and Ainsworth pours a drink on his head. "Not a Navy Lib in sight for the fifty-seventh straight day," Roger shouts, his face wet with liquor. "But after all we're still three miles from Plymouth Hoe. You can't expect *too* much from our pilots."

McCord makes the mistake of telling Doc Parker a "that reminds me" story about England. We can hear his drawly voice in the gaps in the ruckus. Bartlett begins to nod his head and work his mouth in time to what McCord is saying, smirking and flapping his hands. When McCord laughs his choked whinny of a laugh, Bartlett snaps his head back and bares his teeth. We slowly subside and listen.

"So I told Krovalenko," McCord says, "he was going to be one unhappy boy if he didn't get out of there. The JU's were all over the Bay in those days."

"Memories, memories," Bartlett says. "What happened after you ordered the mighty Krov not to fly into the jaws of death?"

"They made some Cocomalt," Ashton says. "Didn't you, Mac?"

"Go ahead and laugh," McCord says. "Krovalenko got the D.F.C."

"So did I, so did I, so did I," Ashton chants. He did too, for shadowing the cans. It was before I arrived in England.

"And Krovalenko didn't get the D.F.C. when you were with him," Bartlett says.

"Hey, Doc, you didn't see the best picture," Ainsworth says pulling a glossy photo from under him.

"Yes, I saw them," Parker says seriously, looking at Tuck by way of acknowledgment. But he looks down at the picture Ainsworth has handed him and there is a roar of laughter as he reacts to the obscene photo. Ainsworth brought a collection with him and has had them enlarged in the squadron photo lab. Parker shakes his head smiling ruefully.

"I'll have to put more saltpeter in the atabrine," he says. "The mystic aerial knights are getting out of hand." He holds the picture as though it were a little hot. Ainsworth puts his finger on it.

"That's McCord down there," he says. "Taken at the Passion Pit in forty-three."

"Mac, and you promised," Bartlett says plaintively. "No pix! Well, get yourself another manager! I brought you up through the dog acts, through the Tia Juana clubs, I finally got you playing the Navy. That's like playing The Palace in our line, man! My greatest triumph—three sailors, a polar bear, and you—and you do this to me." There is a peal of laughter at each innuendo. McCord can only stand a little of it. When it dies down a bit he leaves. Why he comes and starts that inane stuff is beyond me.

"Now we'll get it," Ashton says. "He'll cut off our Hershey bars."

"That ass hole," Ainsworth says. He taps Parker on the knee. "You don't know, Doc. McCord had it all fixed up for us to go to Rome and be a courier squadron. Just fly the mail and maybe Eisenhower around. Said it was in the bag because he had emphasized at some meeting how much time we had on our airplanes, and it would be silly to waste the brand-new squadron next door on something like that." Ainsworth lets off a few words to express blasphemous and obscene incredulity as only he can. "It turned out that was exactly what skunked us—too *much* time on the engines. So they gave *us* brand-new airplanes and when we woke up we were out on Tinian. And *still* pulling our puds!"

"I would have had a villa on the . . . Via Appia," Roger says. "Me and my girls were going to wake every morning to the sound of birds."

Yokum looks at Roger's fat body on the floor with disgust. "Tony Galento goes to Rome. Listen, the girls who will for a Lucky, wouldn't with you for seven million cartons."

"I would have just grabbed the old goatskin and gone off down the road singing and squirting a little wine in my mouth," Roger goes on dreamily. "I blend with a people. I have that knack. You don't, Yokum. I just kind of kick a little dust with my foot, pop an olive in my mouth . . . or a little piece of cheese . . ." Yokum kicks at him. Then he sits on him and delivers the corks for the day's transgressions. Yoke is an artist in the suspenseful way in which he carries out the punishment, driving Roger crazy with feints and practice swings.

Poor Roger. He is really funny-looking. His hair grows at all angles and there is an illusion of roundness about him that comes from some vague distortion in his build. His shoulders slope, his arms curve, his legs are bowed. He looks like he's walking on ice tongs. I regret the relationship he has formed with Yokum, based loosely on the master and disciple principle, because it corrupts any serious moments Roger and I could have. Because of us all, Roger is basically the greatest. Kinder, braver, more loyal certainly, and the only one who is psychically comfortable out here. But he plays the slob and imitates Yokum by baiting everyone. Still, he is always quietly doing other people favors. I have always thought, each time I have lost a friend or a tentmate, and they have bagged about half of both by now, thank God it wasn't Roger.

Tuck has gone to sleep, his mouth open, and a drink in one of the spotted cheese glasses balanced on his stomach. On his way out Bartlett leans over him and says softly, "You know what Sherman said outside the walls of Atlanta, Tuck? Well, outside the walls of Atlanta, Sherman, that great patriot, said to his men, 'Men, nobody shit around here and we can starve the sons of bitches to death.'"

Tuck opens and shuts his eyes and goes on sleeping. On the pillow beside his head Frank Ainsworth leaves the obscene photo. Even sleeping Tuck looks embarrassed. A boy who has just shot down an airplane and killed four people.

CHAPTER THREE

Across the wilderness in a glow
You'll catch sight of rushing streams,
Of steel helmets and sun flags red.

I WAKE up late. I know just about how late it is by the stuffi-
ness of the tent. I have already begun to sweat and that means
the sun is high enough to beat down from above the trees.
I push aside the net and get my cigarettes and Zippo out of my
shoe and slowly and lazily light a cigarette. The smoke is sweet
and sharp and for a while I just lie there contemplating things
with that special sleepy hostility of the first day off. Pretty soon
I start thinking about Corinne and how long it is now since I have
had a letter from her. What the hell can she be doing? I prefer
to concentrate on minor annoyances.

One of these is that we are getting a new tentmate, the ensign
here to replace Neely who finally got a real wound flying with
Prime. He was knocked down by a forty, while standing in the
waist, and broke his collarbone. He also got his pants full of
shards. We get the new one because we have only four in the tent.

Next I realize suddenly that they had eggs this morning in the
mess hall, and I have missed them. Real eggs once a week now,
because, as someone said, F.D.R. is dead. This remark may have
no meaning but it has significance. It is just the kind of half-assed
effort to be funny that you hear more and more of, remarks that
cannot be expanded into anything meaningful. They are a response to hackneyed stimuli, food and sex mostly. Conversation

disintegrates above the stomach and pin-up level. I am annoyed about missing my eggs because I am supposed to be, and while I am not fiercely chaste I could go a day or two without thinking about sex, if it weren't for our heroes. They can't wait to get a woman first and to drink a gallon of milk second, and . . . then eat up all the steak on mother's ration card. These are cardinal war aims.

I can't help remembering England. It seemed to me that the lowliest lance-corporal was grounded in some sort of world perspective, yet even our officers have none. I am sure there are advantages in the so-called democratic army. The chief of these is that no one has to stay in the army when there is no war going on. But I learned to fly in a world now dominated by the cheerfully intractable, elbow-bumping, know-nothing fraternity boys who have come crowding into the arena and reaped ninety-nine per cent of the commissioned rewards of aviation. They have noisily eliminated from the table of values nearly all the things that make a man an officer first and substituted all the things that make an officer a good fellow first. Stuart Ashton and Frank Ainsworth have been loot coms since the October allnav, but who can imagine one of them with a destroyer or a battalion or even a squadron of his own? To Frank Ainsworth Navy Regulations are nothing more than some sort of annoying and primitive taboos. In Ashton's opinion all command is barbaric tumult in a roomful of angry blindmen bent on killing everyone. As for Bill Bartlett, he might win election to the captaincy of a company of Illinois militia in a Blackhawk war if he brought enough grain alky and grapefruit juice to the meeting.

It isn't because they couldn't. It's because they have never been treated as though someday they might have to. None of us have ever been treated as anything except pilots, and although in the States all of us had piddly little collateral jobs—while 400 trained at San Diego I was parachute officer and counted the chutes once a week—out here there are, beyond censoring mail, no additional tasks for anyone, not even lieutenant commanders. There is, however, a great deal of additional pay.

I admire the English. There is no nonsense when they fight. They reduce everything to the act of fighting and their men are just as comfortable in war as ours, perhaps more so.

The best thing about being on this island is that that whistling, rocking, slavering insanity known as the U.S.O. hasn't found its way here. We are too small. I suppose everyone misses it except me, but I remember on Tinian how they came in their low-cut dresses and teased and patronized us as though we were feeble-minded children. They call it good clean apple pie and mom's biscuits fun, the teasing, the gratuitous kiss and the brief dance that some red-faced sailor from the audience gets from the star on the stage. They say the kiss is bestowed in the names of all the kid sisters back home. Only if you are a dirty-minded little boy can it demoralize you and send you home to masturbate. Well, if the roar that goes up and the inflamed remarks you hear afterward can be translated into heightened morale, if women's underthings and all the other totems of the flagellants are healthy goads to courage, then Hollywood is certainly winning this war for us and there is some good in the tyranny it exerts over us.

Skindome Dougherty is one man who doesn't think so. His airplane is the only one in the squadron that lacks the standard oriflamme, a nude girl. He has a huge gaunt devil with a trident, and the devil is chasing a little buck-toothed Jap in a kepi. For this departure from the etiquette Skindome is believed to be impotent, or perhaps queer, as it is necessary to prove a continual and emphatic interest in sex at all times, even while flying. Dougherty is queer, all right. He's sunk thirty-six ships and knocked down four airplanes. Only Prime has more airplanes and no one has that many ships. That's fourteen more than Ironhead Backus, twenty more than Ashton, and exactly thirty-three more than Kirby Stevens. But Kirby can catch him in the next war.

The sweat begins to puddle unpleasantly in the small of my back and I make myself sit up. I sit in utter boredom on the edge of my sway-backed cot and try to decide what to put on. Everything stinks. I put on the last pair of clean socks from my parachute bag, the same dirty shorts, and run a nose test on three

green shirts hanging on a string stretched to the tree outside. I
leave them there to freshen up, but today it is no use. Smelling
the armpits is like putting your face in an ether cone. Some of it
is me and some of it is the animal-fat soap of the laundry. It tags
you all day long. Every time you turn your head you get a whiff
from your collar, and it is necessary to go around like a pointing
bird dog to escape the odor.

Finally I wrap a towel around my waist and take the Coleman
stove outside to the "rock garden." Today the pillows nailed to the
chairs stink too because we forgot to protect them from the rain
last night. I light the stove and dig in the ammo box for cocoa,
crackers, jam and sugar. Some of my pictures are in the box too,
and while I'm waiting for the water to get hot, I look at them and
feel absurdly conceited because they seem so good. Conceit grows
where the facilities to make comparison fail, and of course there
is nothing to compare them with here.

I don't think they are *too* bad. Most of them are simple scenes
with natives hauling light, shadow-lined boats from the water, or
beaches with feathery palms behind them. My best is one of the
carabao wallow down the road. The animals are lolling in the mud
and I got what I wanted, a sense of the heat and the feeling of
the sucking mud and the smell, the real mephitic stench of the
wallow. I sent it home and Corinne wrote me how everyone raved
over it, especially her mother. I can see Mrs. Doerflinger and the
plump ladies of her church group clad in flowered spring dresses
and white shoes all exclaiming loyally over my picture. My
mother-in-law is furious with me because I have announced I am
not coming back to Madison after the war. She has written me
two peevish, or at least querulous, letters about it and there are
lines in them right out of Gilbert and Sullivan. What, never? (No,
never! no never! am I ever . . .)

It is quite typical. With their son-in-law ten thousand miles
away in the middle of a war, the Doerflingers can manage to be
indignant over a thing like that. All my married life they have
become embattled over the blunt beginnings of things because
they can't see open or ambitious endings to them. They can't

understand that I want to go somewhere where I can be exempt
from campus shenanigans and *Kleinburger* mores. It's not the
Midwest. I come from Albert Lea, Minnesota, and I'm about as
Main Street as anyone can be, but now I know I'm through with
Spoon River and Gopher Prairie and all the tree-lined, crossroads
of America. I'm through with people who think it is important
to keep ash trays out of the living room, who militate against anything they can't profit from or understand, who consider the war,
even, as nothing but a personal and abominable insult to themselves, an unanswerable and staggering injustice to the parents
of the young bucks on the block who (every third or fourth one
of them) may someday get shot at. At the same time it is these
brave Christian boys whose efforts will someday make everything all right. No one else is involved, no Russians, no English.
No one except some monkey people called the Japs who are
formidable only because they don't fight fair. Someday, of course,
the kitchen will be festooned again with church festival pies, and
Mr. D., free to take up his inner life of consumer-research prej-
udices once more, will be down in the cellar gosh-darning the
new lawn mower . . . but I won't be there, and neither will, I hope,
Corinne. My medical career is shot, I will be too old, but there
are other things. We can go to Sweden and learn how to design
decent houses. Or to Ephesus to dig for John's tomb, or among
the Hottentots to teach birth control. Who cares?

Yokum and Roger come down the road with the new ensign.
He is all dressed up in new khaki pants and even has wings
pinned to his shirt. Yokum has by contrast his old battered papier-
mâché sun helmet on his head, a dirty towel around his waist,
and G.I. shoes from which he has cut away the tops. He has also
slit louvers in the toes, dyed them yellow, and worst of all
fringed the tongues, to make what he calls "Lesbian boots."
The Navy is full of boots and boot fetishes, Yoke says. People
wear fighter boots and combat boots and Natal boots. Why not
boots for the few Lesbians? Yoke says he used to be a fag. But
then one day he discovered women and he went for them so hard
that he went right on through the barrier and out the other side

into Lesbianism. Only a Les can feel about women the way he does, Yoke says.

Roger is wearing his farmer's straw hat with the top cut out. His ginger mustache droops almost to his nipples, but his ginger hair sticks up through the hole like a rooster's hackles. He brought the hat with him from the cranberry bogs of Cape Cod, where Roger says his whole ambition lies. Lyin' in a bog and pettin' his hog. Someplace called Wareham on Buzzard's Bay. Roger is wearing the standard towel too and resembles an albino native prince with his fat white stomach. Only the flamboyant mustache ruins the picture. Walking beside them the new ensign looks like the Duke of Wellington.

As they get near, one of the laundry girls comes out of a tent and Yokum takes off his hat, bows, and offers her his arm for the walk up the road. The girl giggles and shies away, heaving a huge bundle of laundry up on her head and starting for home through the trees. Everyone of course watches her. She is very unattractive and very artless and often stops to let fly in the dust without taking the bundle from her head. A controlled stream, as Ainsworth says, just like a man, and he sometimes has enough time to snap a picture. The girl has a dusty, grayish complexion and thick legs with splayed toes. In addition she is hairy.

"Listen, listen!" Yokum says in a tone of quizzical outrage that has gradually become a habit. "Shave up those legs before tonight. I don't want to rub shins with a bear." He flops in a chair and shakes his head. "You know, I can stand the kind of legs that are a little thready-looking through stockings," he says to the new guy. "Like a dollar bill, kind of thready. But when you look down and you think a bear has got its legs under the table with you . . ." He digs in Roger's brassiere for cigarettes. For once Roger doesn't object. He is busy sniffing the air and snorting with disgust. It stinks all right. 420 has been giving us the treatment. They cross the road and urinate on our side in retaliation for what we do to the well.

"One giant latrine," Roger says sitting down. "Why do they have to come to our tent? They could spread it around a little."

"Well, they say that's just old Fatfag Smith," Yokum says. "Everybody pees on him. Why shouldn't we?"

I shake hands with the new ensign. His name is Arnold, and he arrived two nights ago in the Fat Cat. He doesn't know he is going to fly with Prime, and we don't tell him.

"They haven't told me a thing," Arnold says bleakly. "Hell, I haven't flown for two weeks. I've forgotten what a 4-Y looks like."

"Very sensible of you," Roger says. "Now that the Mexicans are in we can all quit flying."

"The Mexicans?"

"Yup. Six P-51's full of Mexicans are here. It's like saying the war is over. I forget whose side they are on, but they'll wind it up fast. Those Mexicans can fly." Roger makes an emphatic sucking sound to emphasize his admiration for the Mexicans. Arnold squats on a rock and then stands up again.

"Mr. McCord told me I was to move in with you guys if you don't mind," Arnold says.

"Sure," I say. "Where have you been sleeping?"

"Well, it was kind of late when I got here. I slept down there where that guy is all alone." Arnold points down the road where there is one tent at the end, rather isolated from all the others.

"Jesus!" Yoke says sitting up and looking. "You mean you spent two nights with Standing Room?"

"His name is Mara, I think," Arnold says meekly. "Something like that."

"Jesus!" Yoke says again looking at us in distress. "The guy spent two nights with Standing Room." Roger clucks and shakes his head and I make appropriate and lugubrious sounds. Standing Room Mara is something. He is our hermit, a morose and unhappy misfit in a world of superior and adjusted denominators, if you want to believe the propaganda of the Flying Cadet selection boards. He has low basal metabolism or something, drools, breathes exclusively through his mouth, and falls asleep while flying. God only knows how he got through the syllabus and made it to a squadron. Worst of all he seems pathologically given to living in filth. He never bathes, sleeps on a bed that is broken in the middle so that he is half on the floor, and he is usually covered with some sort of ugly rash which he treats by dusting himself with zinc powder. He is called Standing Room for a reason I have never been completely able to understand, except that it stems from the fact that when he enters the mess all of us take up as much room as possible on the benches to keep him from sitting next to us. Even Roger can find no sympathy for him and the rest of the squadron bait him continually.

"What's the trouble with that guy?" Arnold says sensing that he is on firm ground. "How long has he been sleeping in that busted bed?"

"You were lucky to get out of there alive," Roger says.

"He's a real squirrel," Arnold says. "I didn't unpack anything. If it's okay with you guys, I'll go down and get my stuff."

"We'll help you," Roger says. "Come on, Yoke, you haven't been down there in Gangreneville for a long time." Yokum is up at once. Baiting Mara is one of his favorite games. He pretends to look earnestly at each of us in turn.

"Just remember, you asked for it. I got a feeling it's gonna' be pretty grisly today." He tips his helmet deep over his eyes and goes ahead of us through the trees toward Mara's tent. When we get close we tiptoe. It is ten to one that Mara will be asleep.

Yoke goes up and peeks inside the tent. He comes back clutching his throat with both hands. From the tent we can hear loud snoring. "Don't let me run away," Yokum whispers pleadingly. "Hold hands. Don't let me run." Roger giggles at this and the snoring stops with a piglike grunt. In a few moments it resumes again, but with a rather wary tonality. We creep softly into the tent. Standing Room is asleep but I don't know why. Only his upper back is on the part of the cot that is still upright. His body and legs trail off on the floor. A single twisted and filthy sheet is jammed into the wreckage of the bed and one of Standing Room's feet appears through a rent, his long discolored toenails packed with earth. He has a half-buttoned shirt on, even in bed, and there is a line of red dots across it from the eruptions along his collarbones which he has scratched and made bleed again and again and blotted with the shirt. His face has a clogged look, like chicken skin, and is the only part of him that isn't wet. Everywhere else sweat bubbles from his shuddering body. It runs down his chest through little grooves in the caked layers of zinc powder, and the shirt is streaked with ancient sweat trails. Scattered on the dirt floor are some pieces from a small chess set and among them an open can of flight ration bacon, half-eaten, with sand adhering to it in greasy handprints.

Yokum stands there silently wrinkling his nose and then he lights a cigar, pretending to be very careful with the match. "The whole thing might go up," he says to Arnold.

Roger has gone closer and is bending over to examine one of the rivulets coursing down Mara's ribs. "Look," Roger says, "a flash flood. Just look at those boulders grinding along in there." Mara stops snoring and opens his eyes. He shows no surprise and doesn't even look at us.

"You guys," he says listlessly.

"Weel naow," Yokum says, "if it t'isn't Bridget O'Mara's foine broth of a buoy, and it's awake at last he is, him with the face of an angel and the foine milk-white skin of his mither, at t'all, at t'all." Mara raises his eyes wearily to the ceiling. There they stay.

"Standing Room," Roger says through his cupped hands as though he is some distance away. "They need a strip over at Towi right away. I told them you could level about ten acres an hour if you really got that old acid bath going and they said they think you might be their man. How about it?"

Yokum points at a bucket half full of water in the corner. "Jesus, it looks like he's weakening it with water these days."

"Oh no, you haven't done that, have you?" Roger says with fake calamity in his voice. "No, no, of course he hasn't. Old Standing Room wouldn't do a thing like that. We may have to dilute her down anyway. We have to lay mat in there and that means trimming her up with bulldozers and sending men in there, and sure as shooting some dumb Seabee will fall off his stilts again." Roger turns to Arnold who doesn't understand any of it. "I saw it, brother. The poor guy stumbled . . . there was a sizzle and a little puff of yellow smoke, and pffftt!" Roger snaps his fingers. "So long, one badly needed carpenter's mate!"

Someone calls from outside. It is Passage, the duty yeoman, with the schedule, tracking down the day's victims. I feel secure, having just flown yesterday. "Well, here comes tragedy and heartbreak for somebody," I say. "Come on in, Passage. You got a whole corral full."

Passage comes in, looks at a sheet in his hand and then around at our faces. "Fine," he says. "You're all here."

"What do you mean, we're *all* here?" Yokum says belligerently. He knows he has to fly but he never allows anyone to tell him without making some kind of counterattack. He has learned how to be difficult from Frank Ainsworth, the real master at it. Make it tough on them, Frank says, and someday when it's up for grabs who to pick on, they'll remember that the other guy won't complain so much and choose him.

But Passage just grins. He knows his power. The duty yeoman is the only enlisted man with the perpetual power to torture officers.

"Mr. Mara, start with you, take off oh-two-thirty, Crew Eleven. Okay?" Mara nods and Passage makes a check on his sheet. "Now, Mr. Arnold. You go out in Crew Nine with Mr. Prime, same time. That's tonight. Cross you off?"

"Sure thing," Arnold says coming over behind Passage to look at the sheet as though on it he will at last find a straight answer. "Who is Mr. Prime? Nice guy?"

"Congratulations," Yokum says. "Not everyone gets to start right out on the Orient Express."

"And Mr. Yokum, day hop at six and you'll probably have Mr. Beppolini and one of the new ensigns with you."

"And of course a great crew," Yokum says. "I hope they're not baking bread tomorrow so the cooks and bakers have to stay home. Listen, Passage, you tell Stevens I'm not due. I'm tired of getting stuck so often." Passage shrugs and shows Yokum his name on the pain sheet. It is a short all-daylight hop to

Borneo, only ten hours, and Yoke should be delighted to get it.

"Mr. Stevens makes out the schedule, not me," Passage says, making his eternal and banal reply to all protests.

"And lo, Ben Yokum's name leads all the rest," Roger says.

"I'm not due," Yokum says again. "But I'll go if it will help the squadron."

"Mr. Smith . . ."

"I already know."

"Zero-three hundred." Roger flies with the Captain. He is a little behind the rest of us checking out. "And Mr. Iverson." Passage's voice modulates unpleasantly upward.

"Whoa! Not me. I flew yesterday."

"Yes sir, but we need a stand-by copilot and Mr. Stevens said to use you."

"Stand-by for what?"

"Well . . ." Passage rubs the pencil eraser across his brows. "About an hour ago, the Captain give Mr. Brady the ungarbled word. I ain't supposed to know but I do. Fly or quit. If he quits he's gotta stay out here until the squadron is relieved. Do some kind of work. If he flies, it's gotta be now, tonight."

"With whom?" I feel a nervous flood in the region of my bowels.

"Well, since Mr. Foy has gone to Owi for six days, they give him his place." Foy is Prime's other copilot. He has only been at it a few weeks, but like all the rest, the extra burden of fear has reduced him too. Ironhead gave him a rest by sending him down to Owi to see about a new airplane they are getting ready for us. Since Neely got hurt, there has been a sort of girlish intrigue going on among the new copilots by which they seek to avoid flying with Prime. Recently Stevens hasn't bothered any of the old guys.

"Why me? Why not one of the new apes?"

"Mr. Prime says he don't want two boot ensigns. One is enough." Passage looks at Arnold. "He says he wants a good guy to handle the radio reports."

For that I have to stick my neck on the block. Brady will never go, not if he has to stay out twenty years. I am thunderstruck with my misfortune. "I'll let you know at six," Passage says. "Mr. Brady has till then to decide." But he smirks to show how futile it is to rely on Brady coming back.

"Oh crap," I say miserably. "Why me?" If I had only known I could have escaped in a variety of subtle ways. I understand Kirby Stevens' mentality, where the newer guys don't. They herd around his desk, speculating openly and cheerfully about their chances of flying with Prime, and hoot and holler as though it is some form of roulette. It is fatal to be cheerful or gallant in front of Kirby, but he dislikes a certain kind of personal argument that I have learned to give him, and if I am warned, I can usually make him shy away from me. Now he has surprised me and I have bought this one before I knew what was going on.

"You can show me where to go and what to take along," Arnold says to me. He looks contented. "How do you wake up, anyway?"

This gets a loud guffaw from Mara. He is enjoying himself because he knows how shocked and terrified I am. "Don't worry, junior. You got a built-in alarm clock sleeping right next to you. It will go off about every three minutes all night long!" Passage laughs. I hate him too, because he has conquered me so easily and remained so secure himself. His job is safer than being a street cleaner back in the States. Mara I don't mind, in fact I feel a sudden remorse that I have been along for the baiting. Mara is intelligent, perhaps not as blackly intellectual as he pictures himself, but he has ideas. People hate him for those, as well as for his habits, but at least he thinks. Too often he is merely the arrogant voice at midnight, denying God, or cutting across some other line dear to men isolated and forced together in numbers, with that vulgarity that is so exasperating when it comes from unpopular people. But he has brains.

"Foy, that chicken," Roger says. "If everybody can just go dick off down there at Owi when they don't feel like flying . . ." Roger has flown with Tommy Prime. For a second I feel that he is now making a diversion because he is afraid I may try to involve him again. Then I really feel like a turd. "Tell you what," Roger says. "I'll grab this one and you grab the next. It's all the

same to me, if I get it in the ass tonight then I don't get it in
the ass next week. Because there are going to be a lot of these.
I can smell it coming. Ironhead won't mind."

"No, no," I say vaguely. "I don't give a damn." Only Arnold
doesn't know what a liar I am.

"Just make sure I wake up, will you, Iverson?" he says earnestly.
He begins to collapse his bed and assemble his things. Passage
leaves, followed closely by Yokum who is still admonishing him
to watch the rotation on crews more closely. I absent-mindedly
pick up Mara's chess pieces, blow the dust off them and set them
in a row on one of the tent frames. Roger picks up the can of
bacon and puts it beside the chessmen. It towers over them like a
shiny tin monster. Mara watches us glumly. Then he begins to
pull on his pants. He does it without getting up, wiggling his
behind in an exact parody of a woman slipping on a girdle.

"Okay, Samaritans. Thanks for picking up my toys. Now how
about getting the hell out?"

"Sure, Standing Room, right away," Roger says gently. "But
aren't you going to . . . scrape . . . or something? At least toss a
little zinc in there. The Seam-squirrel Miners Union will go out on
strike . . ."

"Ha, ha." Mara shakes his head in pity. "Honest to Christ. The
cheerleaders of America. Let's all wear Yankee ball caps. Let's
all paddle somebody's ass with a paddle. Why don't you squeal
louder, Iverson? Tell Ironhead it's unfair to make you fly with
Prime because you aren't fraternity brothers. Besides, your ball
cap hasn't come." Mara rolls on his broken bed in simulated
ecstasy. "God, God, I can hardly wait. When we invade Japan,
or in the next war, maybe. The screams we'll hear when three out
of four get knocked off because the other guy finally holds the
cards, or because his machinery is as good as ours at last. He's
already got ten times the guts because he's not all wrapped up in
ball caps and jerk-off literature!"

"Come on," Roger says to me. "Or we'll have to listen to the
big post-war, glacier-coming-thing again." It's Mara's constant
theme. All about the political and moral icing-up of America, the

debasement of all taste, the smothering of all ideals in a welter of billboards and cheap diversion.

Roger and I carry the bed and the extraneous gear and Arnold lugs his big parachute bag. It looks very heavy so perhaps there is some whisky in it. "Goodbye, Standing Room," Roger says. "And give those seam-squirrels a break. Put some blowers down there in the zinc mines or something."

Halfway up the road Arnold stops to take off the new shirt, with the wings pinned to it. His back is dripping from carrying the bag just a few yards. He ties the shirt around his waist by the sleeves and prepares to lug the bag further. "Here," I say, thinking about the whisky, "give me one of the handles." We carry it together and Roger takes the cot by himself. The bag is heavy and bangs against our legs. The sweat squilches out of me in torrents. We stop to rest and Arnold looks back at Mara's tent with a smile of faint disgust, the first tiny sign of personality he has dared to reveal. But now it will come faster, and after the trip with Prime he will feel solidly in place.

"Don't the Captain ever tell that guy to take a brace, get cleaned up a little?" I don't know why, but I resent Arnold terribly at the moment.

"What for?" I say, striving to get the contempt, amusement, patience, and superiority of the old soldier at the front to the new downy-cheeked recruit into my voice. I get it. Arnold looks embarrassed.

"I don't know . . . morale. As an example. Having a dirty guy like that around, an officer, it must make the enlisted guys . . ."

"Maybe. But we have enough morale. Ironhead doesn't mess with it. We all know he thinks Mara is a dirty pig. It's worth more that way."

The con game. I make something up and Arnold nods several times with his mouth open as though discovering in what I have said the answer to a deep riddle. I don't know why Ironhead doesn't get rid of Mara for sanitary reasons. We tried, once, long ago in Tinian. We threw Mara in the sea. To teach him. But he remained in the water for hours, imperturbably swimming in his

clothes and robbing us of any satisfaction. And he didn't change
a bit.

Arnold gives me a cigarette, a Camel. I haven't seen a Camel
for weeks despite the billions supposedly shipped daily overseas.
I ask him about replacements. He says there are plenty but they
take much too long getting through all the syllabi. He was three
months in Kaneohe. I picture the man who will replace me spending days learning how to make salad out of palm shoots at the
survival lectures out at the Bishop Museum while I sit and wait
for him.

"I was in a crew but they busted it up," Arnold says. "We had
a smart aleck plane captain who got to crawling out through the
nose wheel doors and one day we ran over him."

"Kill him?"

"Damn right. Then the P.P.C. was check-out happy. He liked
to get things in his log book, you know, that he's flown a PBM
once or something . . . so he'd go down to the ramp and mooch
time. They finally let him make a jato take-off in a Duck and the
cockpit collapsed on him. He went to the sick bay all stove in . . .
then a radioman got an appendix attack and the other pilot
besides me broke a rib swimming there at Mokapu, where you
aren't supposed to go in. They broke us up."

"You've had a tough war already."

"That same guy went to Clark and the first patrol he went on
the airplane didn't come back. I heard it in Leyte day before
yesterday. I heard there's a squadron there lost sixty per cent of
its crews in about one month." Arnold looks at me solemnly.

"That's a madhouse," I say. "I was there for two weeks. I was
plenty happy to get out."

People are drifting by going to the mess hall. It is a good
morning, with high white clouds over the mountains, and despite
the heat, a fresh little breeze coming from somewhere. Out over
the Sulu there are more clouds in big pearly heaps. A fine day to
die, I think inanely. Yokum and Roger are standing in the road
calling to us. "Slop down, fore and aft," Yoke shouts up and down
the street.

We carry the bag to the tent and I put on a pair of green dungaree pants. Engelson has forbidden eating without shirt and trousers. Roger looks at Arnold appraisingly as we come out again. "The big problem was to get the kid out of there before he caught the yaws or something. I think we made it." He signals to me to indicate that Arnold has taken the wings off his shirt. "He'll make a good squirrel hunter," Roger says in a fatherly way.

The hot lunch of pork and beans and string beans swimming in their own water makes us sweat harder than ever. Sitting in the crowded mess shack is rather like staying with your head under a blanket for too long a time. You breathe harder and harder but it doesn't seem to do any good. The bodies around you seem to compress the heat and force it into you, and even though I sit by a window screen I feel as hemmed in as though surrounded by steel walls. It takes us about five minutes to eat.

As we go out Tom Parker notices the tomato remnants bubbling in the first big steam caldron where the enlisted men slosh their trays. Since we didn't have tomatoes today, the residuals must be from yesterday. Parker swears and charges into the galley to ream out the cooks, and we watch through the screen. Nobody can score on a cook. As Parker roars they just twist their necks and pull at the sleeves of their T shirts, scratching among the hair on their arms like perplexed monkeys while they give Parker some version of the standard "beats the heck out of me, sir, I ain't the regular mess cook Tuesdays."

We wander slowly back to the tent and sag into our chairs. At two there will be a lecture on the use of morphine. Since it is compulsory to attend it once, and since Tom Parker has already given it twice and this is the last time, we will have to go. It is irritating to me because I am downright nervous about going out with Prime. I want to go off and be alone. I know Brady won't make it. The lousy lunch was a milestone on the way to complete terror, and now there is only supper and the night between me and the reckoning. I don't count tomorrow's breakfast which will be simply a gagging horror of adrenalin chills, oily coffee, and too many cigarettes.

Arnold goes off to prowl for lumber. He wants to have a chair too. We used to have six, but dead men's chairs disappear quickly when the mortal adventures of their owners are over. Segrave's has found its way over to 420. I have seen it there with his name stenciled on the back. I don't know where Honey's is. Glenotre never had one. He had a hammock instead, but that was always full of rain water and finally rotted away. Glenotre and Segrave have rotted away too. They have been a long time moldering in the depths off Catanduanes.

Yoke heaves himself up and helps himself to Roger's cigarettes in the brassiere. To annoy Roger he rummages around in it a long time.

"Watch your filthy roving hands," Roger growls feebly. We sit and listen to the flies buzzing inside the screened head down the road. The net effect is the sound of an erratic dynamotor. They burn and spray and trap the huge dreadful flies so that they die by thousands and form a carpet on the ground, but still they come on, beating the screens with that unnatural, needless strength that, most revolting of all, they seem to draw from the reeking pits underneath. Arnold comes back. He has been intercepted by Fred McCord and handed a stack of bulletins and booklets he is supposed to read. Radio procedures, encoding tables, emergency procedures, cruise control. He squats down and shuffles through the books. "What should I *really* know?" he says to me. I look at the stuff he has. There is even a loran handbook but there is no loran out here.

"When you first get inside," Yokum says sleepily, "you'll see a . . . what, class? Right, Copilot Fatfag! A wheel. Like this." He makes a pie-sized circle with his hands. "Wheel, steering, mark five mod nine, and don't touch it. Have you ever noticed the wheel up there in the front of an automobile? No? Ah, some of the class, yes? Well, it looks exactly like that little old wheel. Now keep your eye on it because in less than fourteen years you'll be steering with it!"

Arnold laughs weakly. "You mean I don't get any landings?"

"*Sure* you do, *sure* you do. For example in forty-three I had a landing. Two, in fact. They really piled them on me that year and the result was I was overtrained."

Yokum pulls one of the binders out of Arnold's stack of books. "Now read this . . . this is word. Field Service Bulletin twenty-four able," Yoke reads. "Fuel transfer procedures in B-24 airplanes paren applies through serial numbers four-oh-one-one-one-nine-three-eight, unparen. And you won't get confused either because every one of our goddam airplanes has far higher numbers than that and none of it applies to any of them. Jesus Christ!" Yoke throws the booklet helplessly up in the air over his head. "You too can win your Navy wings of gold! You know that poster, Arnold? Do you have that something extra? There's a guy and a Corsair and a lot of beams of light streaming down on them? Well, behind that Corsair, there's another guy. You can't see him but he's there. You'll find him wherever you go in this man's Navy. His name is Commander Bigfinger and that's just what he's got, ready and waiting for you. That big finger is the only thing you'll ever fly." Yoke shakes his head slowly and sadly. "But even giant warthogs get through somehow," he says. "Giant, fat-assed, blubbery, disgusting warthogs from Cape Cod."

Roger eyes the distance. Yoke is slumped down with the sun helmet over his eyes. Still, Roger never knows if he is watching. Roger eases forward in his chair. Yoke doesn't move. The hat is tilted so far forward that it covers his face down to the tip of his nose. At regular intervals his cigarette makes the trip from his knee to a point just off the brim of the hat, hesitates a moment like a mud wasp seeking it's home in a cranny, and then goes in under the hat. Masses of smoke billow out. Yoke seems able to inhale and exhale at the same time. It makes you dizzy to watch him.

"By God, I think Midway broke our back," Yoke continues. "Took the cream except for a few guys like me. They just don't send us the kind of boys they used to. Just fat bastards in straw hats with harelips. I sawr a bananer in the winder of a cah in Canader. People who talk like that should be exterminated."

Roger jumps up and tries to pound him. Yokum whips from

the chair so that Roger's fingers crack the wood, and like lightning he has hit Roger hard on both arms. Yoke taps his chest. "It's not the iron in the ships, Arnold. It's the iron in the men that counts. Come on, it's five of." He gets up, wipes his stomach with a towel and meanders off in the direction of the dispensary tent. We follow wearily.

In front of the dispensary there is a small table with a single wilted orange on it. Fifteen or twenty men are sitting on the sandy ground smoking and reading mail. In the road Zalewski and Cunningham are tossing a softball back and forth. Zalewski was a semi-pro softball pitcher in Detroit and very good. He throws with incredible speed and all kinds of stuff on the ball—so much so that when we used to have intercrew games he would pitch no-hitters nine times out of ten. In the last inning the rest of us never took the field, only Zalewski and the catcher. Now no one plays any more.

Tom Parker arrives with a small chest. He unlocks it and takes out a box of morphine Syrettes, then carefully locks the chest again. The Syrettes are worth twenty-five dollars apiece in Honolulu and were stolen so often that they are no longer left in the kit on the airplane.

Jericho, the fairy corpsman, comes out of the tent, is seen and jeered by the men on the ground, and takes up his stand beside Tom Parker, posing like some magician's assistant. There are snickers at his girlish, hippy motions. Jericho is probably the brainiest guy in the squadron, with several degrees, and very nice too. He is not aggressively or even passively up to anything around here, and whatever he is he keeps it down. He seems more like a boy who was raised by old maid aunts, or slept in his mother's room till he was seventeen or something, than a fairy, but who knows? Standing Room Mara is highly touted as a great chess player but I have seen Jericho beat him easily in a handful of moves.

Now McCord arrives to take attendance. He wanders through us like a diligent overseer, tells us to settle down, tells a mumblety-peg game to "belay that," tells us, as though making some kind of dispensation, that the smoking lamp is lit. "Pay attention," McCord says. "This may save your life. Three men died at Morotai the other day because someone didn't know his ass from a tin cup and gave them too much morphine."

Behind me there is soft muttering. "No shit, Mr. McCord? Now hear this men, Mr. McCord has kindly lit the smoking lamp for us." There is quiet derogatory talk about Mr. McCord everywhere. Just soft enough so that he can't hear anything specific. Someone nudges me. It is Andretta, our radioman second.

"How you makin' out, Mr. Iverson? You gonna beat the rap?"

"What do you think?"

"Well . . . it's fourth down for Mr. Brady. He may make it."

"You better stay with us," Cunningham says. "Mr. Ashton says from now on he don't go after nothing unless he can see oarlocks first."

Wouldn't I like to! Every time I think about it I feel my glands flush something through me, and automatically I begin an inane conjuring process to try to eliminate what *could* happen. I pray, I rub my wedding ring, I cross and uncross my fingers in a ritual I have developed. But before I have finished with one terror, I have already thought up another. In the odd moments I wish I had never joined the Navy, never left Albert Lea, and was 4-F and driving the Good Humor wagon as I used to do in the summertime in my high-school years. My God, I think, I could spend the rest of my life on that wagon listening to the tinkling bells and being neighborly. When I am scared I long for life at its simplest level because it somehow seems more likely to be granted to me there.

Parker has the orange and stands there tossing it from hand to hand, waiting for the noise to subside. He is still too much the civilian doctor to order it to stop.

"Okay, Zalewski," McCord calls nasally. "Waiting on you. Or maybe you'd like to give the lecture?"

A few men guffaw. "What on?" somebody says. "How to adjust a prophylactic bag?"

"Whorehouses in Hamtramck," Cunningham says. Zalewski

gets on his knees, removes his baseball cap and bows all around.

"I want to show you how to use a morphine Syrette correctly in case you have a wounded man on board," Parker says. "And so you won't make a mistake and kill somebody. Actually only one man died at Morotai . . ." He looks at McCord who shrugs to show he is not responsible for bum word ". . . but a couple were so narcose they would have died without prompt attention."

He opens the box, takes out a Syrette and unsheathes the needle. Jericho flashes around tidying up the table. Parker takes the orange and in an easy fluid motion sticks the needle into the carcass of the orange. There are immediate moans all around. "Remember each Syrette has a quarter grain. I might add that the standard hospital dose is an eighth, although it isn't used much any more. So be careful. Keep track of what you're doing. Don't jab a man every time he howls." He demonstrates again, jabbing the orange several times.

"That's enough, Doc," Cunningham says. "My cheeks are hard as walnuts just watching that." There is a titter. Parker smiles patiently. He starts to explain shock. Almost at once the needless questions begin. People don't ask for the sake of knowledge, they are simply projecting themselves, being heard. Cunningham is like that. He gets involved in a train of progressively more pointless questions and soon the audience is groaning each time he says something.

"Well, what is shock exactly? You mean like losing all your blood?" There is a scattered cheer.

"Shock is a marked lowering of all the vital activities of the body . . . that follows an injury . . . a wound. Particularly a penetrating wound. The body becomes cold, the pulse thready, breathing shallow, and so on."

"The way you feel all the time, Cunningham."

"Oh, that's what killed the guy at Morotai, huh sir?" Groans.

"No, he fell in the head and the squirrels ate him up. Jesus weep!"

"No, I just said it was too much morphine."

"Yeah, well what I mean is, what happens when you slug too

much morphine in there, you go into shock?" There is a wail of
derisive laughter. Cunningham is not that dumb. He is enjoying
himself.

"Morphine depresses the apparatus with which you breathe.
The point is that the man who died was only superficially injured
and would not have died of his wound. But because he kept
groaning, some ignoramus kept sticking him with these." Parker
holds up the box. "He had about three grains in him."

"I hear they killed eight guys that way after Balikpapan,"
Cunningham says.

"If Cunningham heard it, you can divide it by twenty," someone
says.

"Unless he's talking about tail. Divide that by four hundred."

Parker is foundering in questions and would-be wit and since
McCord has left there is no one to save him. We are the only
officers and outside of an airplane none of us would dream of
issuing an order, especially one that might lead to unpopularity.
But Parker heads off the trend by talking rapidly and without
stopping until he is finished. A final admonition or two and he
picks up the chest and is gone.

The people get up but there is no hurry to leave. There is no
place to go. "Hey, pogie bait," someone calls to Jericho who is
collapsing the table, "is it true you was gettin' forty bucks a shot
in Kaneohe for the stuff and spendin' it on nice young Jap boys?"

"Eighty," Jericho says smiling. "Ask Cunningham."

"Ask Cunningham," Zalewski says. "Like that time on Guadal.
They caught some nurse peddlin' her ass at a hundred a throw,
see? She had about five thousand bucks already. But Cunningham, goddam his soul, told me she was gettin' five hundred a belt
and had eighty grand in her mattress. So I didn't go over."

"What are you, a tightwad, Ski?"

"That's when he learned how to build orangutang traps."

"Well, Cunningham told me it was pretty good stuff."

Zalewski flips the ball to Cunningham and they begin the
eternal game of catch, backing away from each other, Cunningham squatting professionally to receive the pitch. Zalewski holds

the ball a fraction of a second in a peculiar way just under his chin, then whips it out. The ball flashes through the mottled shade and light under the trees and plunks into Cunningham's mitt. With each pitch I can hear the clank of Zalewski's dog tags and holy medals. It reminds me to say a Hail Mary (which I have learned because it is short), to rub my ring and, pretending I am just doodling, to rap my knuckles on the trunks of three palm trees in succession. Like birth pangs, the flushes of fear come more and more often. Maybe I'm dilating, as they say. Around in back.

At five o'clock I hear that Ironhead is having another talk with Brady. I can picture the scene, Brady going deeper into the shifting sands of his imagination and telling the Captain he should have gone into submarines. My God, picture the scene! The lights are going on and off, jets of water are shooting in from the bulkheads, Brady's face is growing pastier with each illumination. Then in the middle of the canning, Brady finally tells the skipper he will have to come up and quit, his tympani are hurting him again. Perhaps he has convinced himself he does have an ulcer, unbearable sinus, migraine, earaches. But he should never have retreated from his stomach and let himself be cornered in an outcropping like the ear.

Well, who am I to scream saffron at anyone? I am as chicken as anyone can be; it's just that unlike Brady I have never had the chance to consider myself important or indispensable. In his world, if I *had* been good at football, let's say, I might have spent the whole season on the bench because of a morbid fear of fractures.

I sit in the tent and wait, a little hopeful, in spite of myself. I watch Arnold innocently and meticulously sorting over the articles in his survival kits. He uncorks the halazone pills, sniffs and corks them up again, fiddles with the signal mirror, stretches a condom over the muzzle of his pistol. Roger and Yokum come in.

"Well, what's the poop on Fighting Tim Brady?" Yoke says.

"None that I know of."

"Yes sir," Roger says. "Old number seventy-eight has got to

throw a block now or turn in his jock. Your boy, Mom, is entering
a big new world, Mom. His letter up at State U don't mean a thing
out here, Mom. He's in the Big League now. The biggest League
of them all, Mom."

I have to leave. Just a little bit of Roger and Yokum will drive
me crazy right now. I see Monty Herbert go by on his way to the
late confab in the Wing Quonset. The sun dips. Milestones. I
wander among the trees, come out on the beach and hurry
stupidly over the barriers of fallen palm trunks and rotting fronds.
On the beach the sinking sun still catches the sand and I run
through the glare until I come to a shallow pool in a basin of rock.
I make myself squat beside the pool and study the life in the
water as though salvation somehow depends upon an immediate
and deep concentration on it. A spider starfish is moving slowly
along the bottom and I take a stick and gently flip him over on his
back and watch as the feathery arms contract to bridge the body
like a wrestler and to twist it suddenly rightside up again. In the
meaningless moment I wish I had become a naturalist. It is almost
as silly as the Good Humor wagon escape. Life, that's what I
want, in a flat, solidified plane. In a quiet museum. In a music
box on wheels.

I try to think about Corinne and me in a cottage, in a permanent heaven made out of song lyrics. How she would hate it. I
think of our goodbye and how much I hated the way that went.
No fine remembrance, no picture to hold in my mind, just a
jumble of ridiculous remonstrances from the Doerflingers, as
always onstage, and then the very real failure between Corinne
and me. Finally the entire incomplete and ragged scene moving
away from me—Corinne already leading the dog toward the car,
street crossings becoming more and more unfamiliar as the train
leaves the town, and in a last look back through the curving
smoke and wheeling buildings, their car cutting the track behind
me, severing the lifeline.

I lie on my back and look off at the white clouds billowing over
the mountains. A gaggle of P-38's comes in from the southeast,
flying low over the field and then making a great arcing, exag-

gerated turn to get into the pattern. I begin again to imagine the spar-cracking, dizzy, gyrating bedlam that will take place in Prime's airplane. Super-flying. I hate it more than war or weather or anything. It is the way the Primes fly, beyond the limits of my understanding, beyond the limits of the airplane itself, a form of super-flying that must be instinctive. Prime was born with this ability, just as a mongoose is born with the ability to conquer snakes.

In a shock of new apprehension I sit up. Someone is responsible, but who? God, maybe, but I don't believe in him. What a convenience if I did. Roger is a Catholic but I don't know how far he takes it. Does he ask God to soften the jarring blows of the air, stop the electrical muttering, watch over him on the schedule? God, God, God, clanking on the end of a chain under ten million skivvy shirts . . . have you still got time for me? God, sitting in the center of a huge vibrating web, sorting out the few worthy signals from the hopeless jangle going up, listening for the bleats of the righteous in the storm of mechanical noise . . . God, while I lie waiting tonight, seemingly balanced on nothing but my elbows and the two cheeks of my buttocks, I will ask you to stir the air from above. Leave off the direction of a billion moons, ten quadrillion orbits and look out for me . . . and of course, God, I'll never ask you for another thing!

It is after six. I get up, brush off the sand calmly enough and start back. I walk around through the trees until I can see our tent. One look tells me the story. Roger and Yoke are there and Beppo and Cox and some others. Roger is draping the front fly of the tent with a long piece of black mosquito netting. They are getting ready for me. The Funeral March hummed, the mock benedictions, the sort of Grand Guignol pantomime that is Yoke's specialty. "You've all experienced blacking out, class, well Priming out is merely an extension of it. It occurs when the eyeballs have been sucked far enough down in the belly by centrifugal force to pass the a-hole which is on its way up to its permanent new location in the throat . . ."

I get out on the road and begin to trot. After a bit I slow to a

walk in case anyone should see me. There is an illusion of successful flight walking down the road and away from the camp. I
am at this moment actually walking toward San Francisco.

Up on the mountains there is an area of colorless gloom under
the big clouds. It is already sliding down the dark green hills,
blotting out the details of the land. If I go back now I will be
ready to bathe when the evening shower hits the camp. But I
go on. To be clean is not a virtue when you are riding shotgun on
the Tombstone Express. Courage is the thing that counts.

Eight o'clock. I take Arnold and go to find Tom Prime—Tommy
that is; it sounds more deadly as a diminutive. Billy the Kid might
not have scared anyone if they called him Bill.

Prime is playing poker down the road with the Army Engineers,
where a game is in eternal session, moribund only in the twilight
before payday. There are half a dozen players around the blanket-
wrapped table. Prime is wearing his hat with the tarnished and
unraveling braid on it, and he has pushed it back so that a lock of
dark curls hangs boyishly down from under the vizor. He is very
handsome and has the delicately dangerous air of a story-book
Mississippi gambler. One of the watchers tells me reverently that
there is a very big pot on the table. Around six hundred bucks.

I have an immediate feeling "The Prime" will win it. It is
apparent in the red and sweating faces of the others, in their
despondent eyes and twisted lips and weary grins. Prime wins
continuously. Not just at cards. He wins the women, good whisky,
cameras and convertibles. The things that make up a brimming
life for people like him seem to come effortlessly into his hands.
He is always trading, selling, dealing—and winning. I have noticed
that wherever we go—that is, any place half civilized—Prime inevitably appears inside an hour with the most gorgeous girl in the
world. He doesn't turn them up in the middle of the Gobi, where
they would be relatively much easier to find, he turns them up in
Norfolk or Honolulu where it is impossible. The girls are always
well-dressed and made up even if it is nine in the morning. They
must live in costume jewelry and lacquered hair waiting for him,
for the call, like firemen, and it becomes almost impossible to

imagine them in anything else, in slacks or a bathing suit—or even naked. After a while, when you have seen them that way, sitting around in convertibles or in the lounges of B.O.Q.'s or too early in the O Club, they begin to express a dullness and a repetitious formula that discounts their heavy physical charms. Their faces are all beautiful, contented, passionless, as they sit around waiting for Tommy Prime.

It has always been hard for me to think of extraordinarily handsome people ever being very intimate with one another, but it is impossible for me to picture Prime and his women as animated or cruel to one another or at all passionate. Prime seems unaffected by the ordinary currents of life, never seems to eat or sleep, gambles endlessly, smokes enough cigars in a night to gag five normal men, and in his spare time works lackadaisically at the job of staying abreast of Skindome Dougherty who devotes full time to his work. Dougherty has thirty-six ships and Prime thirty-four, but in one of his spasmodic fits and starts Prime is liable to go ahead by five in a single morning's madness. . . .

Arnold and I wait and watch. There is only one man besides Prime left in the hand, a major, who gazes stonily at the crumpled bills and faded chips on the blanket. Now and then he slides his cards up his chest in a stealthy way to look at them as though he has forgotten what he holds. Prime sits among his props. In front of him, pinning down a thick sheaf of money, is a polished fifty-caliber slug on a gold chain. At one elbow is an alarm clock set to ring at the time specified for the end of the game. The Major waves irritably at the layer of cigar smoke and swipes viciously at his nose. Prime whistles a scrap of a tune in an incredibly high register, warbling and trilling like a bird. It is one of the inconsequential talents that he has, along with the card sense and flying.

The major is acting like a dog who is afraid to jump from a high place. Prime picks up the slug and twirls it dreamily. Under his cap his face shines like ivory. He winks at me. "Malaya," he says to no one in particular. "We ought to find something in Kuantan."

"It's the sector below," I say in a tone calculated to play down the potentials of the flight. "Not much in it."

"We'll find something," Prime says. The major slides his hand up his chest for the umpteenth time. I feel inexplicably sorry for him and wonder if he would feel sorry for me if he knew my predicament. Prime sings, something about being "just a sand crab from San Diego." Someone snickers and Prime rewards him with a smile, flashing his white teeth.

"Kings over eights, goddam it," the major says turning up his cards.

"I think you got him, Paul," the man beside him says.

"And you pushed out a little gietus?" Prime says leaning forward a little.

"It's there," the major says sarcastically, tapping some bills he has advanced a few inches in front of him. Prime fans his cards on the table. He has aces and queens.

"You, you goddam sandbagger," the major says bitterly to the man next to him.

"Like hell," the man says. "I got about one-five-oh in that pot myself don't forget."

"More?" Prime says picking up the pot. "A friendly game . . ."

"Screw that," the major says getting up. Prime shrugs and looks at me again.

"This is Jim Arnold," I say. "He's going with us. His first trip." Arnold takes an awkward step forward but he can't get close enough to shake hands and Prime doesn't look as though he wanted to. He just nods at Arnold.

"Just make sure you got everything. Neely always handles the code stuff, sends the weather . . . all that. So you do that."

"Okay."

"And I like to leave a little early. Say a quarter after. The days are getting longer and the sun is up before you get anywhere."

"Okay."

"I don't eat so I'll see you at Early Bird the Turd's." He is referring to Monty Herbert, for whom he has no use at all.

"Okay."

Outside it is dark with no stars, but the road shows as a tawny streak through the blackness under the trees. The illusion of this afternoon is gone, the road doesn't lead toward San Francisco. It is simply an alley, bounded by darkness, leading only to fear.

From the tents come the routine post-movie obscenities. Arnold and I walk along between the fingerlings of faint light that stab out from the tents and even he is quiet now. As for me I have hit the maximum drag. Anxiety is at its peak and can go no farther.

Roger and Yokum come home early but I pretend to be asleep. "Lucky Pierre," Yokum says. "Well, scratch one more roommate."

"Chances are it will be quick and clean," Roger says.

I sleep a little but wake every few minutes to look at my watch. My eyes oscillate from fatigue. Once the dial seems to read three o'clock and I am flooded with sudden hope that the flight has been canceled. But three o'clock becomes quarter past twelve when I look a little harder. I am up and half-dressed when Barker, the other yeoman, comes to wake us.

Arnold comes over on tiptoes, like a conspirator. "What now?" he whispers.

"Eat. You got everything?"

"I hope so. The chute harness is too big. I don't want to be deballed." He snickers. I don't bother to tell him he'll never need it. There's no sense in jumping out where we're going, and if there was we can't do it unless we have plenty of time and altitude, things nobody ever has in masthead bombing.

Roger isn't flying until half an hour after us. He sleeps soundly always right up to the last minute.

The mess shack is full this morning. Beppo is there, going out with Frank Ainsworth, his regular job. He looks at me in surprise. "What the hell are you doing?" The little runt knows damn well. But to be congenial on my last day on earth, I slowly raise the middle finger in the time-honored gesture, peel it like a banana, and jab it in the air.

"Too ambitious," Beppo says. "Me, I was all set for lunch with Yoke over Great Natoena today, but that mother Stevens dropped a crab in the beer."

Natoena is an island off the Borneo coast with nothing on it but an abandoned airfield. It is a wonderful place to dick off. You can bomb the deserted hangars and strafe the old wrecked airplanes lying around and not so much as an enemy seagull will you see. Neutralizing Natoena, it's called.

Beppo wails and moans about his life with Frank Ainsworth and I gripe about the deal handed me. This pleases Arnold. At least he looks pleased. He is glad to be here in our darkest hour.

It is a lonesome walk to the ACI tent with this strange crew. They are a glum crowd of shufflers and say almost nothing to each other in contrast to the magpies in our crew. It occurs to me, of course, that there is a good reason for this. I say goodbye to Beppo and really mean it. In a few hours we will be two thousand miles apart.

When Prime arrives at the ACI tent, tarnished gold eagle and all, Monty Herbert gives him a special little smile. Herbert is a great admirer of the killers, and in particular Prime, whom he looks upon as a sort of wonderful, murderous baby. He reminds me of an aging businessman squeezing Joe Louis's muscles and gasping in overworked awe. It makes no difference that Prime despises him and all other "grounders," he hurries to give Tommy a special report on some shipping that is supposed to lie in a harbor called Raja Wali inside our sector. Prime reads it with no show of interest and spends his time studying wall maps, while Herbert is giving us his counsel. Skindome Dougherty listens with his head bent, Frank Ainsworth sits correctly and dispiritedly slumped in his "attract no attention" pose, Bill Bartlett dozes. If Herbert says anything unusual, Ainsworth will bitch quickly, out of sheer policy. Skin-conscious Frank is a scientific griper, incorporating the voices of his satrap copilots, Beppo and John Excel, into a storm of protest designed to fend Herbert off from trying to promote any of his little additions.

"No bull drop today," Ainsworth says eying a bale of leaflets on the table. "I only got thirty-one fifty on board. I'll be lucky to make it home."

"They're not for you, Frank," Herbert says gently. He looks at Prime's back, over at the map. "It's all little stuff, Tommy, but

you may root out a Fox Tare Charlie. Four twenty claims they
saw one in the bunch."

"Why didn't they nail it then?"

"No more bombs. They dropped them all somewhere. And there
is nothing in around there to give you trouble, as far as I know."

"How far is that," Prime says, "about a pecker length?"

Herbert shrugs. "The distance to Singapore where the nearest
fighters are. Joe Norton wanted this one in the worst way, I can
tell you that, so it must be good."

Arnold smiles merrily at all this. He will make a fine idiot,
applauding all the people who are trying to kill him. Sure mister!
Swamp the pissers? Glad to. Suck eggs? Geek? Sure mister, I'll
geek, till something better comes along.

Darkness, dust, truck noises, a flashlight on an airplane's nose.
This time it shines on the figure of a nude seen through a keyhole.
The *Snooper*. I watch Prime closely. He has pulled on thin leather
gloves and his hands flick here and there among the gadgets, like
some sort of aerial surgeon arranging his instruments. I wish I
could see in this an omen of conservatism, but I know better.

I deal with a voice from the tower, that eerie green cavern on
poles.

"Greetings."

"Yo."

"Eleven Victor?"

"That's right."

"Clear down east end, make your run up well clear, we have a
boxcar coming in on three." The voice has a slight cant but no
Collier's stuff.

"One of ours?"

"One of ours." The Army has half a dozen Liberators here used
for much the same purpose as ours.

We taxi out, stop at the end of the taxiway and swing around.
Prime runs up carefully and precisely, checking everything. He
turns the fluorescents down until the instruments are no brighter
than watch dials, unlocks the yoke and works the controls around.
"Tell the man," Prime says.

I call. The boxcar on three is still far out and we are cleared. Prime does not even grasp the yoke until we are far down the runway and going quite fast. At the end, as the three red lights come rushing to claim us, he looks indifferently at the air speed and heaves. The red lights shoot by perhaps ten feet under us. Prime raises one hand, palm up. I yank the gear handle. It has been just about as close as ever but seeing Prime, already settled comfortably, his elbows on the arm rests, only the tips of his fingers on the wheel as he holds the hard-to-get altitude foot by foot, it is difficult to realize it.

The time goes by. Subtly the keynote of my anxiety changes. A new set of symbols replaces the old. The fear of Death in the Machine, the impersonal and meaningless death of accident, slowly gives way. Fear of Death at the Hand of Man enters. Fighters. Flak. Spinning-in in some stupid attempt to do the impossible. There are those who like to say in a beleaguered way, "Christ, just take away the overload and keep the thunderheads off my back, and you can bring on the fighters," but not me. Statistically they are sound. We have a definite psychic domination over the Jap fighters we meet and they get very few of us. But despite the statistics there remains something incandescent about the word fighter, and I am always more unnerved when I know I am on my way to the country where they can be expected. There is a loneliness and the most dreadful feeling of space when I see them. Only fighters betray the awesome distances. They seem to career through a lofty chaos like implacable meteors, their orbits continuously rebent through me. In their trackless sweeps the miles become moments. We have no real defense except to turn into them tightly, to crowd them into turning tighter and tighter to shoot. The fact that this seems to confuse the latter-day Japs is small comfort. Our own fighters, or the Germans', would kill us in nothing flat with a couple of co-ordinated runs from overhead. The Japs can improve. So far they haven't. To reassure myself I build a mental pyramid out of a heap of material labeled "The Facts." Distilled, the facts are that in eight contacts with Jap fighters to date no airplane I have been in has been more than superficially damaged and no person has ever been hit. We did lose people at Iwo and Okinawa but it wasn't surprising, the things that Norton and Dougherty and Prime were doing, following the Japs right into their own traffic circle.

Prime touches my arm and points at the wheel. I begin to fly and he slouches in his seat and goes to sleep. In a few minutes I slip into an illusory reverie in which I review the steps I might have taken to get into NATS. I even imagine myself in a big Douglas transport, a great big nice new one, cautiously threading my way through the little innocuous islands between here and Honolulu.

I monitor the instruments unconsciously and only wake up when we flick through a rain shower or a rough cumulus. I can see the dark masses of the really big cus in time to weave around most of them, because they are a shade darker than the night itself and tonight are not so thickly massed as usual. Arnold stands beside me and talks. I can see he is striving to find some mutuality in our aviation careers but I went to Pensacola and so can't discuss the celebrated idiosyncrasies of the instructors at Corpus where he went. I also escaped the horrors of pre-flight. Arnold expresses the classic outrage. He tells me that in two years of pre-flight at three colleges he broke his wrist wrestling, got a concussion from boxing, and was injured, as he says, seriously about ten times. During the period he never saw an airplane.

He shows me the DR he has been running, drawing position lines at ten-minute intervals on the chart. It is elaborate and needless. Prime knows where Malaya is, he knows the wind without running a wind star, and he knows when he will get there. It is a one-man expedition.

The hours slip by. Suddenly first light shows in the east. The day breaks with fantastic speed down here, so fast that I often burn myself on the fluorescent lights that I have not turned off because the oncoming daylight pales them so quickly I don't notice they are still on. I wake Prime. He flies again and we start letting down. I drink coffee and smoke one cigarette after another.

Any minute now we will sight the coast. The light grows and then all at once there it is, a dark smudge without detail. But Prime sees or senses something that eludes me. He changes his heading radically to the west, but keeps going down until at last we are right on the water. We fly at zero feet on the altimeter and under us the ocean heaves gently in long faintly wrinkled swells.

Now I see what Prime is after. He has spotted some small sailboats. There are three of them with lateen sails in the faint rose ahead of us. They are becalmed until the morning breeze picks them up. Prime heads for them. An instant before we reach the first, several figures appear at the stern and dive over the rail into the sea. We are so low it appears we will hit the mast, but Prime flicks up a wing and turns to head for the next one. I look back through the blister window and can see the tiny boat rocking wildly, its mast almost beating the water on both sides. I don't know if this is the effect of the slip stream or of the men jumping overboard. In the second boat one man remains standing upright and looking up at us with an expressionless face. The others go over the side. Prime laughs. "Look out for the sharks, fellahs!" he says. It is needless to do this sort of thing. The men are Malayan fishermen and now they will hate us. It is so easy to yield to this sort of irresponsibility in an airplane.

Prime has a cigar in one hand and the mike in the other, but despite this he is lower on the water than I would go with both hands free and my complete attention on the job. There is an illusion that the slowly heaving ocean sometimes reaches higher than our wing tips, and I almost have to sit on my hands to keep from involuntarily pulling back the yoke when Prime takes a hand off to smoke or to talk into the mike. "All right," he says lazily clicking the mike button a few times to get everyone's attention. "Let's start in the bow. Larabee. The bombs the same way we had 'em last trip. G.P.'s first and one at a time. But if I tell you to shag your ass back to the intervolometer you get there in a hurry. Have you checked it?"

"Yes, sir. She's okay." Prime makes the rounds, turrets, waist guns, tail, cautioning each station in some particular way. There is no levity as there always is in our crew. "Now if the joint is loaded," Prime says at the end, "take it slow. Don't burn up the ammo in ten minutes. We'll be coming around a little hill into the harbor, if my poop is right, and the sun will be behind us. I doubt if they can hear us and I doubt if they will catch us on radar if I stay flat. But no shooting until I give the word. What did I just say, Jenkins?"

"No shooting until you give the word, Mr. Prime."

"That's my boy. All right, kiddies, test-fire the guns." Prime's voice has become absurdly caressing. I begin to think it may not be so bad. There is nothing alarming in what he has said, and he has told everyone to exercise restraint. Perhaps it will be a blank anyway, if someone was in here yesterday. They don't keep convoys hanging around in little coffee bowl harbors these days.

The guns thump briefly from all around the ship and the men call in the "manned and ready" from each station. Prime acknowledges by clicking an R on his mike button. We are so low it seems to me that every swelling rise of the sea will wash against the belly of the airplane. I can't look. I fix my eyes on a dark green knoll ahead and search around it for signs of a harbor or a town or shipping. I can see nothing except some hazy mountains further inland and the broken purple and green foreshore. Prime flies confidently toward the knoll as though it is a landmark he has grown up with. He lounges sideways in his seat like a Sunday driver, an occasional puff of cigar smoke jetting from his lips. His only other movement is to twist the pickle around on the yoke to where his right thumb can find the firing button easily without any motion of his hand. I tighten my belt, raise my seat a little, and begin to strain forward.

We cross a narrow beach, brush a patch of jungle and follow a contour around the green knoll, pressed flat against the tops of the trees. Prime raises a wing tip now and then to clear one, and each time he does, Arnold, standing between us, makes a little oh-h-h of excitement. I look up at him once, see his foolish grin, and then keep my eyes ahead.

Prime takes off his cap, puts it carefully behind the seat, raises the mike. "Open 'em." There is a rush of air all around us and Prime's black hair dances on his head. We have to squint for a moment because opening the bomb bay doors blows dust up from the flooring and into our faces. In a few seconds it is blown away.

Ahead there is a notch in the trees. Prime sinks into it, knifes through. One moment I am looking up at palms and the next we have come out into a neat little harbor which has been hidden behind the knoll and whose narrow entrance is nearly overgrown by the trees. There are ships, black in the coppery bath of sunlight on the water, and a town all around one side of the harbor.

The first ship is a small rusty-looking freighter, a Sugar Charlie in the code name. It has a single stack far aft and a lot of wood and latticework over the stern half. The foredeck is the usual jumble of coiled lines, netting, lumber and barrels. In a fenced-off pen on top of the latticework is a single twenty-millimeter gun in a canvas jacket. It points at the sky. No one has heard us.

We dip, lower than the ship itself. "Begin," Prime says into the mike and then drops it. There is an almost unbearable concussion as the crown turret fires forward, the muzzles of the guns only a few inches above our heads. Things rain down on us from the overhead—handles from the ADF receiver, fluorescent lights swinging on their long cords. In the water great churning splashes move quickly toward the ship. When they reach it pieces of the latticework begin to fly in all directions. Some of the bounding red balls carom off the deck and curve away like falling stars. At the last second a man comes out of the head which is built to hang out over the port quarter of the ship. He has a rag around his head but no clothes and when he sees us he raises his arms as though stretching and sinks to his knees. The splinters of wood fly up all around him. Prime grunts loudly as he presses the pickle, and we shoot up and barely over the mast.

In the next instant I am sure we have been hit. We seem to be snapping over onto our back. My cheeks sag, my flesh quivers, my vision grays, and I try to shrink feebly away from the forces and the motion. I am aware that Arnold is on his knees, that his head has come over onto my shoulder and that he is gripping my knee. Then we are high, spinning, unbearably slow, falling, the sounds rising again, the forces shifting. I am lost, but when I catch sight of the needle and ball, I notice that while the needle is completely to one side, the ball remains glued in the center. It must be stuck. I have never felt anything like this in a B-24.

Then suddenly we are banked at a mere forty-five degrees again and dropping down toward a ship. I hear the thud of the first bomb. The fuse is a delayed one to give the airplane time to clear. "Wahoo!" Arnold shouts in my ear. We are on top of a wooden-hulled thing with some old and brittle-looking palm fronds draped over it for camouflage. I have a glimpse of three or four men hanging over her sides on fender lines. Another in a white skull-cap is crouched behind a barrel on the deck. The guns begin, splinters fly, yellow flashes wink around the men. They let go of the ropes. I close my eyes, feel the beginnings of the sickening pull-out and roll, and this time actually black out. I cannot believe that the wings will stay on but they do and there we are again, a hair above stalling speed but poised and perfectly aligned with another ship. It is a beautiful thing, a sort of wingover that Prime does, pulling enough G's to kill a horse and going damn near on his back to get around without using any space.

Now they are shooting. I can see stuff going by from two different sources, but it is high and Prime is going under it, down and down to the water, over the third ship and away across the land still low. The shooting stops. Prime taps his head gently with the heel of one hand. I breathe deeply in the respite and sink down a millimeter or two off the cheeks of my buttocks. Arnold runs a hand over his hair and grins stupidly at me. He is very white.

Now we can see the harbor behind us. The first ship is broken in two halves, both resting on the bottom. The water is up to the twenty-millimeter gun on the stern piece. The second ship has disappeared, where it was is a sea of floating junk. Smoke pours from the third but it is still intact. "I missed that one," Prime says laconically. "I squeezed her too late."

"Parts of that second ship flew up about a hundred yards,"

somebody says. "I seen a two-by-four way the hell up in the air about a mile!"

"Like a roller coaster!" Arnold shouts to me. "I'm either on my knees or plastered against the overhead the whole time." He looks happily ahead toward the next event. Prime is circling well inland. I am wondering if he will go back in. At the moment he is interested in something below us. I can see some shacks with pyramid-shaped roofs on the slopes of the hills and there are narrow-gauge tracks going through them, and a big tank mounted on stilts. We go up the tracks, passing the gray tank. Jammed at what seems to be the entrance to a mine are some diminutive railroad cars.

"Ore trains," Prime says. "See the mines?" He points at some ragged gashes in the red dirt sides of the hills. "Tin mines," he says. He goes wide away from the tracks and then cuts tightly in again behind the line of cars, picking up speed. He is going to try to sling a bomb into the main mine tunnel where the tracks lead.

He tightens and tightens the bank until I am sure we will spin it. The feeling is such that I can barely keep from grabbing the yoke. Then we are flat and skidding, the airplane vibrating as though something integral has fallen from it. There is the hole, we yaw violently. The hills rear high above us and seem to suck us toward them. I close my eyes. When I open them we are going up and over a low spot, getting out. When I see the shaft hole again it is almost obscured in red dust. He has put the bomb inside and several feet of earth have fallen down from the roof of the tunnel onto the tracks.

"Take the cars," Prime says into the mike. We are flying straight and level and parallel to them. They are on my side. Fifties carom off the steel sides knocking dust into the air in big red spurts, but they don't do any damage. "Shit, they got the engines hid in the mine, I bet," Prime says in faint disgust. "Okay, now the tank."

"Holy man, can he do it!" Arnold says repeating himself over and over in inarticulate ecstasy. "What a touch!"

"Where's the tank?" someone says.

"Where do I usually put things for you?" Prime says genially. "Ah hah, dead ahead! I see it."

The bow fires, followed by the crown. The smoking red arcs pour into the hull of the drab gray tank and disappear. Nothing happens. "Balls," Prime says. "Must be water." He begins to turn. We are perhaps two hundred yards from the tank, turning, when there is an explosion that seems to batter us to the ground. It comes in waves, sucking us down, up, rolling us over. The ship snaps and quivers like a limber pole. Prime struggles, his face surprised, and then as he sees he still has control, he looks almost pleased.

There are ejaculations from all over.

"How does she look, Hank? Did we warp the wings?"

"I don't think so, sir." Then having obtained a consensus of opinion from the waist, ". . . looks okay, Mr. Prime. What the hell was that, nitro?"

"There's a column of smoke half a mile high already," the tail gunner says.

"Gas, I guess." Prime shakes his head. "I was a little afraid of that goddam thing. I remembered that deal at Okinawa." I shake my head wordlessly. I don't know what deal he means but obviously he has experienced this sort of thing before.

"You popped some rivets," a voice says excitedly. "And there's a big hunk of skin hanging down—I guess it's a piece of one of the doors."

"It's the starboard door, sir," the man called Hank says more positively. "It's out of its channels and drooping down. It's okay. If it goes it'll miss the empennage I think."

"You think?" the tail gunner says. "Goodbye to my buddies. After that blast the whole ass end is only hanging by a thread anyway."

Prime has stopped thinking about the tank or the damage. He is looking ahead at the clean white buildings of the town. I have a feeling where he is going. On the waterfront I can remember a large wooden building with a flag over it. We still have the incendiaries. To confirm my fears he calls Larabee back to rig them on the shackles.

We circle a minute and I watch the sky. We have been here fifteen minutes, long enough for fighters to arrive from any one of several places. Larabee scuttles back and forth, fiddling. Once he asks Prime to squeeze the pickle for him. The smoke has risen high enough in the still air to cast a wispy shadow on the ridges of the hills. It boils up from the collapsed tank, black and gnarled like the trunk of an old tree. In the harbor the ship still burns, but the smoke from it is gray. I can see a couple of small boats around it. "Okay," Larabee says with his inevitable preface. "Okay, I guess we're ready."

To my surprise Prime slacks the boost, pulls the nose up, slowing. At a hundred and thirty he drops twenty degrees of flaps. We go out over the harbor behind the silent ships and begin to sink as though we are about to land among them. It is agonizing to go so slowly toward the ships and to wait for them to shoot, as they surely will now. I can see people on the ships and though some are springing from the rails others are not. They are bunched on the deck or on the bridge around a gun.

"Pop those bastards," Prime says. "Then pop the bastards in the water." We drop slowly down onto the ships. The first fire comes up at us. It seems headed straight for our eyes but in the last second the tracers veer and go over us. It is an optical illusion but very unpleasant. The airplane shakes with our own gunfire. It seems far heavier and faster than what is coming up at us. The fluorescent lights jump from their sockets again and swing crazily in front of my eyes. I have been putting them back all morning, now I leave them there. The shooting from the bow and crown is amazingly accurate. It pours into the ships until nothing more comes back from them, and then beats the water where the small boats are frantically spinning on their oars. Prime swears and opens his side window. He reaches back, snags the thirty-eight from the holster hanging on his armor plate, and begins to fire the pistol out of the window. The rounds are all tracers and I can see them go out, streaking red but almost at once corkscrewing wildly. Prime is laughing, flying with one hand and bracing the pistol against the rush of air from the open window. We are going maddeningly slow, but nothing is coming up at us.

We cross the line of ships and head for the town. The first load of incendiaries goes into a row of lighters moored rail-to-rail at the jetty. Without turning we come down directly over a narrow alley. Prime is sprinkling the incendiaries along the way, in an open corner where dozens of bicycles are parked, on an old-fashioned touring car standing in the middle of the alley with all its doors open, on the roofs of the shacks twenty feet under our belly. There are no people but I see a goat tethered to a porch. It whirls and yanks on its rope without looking up. Arnold leans over me and grins when he sees the goat and I push him back and swear. At a hundred and thirty knots we crawl over the roof of the town toward the big white building.

"The big place with the flag," Prime says into the mike. He is smiling a slick smile, perhaps visualizing the building with glass showering from the windows in bright streaks and that funny way the smoke has of seeming to jump out when you get something inside a building, and then abruptly stop and hang like a curtain around it. It must be the way a firebug smiles in a moment of rapture.

It takes forever. It is not a cliché, it really does take forever. We hang above the alley, above the bicycles, above the goat, above the pyramid roofs, the airplane shuddering as the fiery golf balls fly out of it toward the blank white face of the building. I look at the air speed and I watch the white building growing taller in front of us and I hear the settling sound that an airplane makes when it is uncomfortable. I fight the resentment of my inadequate flesh in the way I have learned—squeezing it between my locked ankles and straining buttocks and clenched teeth— while judgment screams too low, too slow, and raves inside me like a mad thing, but I know I will do nothing. I pinch off reaction like blocking the passage of a turd, and I will ride this fantastic contradiction to my death without protest and without knowing why I cannot protest.

We are there, lower than the roof. Prime wants to sling the incendiaries in through the windows in a final burst of technique. For some reason no one is shooting now, at least not ahead. I hear

Larabee from the bow say something. He is having trouble or has
run out of ammo. The crown pounds twice and goes no more.

My God, the roof! It comes at us from two places, the sources
hidden by sandbagged rings. It is wide on the right, high on the
left, but then the two streams flick together and in a single instant
there are half a dozen yellow flashes in our faces and a multiple
pinging sound. I duck under the sudden rush of air and cigarettes
and bits of paper, and unidentifiable small objects whirl around
my face in crazy eddies, as though caught in a twister. The engines roar, I am pressed down, my head behind the pedestal. I
feel us mounting, staggering up, and hear a sharp metallic snap.
We have hit something but we are still going. Now there is smoke
and an electrical stink. The smoke whips along the floor under
my hand, spread like a claw on the vibrating metal deck.

Arnold is leaning on me and when I try to rise I find he is across
my back. I heave against his weight and his feet slide backward,
his body spins and falls forward over the pedestal, rolling onto
me again. Prime is yelling but I can't hear what he says, the noise
is deafening. I can see blood on the sleeve of his flying suit and he
seems to be holding one hand to his face. I push Arnold off me
and scrabble with my left hand until I find the rpm toggle and
shove it forward. The engines surge but the new sound is more
reassuring. The airplane is flying.

The smoke is suddenly gone. We are out over the water and
have climbed surprisingly high. Prime is still yelling but into the
mike. When he takes his hand from his face, blood wells from his
right eye and runs down his cheek. He squints and blinks and
holds his head tipped back as though he is trying to see over a
high fence. My earphones have fallen off and I can't get them, but
I turn and scream back through the nav compartment door. In a
moment a stricken face appears. Then another. "Get him off me!"
I yell. They pull and tug at Arnold. There isn't much room and it
is hard to get the leverage to lift him, but I help by raising Arnold's head from the pedestal. There are strings of something
cleaving to the knobs of the radio receiver on my side. As I lift
his head the strings stretch, grow tense and come away. In the

sunken dials on the receiver bloody froth dances in the storm of wind.

"Fly!" Prime yells. He lets go of the yoke and I take it. I get the flaps up and the throttles back and when I look again he has a handkerchief pressed to his face. He is swearing in a funny bereaved way but all I can hear is "son of a bitch," which comes out louder than the rest.

"Where did it get you?" I say. I hold his arm, try to make him let me see but he keeps the handkerchief tight against his face.

Arnold lies half in the nav compartment and half in the cockpit. The radioman is supporting his head in a tender but senseless way. I know he is quite dead. There is not a tremor in his body, not a twitch of arm or leg. Something has gone off in the middle of his head.

"Never mind that!" I yell at them. "Get the kit and help Mr. Prime." For the first time I take a good look at the damage. The canopy is pierced and starred everywhere, most of the holes at eye level. It is difficult to say where the hits went afterward. There are rips and holes in the skin beside me, gashes in the overhead, bakelite fragments all over the place. The armor plate in front of us has stopped some of the rounds, but some have gone right through into the nav compartment and out through the skin. I get my earphones on again and break in on the excited chatter. There is a great deal of solicitous cross-checking, but the rest of the ship has no idea what happened up here with us, and their greatest excitement stems from the fact that we missed hitting the building by inches and even knocked the flag off the roof as we grazed by. I tell them that they must watch for fighters until we are well away from the coast.

The radioman has a compress but when he applies it to Prime's eye the blood continues to drool out from under it. It looks to me as though the eye is gone, the socket seems flattened and elongated, but there is too much blood to tell and Prime can't stop the horrible winking. When he asks if the eye is gone the radioman equivocates.

"Well, there's so much blood it's hard to say," the radioman

says. "But just take it easy, sir, and we'll get you back to Doc
Parker. He'll fix you up."

"Iverson," Prime says loudly, "look and tell me."

"Just a second." I am plugging up the holes in the windshield
with the cloth survival maps I carry in my knee pocket. Gradually
the blast of air inside abates. I lean the mixtures. We have a long
way to go and I must start thinking straight. For lack of a heading
I take up the reciprocal of the one we followed coming down. I
will at least make a landfall somewhere and recognize something.

I motion the radioman. He swabs with the compress and then
leans quickly out of the way so I can see. I am sure there is no
eye there any more. There is an enormous slicing cut across the
brow and through the eye and deep into the cheek bone. Something is sticking in the bridge of Prime's nose.

"I really can't tell, Tommy."

"Don't shit me! Is it gone or not?"

"No, I honestly can't see. You better pull that sliver out of his
nose, there," I say to the radioman. The radioman picks gently.

"I better leave it alone. It's probably plexiglas. I'll put some
sulfa in there, though. That'll help."

"Not in the eye!" Prime says vigorously. "You don't put sulfa
in the eye."

The radioman looks at me. "I don't know what you do. Radio
the base. Tell them we have wounded. I'll come up with an ETA
in a little bit. Ask about the sulfa. Before you do that the two of
you get Mr. Prime into the nav compartment and get him some
blankets. You want a morphine shot, Tommy?" He shakes his
head.

They help him out of the seat. He has to step around Arnold
still lying half in and half out of the cockpit, his body arched over
the steel threshold. "And move him somewhere," I say.

The Plane Captain comes up and sits with me. He figures the
gas and tells me we have enough to go a little faster. But after a
while I get anxious about the gas and take off the extra boost. It
will only be a matter of a few minutes in any case.

Prime refuses to lie down. He is in a terrible hurry to settle the question and will stand for nothing else in the meantime, not morphine, not rest, not even comfort. In a little while he is obviously in great pain and begins to jitter. His hand shakes so badly he can't light a cigarette and his good eye wells tears. He swears and bangs his fist on the nav table. The radioman rubs and pats his shoulders and keeps drawing a blanket around him, but when he says something calculated to cheer him up Prime says, "Cut the shit!" in a broken, bitter voice. It is strange to see Prime reduced, to find he doesn't have unlimited resources. It is hard to realize that in a single moment over that building a tiny bit of the violence that had been going on down below us the whole morning found its way up here to us—or rather to Arnold, stiffening there under the turret, and to Tom Prime, master of violence.

I sight Mount Kinabalu at eleven, at the north end of Borneo, and before one I am home. As I come in to land I see the ambulance begin to roll down the edge of the runway. I land fast and stop far down the strip. Parker is inside before the engines are dead.

"Just Tommy?" he says. I nod. "Nobody else hurt?" I shake my head. I wonder if perhaps he is disappointed. When I get up to go out they already have Arnold trussed in a blanket and lying on the bomb bay catwalk. I wait till they take him.

I am tired and begin to cry and when Ashton hugs me I cry even harder. He gives me a half tumbler of whisky on the spot and we stand around the airplane gabbing like women while an enthusiastic crowd of mechs and bystanders tallies the holes and hits on her. There are a great many more than I would have thought, in the nose, in the inboard starboard nacelle, in the starboard wing. Inside it looks worse. It seems a miracle that we were not all killed until I reflect that a great deal of the mess is shattered radio gear which gives a false impression because it goes to pieces so readily. Still upwards of twenty rounds hit the ship, cannon or large caliber machine gun. A great many more than were necessary.

Prime has paid for his brashness, stupidity, recklessness, or whatever it was. He has lost his eye and the thing that destroyed it was a sliver of bone, more than two inches long, that was blown sideways from Arnold's head, passed through Prime's eye and finally bedded itself deep in Prime's nose. It was a freak accident. Nothing else touched him.

That same night Prime is flown out to Leyte and I go to see him and say goodbye. I am uncomfortable but my sympathy is not very deep. He has not once mentioned Arnold. Beyond that it is somehow impossible to think of him as seriously handicapped or really reduced in any way from The Tommy Prime. But he is. He spends the whole time I am there cursing the "lousy break" he has gotten.

In the evening Roger and I do Arnold's stuff. It is easy because everything is clean and most of it still unpacked. There is no whisky after all. All we take are the cigarettes. I keep remembering that when Segrave died we had to hunt through every nook and cranny for dirty pictures to be sure they didn't go home to his mother.

CHAPTER FOUR

Just see how they are patting their horses,
Nothing of the morrow they would know.

THE DOLDRUMS. On orders from Ironhead I get five days off. I could go to Manila but there is nothing there. We drove down one time from Clark in a jeep. Seventy-five miles each way and when we got there, there was nothing. So I sleep, I swim, I smoke myself sick, and I write to Corinne. Because I seem to hold a brief psychic advantage over Kirby Stevens, by chiding him about his efforts to have me killed, he leaves me alone after the five days are past. Eight days go by without my flying.

Ironhead gives Tim Brady another chance. Apparently Brady asks for it. Maybe he is conscious-stricken about Arnold or perhaps his courage has revived with the certainty of never again being scheduled with Tommy Prime. He flies twice with Ashton, both negative patrols, and then is up to go with Skindome Dougherty. Skindome takes Brady down to the strip to help him check out the airplane, as he always does, with his entire crew, but Brady doesn't like it very much when he sees the clusters of six-sided napalm cans going into the bomb bays. He heads for the dispensary on the double. There he gets nowhere and so he waits until he can pull the very last rip cord. When Passage wakes him at one o'clock for the trip, Brady pretends to be so startled by merely being touched that he vaults out of his sack and falls on his back on the floor. Naturally he wrenches his back.

It his last performance. They make him some kind of liaison officer between the squadron and the Wing and he has to spend every morning at the strip from 1:00 A.M. until the last flight goes, and then meet them all again on their return. No one knows what he does but it can't be much. I'd like the job.

Yokum and Roger go out together on a night patrol. They are supposed to go to Manado, in the Celebes, but get no further than the end of the mat where they run off into the water. They are lucky, nothing explodes and everyone gets out. Of course the airplane is gone. Both insist it was too heavy and wouldn't leave the ground, but Swede Engelson wants to hang pilot error on them. They are confined to the tent for several days while the investigation proceeds. They aren't supposed to drink or have visitors but both of these rules are broken every evening.

"Tell us what happened, Rog."

"We submerged. Glub, glub. The skip took us down."

"*Smith* wrecked us," Yokum says. "I gave him a take-off and he pranged us."

"P.P.C.'s that lie . . ." Roger says, adding up corks.

"Copilot Fatfag just pulled a couple of the wrong handles. He let all the air out of the saddle tanks."

"We were riding the vents, when the order came down from scope con to flood Kingstons." Roger shouts, cupping his hands to his mouth and gradually diminishing the volume as though the commands are echoing deep inside a sub. "Flood Kingstons, flood Kingstons!"

"Well, the skip had done it again and we knew we had to die. Just couldn't line up those three little peas in the little box and get those mothers all in their holes at the same time."

"I said Skip, this is it, and you go first as usual. We leaped to form a ladder of human flesh for our beloved skip to ascend. There was no panic. The years of rigid training under Patrol Plane Commander Yokum were now to pay off. Those Christmas Eves spent in ditching drills, those silly seventy-two-hour liberties when everyone else was getting laid and drunk and we were down in

the old survival tank at midnight with the yellow rubber goods
and laughing ourselves sick because we knew what a jump we
were getting on the other fellows. So when the skip came along,
wearing his pole climbers and started up our backs, we knew,
from timing it in practice, that if we could hold our breaths for
just fourteen minutes, we were gonna get out of there, because
that's what it takes him to climb on the nav table and out through
the hatch."

"I stepped aside," Yokum says. "There was a certain particularly fat ass jammed in the hatch, one we all know. I tried to tell
the men trapped below how sorry I was that we wouldn't live
now to see the brave new world which their efforts were helping
to create. This was hard to get out with Smith and his enlisted
friends standing on my face . . ."

"Were you guys under water very long?"

Yokum looks astounded. "If you floated down the Niagara on
a water-logged telephone pole . . . with nothing to pull on but a
frayed yo-yo string . . . and then went over the falls, would *you*
be under water? But watch out for those fat copilots. They lose
their heads. You have to have somebody body-check them hard
until you are out." Poor Foy, who was with them, doesn't say
anything. I guess he wishes Tommy Prime were still around.

I write to Corinne every day, spending an entire morning on
each letter and maintaining a loose continuity as though we were
talking to one another. I enclose with each letter something that
I think might be peripherally interesting to her—photos, a drawing, a peculiar leaf, one day a poem. It is a bad poem, overblown
and pretentious, with lines like, "I must guard the feeble candle
love, and nurse its fitful flame." Fitful is the word, all right. I
haven't had a letter in three weeks. I tell Roger but nobody else.
About three months ago he got dusted off. They weren't married
but they had gone together since high school and were being
sensible about the war. His D.J. was a pip. After the usual plati-
tudes came what to me was the real horror, the effort to make it
sound right and plausible at Roger's expense. She told him all the
things he never had been for her. She told him she realized it as

soon as she had begun an affair with someone else. She said when
he got over being angry, and *met* the new guy, and could see how
right everything was with his own eyes, he would be the first to
agree that it was for the best. In fact, she told him, she would bet
anything that the new guy and Roger would become fast friends
. . . he is just the kind of man you *do* like, Roger!

Of course I feel terribly in love, which is something of a paradox
because I didn't feel *terribly* in love when I left. Anxiety is a more
effective whetstone than absence in making the heart grow fonder.
Roger says I must be blasé, turn the tables, reverse the tide. This
is pretty primitive advice. And from a loser, too. I do draw casual
cartoons, showing me seated under a palm tree taking a swig from
a bottle with three X's on the label, and surrounded by hula girls.
In the background is usually a bewildered-looking airplane with
a crumpled body and a dizzy swirl spiraling up over it. The
aviator's life in the romantic South Pack. But in my letters I make
extravagant and worshipful love to Corinne, with a show of basic
passion that must astonish her. At the same time I am faintly
aware of how unreliable my opinion of her beauty and intellect
has become in the pervading loneliness. I dally with the letters
afterward, drawing elaborate Air Mail instructions on the envelopes in red and blue crayon and dripping sealing wax on the
back. I press the embossed part of a gold ring she gave me into
the wax and it makes a seal, although my initials appear in reverse like some ancient hieroglyphic. I get around the censoring
problem because Ashton is one of the head censors and keeps his
stamp in a moccasin under his bed where his friends can find it.
I stamp the letters in his tent and sign his initials in the circle.

I write to my father too, and send him a little gold cloth anchor
patch from the cap of an Imperial Landing Force private. I got
it on Tinian and I tell my father how we found a pillbox on the
beach with six dead men in it and how they had apparently killed
themselves by firing their rifles with their toes and how I held my
nose when I tore the cap off the dead man's head. One side of him
likes that sort of thing, yet the other is wonderfully gentle and
full of a sort of natural theology that is sometimes embarrassing.

"Now, boys," my father will say to men in their sixties, "I hear you talking about trout, and sure, that's where the pretty poetry is. But a musky now, there's a spark of divinity in him! He'll charge the devil. You travel all night and cast all day and spend months after him, and you trick him and gag-fish him and some of you even shoot him, but he keeps his humor and his fight and his disdain for the lot of us."

My old man. He owns a bar in Milwaukee now, the kind of place that has hard-boiled eggs and pigs' feet on the counter, and he tells the customers endless and tedious stories about his son Carl, the pilot, who was once a great fisherman. They are the kind the people interrupt because they know or can guess the ending but my father keeps right on, cheerful and undismayed to the very end. "Well sir, that little fellah had hooked into the biggest walleye I ever saw up there around Wausau, and Carl was only as big as a minute," my father will say, demonstrating with his big vein-ridged hands how big a minute is. "Now he's a pilot, you know . . ."

My father has lived like a carp ever since my mother decided that her insights and secret communions with spirits should not be handicapped by having a garrulous fisherman around. He lives alone in a single room behind the bar. There is a gray towel on the doorknob each time I go there and a dirty comb full of gray fur on the window ledge and dead roaches scattered on the linoleum floor. My father says they are wanderers who have lost their way on a huge glazed desert. Think with what high hopes they may have set out to cross it, he says. He makes their deaths seem the end result of some noble purpose. He left Albert Lea because my mother told him to, but he still sends all his money to her and refuses to treat her as the hopeless neurotic she is. For years now at night she has seen the Goodman or the Badman appearing on the wall. "Mr. Goodman came and told me all about you, Carl. He said he was sure you could spare your mother some money for her teeth."

I send them both money when I can and so does my married sister in Eau Claire, but my other sister has given up. She says she

can't stand it any longer and she says one of us is going to get
trapped and it isn't going to be her. She doesn't even write to
them. "Ginny," my father says. "That Ginny must have a heart
full of sawdust. She's forgotten us. You know I once asked her if
she knew what a robin was really after, hopping along over the
grass and listening like he does. Money, she said, if he's got any
sense. Just like that."

The world is so full of cruel abstractions. I know Ginny is right
and I know I can't go home to that, any more than I can settle
down near the Doerflingers. It's only since she met me that
Corinne stopped believing that hellfire awaits you if you grab
your napkin before grace. Some of those Navy parties must almost
have killed her. Especially the last one we had in San Diego the
week before we left.

That night she tried as always not to be a liability on the carni-
val spirit and set herself stubbornly to weather it out. Billows and
shock waves of blasphemous, drunken, and dirty sound rolled
over her but she stuck it until the last ensign was hung. This happened to be my friend Segrave, who when sober was fond of
saying rather traditional but harmless things, like "Who has more
fun than people?" or when he felt a skeptical turn, "Don't romance me, gal." But when Segrave was drunk his speech became
more pliant and full of picturesque and accentual variations for
the words of four letters. He and Corinne were natural enemies
and it was awful to hear them argue over morals and gin, Segrave's only known tilting grounds, and to see how a voluble and
quick-witted ignoramus could overwhelm my intelligent wife
who was on her way to a Master's degree in art. Segrave shattered
what he considered her flimsy convictions with a well-planted
"crapola!" here and there, and told her with patient good humor
that "the Lord put that thing there to be used, gal!" meanwhile
blowing Southern Comfort fumes in her face. Nobody won the
argument but I lost it, because Segrave managed in an hour or
two to wrench my sex life out of gear for almost all the time remaining. Poor Segrave and his dismal yardstick for women—no

scale, no degree, just "would-I-or-wouldn't-I?" I hope his ghost isn't watching the night I get home.

One afternoon I am called to the Wing Quonset. Swede Engelson is holding one of his biweekly "talk outs" with the captains and execs of the two squadrons. I don't know at first why he wants me but when the meeting begins with a rather silky lecture from the Swede on "your people's primary job," it seems clear that he wants to aim a reprimand at Ironhead Backus because he allows "prima donnas" like Prime and Dougherty to violate Wing directives in their efforts to run up scores, and that I am there to give evidence of some kind.

It is cool in the Quonset set deep in the trees. There is an open parachute bellied out against the ceiling to insulate the room and somewhere overhead there is the pleasant sound of water trickling. It is probably going into the tank that supplies the Swede's indoor shower. In one corner of the hut is an inverted astrodome and some brightly colored fish about the size of cigarettes are swimming around in it. Engelson lives here in regal isolation with his fish and Travis, his personal mess boy.

The Swede looks at me without recognition two or three times while he is talking, and then suddenly asks me why it was that an approach to a target was made with the flaps down and at such slow speed.

"I don't know, sir," I say, unconsciously imitating the tone of incredulity in his voice. That is the extent of my evidence. He crooks one hand and scratches a place on his scalp with a little finger, being careful not to disturb the thin black hair that goes back over his head like harrowed furrows. Then he blows air through his clenched teeth a couple of times and looks at Ironhead.

"Juilly," he says slowly, "your people just haven't grasped the doctrine." We sit while Engelson rants at us like a harassed football coach. The team can't seem to learn his favorite play, so he must conduct a complete review of the game's fundamentals. Ironhead is hardly listening but Kirby Stevens is nodding penitently beside me. There is a disgusting shine of reverence on his horsy face and a look that says that we are now hearing just exactly what Stevens has long been meaning to bring up at a meeting. This is the sort of urbane disloyalty that I hate and if I were Ironhead, Kirby would have nodded his way back to the Camp Kearney pool long, long ago.

Kirby wants to tack on to the Swede's coattails, and with reason. Engelson is already well-known in the Bureau as a mild wonder-boy for the way he has met the unique tactical situation that develops earlier and earlier around our bases. It is simply that the quarry disappears from the frontiers faster than the eager hunters can catch up with it. The Swede's creative agility consists of moving his Wing forward to the worst and smallest and farthest advanced fields to be found anywhere and then getting his air-craft further out than was believed possible. He plans it all out on his Big Game Board, jazzing the colored pins around and fighting one hell of a war. But Engelson is no fool. He has clearly identified himself with the powerful and popular and enthusiastic needs of Naval Aviation, his object is to advance with these needs, and his opportunity is now. Perhaps he'll take a few people with him and this is what Kirby is after, because, as Ashton says, after you make lieutenant commander, then they start using ropes in the climb, and that means the end of Kirby.

"Now the other day this man Dougherty . . ." the Swede says taking up a new cudgel. "Perfect example of what I'm talking about, Juilly. I don't put out Wing Directives because I like to type." Skindome Dougherty has violated a Wing Directive for the third or fourth time by going outside his sector. He has an island where he once found a ten-ship convoy, including two Fox Tare Charlies of around three thousand tons. Unfortunately the day he found this deer park, he had already dropped his bombs some-where else. Now he visits there when he can, hoping they'll come back.

The Swede rises and goes to the wall where the huge wagon wheel is drawn in red ink on his maps, the spokes radiating out to show all the sectors we fly. He reaches out and spread-eagles his fat fingers over some blue sea, and starts them inching over the beaverboard like a measuring worm. "Nine seventy," the Swede intones. "Three fifteen. That's twelve eighty-five. And now back. That's twenty-two eighty-five." He pinpoints a spot on the map with one finger and looks balefully at Ironhead. No one has been adding the mileage with him, but it is obvious that Skindome has gone way out of the sector he was in. No one denies it. Nevertheless Engelson must talk as though there is still someone to be convinced.

Ironhead clears his throat and says mildly, "John, he went over there on top of his search. I can't see how you can object to that. He was up all night shoe-horning the gas in. When its cool you can get a hundred or a hundred and fifty more gallons in. He was out damn near seventeen hours."

"Ho . . . ho . . . ho," Joe Norton says derisively. "That is one hundred per cent pure hocky. I can't stay out that long." Norton is a pudgy man with bristling close-clipped hair and a neck that looks as if a fly swatter has been pressed into it. He has a big red mustache that goes up and down over his mouth like a roller door when he talks. He never swears or uses dirty language and hocky is one of his more famous substitute words.

Ironhead gives Norton a little bow with his head. They dislike each other intensely. "That doesn't make it impossible, Joe."

"You're ding-dong right it does!" Like his nickname, Cap Ahab, Norton is all caricature, but the kind who is talented and dangerous. He gets a lot of leverage with his affectations, leading 420 as though to some jihad, with slogans and the nonsense about "The Blue Raiders," and a weird sort of journalese speech that would embarrass us. But his squadron is nearly all new and the P.P.C.'s have come from being buried in Hedrons for several years, or else they were instructors or part of one of the deeply rooted families of a Naval Air Station.

"I think it's impossible to fly three thousand miles no matter how much gas he took," Engelson says. "He left his track and when he did he gave something time to slip through." It would suit the Swede if we could fly four thousand miles. We could see if there were any Sugar Charlies hiding in Lake Baikal.

"But we do it all the time," Ironhead says. "I mean give them a chance to slip through. Right now, for instance, there is no one out at the end of any sector. And all night."

Ironhead has hit the bait. Now the master planner can explain his master plan. We have *forced* him to, with our ignorant replies.

"To get to sector seven, let's say, unseen, a force would have to run four, five, and six at night. They could do this but they would show in seven in daylight. If no one spotted them, they would have the chance to run eight and nine at night, hole up again in ten, and the next night get clean away." Engelson goes on and on, finally winding up the speech by repeating "the Wing's definition of search doctrine" lecture. Everyone is bored stiff except Kirby.

When he is through, Cap Ahab makes his weekly complaint about the well. "Someone pitched a lot of hocky in there again last night," Ahab says. "It's gotta cease and desist."

"It wasn't us," Ironhead says. "I just had it bailed out."

"It wasn't bad this time," Herb Millar says. He is Ahab's exec, a mild-mannered mustang about forty years old who is supposed to have nine kids and three ex-wives. "It could have been accidental." Ahab pays no attention to this craven admission.

"If I catch the son of a rip . . ." He gives me a menacing smirk.

"Why don't you share the water?" Ironhead says benignly.

"There isn't enough. By Christmas! I'll put a man with a carbine down there."

"It might help more if you asked your men not to urinate in our area."

"The woods are free."

"So is the water. Come on. Let's knock off the childishness all around. Fouling wells is pretty infantile, I'll admit, but sneaking around pissing on someone's doorstep just because they won't vacate the premises is even more so."

There is a mild explosion and the argument gets nowhere. Ironhead wouldn't do anything to please Cap Ahab if his life depended on it, and rightly so, because Ahab does him dirt whenever he has the chance. Ahab is a loudmouth and he has a loudmouth's surface insistence on fair play, but at a deeper level he is plain treacherous. He intrigues with everyone, all the way back to the Bureau, and he seems to get what he wants—the publicity, new airplanes, replacements, medals.

Engelson closes the meeting with the blistering announcement that the capture of the officers who have been selling liquor to enlisted men is now imminent. He has been saying this since we left Tinian four months ago. "Pass the word. When I get 'em, I'll burn 'em. And I mean the real burn, all the way to Portsmouth." I take this to mean that 'em, whoever they are, can still save themselves by a timely reformation. As we go out I hear Ironhead telling Kirby that he is not to talk to Dougherty about his transgression. Ironhead knows exactly what Kirby would say. Some dreadful platitude for ex-enlisted men who have become officers, from an ex-reserve officer who has become regular, if there is anything so horrible.

Near the door is a small visitors' bench with a sign over it that says: "If thou desirest rest, see that it be not for too long here." Stevens laughs a sniffing little laugh of homage for Engelson's wit. He also stops to make sure the outside screen door doesn't slam. Everyone has heard about this. When the door slams the ping-pong balls that are resting in the curve of the paddles on the Swede's ping-pong table are sometimes jarred loose and roll around on the porch floor where people step on them. Perhaps the taxpayers have been writing, because the Swede is very sensitive about this. Perhaps Kirby figures that if he catches enough screen doors he may make it up the old slag pile. If he does and Ironhead is passed over again, Kirby will rank him. Ironhead is a man who finished inside the first twenty-odd numbers at the trade school on the Severn, who was an athlete, was a handsome and personable man. He still is a fine human being. Stevens is a man who, intellectually speaking, is quite stupid, who went to some dime college in the boondocks for a year or two, never played anything except other people, looks like a horse, and is small-town, lower-echelon, bourgeois, through and through. The whole thing is more depressing because it proves how few real *people* are necessary in the great sprawling movements of America in war. So few seem embattled except on the petulant level of a Norton or the selfish one of an Engelson. So few seem informed or resolute or devoted, as they have been in other wars. We have our leaders but they become heroes by getting up there on the bridge of the *Essex,* pointing their swords at Tokyo, and saying— over the bull horns of a thousand ships—follow me, men! Enough ships debouch from Ulithi—perhaps a sixth of the total there—to outnumber the Imperial Navy ten to one. My four-year-old nephew could do that, if he could manage the ladder and someone would tell him which way was north.

Ashton says I read history all wrong, that it has never varied, that war remains war, and warriors warriors, and effective ones have never been attractive types. Jackson was a bigot, Custer a murderous fop hated by his men, Nelson poisoned with conceit, Teddy Roosevelt so in thrall to his bully-boy mystique he could scarcely wait to shoot a Spaniard with his revolver from the *Maine* —or to say he had. It is from their inversions that they draw the superhuman energies they need for such success. Perhaps he's right, but as I told him, I read the life of Sir John Moore not long ago, and there aren't any of him around any more. Nor do theories about warriors help to explain Kirby Stevens. They have nothing to do with *him!*

Furthermore, Ashton says, the congenital chickens lose the right in wartime to jeer or hoot at the absurd people, who for all their absurdities do a hundred times as much to win wars as the so-called intellectual class of warriors who make up the bulk of the chicken population.

Cap Ahab was at Hainan one day, trying to prove the validity of one of his dogmatic utterances. "There is no flak in the Pacific I can't fly through at five thousand," said Ahab. He was exactly at five, circling, when something hit the fan. Two men were badly hurt. Ahab's reaction, instead of being like mine, remorse, or fear of a court-martial, at least fear of surrounding opinion, was absurd. He had himself photographed measuring the size of the flak hole with a yardstick.

We doubled up laughing. Ahab was new to us, the most ludicrous thing we had seen so far, an Annapolis prick destroyer sailor with only five or six hundred hours flying time who until that moment had done nothing but issue edicts threatening punishment for what he outlined as "unnatural acts." He spent his time confiscating all the books and magazines that he considered too provocative for his fighting bulls, and preached that Gene Tunney nonsense about continence, throwing in all the good old boy scout fears plus a few new ones of his own. How we went to work on *that* one! Self-abuse can be stamped out! Why not see your chaplain today about the new easy, voluntary, castration plan? Defeat The Hand in your bed with the newest, most effective weapon yet! No more sitting around with the old-fashioned "just put it out of your mind" method. And more.

Since that time Ahab has sunk about nine thousand tons of shipping by himself, and goaded, bullied, and horsewhipped his squadron to the brink of a Presidential Citation. Perhaps he is crazy, impotent, a liar, treacherous, but he is doing what he is out here for. And the rest of us? Ain't nobody here but us chickens, boss!

Throwing his cap into the air, young Iverson vowed he would never leave the sea!

After lunch I sit in the rock garden and try to read a book that someone has lent me about the RAF. It is a good story about reticent English pilots doing wonderfully active things without comment, but suddenly the book will go over into formlessness and ambiguity as the author tries to resolve fear, hatred, sexuality and other rather non-British emotions into words, and to be knowing about it. In the first sex passage I learn that "it" is there, that "it" is bigger now, bigger than both of them and the whole war, a warmness spreading, a wet urgency. It is clear that the writer's fantasy life is more vivid than his real one. It is also clear he has never flown an airplane. His sensations are too uncertain. As usual the hero has formed a relationship with the only girl in a thousand miles and is successful keeping her to himself in the face of armies. Occasionally the warmness spreads, and he seems very adjusted. No dirty secrets. No filthy admissions. When I think of the carefully guarded fantasy lives all around me here, hundreds of people living out of their imaginations or recollections or from pictures or books, it is rather terrifying. Not very nice for the noble mothers to think about. One day I saw my boy doing a dreadful thing in front of a picture of a movie star . . . I realized I hadn't really known my boy at all.

I am bored with the book, and with my thoughts, and with listening to Yokum and Roger who are on their third day inside the tent. They are playing showdown and of course Yoke is winning because he changes the rules to suit his game. I go over to the operations shack to do my stint at censoring mail. There is no one there except Barker, the yeoman, a pale, skinny nineteen-year-old with a mass of oily hair piled on his head. He is singing a song which, because it is obscene and disrespectful, has officially been banned. "Oh, Eleanor lay on her bed a cryin', when she got the news that Franklin . . ." Barker stops and then continues.

He is testing me, for with Barker the real war is the one against officers. His weapons are insolence, deception, and constant readiness to betray the slightest trust placed in him. He is the author of dozens of stories plotted around the incompetent or abusive conduct of an officer. To make them more popular, most of the stories contain an enlisted hero. Quick thinking in the ranks inevitably succeeds in retrieving officer failure, enlisted spunk shows itself in the nick of time to balance commissioned cowardice. Barker hates officers the way a bank robber hates the police, with a good deal of the same kind of bravado. No one *likes* officers, but Barker's hatred is pathological. What he doesn't know is that the power he loathes is the very thing that defines him. It gives him being and without it to fight he would be a cipher.

He begins to wipe a comb, with which he has been laying up his hair, on the front of his denim shirt. On his forearms are the daily crop of tattoos in ditto ink. I can see a fat buttocks with a harpoon through it. Barker sometimes amuses people by manipulating the skin on his arms in a place where he has drawn some such pay-toilet art. He bobs around behind the mound of log books he is working on, sings, whistles, burps.

Kirby Stevens appears in the doorway. His approach has been noiseless in the dust. Barker sings boldly on, glancing over the mound of books at me occasionally, his little bittern eyes bright with accomplishment. Kirby stands there, his finger on his lips, and listens.

"Belay that, Barker!" Kirby steps inside and glares at the yeoman. "How many times would you say you've been told about that song?" Barker shrugs. "That's the President of the United States you're razzing . . . stand up when I talk to you!" Barker gets up slowly, waiting just that extra moment before he takes his hands from the desktop that makes the whole action insolent. He lets the comb slide into his shirt pocket, folds his arms, unfolds them again. His eyes seem permanently focused on a plane about five inches in front of his nose.

Kirby examines him with as much loathing as he is able to show. He finds that Barker has again grown an inch-long nail on one little finger, which, filed to a point, he uses as a tool for endless probings in his ears and nostrils. But there isn't much Kirby can do and Barker knows it. They are the most natural enemies, but they are used to the bare, dull combat they have been waging all these months and they both know there are no new moves to be made. Barker's sins are only sins when they are committed against the orderly Stateside Naval Establishment. We have no Captain's Mast and Kirby is impotent to do anything to Barker that Barker will care about. So he delivers a few indefinite threats and sends him off to clean his arms and cut off the "breadhook." Barker's head flops on his skinny neck with just the amount of impudence that the law allows as he saunters out. Now Kirby makes a great deal of noise in yanking his chair out and shoving his desk, as though the energy he is unable to spend on Barker is still with him. He looks at me as though he might reprove me for not doing anything. But if he can't conquer Barker officially, how can he conquer me? Nevertheless, I make a ponderous effort to be genial. Kirby still makes out the flight schedule.

The shack fills with the afternoon workers. Fred McCord arrives, trailed by the dutiful Passage. They are discussing something that allows McCord to use his favorite expression, "yea big," several times. Two ensigns come to help me with the mail. We sit at a long table with letters heaped in front of us and read. Because they don't know me very well, the ensigns don't read choice excerpts from the letters to each other, as most of them do.

I gather all the letters I can find written by my friends and seal and stamp them without reading them. It is a courtesy we all extend to one another. But evidently McCord is watching me. He begins to complain, not about me, but about Ashton letting people use his censor stamp without supervision. From this he goes into trouble in every oblique shape and form, every niggling thing that happens, or doesn't happen, or might happen. The memo requiring the wearing of long-sleeved shirts on operational flights isn't being obeyed, the Captain has not yet set the limit on enlisted men's War Bond allotments, the scrub typhus immunization records are incomplete; it pours into the room in nervous bursts. As he talks, McCord's fleshy ears leap about like Punch and Judy above the pits and craters that make his neck look like a map of the moon.

I feel only an obscure contempt for him, sitting there bent forward in his chair, the jockey riding a close race. He has that air of the man without a moment to lose. Day after day he sits here in this stifling hut, like a doomed chicken in a crate. Yet when he gets home he will tell awesome stories to the civilians, possibly be a big shot down at the V.F.W., augmenting his flabby personality with the muscles of other men's words and deeds. "When I was in the South Pack . . ." No one will know that it is all padding. Probably no one will care.

Ironhead comes in and McCord subsides. The Captain sits at his desk for a moment, mops his stomach with a towel he keeps in a drawer, and sighs audibly. We all look up at him and grin. "Hot," he says. I can feel my thighs sticking to the seat of the chair like suction cups. "Passage," Ironhead says wearily, "Will you see if you can find Mr. Dougherty?" Passage nods, gets to his feet, rolls a pack of cigarettes into the sleeve of his T shirt, and starts out.

"And tell your buddy to get back on the double and do some work," Stevens says to him.

"What did Dougherty decide?" Ironhead says to Kirby. "Does he want the first one, or not?" He is talking about replacements and the fact that Dougherty is first on the list to go home if and when any come.

"I don't know. You said you were going to ask him yourself."

Ironhead considers. "All right, I will. If we get six crews on the first, which is what they are now talking, that will mean Dougherty, you, Ainsworth, Bartlett, Ashton—and one to grow on."

"Maybe they'll just consider the first three as replacing losses," Stevens says seriously.

"Uh-uh. We've got along with fifteen crews for a long time now. As far as I'm concerned that's our strength from here in. We don't need replacements for the dead, just the living."

Passage comes back. "Mr. Dougherty's coming, Captain." He squints after coming in from the brightness outside.

"Thank you, Passage."

The enlisted men don't like Skindome Dougherty, despite the fact he was once an AP. He could have been their champion, the proof that you can defy the prescription for "officer material" and then outrace all of those who have drawn wider circumferences around themselves with education and airs. But he is only an older and grumpier officer, oblivious to their overtures, unforgiving in the light of his knowledge of their traditional sins, lost in a crabbed, narrow, obstinate world of his own—the B-24. He can probably conduct the most rarefied forum in the world on this airplane which he has studied in the way a lawyer might study a case that will last his lifetime, and he is in a constant distemper with people who say the Lib is a dog, which is the popular feeling. On the silent ocean with the clamoring people warring all over it, Dougherty has sometimes proved that it isn't.

I imagine Dougherty's whole life has been circumscribed by one ambition, to be in the Navy. Expression stops there. As an enlisted man he had to fight like a tiger to get flight training, the rewards of which are even then mighty slim. Catch the buoy in a P-boat. Fly a JRF once in a while at some Naval Air Facility.

If you asked him why he did all this, which no one would, he would never say that he loved the sea or ships. He would never repeat the practicalities of Navy life that he has read on the posters. His real union with the Navy is in sentiment and I am sure that years ago, perhaps, even Dougherty felt some strange heightening process inside him, felt esteem and knowledge grow with his responsibilities. It has been satisfaction enough.

Barker and Dougherty arrive at the door together. Dougherty is still buttoning up a clean short-sleeved shirt and he lets go of it a moment and makes impatient gestures for Barker to go in ahead of him. Barker turns sideways and scuttles inside as though he thinks Dougherty might kick him in the seat. He might, too.

He is a short powerful man with flaring nostrils and a valence of blond hair all around his bald head. His arms and face are darkly burned and there is a triangular patch of dark skin where his shirt is open at the neck, but the rest of him is of the whiteness that never sees the sun. When you see him in the shower the contrast in the skin tones gives him the look of a laborer who has no leisure. It points up the utter lack of frivolity in him. Dougherty is thirty-six, older than the Captain.

"I hear it's another gripe, Captain," Dougherty says. He stands there in his clean shirt and faded but spotless pants and looks calmly at Ironhead. Anyone else would have come wrapped in a towel.

"I'm afraid it is. The same gripe."

"Yes, sir." Dougherty's mild blue eyes show no surprise.

"What the hell, it's a sensible gripe," Ironhead says. "Engelson has to do things the way he sees best. The point is you and I have to watch it. The old days will be back . . . we'll be bumping into all these people again."

"And the biggest thing the commander will have on his mind will be some new order for the Shore Patrol to really bear down on guys who don't square their hats," Dougherty says tucking his shirt deeper under his belt. "The trouble is I'll be wearing one."

"Maybe not. With your record you can probably stay up."

"I'd lose all my time." There is a blank impenetrability about Dougherty, a mingling of ignorance and insight, the thing he levels at authority and possibly at fate. He is not going to be deflected from the way he flies by a little fat man in a shaded Quonset and he is not going to allow anyone to alter the way he plans to live.

"Anyway," Ironhead says smiling, "stop violating Wing Directives for my sake."

"I don't. I finish every search no matter what the Commander thinks."

"Did you the other day?"

"I come in to the reef where the sub hulk is. That's twenty-eight minutes from here."

"How long?" Stevens says chidingly. He is disappointed that the Captain seems to be commiserating with Dougherty instead of reprimanding him. Dougherty looks at Stevens.

"For one hundred dollars. I'll start at a thousand feet over the hulk, I won't use more than thirty inches at any time, and I'll be on the deck inside of twenty-eight minutes." Stevens manages to look skeptical without having to accept the challenge.

"Most guys search at ten thousand," Dougherty says turning back to the Captain. "They don't look under clouds. They read and they eat and once in a while they look at the flux gate and twist a tit on the auto pilot a little. Maybe they look outside once in a while to see if there are any thunderheads. The radioman sleeps. He looks at the radarscope about as often as the pilot looks outside—and half the guys don't work the sets right anyway, if there was something under the cloud deck they'd never see it. Sure, when they get out to the end they wake up, but in close . . . The *Yamato* could sail right up to this island just about any time she wanted to, but she wouldn't come down a sector I was flying."

Ashton has entered during this speech. At the end he claps. "Nah, you have to have chicken inspectors, Dougherty," Ashton says. "It's in the by-laws of The Club." Ashton has become the

rhetorical voice of all civilian antipathy toward what he calls
"The Club," the silly, hermetic society of the stupid, the false,
and the inane, the United States Navy.

The ensigns laugh, pleased with Ashton's daring in front of the
Captain. Ashton grins, picks up one of the censor stamps and
stamps my shirt. "You see John Paul Jones knew that someday
there would be flying, and . . ."

"Okay," Ironhead says. "Enough lobbying."

"Excuse me, Captain, but that cons me. They let words get in
there. Strategic Surprise. Target of Opportunity. Well, for the
love of God, what are we, lexicographers? What does Engelson
know about it? Where did he learn the breaks and holds? By
circling around his darling very own cruiser twice every year for
ten minutes in an SOC?"

"Take it easy," Stevens says in his patronizing, go along with
you, mate, but not too far, voice. He reserves this tone for braking
actions in the presence of the Captain. "There's no place to put
you here except the generator shack." Kirby is referring to the
time on Tinian when Engelson gave Ashton five days' hack in a
store tent with a marine guard, no liquor and no visitors stipula-
tions in force, because Ashton popped off about the stupidity that
characterized the handling of a trip to Chichi Jima. 420 had just
arrived and were already busy attacking destroyers, and of course
enjoying a chilling casualty rate, and they got us involved in one
of their minor massacres. We lost a crew.

During the big Christmas Eve air raid, Ashton sneaked out and
came to visit us. We were all up on the roof of a Quonset watching the show across the channel on Saipan and listening to the
would-be Bill Stern who was announcing the raid on the loud-
speakers. It was like a football game, and we had whisky and
plum pudding and cigars to help us pass the time. Suddenly a
Betty glided in on us with its engines cut and laid a stick across
the camp and we all slid off the roof. Ashton twisted his ankle
and then ran smack into Engelson in the darkness. He got five
more days in the store tent.

Kirby's remark makes Ashton angry not because it refers to this but just because it is the same old effort Kirby always makes to kill off the fun and leave behind only the senseless torments. There is no suitable riposte to Kirby, other than to portray dumb agony. This we do at the drop of a hat. For example when Neely, who is a wonderful jitterbug, does his stuff at a party and Kirby steps out and by way of competition begins clumping around in the Cossack dance, we groan and make our hopelessness so naked that Kirby has finally stopped *that* one. But he is not really rebuffed, or self-conscious, or even faintly embarrassed, and his "personality" only crops up again in an evening of cockney dialect or dreadful fraternity house toasts. These are impossible to kill off.

Ashton looks at Kirby, trying to think of something extra derogatory to say to him. "Kirby," he says slowly, "now that you've taken out a life membership in The Club, you'll have to think about these things. Who you can put in where. How far you can ram that Regular Navy anchor up someone's butt. It's not going to be like the old days pumping gas down at the Shell station."

"Where you'll be, if you're lucky."

"Doesn't the idea of remaining a moron for life bother you at all?"

"Thinking of you down in that grease pit will keep me happy, Ashton."

"Now, boys," Ironhead says. They are getting quite angry.

"Well, with my diploma from The Club they may let me run the lube rack up and down. What the hell, you can't *buy* this sort of training. And with what you learned down there at South Central West Virginia Polly and Aggie, Kirby, you're equipped to go places. *You* have that something *extra*."

Stevens shakes his head pityingly. "Okay, okay. I'm stupid. I didn't go to Princeton like you. I'm a poor USN moron. Now how about you hittin' that old mail? Iverson isn't supposed to be signing it."

"I'd like to, Kirby," Ashton says. "I really would. I'd like to get in there and get on that old ball and really hit that old mail. But I just can't. I'm too low. My mom's pie didn't arrive this week."

Dougherty rises and his big hands grip the back of the chair

to move it out of the way. His knuckles come through the tan skin
like white chicken bones. "If that's all, Captain . . ."

"That's all, Bill."

Dougherty nods and then his face flashes with sudden amusement. "You know those guys kill me," he says nodding his head
in the direction of 420. "That Tindall—he is still discovering stuff
on Natoena. All them dummy planes, the weather station we
wrecked when we first come over here, them two ships the Japs
beached. Some guys even reported return fire and people running
around. Christ, there hasn't been an unfriendly seagull on that
island for months. They see their own tracers bouncing and think
they're being shot at." He shakes his head sadly and goes out. I can
see him through the rolled-up sides of the shack, striding away like
a powerful troll. I have heard he has wife troubles like the Captain's. They are alike in many ways, a shaky career, a standout
nickname, a sand crab wife. It is said that Dougherty's wife has
told him that she hopes he never comes home.

"Okay, let's go you guys," Kirby says to me and the ensigns.
Ashton is looking at the pain sheet and pays no attention to him.

"You are hereby ordered to participate in an aerial flight in
accordance with Fleet Air Wings, U.S. Pacific Fleet, Philippine
Sea Frontier, letter number four million three hundred thousand
and . . . duty in and around tall buildings shall, in some cases,
be deemed sufficient to meet the requirements of this . . ."

"Okay, knock it," Ironhead says good-humoredly. "And let me
see that thing."

I have watched the Captain read the schedule many times. I
have seen the tiny gust of excitement sweep across his face when
he comes to his name. It is some sharp, sweet shock that he feels,
perhaps a tiny insinuation of hope, that this time . . . this time!
He moves slightly in his chair and blots the towel against his
stomach and chest. I wonder if he feels the temptation to pick
plums, to say to hell with the bumbly fair play where everybody
goes out on rotation.

The shack settles down, stabilized by the presence of the Captain. The ensigns read and stamp and I sign and seal.

CHAPTER FIVE

When the curtain of darkness falls,
Swords, guns and even tanks are gone.

O N THE tenth day I fly again. They have organized a strike on a tiny island in the South China Sea named Itu Aba where there is a weather station and a few installations. It is the island where Skindome Dougherty found his convoy, and to which he returns like a Capistrano swallow every time he gets the chance. There will be six Libs from the Wing, six from the Army, some B-25's and a few P-38's. Ashton, Bartlett and I are flying the delegation from 400. Foy and Beppo are my lucky copilots.

Bartlett suggests that Frank Ainsworth be allowed to lead the array since he once hit the armored launch from twelve thousand feet with a water-filled on the Salton Sea, but Frank obscenely declines the honor. Since we have long since dispensed with Norden sights and oxygen gear, we will have to bomb on a signal from the Army at around nine thousand feet.

Of all people to want to fly such a trip, Norton appears at the briefing. He has more than the usual props, which is disturbing. Natal boots with the legs of a shiny new Flash Gordon suit stuffed into them, a new oversized patch on his left breast, and mother's wedding ring clamped in his right ear. This is significant because he only wears the ring there when he hasn't killed recently. If it is true as it is said that Ahab promised his mother on her deathbed never to use foul language, I only hope she died before he had time to work out all those tedious derivatives.

The patch on the nylon suit is exquisite, a piece of yellow cloth the size of a dessert plate upon which is sewn a red Flying Whale, who is, of course, carrying a bomb in his flippers. The whale is snarling with determination and a live fuse hisses in the bomb. I don't know why Cap Ahab should want to go along on a puny little strike unless he wants to preview his new patch for us, but there seems to be more than the usual jauntiness about him today. He seems to strut even sitting down. He doesn't mingle with us but goes over and comrades the hell out of it with the Army boys. Now and again we can hear overtones of what he is saying about "the honorable sons of rips." There is an Army major with a broken nose and rolled-up sleeves and pencils stuck in his suit talking to Monty Herbert, and a flock of guys wearing khaki caps with the bills turned up. We are all very picturesque but Ahab's red whale is far and away the most aerial-combat of the fetishes. It is really big medicine and everyone notices it.

We wait and finally Swede Engelson comes in and confers with the group around the major. It must be very important, this island. Perhaps Tojo is spending a holiday there.

"There is Donald Crisp," Ashton says to Bartlett. "And there's a guy who looks a hell of a lot like Reginald Denny. Just a hell of a lot. But where is Richard Cromwell and his dog?"

"No stove," Bartlett says. "There has to be a stove where that extra hairy dog with the litter of pups can lie. Everyone is terribly fond of that dog. Even Crisp."

Engelson and the major are very animated.

"Do you suppose they are talking about steak, or milk, or lettuce?"

"With their hands?"

"How else can they talk? These men are pilots!"

"I bet I could eat five heads of lettuce and drink two gallons of good old milk, I bet, because that's what I'm fighting for."

"Nice to fly with you, fellah!"

"And the wheat, of course. At haying time the wheat in the upper meadow looks like cloth of gold."

"Fight for the wheat, Americans! Fight for Bess, there, under the stove. Let her have her pups in a free land. Fight for your corner drugstore . . ."

"Okay, pipe down, pipe down, everybody!" Engelson has the kind of high twangy voice that you can hear above the engine noises on a ramp, the voice of the sedentary officer I used to hear at Pensacola who had come out from behind his desk to try something physical that he was slightly afraid of. Like flying.

"Major Macmoriarty is going to tell us about the operation," Engelson says. "Since he is going to be in command, I urge all of you, the Navy people at least, to pay close attention. We don't need a snafu on the part of the Wing."

"Major O'Macmoriarity did he say?" Ashton whispers. "There's one. O'Macmoriarity stuck an unlit fag in his broken-nosed, freckled face." Bartlett makes a sign with his thumb. It means they have just cast a new character in their endless serial. He will join the kid Yid, Davy Cohen, who carries everybody's packs, unwillingly of course, and Kindly Father Killarney, always up in front with his buoys, and Second Lieutenant John Fuckjohn of the RFC, usually known as Second John John Fuckjohn, and many others. It is reasonable to suppose that the major, now stepping forward, rubbing his bare arms and staring at the floor in a highly dramatic fashion, will find a leading place among them. He briefs us, calling us "gentlemen" about every five words.

There will be six of their Libs, here from Mindoro, six of ours, nine 25's and six 38's. The idea is to level the place. We will drop on a voice signal preceded by a count, from him. The 25's will strafe with their package guns, the 38's will get the flak out of there.

There is a lot of confusion at the take-off. It is still dark and everyone is trying to be last. Just as I take the runway I hear excited voices on the VHF. One of the Army Libs is in trouble. He is coming back and going to land downwind. Behind me are airplanes jamming the taxi strip and I can't get off the mat. We sit and watch the winglights approaching.

Because he is coming with the wind and because he is nervous with his trouble, the pilot doesn't touch until he is far down the runway. He comes straight for us, very fast. For a moment everything seems to be in order, I can see the winglights bouncing gently up and down as he brakes. Then something gives way, the red light arcs up and over, the airplane stands on edge and veers off to our left. It looks like a wheel has run into soft sand off the mat. The airplane rends itself apart and twenty-five hundred gallons go up about two hundred yards away. People run toward the wreck but they can't do anything. As if by miracle two figures come walking out of the flames. The fire trucks blanket everything with tons of foamite but it is of course too late. We are delayed ten minutes. When we go the fire is still burning and it makes the take-off easier because the steel mat glints with red light along most of its length.

We begin at once to siphon. I rock the wings, trying to break the suction, but it doesn't stop. Because of what we have just seen, we are more terrified than usual. Beppo is crossing himself every five seconds, only Foy is cool. He shuts off everything electrical and I come back on the turbos as far as I can, and still stay in the air. Even so sparks and chunks of red hot carbon go flying back under the wings. I sweat like a pig, rock the wings, pray. At last it stops and Beppo and I come down off our butts with a sigh.

I can't find Ashton and Bartlett, so I follow a three-plane section, flying well down in the hole under the V. As daylight comes I see they are Privateers. I join up and for an hour all I see is Ahab's tail turret, the two big blister mounts, and the retracted radar dome, swaying a hundred feet above me. A Privateer has more guns than a porcupine has quills. Beppo and I take turns practicing formation flying, drink coffee, smoke, and insult Cap Ahab. Beppo says it took him seven hours to bail out the well and he ain't going to forget it.

I have never seen the island and am surprised at how tiny it is.

It is pear-shaped with a long sand bar running out where the stem would be, and the whole thing isn't more than a mile long. There is a slender jetty on the leeward side of it, some block-houses, and what looks like a lot of beehives scattered about. Around the entire island is a collar of white surf. "Jesus, all this for that little dump?" Beppo says.

I locate Ashton and Bartlett, drop down and let them pass over me, then climb up again and get in on Ashton's left. "You just come on back here with Richard Cromwell," Ashton says on VHF.

"Nice to fly with you, fellah," Bartlett says.

"That's changed to fry. Nice to fry with you . . ."

"Knock it," says a voice. It sounds like Ahab's.

"Who is that, Crisp speaking? Nice to die with you, sir!"

"I said knock it. By Christmas, that means knock it!"

It is Ahab. Nobody says another word. He might shoot us down.

We have to put on a lot of boost to catch the five Army ships. The 25's are below us and far to our left, the 38's are up ahead just above the army Libs. It is quite an armada for this little place.

We fly directly over the island and the lead Army element makes a slow turn so that we can cut inside and catch up. At last we are joined up in a diamond of three-plane sections, two brown and two blue. One of the brown has of course only two in it, but it is a very pretty sight nevertheless, and one that we don't see very often in our business. I work hard to keep in tight so that the Army will have nothing to say.

The major calls on channel B. His bombardier will give the drop signal the instant his Norden releases the bombs. The tiny hesitation, coupled with the spread we get from our intervolom-eters and the fact that the airplanes are scattered a few yards apart, should give good coverage. Pretty scientific, what with Nordens and bombardiers.

It is a long run, and we make it with the doors open. The air rushes in and blows sand in our eyes. Foy spots the first flak. The puffs are small and black and the cycle is slow. Now the P-38's peel off. They seem to go straight down. They dive down the streaks the flak makes coming up at us and fire right into the

nests. The way they package the fifties nowadays, you can saw
a cruiser in two with them. I can't see much, I am too busy staying in there, but there seem to be a lot of red golf balls bounding
around down there among the beehives, which Foy tells me are
tents, pitched in an orchard.

A voice is counting and I get my thumb over the pickle. We
seem to be turning and it is hard not to skid. If I drop while skidding I will sling the bombs out into the drink. I am at the end of
the whole boodle, with Bartlett, and our movements are exaggerated, like the last man in crack-the-whip. But now we are
straight and the air is smooth. "Drop . . . drop . . . drop," says
the voice. I squeeze the pickle and the airplane bucks slightly as
the load leaves. We turn and head out to sea. In a moment the
island seems to erupt in smoke. A few bombs make roses in the
sea.

I see a blue airplane dropping away on our right. There is another and another. It is Ahab and his boys. All at once I am alone
up there with the Army. Ashton and Bartlett have gone down too.

"What the hell," I say to Beppo.

"Sure," he says. "Why be the only ones?" Down we go.

Airplanes are crisscrossing the island at low level from all directions and tracers are winging all over the place. The 25's are
dropping napalm. I see one of them lob a can right into the window of a blockhouse. There is a white bloom, with jagged tenta-
cles coming out of it, and then a solid percussive billow of greasy
smoke coming from all the windows of the blockhouse and up
through the vent in the roof. They drop others down among the
trees of the little orchard where the tents were pitched. When I
pass the trees they are burned to the ground and the tents have
nearly all disappeared.

Airplanes come diving down from all directions. They go under
us, over us, past us, as we lumber along. Everyone is shooting
from our airplane but my only maneuvers are to avoid ramming
other aircraft. Twice I see figures running on the ground and each
time they are hunted by the fire from two or three airplanes, all
jockeying for the same target. In five minutes the island is a

smoking wasteland. The skeletons of the blockhouses remain, but not a shack, not a tree is left. The camouflage has been seared off the single flak battery and the guns are exposed, twisted and bent like pretzels. I don't dare turn, there are so many airplanes whizzing around us. A 38 comes skimming in from the water, hops over the jetty, which is still intact, and comes curving in straight at me. His tracers go by less than ten yards from our left wing tip. I have never seen so many coming from one airplane. The fire from a Jap fighter is puny in comparison. I pull up and turn gently but there are airplanes on my right and behind me. Everyone in the crew seems to be reporting an imminent collision. I fly straight ahead, out and away from the chaos. On channel B there is now a great deal of yipping and blasphemy.

"Mike, you bastard, you're eating grass!"

"God damn it, stay in the pattern, chiseler!"

"Get your ass out of the way, you Navy boxcar!" This is probably directed at me by the 38. It is exactly what I am doing. The thing is so out of hand it doesn't seem possible that anyone will reorganize it. We start home alone, climbing slowly.

It has been the most gigantic expenditure of power on so small a target I have ever seen. All the installations on the island weren't worth a tenth of the price of the munitions expended on wrecking it. Since the island is flat and, unlike Iwo, devoid of any rocks, there couldn't have been any place for a mouse to hide. Behind us the bedlam continues. "Stand back, men, I am about to let the bastards have it through the relief tube," someone says on channel B.

Half an hour after we land, I am summoned to the Wing Quonset. I hike through the hot sand and Travis, the mess boy, grins as he lets me in. I hear Engelson's angry voice talking on the telephone.

"What's the matter with him?"

"He mad about sump'n," Travis says.

Engelson comes in from the back office, sucks his teeth and stares at me. "Where are the others?"

"I don't know, sir. They hadn't landed when I got in."

"There's going to be hell to pay, rioting around like that. The Major just told me that you joined right in . . . all of you!"

"Not me. I just flew over the island one time."

"At nine thousand?"

"Well, no sir. I meant I flew over once at low level just looking."

"And shooting!"

"Some . . . yes, sir."

"What at, the B-25's?" Engelson is already bored with me. He wants to deliver a blistering lecture to a large audience and it seems hardly worthwhile to waste any of it on one meek little j.g. He tells me to come back at two when there will be a meeting of all pilots who took part in the operation.

The meeting is never held because in the meantime it is discovered that Joe Norton is missing. Nobody has seen him. Engelson questions everyone and tells each of us that through our personal foolishness the commanding officer of a fine squadron has been lost. But not even Tindall has seen old Ahab since the moment he ducked out of the formation. Tindall sits in a jeep down at the field like a grieving sheepdog until after dark, telling everyone he just can't believe they finally got the Captain.

We finally got the Captain, is the way Ashton puts it. Ashton says he personally got good hits around the cockpit and some day he will show us all the pictures.

No one got Ahab. A Dumbo PBY locates him out on the end of the sandpit off Itu Aba, but since their radio is out no one knows the story until late in the evening. Norton has been hit by something, probably a wild burst from a thirty-eight, and set on fire. He has to land and manages to do it so that he winds up wedged on the sand bar with the airplane just awash. This is a neater trick than it appears because he has landed in breaking seas, the aircraft on fire, and no hydraulics for the flaps. In the landing Ahab gets a blow on the head and nearly drowns. After everyone has left without seeing the downed Lib with the crew waving and firing flares from the wing, some Japs come out in a boat. Ahab says there were plenty of them left alive. He manages to get the crown turret trained on them manually and

when the Japs row into range Ahab personally lets them have it.
He spends the afternoon under rifle fire from the island, occasionally pulling one of his crew back from the water where they are
being washed by the heavy sea. After all this he manages to be
chesty when the Dumbo arrives. "If you sons of rips hadn't got
here pretty soon," Ahab tells the PBY crew, "I was going to have
to swim over there and take that island from the honorable sons
of rips." Then with admirable energy he boots the j.g. out of the
left seat and flies the P-boat home.

That is Norton's story and I for one don't doubt very much of it.
The word is out that he will be recommended for three medals
simultaneously. The D.F.C. for the water landing, the Silver Star
for killing the Japs in the boat, and the Soldiers and Sailors Medal
for saving his crewmen, one of whom has a broken back. Engelson, of course, does nothing to discipline anyone.

That night, during the celebration over in 420 there is an air
raid, probably a feeble retaliation for the attack on the island. A
couple of single-engined airplanes come down the glade behind
the camp and fly a bit clackingly to the airstrip where they begin
dropping some small bombs. Roger and Beppo and I are at the
movie and when the twenties begin to come low through the
palms and to carom off the trunks, we have to run for it. The
gunners down near the strip have depressed the guns very low
to fire at the Japs who are flying up and down the runway, and
they forget that the shells come right into camp.

We run through the trees away from the darkened movie, trip-
ping and cursing while things blaze red in the blackness all
around us. One of the airplanes seems to follow us. It comes over
the camp barely above the trees, flying very slowly with an archaic
popping sound in its engine. Once the pilot cuts the throttle back
as though he is considering landing on us.

Now the noise is dreadful. There are quadruple fifties firing
from the camp and the people of 420, who are drunk, come
running out of their tents and fire carbines into the air. The tracers
loop overhead, in long red arches. Ricochets whine from the
trees. You would think it was a fifty-plane raid. One Jap begins

dropping daisy cutters in the tent area and we run for our private shelter—the big steel scoop of a steam shovel the Seabees are using nearby. The scoop is big enough for three to stand in and its steel sides are several inches thick. We make this with a lot of yelling and excited laughter. The bombs crack, every gun around is blazing away into the night. Just outside someone is firing a carbine and laughing like a maniac.

"The stupid bastards!" I say panting. I hit my ankle on one of the steel teeth getting inside the scoop and now I am furious with everything. I decide to hell with sitting in here and smelling everyone's breath, I am going to strike back . . . but at what? The Japs don't irritate me—420 certainly does.

"We'll never have a chance like this again!" I shout.

"For what?"

"The well!"

"Christ, come on!" Beppo says. We run for our tents. I rummage frantically around and come up with half a can of rancid bacon, a can of Aerosol, and a box of soap flakes. On the way out I rip two packets of yellow dye marker off the Mae West hanging on the wall. It doesn't seem half poisonous enough. Roger is giggling. I have no idea what he has found. We pick up Beppo and run back through the noise across the road and into 420's area. Beppo finds the iron pipe that leads from Norton's tent to the well and we follow it off into the trees.

We go to work ripping open the dye marker and soap containers and punching holes in the Aerosol cans with our knives.

"I wish I had time to take a big hairy Annapolis in it!" Beppo says.

"Stand back, I'll give it the treatment," Roger says. He has something oblong in his hand. He slams the object on the iron pipe and drops it in the well. We run hunched over. Behind us there is an explosion. It is a Jap mortar round, one of the things we often denature and use for a sort of scrimshaw souvenir. But they work fine, just like a grenade, if you bang the nose on something hard.

It is much quieter but there is still one airplane around somewhere off the beach. The popping sound of the engine is more pronounced.

"He's losing a jug, poor guy," Beppo says. When we get to the tents the firing has stopped completely. Somebody peeps the siren playfully. It didn't blow at all to announce the raid.

The next morning they find a dozen unexploded daisy cutters in and around the camp. They seem to have been dropped too low and consequently didn't arm themselves. But a shard from one that did go off struck a radioman in CAC 11 on the head and cut his scalp rather badly. Down on the strip five airplanes were hit but none seriously.

As the imaginative Cunningham first told the story, a chief and two other men were lying in their sacks down the road where the Seabees live, contemplating the fact that they were going home the next day after thirty-six months. A dud bomb fell in front of their tent and a dud just behind it, but a live one fell right in the tent, killing all three of them. They lay in their tent, Cunningham said, just as they had died, with their hands still folded behind their heads.

The next day we see two men with a gasoline pump, bailing out the well and in the evening there is a swabbie with a carbine on guard over it. No one could look more embarrassed.

CHAPTER SIX

But when I dream father urging me,
To fight to death for the country,
How I'd outface foes in front.

"IT HAS come to the attention of this comm-a-n-n-d . . . that some of you me-yen . . . have been . . . breathing! This practice will cease and *de*sist . . . eeemeelialy!" Yoke whips his cigar into his mouth and quickly out again. "Sign that one . . . Gawd! Commanding cinc univ! Copies all flots divs, desrons, croutons, morons, and hardons."

It is the hottest morning in weeks, not a cloud in the sky, not a sound except Yokum and the clanking of the new washing machine down the road. The machine arrived the day before yesterday and has been going steadily ever since, and a huge puddle of soapy water has spread across the road and into the jungle. The machine is hooked to an extension cord running to the generator shack that is over a hundred yards long. We three are next after Beppo and before Standing Room Mara, who mysteriously enough is maneuvering to use it too. He comes to the door of his tent every few minutes to see if it is available. We have to beat Mara to the machine, otherwise we'll all die of zinc poisoning. But perhaps he only wants to wash his chess set.

Roger is lying on his back in his chair, his fat, unself-conscious stomach exposed to the air, and from time to time Yoke dumps cigar ashes on it. Roger doesn't bother to brush them away unless they are hot, and Yoke pumps on the cigar like a forge to make them so. Roger finally yelps.

"That's it, boyee, suck up them entrails," Yoke says. I mean *suck* up them entrails! Till they right where you brain would be if you had any. You in the Mareen Coah, boyee, you ain't home with you mother-fuckin' mother! Speakin' of you mothah show me again how you'd give it to her if she evah tried take that refle fomya, boyee!"

Roger flutters a hand feebly. "Why, Sarge, I'd just naturally give it to her right in her mother-fuckin' entrails, that's where."

"Boyee, you got esprit de coah! Now we gonna have a little PT, boyee." Yoke tips his hat down over his face and sinks lower in his chair. "The next exercise will be done in the following manner. Ready, begin! Hip . . . harr . . . hup . . . harr . . . hip."

Swede Engelson goes by, closely accompanied by Monty Herbert and the ACI officer of 420. The tetrarch followed by the canephorae. Yokum leads us in a line or two of "Veiled in flesh the godhead see," and speculates obscenely on what would happen to the noses of intelligence officers if the execs of air wings stopped too suddenly while walking.

"*E*effective *ee*melialy, all personnel in this air-reah shall render the kneeling salute to executive officers of air wings at such times and places as shall be deemed appropriate. In other words while swimming, flying, sleeping or in the head, and at all other times. To properly render this salute, place the elbows firmly on the deck, buttocks slightly raised, lips open and pursed, and . . ."

"Well, I see nothing's changed. You guys haven't moved an inch in three weeks." It is Neely back from the hospital in Leyte. "I feel like I was never away, hearing Yokum again."

"You been somewhere?" Yoke says. "Oh yeah, you the one went chicken S. Name's Brady or somethin'."

"I hear he finally made it carrying those hundred-pound wings to Ironhead's desk," Neely says. "Well, you can't keep 'em unless you flap 'em."

"Unless your name is Engelson," I say. "Or Cassowary."

"They did a terrible thing to that boy," Yokum says. "A boy with his heart in the sky like that. Why that boy just lived to fly."

"What's he doin'?" Neely says.

"Why workin' his ass off! He has to drive a jeep *around*! Has to go down to the *line*, sometimes twice a *day*! To see that the mat isn't getting rusty or the coconuts aren't falling on it. Then . . . he runs the library. Big job . . . must be thirty . . . forty books to keep track of."

"I hear you two guys went in the old *agua*," Neely says. "Foy said it was pretty shaky."

"Yes, well, Foy. As a matter of fact Fatfag and I did put in a little sea time one evening. What you been doing, Neely? Did you belt any of those nurses?"

Neely looks at the ground and licks his lips. "You won't believe this. But I did. The last night. You know, she took care of me, and you kind of get to know them. We went to the club a couple times, boy, you wouldn't know it any more . . ."

"The *nurse*, Neely."

"Well, the last night I finally got her in the sack and the next day I had to leave. Boy, does that feed me."

"That's war, boy," Yokum says. "Now don't ruin the first good story we've heard in years by telling us she was good-looking."

"Not too," Neely says. "But not bad, either. I'd forgotten what it was like."

"Let's see," Roger says. "How *does* that go? You put your left arm under her right knee . . . no, your right hip against her . . ."

Neely giggles and tells us the details. It is preposterous the effect it has on me and how much I envy him. My lethargy vanishes. My imagination runs away with me, my libido comes out like a genie from a bottle, swelling and growing with each word.

When Neely stops, Yokum, the only one not transfixed, looks at him and shakes his head sadly. "Lord save us," he says like a startled old maid. "Good clean fun down at the roller rink would have been one thing, but . . . Smith, what have you got to say to this dirty little boy?"

"Like to see you over in the chapel a little more often, fellah. We got a new dart game in the basement and magic lantern slides every Thursday."

"I bet you're glad to find Prime gone," I say to Neely.

He trickles sand through his fingers. "What do you think? You had a nice rough ride with him, from what I heard."

"I hardly miss him," I say.

"I was the sixth Purple Heart in the crew. Prime makes seven and the other guy . . . Arnold . . . eight."

"Did they give you the medal?"

"Yeah. A guy came along and dumped it on my bed. The scuttlebutt is that Prime will get a Navy Cross, to make up for the eye."

I see Tindall from 420 coming rapidly and purposefully down the road, straight for us. He walks with his hands clasped over his steerhead belt buckle and his shoulders hunched forward to make his muscles stand out. He stops, three feet away, throws one leg forward and one shoulder back, scowling. "Ah don't know which one of you jokahs did it . . . ah aim to find out." He looks from one to the other of our faces. "When ah do, well what ah give that little dago is child's play to what ah'm gonna give this jokah."

"Mr. Tindall, suh, whatever do you-all mean?" Yokum says innocently. We all gawk at one another in feigned amazement.

"You know goddam well what ah mean, Yokum. And if you don't, ah ain't about to explain. Ah'm just naturally gonna beat somebody's bag. Maybe ever'body's bag."

"I think you'll find that it's bags in the plural," Roger says.

"Never you mind, fat boy, ah pound just as hard in the singulah."

"Let him start beating bags," I say. "Tindall, you're great at beating up runts like Beppo . . ."

Tindall comes in close until his face is inches from mine. He twists his mouth, pounds one fist into the other palm. "You want some right now, you skinny son of a bitch, because ah swear to God ah'll give it to you?"

"Try it and you'll get a carbine butt across your head!" Roger says sitting up.

"More than that," Yokum says. "We'll kill you. We'll shoot you."

"Yeah," Neely says. "Crank something up, mate, if you want

your ass in ribbons." He must have been fed raw meat during his convalescence. Tindall glares at each of us in turn. He probably isn't scared but he is surprised by the unexpected show of solidarity. No more surprised than I am, though.

"Don't shit me," Tindall says scornfully. "Not a one of you guys could fight your way out of a two-bit shirt. Smith might could if he fell through it. Ah'm gonna have me a little talk with Ironhead and then we'll see whose ass is gonna have ribbons onto it."

"Ah, Tindall, blow, will you?" Yokum says wearily. "Go get some more tattoos. At least get out of here. You feed me." Yokum is the only one of us who has not unconsciously shifted his position. Tindall smiles and then giggles. His voice is that strange shuddering alto I have often heard when southerners are angry. "Boy, you just dyin' for it, ain't you?" He looks us all over one by one again. "Well, you'll git it. See if you don't. Ah'll find out." He nods emphatically, his head bobbing like a woodpecker, then stalks off, the muscles on his broad back rippling awesomely.

"Don't tell on us, please, Mr. Tindall, don't tell on us!" Yokum calls after him. "But goddam me, he's big," he says to us shaking his head. "Did you ever notice how much bigger their guys look than our guys? We must have every runt in the Navy. And Smith. Two hundred and ninety pounds of fighting fat."

"It's because they're all ex-instructors. They just seem big."

"Shit on him. The four of us can whip any man in the house."

"What's he griped about?" Neely doesn't even know.

"The well. We gave it the deep six again last night."

Tindall probably *could* whip us all at once. Yoke and I are thin and light, Roger is fat, Neely hasn't a single visible muscle anywhere. But our fighting mood, and the solidarity we have discovered among ourselves for the first time, work like an emetic on us, and we bubble with loyal declarations and high-blown promises of mutual support. We talk about what we will do to Tindall if he tries anything. We will even kill him, if necessary.

Beppo whistles from the road. We take our dirty clothes and go down to where the big puddle of soapy water lies across the

road. Neely tags along. He says he is in no hurry to check in
with Stevens.

Beppo has hung some sheets on a line strung between two trees
at the edge of a thick patch of cane. His wet laundry is stacked
neatly on a table the Seabees have made us to go with the washer.
He has even washed his shoes in the puddle and put them on a
stump near the sheets to dry in the sun. Beppo looks pleased with
his morning's work.

"As soon as it drains you can have it." We sit down on a palm
log and smoke and tell Beppo about Tindall. Beppo spits into
the soapy lake and scowls formidably. "He ain't fooled with a
fightin'-mad dago. I'll cut that mother wide open, from behind,
and in the dark," he says fervently.

Maybe Beppo would chop him up with a machete, but I remember the night the Japs came through the camp on Morotai.
There weren't more than a dozen of them, but there we were,
hiding under the beds, terrified out of our wits. Beppo wasn't
cutting anybody up that night. He was lying with his back against
mine, mumbling Hail Marys so loud I was sure that every Jap
in the place would home in on us. Yokum almost got shot by the
Rangers because he had "to see what was going on."

Roger was flying that night, hence forever after denied admission to our exclusive "Hand-to-Hand Combat Club." Of course
I have never been admitted to "The Ditchers Club," "The Bail-
Out Brotherhood" and many other organizations some of which
contain only one member.

We sit lazing in the hot sun. I have my back to the others and
face toward the cane patch and the line where Beppo's sheets are
drying. The sheets droop down to within a couple of feet of the
ground, and from where I sit, they hide the stump where he has
put his shoes. Suddenly I see a pair of legs moving behind the
sheets. I wonder idly who it can be back there. The legs are
strangely thick and peculiarly clad. They go to the place where I
know the stump to be, pause, and then move rapidly on.

I stand up. A Jap is running over the rough ground toward the
cane. The earth has been ripped by bulldozers and he staggers a
bit in the uneven places. Just as he reaches the cane he looks

back, sees me, and dives into the stalks. The tops wave briefly. He is gone.

"Hey!" I shout, half at the Jap and half to the others. "Hey, I just saw a Jap!" The others turn around.

"Sure you did," Yokum says after a look. "It was Frank Watanabe and the Honorable Archie . . ."

"I'm not kidding. He just disappeared in that cane." I duck and peer under the sheets. "If you don't believe me, where are Beppo's shoes?"

"He took my shoes?"

"They're not there any more." We all run over to the stump. The shoes are certainly not there and we find some tracks.

"I'll be a son of a bitch. That's where they were."

"And that's where they went." I point to where the Jap vanished.

"What do you know?" Neely says and giggles. In the giggle is reflected the first mild consternation we all feel. We are taken aback to have been, as it were, in the presence of the enemy in such a personal way. It isn't exactly new. We have seen Japs at close range. In caves, hiding inside our camps, inside barrels even. We have seen people kill them and we have killed them from airplanes at ranges of twenty or thirty feet where we could see their facial expressions. But always there was protection for the thin-skinned aviators. Soldiers or marines or the fact we were flying. Here there is no one except the Seabees, who are about as pugnacious as we are.

"I don't know about you guys but I'm doing a ten-flat hundred out of here," Neely says.

"And you're the guy who's going to do what to Tindall?" Yokum says disdainfully.

"There may be a dozen of them, right in there." Neely gestures uncertainly at the cane, ten yards away. "Maybe they're watching us right now."

"He wasn't carrying a gun," I say.

"Hell, I'm gonna get my shoes back," Beppo says loudly. "No chintzy Jap is gonna steal my pet gunboats." He affects an outrage that I am sure he doesn't feel.

"He was bigger than you, Beppo," I say. "He was four ten."

"That's okay. I'll knock him silly with left hands." Beppo spars around. We laugh. No one knows what to do. "What the hell," Beppo says. "He didn't have a gun, did he? Let's get the bastard. He's probably the only one left on the island."

"I think we should have a little private Jap Hunt," I say. God knows why I am so eager. "Of course if you guys are chicken . . ."

I stay and watch while they go to the tents for weapons. Roger brings me my carbine. He has his Jap rifle and three clips of ammo for it. We stand at the edge of the sugar cane feeling a bit foolish.

"Now, men," Roger says. "Get in there and flush the dirty yellow bastard out so I can shoot him. I do it best from an elephant but . . ."

"Holy Mother, watch out where you point that thing!" Beppo screams. Roger has waved the muzzle of the Jap rifle right across his chest.

"Don't be scared," Roger says. "Remember it's the *un*loaded gun that always kills you. This one is loaded, cocked, and the safety is off. It can't possibly hurt you."

"Who is going to charge in there?" Neely says.

"All of us together," I say. "Let's get a few feet apart and just go in abreast."

"Okay, but don't shoot unless you can see what you're shooting at."

"Unless it's Fatfag," Yokum says. "Then blaze away."

"Just watch out," Roger tells him. "I can kill you officially with this. No one will know. A genuine Imperial Landing Force Arisaka Year Forty. Well-made, too." Roger reaches up and slides the wooden forepiece of the stock back and forth. Every time he has fired it the piece slams back against his fingers.

"Maybe it's a pump gun," Neely says.

Beppo snorts. "Well, we've had a nice little talk here," he says scathingly. "Now let's go home and put our toys back in the box and get our didies changed and ask Ironhead if we can have our Pablum. Jesus Maria, let's go, if we're going!"

We part the stalks and step gingerly in. The cane is up to our

chins and crackles and snaps with each step. Neely is a few yards
off to my left, the others to my right. We sound like carabao
stampeding with all our thrashing and grunting. I take a few
steps and stop. I hold my carbine as high as I can above my head
by the barrel and whistle. "Can you see this?"

"My God, a Jap! Kill the bastard," Roger says.

"We're making too much noise. But if I hold this gun up every
minute or so, we can at least keep track of each other without
talking. You guys do the same."

"Okay, Commander, but which hand shall I hold it in?"

"The one you hold it in every night."

"Let go of my ears, I know my business!"

"Honest to God, are we really winning this war?"

We move slowly ahead. I push the stalks aside with the muzzle
of the carbine and then hold it at the ready until I see that it is
clear for the few feet ahead of me. The ground is rough and I
have to keep looking down at my footing, and sometimes when I
look up again I think I see the Jap. The cane gets higher and
thicker until at last I can't see anywhere except straight up. I
keep the sun over my left shoulder and try to go in a straight line.
Occasionally I hear swishing noises from the others but they seem
further off than when we started.

I hope now I won't see the Jap, even unarmed. I am afraid of
him and I don't want to face him alone. It is just what Mara is
always saying. We are so soft that without our reliance on the
fastest, safest and most numerous aids to battle we wouldn't
fight at all.

I know we took some beatings early in this war. The Philippines, Rabaul, perhaps sometimes on Guadalcanal. And I know
we lost plenty of guys at places like Tarawa under the most
murderous conditions you can imagine. But very few people took
part. The average American still is out of it, and I will bet that
when it is over not one in eight or nine servicemen will have seen
combat. Not so the Japs. All of our setbacks or defeats are minor
compared to what they have taken in the last two years and they
still have nothing but guts.

Joe Norton might have done what the Japs did up there in the Marianas, but none of my friends would. They flew down to Tinian and Saipan night after night, a dozen old Bettys, all the way from Japan, staging through the dark, bombed out airfields on Iwo and Pagan, and they hung around bombing and strafing a place as hot as Isley, with night fighters swarming all over them and flak that wouldn't quit, until they lost eight or nine airplanes. It was nothing to see three of them on fire at the same time. Monty Herbert says they found out that the pilots who survived came down the next night, and the next, until they were killed too, the method being to feed a squadron in until it was annihilated, then put together another.

I wonder what they would do with Brady in the Jap Air Force. I wonder what they would do with me! I wouldn't even taxi airplanes like that, the easy way they burn.

I break out of the cane and see a low ridge ahead of me, the first of several that go back into the mountains like ripples. The ridges are partly covered with trees and cut by deep gullies where the rain has ripped through them. Neely appears at the same time and comes over to where I am waiting. He shakes his head. "How would you like to do this for a living?"

"Well, I was thinking of joining the Marines, but a little of this would cure me."

Now we can see Beppo and Roger. They are on the other side of one of the gullies and wave at us to come over. The gully is steep, and when we reach the edge of it, we sit down and wave at them. We signal that we have come partway and will now stay right here and wait for them to come to us. After a moment they begin to walk slowly toward us. They are a few feet away when there is a shot off to our left and in front. We hunch down, all except Beppo. He runs the last few steps and falls flat beside me. Then there are three more shots in rapid succession. They seem to crack out and don't have the rolling rumble of the first one. Roger leaps up and hustles over.

"Jesus, a goddam battle," Beppo says looking nervously out through the grass.

"That's Yokum playing a little game," Roger says panting.

"You think that's Yoke?" I can't see anything.

"He got ahead. Besides he did this to me once up at that Jap dump on Tinian. Sneaking around and playing scout and firing his goddam carbine."

"That first one was a Jap rifle," Neely says. He is still leaning forward as though trying to get his ear closer to the source of the sounds. "The other was a carbine, all right—it goes rap . . . rap— but the first was Jap."

"Well now I flunked small arms sounds at Corpus," Roger says.

"It was different all right," I say.

"It was Jap, I tell you. A seven-point-seven."

"What caliber is this?" Roger says lifting one leg and farting.

"That's a smooth bore," Beppo says. "Reamed to about a ten gauge. Sounds like the breech is blown, too."

Neely giggles. "After four years in the Navy it probably is."

"My God, you guys have a lot on your mind," I say. "We better go down there."

"Us? You mean *you!*"

"All of us. Come on." We go across a patch of torn ground with huge uprooted ferns that have been washed out by a flood, and move slowly through a piece of thin woods toward the ridge. There are clods of red earth lying about that look like human heads. Once I even jump and point my carbine at one of them and Neely giggles.

We begin to climb the ridge. It is steep and we have to angle up it, first one way and then the other, puffing and sweating. Near the top there is a faint breeze. It makes the leaves of the scrubby trees shimmer in the sunlight. Someone calls down from the ridge. It is Yokum. He gets up carefully and takes a few steps down the hill as though protecting himself from something off to the right. Then he comes along the ridge to us. Roger has begun to do the manual of arms with his Jap rifle to greet Yokum, but when he sees Yokum keeping himself down behind the hill he stops and squats down with the rest of us.

"What happened?"

"I found harro prease Yankee sodjer," Yokum says excitedly. "Or he found me. He missed me by about three inches." Yoke makes a knifing motion past his thigh. He is very pale. "He went in there." He points over toward the next ridge on our right. "I thought you said he didn't have a gun!" he says to me accusingly.

"Did you shoot at him?" Neely says. "We heard a carbine."

"Hell, yes!" Neely looks off down the hill as though he expects to see a body at the bottom. "God damn it," Yoke says to me as though I am the only one who will understand this. "He came out of the cane right in front of me, I guess. I thought I heard something but the old brain was up and locked. The first thing I know, cheeeooo! Then he ran. I had a perfect chance but thanks a lot, some skilled craftsman in Chillicothe, Ohio, we just couldn't quite touch off the old blast. Click, click." Yokum holds the carbine out as though it smelled and he was going to drop it in a garbage can.

"What do you mean? We heard you fire."

"Finally. I fired at his wake. I finally got the belt pawl and the feed-pawl slide and the pawl-feed sear and all the rest of that horseshit all lined up like a goddam slot machine. Exquisite workmanship," Yoke says. His disgust is obviously feigned. I will bet there isn't a thing wrong with the carbine. Neely wants to look at Yoke's gun but Yoke pretends he doesn't hear him. "Oh, now it works," he says bitterly. It is the first time I have ever seen Yoke upset. Well, it would have scared me half to death.

We sit on the ridge and have a cigarette and discuss what to do, but it is evident that no one is going down the hill and up the next ridge in a hurry.

"It's time to call for the elephants to come trample the black men," Roger says. He is delighted to see Yoke scared. "Anyway, it's your hunt now. The law of the jungle. You have to go in there and finish off your kill."

"Maybe you did hit him," Beppo says.

"He told me he wanted the fat guy," Yoke says, his courage returning. "For the corporals' mess. He said they could feed a platoon for a week on a guy as fat as that."

"I hope he didn't say anything naughty about Babe Ruth,"

Roger says. "The thing that worries me is what do you paint on your airplane if you get one of the monkeymen on the ground?"

"He probably kept right on going," I say. "The woods are pretty thin and he must have heard or seen the rest of us."

Neely knows what I mean. "You're right," he says. "He wouldn't be in there. Besides I can see clean through it."

I don't want to appear too craven. "There is a thick part that keeps going. He could be in there."

"Where?" Neely says disparagingly. "I don't see any. Anyway it's stupid to go into a place like that where you can't see." If the woods were at first too thin to conceal a man hiding, they are now too thick and too dangerous for a man approaching. No one argues with him. As if to settle it, Neely says emphatically, "If he's in there I'll eat it."

"Show me the man who won't and I'll take his girl away from him," Beppo says. "Which reminds me, it's about time for the mail and I am due for a nice horny reply to the nice horny letter I wrote my girl."

"To hell with walking your tail off for a pair of shoes," Neely says.

"If you guys do catch him, drive him by my tent and I'll drop him for you," Roger says. He pumps the loose piece of stock on his rifle. "With the old Arisaka."

Yokum looks at me. "There goes the posse," I say. "One guy's too chicken, one too lazy, and the other too horny."

"How can his girl be horny?" Yokum says. "That escapes me."

"If you were a guinea, you'd know," Beppo says. "Come on, let's blow." The expedition is over as quickly as it began.

"I pity the serious guys in the Crusades," Yokum says as we start down the hill, "if they had guys like you three along. Beppos that peeled off after every dame, gutless wonders like Smith . . ."

"They would have burned you alive," Beppo says almost vehemently, "for razzing the Holy Grail."

Down in the bottom of a gully we begin to smell something dead. On one side of the shallow ravine the trees are knocked down and have toppled into the gully bottom and the ground is

chewed up by bulldozer or tank tracks. The tracks are old, baked
and brittle from the sun. Beppo spies a Jap helmet. In the front
of it is one neatly punched hole. There are more helmets lying
about and stiffened bits of uniform sticking out of the earth. I
kick one piece and there is a bone in it. Where the rain has
washed away the sides of the gully it has exposed bodies buried
there. The stench is overpowering.

We hold our noses and go further down the ravine. The ground
is littered with Jap equipment. Canteens, red canvas cartridge
boxes, tennis shoes, mess plates. The earth is spurned everywhere
by tank tracks, and judging from the helmets, at least fifty men
died here. They were caught, killed, and bulldozed right in.

The marks and signs of their deaths seem so perfunctory. It is
so apparent that what happened to them in this gully was in
violation of all the rules in which they believed up to the moment
of their deaths. They had expected to fight on this hill, to stand
and fight, but the straw soldiers of the enemy hadn't obliged them.
We had simply exterminated them, and what should have been
the supreme moment, the culmination of all their spiritual prepar-
ation, the kindled pride and national fervor that would take them
to Yasukuni in cherry blossoms and incense, was merely an
exercise for a couple of tanks and a platoon of Rangers, followed
by a few sweeps with a bulldozer blade. They could not even
run as hopeless people have a right to do.

Neely is over under a small tree, gingerly lifting the leg of a
pair of torn pants hanging in the tree. He has found something
he wants, a big white patch on the seat, a laundry mark crawling
with Jap characters. Neely tears away the patch while I hold the
pants for him. "Happy Tokyo days," Neely says. As he tugs some
coins fall from the pants. They are made out of some kind of pot
metal, and are curiously creased and bent. The tank tracks lead
up to the tree and over it, and apparently the tree and the owner
of the pants were run over and pressed flat and the tree has
sprung up again. But not the man who was in the pants. Or at
least not all of him. His money has been bent a bit too.

Nearby I find a fancy celluloid box with some sort of powder in it. The box is also covered with writing and makes a fine souvenir. Perhaps the man whose trousers are in the tree owned it. Perhaps he was the Standing Room Mara of the Jap Army and was always dusting himself.

Roger finds the only helmet without a hole punched in the forehead. All the others, mashed flat or not, have the gratuitous hole. We can't figure this out unless they gave everyone a grace shot afterward. The metal of the helmets is thin and weak and wouldn't stop a twenty-two.

Just below the tree, a face peeps out of the hillside, at me. It has been uncovered by the rain, and dirt has washed by it on both sides giving it the effect of having long brown hair. A pug nose and cheekbones are already pushing through the skin and the mouth is stuffed with dirt, so that it is impossible to say now what the man looked like. Even so I try to visualize the face animated and expressive again. Is it the face of a peasant kid from some bleak farm island in the north, or that of a city boy, possibly one of those reflective diary writers that seem so prevalent in the Jap Army? Monty Herbert has stacks of their stuff, all of it terribly sentimental, and most of it quietly critical. "Today my comrade who has marched at my side for three years was killed by the Americans. Never again will we sing together as we go to battle . . . The Americans are not soldiers. They worship firepower and are afraid of our bayonets . . . Still, I cannot understand why our leaders do not give us better guns . . ." I go over to Roger with my finger through the hole in a helmet I have picked up.

"Suppose you had to wear one of these beer can helmets. Suppose you had to actually use that rifle where the parts fly back and forth. Suppose you had to face all our automatic weapons with it . . . what would you do?"

"I'd go to the flag secretary in Tokyo and get down on my knees and tell him I wanted duty in a local Hedron," Roger says. "I could tow targets, maybe. In a Sonia. Nagasaki Naval Air Station. Every morning a little acey-deucey . . . or mah-jongg if they'd rather . . . about ten cups of tea. Maybe fly someone around the palace once a month in a stagger-wing Beech. That's what you got to have. I could tell the other AP's about how rough it was down on Saipan. The Americans were actually hiding in our footlockers, Saki, and no bull!"

Nobody laughs. We all feel the faint need to be solemn in these awesome surroundings. I toss the helmet gently back on to the hillside near where I found it.

"Jesus," Beppo says, watching it roll, "in one square mile of Pittsburgh, say, I bet they make more helmets, and good ones too, than these kids turn out in the whole country. Even with all the mama-sans working all night in the basement. What the hell were they thinking about, jumping us, will you tell me?"

It is so hard to see what is here. There must be abstractions hovering over this pretzeled ugliness that was life and is now bent and dried and reeking like a fish in the sun. Fifty-odd unities spewed over a hillside. Fifty who bowed and marched into the machine's mouth. Fifty out of thousands, and thousands out of millions marching in springs of blood and the sweat of agonies forever, and finally haunting places like this with their stillborn hopes. You there, rent open and stuffed with earth, what did you believe at the end? In honor still or simply cold despair? Did you wonder how you had estranged some happier destiny? Did you notice that your leaders had lied? Did you dream of living while dying? And beg God, knowing that the beatitudes of very saints die in the treetops over scenes such as these?

We don't often call our leaders leaders although they lie like leaders, but we sometimes call other men our brothers. This is one of the big swindles, the affectations, face in the earth, for we aren't brothers and would have killed one another whether we were told to or not. All the angry and dangerous questions about this can now be answered. You know it and I know it and we must tell the prophets and wise men what we have seen, so they can stop the talk about brothers and brotherhood. Otherwise they will go on nattering for centuries.

Down in the bottom of the ravine Neely is making the noise that is the traditional prelude to stage vomiting. "My God, haven't

you ghouls had enough?" Neely says. We sidestep down the bank
carrying our trophies.

We walk single file out of the ravine and nobody says anything
until we are out of it and on a ridge that seems to lead us back
to camp without our having to go through the cane again. Then
Roger puts on his helmet, but almost immediately decides to take
it off again because of the danger of being shot. By us, as he
says. He hangs it on the barrel of his rifle where it grinds and
bumps unpleasantly all the way home.

Yokum composes a charter for a new society which he will
call "The Man-to-Man Rifle Duellers." He is, of course, the only
member on our side. He plans to drop a challenge to the only
member on the other side from an airplane on his next trip. They
will arrange to meet somewhere in the hills for the showdown.
If he is a hairy Ainu, Yoke says he will kill him on sight and have
the head mounted.

That evening the Wing puts Seabee sentries around the camp
for the first time. They better not be wearing shoes around size
six, or they may be gone by morning. So long, some badly needed
carpenter's mates!

CHAPTER SEVEN

In the battle we fought today,
My comrade has passed away.

M AY STARTS off as a month of unusual events, some of
them the offspring of passion, some of incapacity, some
of neither or both. The replacement rumor is so strong
that people who can see any prospect of it are already giving
everything away in a rash of bequests. There is an almost blithe
mood in the squadron that we haven't felt since North Africa.
We roar out the old songs, "The Chandler's Wife," "Wind up
my little ball of yarn," and of course when overpowered
with emotion, "I Used to Work in Chicago." Obscenity covers
embarrassing sentiment, as the prospect of parting becomes
real.

The Jap radio does its part. There is no longer doubt about
the victory. The Kamis have dispelled it. To impress us with the
earnestness of our situation, there are marvelous stories about the
wind that drove the Khan's fleet from Jap shores, about the latter-
day version of the wind that will destroy us. The best one is the
tale of the mother who commits suicide the night before her son
is due to fly his special attack mission. This was not done in a
fit of depression, the narrator says, because she felt a little blue
about getting his fingernail cuttings and hair in the mail. Far
from it. She was removing the natural anxiety the son had about
leaving her behind. This was sweetly expressed in her death

poem, which has—we hear—thirty-one syllables, a turtle, and a tamarind tree.

Bartlett and Ashton have a good time with it. "As Paddy Watanabe said, this is *it*, Japs!" Bart says into a beer can mike. "If you don't get your Belt of a Thousand Stitches in time for your first solo hop—to the American Seventh Fleet but not back—remember the Geisha have gone to war. Our pretty flower arrangers are making the ships and planes to kill the mechanized barbarians."

Ashton writes a poem. "The turtle could smell the bark of the tamarind tree. In the moat were the silver wings of the little fishes. The Emperor's spirit sang in the tea flowers. Above the turtle the cherry nodded mournfully. In the Fifth Watch of the night the turtle wept by the open grave of the tamarind's sister."

Together they harmonize, "Rove me or reave me, don't ret me be ronery."

Nobody goes home but, wonder of wonders, Fred McCord is transferred. He is going over to Leyte to run the O Club. His replacement is a clever little Jewish boy who will be hard to deal with once he has consolidated his hold on the job. Kirby Stevens gets the word he is going back to the pool to wait for his own squadron, but we all hope and pray that nothing quite so castastrophic for the United States will be allowed to happen. And Stevens is still around two weeks later.

I get a bad letter from Corinne. While her letters are never brimming with passion, they are sometimes warm with innuendo. She often lets herself go with things like "I would just like to put my arms around you and kiss you right on your dear sweet nose." This makes me reel with desire. But this letter is vague and offhand and colder than any I have ever had. It begins with a list of things she has decided not to do any more, such as go to summer school again, it's too boring; visit my father so often, *it's* too boring, they have so little to say to one another (Why don't they talk about me, for Christ's sake?); go to the movies alone, no explanation; wear certain articles of clothing (list of virtually all my favorite things) because they make her look cheap, and so on. She has a job. She got it the first of April but only tells me now. She does the windows in one of the big Madison stores and in June will be allowed to go along on buying trips. Perhaps even to New York.

I am crushed, frantic, desperate to get home quickly because I can see now how the long silence has been merely Corinne straightening her lines prior to the main attack. There is obviously a guy. There must be. A well-dressed, smooth-talking, 4-F floor-walker. A guy who pays instinctive lip service to all of Corinne's tiddly little immature demands. A guy who doesn't mind fooling her. I can see them. They discuss things like religion inconclusively, he being careful not to take a real stand. They dance a lot but also inconclusively like ballroom contest couples. He says grave things about the job, his responsibility to the store. He describes, with what he considers a fair talent, the personalities of the people around them both at the store, his own becoming magnetic as he deftly and slightly tinges with disparagement all the others. Except for old Mrs. Doerflinger. "Your mother is a wonderful person, Corinne. She's so . . ." And while he gropes for just the right word, he lights the cigarettes in a mannered way that Corinne has grown to love. The rest of it is easy. Corinne would commit suttee for a man like that. And I have been sending this girl peculiar leaves in envelopes!

I decide to ask forthrightly if there is another man. Then I decide not to, it simplifies her job of telling me. I don't fool Yokum. But he is kind, for him, and only makes up one or two Dear John openers. Roger supplies my answers. "And if you don't write me a letter, within ten years," he says dolefully, "I may even cut off five per cent of your allotment."

I am so nervous that I take to walking in the jungle. I like the relief of the tiny agonies, the vines that scratch, the creatures that sting, the wetness of my feet. One day I am plowing through a particularly swampy place bordering on a creek. It is hard going, I am half lost and wishing I hadn't driven so far into the muddy part. But I keep going in order to gain the road on the other side. The water is above my knees and I am worried in spite of my sorrow because there are blood flukes in all the inland waters here.

Quite suddenly and mysteriously I come upon a series of low wooden bridges that cut across my track at a slight angle and seem to lead off to the left and deeper into the marsh. They are made of freshly cut planks and lumber, which is peculiar, but more peculiar is the camouflage of fronds and bushes that cover them. It is obvious this is meant to conceal them from trespassers, but who ever comes in here besides guys who are losing their wives?

My first thought is that I have found the secret route by which the Japs come down from the mountains to steal food. In the last week or two, several of them have been sighted at the field and around the camp, and Swede Engelson has brought in a child Marine lieutenant and half a platoon of men to try to get them. The marines have been strolling around in the evenings armed to the teeth and scaring us to death.

I start to follow the line of little bridges. It cannot be Japs, they could never get the lumber or the tools to do work like this. It must be Seabees. The bridges lead cleverly from hummock to hummock, and always they are disguised with foliage. Finally at the end of one of them I see a small wooden house up on poles. It is made of new and freshly cut lumber like the bridges, and under it in the humus-brown water gleam dozens of beer cans and empty whisky bottles.

I go closer to reconnoiter. There is a door at eye level and it is open. By walking on the hummock grass I get close without making a sound. There on the floor of the house are two native girls, and a man lying asleep. The man is wearing combat boots and green dungarees. One of the girls is sitting up braiding her hair. It is the laundry girl with the hairy legs.

I duck down. I have a wild thought. I'll wake the man and tell him that unless I am cut in on the setup I'll give it away. I picture myself coming over the narrow secret bridges every day I have off and life becoming a Tahitian idyl. To hell with Corinne. I'll cut off my ear and send it to her instead of a leaf.

I look greedily again. I can see the man now and recognize him as a chief tin bender from the Acorn. He is a dirty man with red rheumy eyes who is interminably hectoring the crews and at the same time sniggering to officers about women, Sydney, the last piece, the next piece. It is fitting that I should find him here and pay him off, refine his conception of war a little, and the conduct of men in war. I may even forbid him to come for a week.

Now the laundry girl has turned and I see her familiar gross face and the dollops of fat swinging under her upper arms like little hammocks, and her gray skin, dusty, like a snake's. Beside the combat boots are a pair of horny splayed feet belonging to the other girl. The feet of both sleepers are thrust forward in the grotesque perspective of a badly staged photograph. Now there is nothing even faintly erotic about the scene. I give up all thought of blackmailing the chief petty officer, and as Ashton describes it later, stumble broken-hearted and blind with tears back over the tiny log bridges away from Paradise.

There is a sequel to this. A couple of days later Rowland Hill, our alcoholic Wing Captain, drops in for one of his infrequent visits with Swede Engelson. With him are two Red Cross angels, presumably just along for the ride, since they don't hand out any doughnuts or coffee.

People strolling after dark see a lot of unusual things going on in the Swede's Quonset. A ping-pong game in the nude or semi-nude, for one thing. Cunningham's exaggerated account, if exaggerated it is this time, has it that another form of light athletics began to take the place of what had promised to be a damn fine game. Whatever happened, the next morning one hundred and fifty-odd signatures appear on a proclamation spiked to a palm tree near the door of the Swede's Quonset. The undersigned hereby cancel their War Bond allotments. The enlisted men of this Wing refuse to support an officer's whorehouse on their pay.

There is a day of meetings, of stubborn pressures, of quasi-juridical nonsense, and then absolutism wins. In a *coup de main* Engelson descends on the little jungle call house with his new

marine landing force and smashes "the ring." He apparently knew
about it all the time. Perhaps he saved it for just such a time as
this. At any rate deals are made and the powerful petty-officer
faction quickly sees to it that the petition is withdrawn.

The Swede's riposte is not yet complete. He snares the liquor
peddlers. The child lieutenant of Marines dresses up as a simple
swabby and goes out into the jungle one night. As one of the rum-
runners takes forty dollars from him (for a fifth!), he is arrested.
Then comes the staggering news! Tindall, and a companion in
crime also from 420! There will be a special court convened by
the admiral himself and it is certain the two of them will see the
inside of Portsmouth. Beppo is ecstatic. He only regrets that
Tindall can't be flogged through the fleet first, á la Trafalgar days.
He says he himself would immediately strike for bosun's mate
so he could personally wield the cat.

The marines continue to make the headlines. They are Third
Div men and have rat-hunted Japs all over the place in the off
seasons. We have always been around marines but it is hard to
believe how unbelievably tough and competent a certain type of
marine is unless you see it. I wasn't at first impressed by their
skill at hollowing out Jap skulls for humidors, but I was later by
plenty of other things they could do. I am again one night when
they trap some Japs in Ironhead's airplane where they have gone
to pinch emergency rations.

I happen to be around when word comes to Ironhead from
the lieutenant. Sir Tristram wants to know if it's all right if he
makes a few holes in the aircraft. Ironhead and Monty Herbert
and I ride down to the strip to see the show.

There are quite a few people standing around, mostly maintenance men, some of them with carbines and Tommy guns held
at various unprofessional angles. The marines have bracketed
the airplane in the lights from three jeeps and it's kind of like a
scene from a Cagney movie. Only everyone knows the gangsters
won't be invited to come out with their hands up.

The lieutenant and Ironhead confer and then the lieutenant
talks to his children. They are literally only seventeen and eight-

een. Only two can go in after the Japs with the lieutenant because of the danger of shooting each other. The three choose weapons for the job with the air of studious golfers selecting the right clubs. One of the kids rejects the offer of a Thompson with a laconic "I ain't qualified on the sub." They all take carbines and a couple of grenades.

"We'll try not to blow up your airplane, Commander," the lieutenant says. "But we can't guarantee anything." He posts the other marines in what he considers to be tactically sound positions of support, and then he and his volunteers flop just out of the jeep lights and begin to belly up to the airplane. At a signal all the jeeps douse their lights. I feel a little foolish when I think of our foray after the shoe thief or my daring at snatching the caps off the heads of people who are already dead.

The three disappear in the darkness. A couple of minutes go by. There are some indistinct sounds from within the hull. A Jap is in the crown turret and trying to work the guns. People scurry for cover. It is a Martin turret, hydraulic, and impossible to work unless you know the procedures. You need power, you have to turn on the pump-motor switch, the combination trigger and reflector sight switches, dead-man switches; you have to know how to charge the guns with the charging valve, wait for 750 pounds pressure, and so on. Nevertheless we lie flat on our faces. The guy may be an old Martin employee.

"We don't need to worry if my ordanceman calibrated the ammunition," Ironhead says. "That fellow won't get three rounds off before he gets a stoppage."

A moment later there are three shots and then the blast of an American grenade. This is followed by two shots, an interval of silence, and a multitude of carbine shots. Someone calls nonchalantly for light. The jeeps light things up again and we approach, warily screening ourselves behind one another.

There is a Jap lying dead on the catwalk in the bomb bay, his head lolling down and blood running from his hair. There is another in the nav compartment blown to smithereens by the grenade. The third is in the crown turret. A marine poked his carbine up into this one and gave him a clip and his clothes are burned. We are advised to get them out quickly as they are bleeding all over the goddam place. This is gingerly accomplished by a detail of body handlers under Monty Herbert. Then we crowd around to inspect the enemy.

They are all in poor shape, thin and ragged, and covered with sores. Two of them have sacks around their necks in which are some things they have stolen from around the camp. None of them have any weapons. One of the marines says the first Jap tried to fake him out by pretending to bang a mortar shell on the catwalk, but when that didn't work he just sat there and took it.

The damage to the airplane is considerable. It is a coincidence because this same airplane was damaged down on Peleliu the night a Jap j.g. led his carpenters and Chamorro workers in the big January Banzai. They rowed over from Babelthuap and screamed and threw things for a while until they were killed. The brave men of the 400 detachment lay in a hole in the sand trying to get under each other like cold puppies.

There is a sentimental payoff. The Jap up in the turret is found to be wearing G.I. shoes and sure enough inside the tongue of one of them, written in green ink, is the name "A. R. Beppolini." I take the shoes home and give them back to Beppo, but not he or Yokum or anyone else is happy that our Jap is dead. In deference to his memory, Yoke solemnly dissolves the society of "Rifle Duellers." The odd thing is that the only other member of that society forgot to bring his rifle to the last meeting.

While all this is going on down below, the air is lively too. Ironhead bags a Jake and the whole thing is ludicrous. He is at eight hundred feet when the Jake, a cumbersome single-engine float plane, passes just underneath him. Ironhead starts after him, but before anyone can fire, the Jake pilot looks up, sees him, and dives into the sea. The fuselage sinks but the floats drift away with the Japs still clinging to them. We are mystified. As Bartlett says it was probably a student out on his nav check.

Skindome Dougherty distinguishes himself in a new field. He is up near Hainan to rendezvous with a British cruiser that has been damaged and is limping out, and he comes on a big sub. The ban on dropping on them has been lifted for the moment because of the cruiser, but a sanctuary has been laid out. Dougherty checks and finds this one is well outside it, according to him about eighty miles outside. He flashes the recognition signal and gets nothing back. The sub is diving. This is enough for Skindome and he lets go with G.P.'s, straddling the submarine aft. Had they been depth charges the sub would almost certainly have sunk.

As it is, the sub is damaged enough so that it has to return—to Manila. It is the U.S.S. *Yellowfin,* out on a war patrol. They of course dispute everything—position, recognition exchange and so on. There will be an investigation. They are lucky. It's the first time I ever heard of Dougherty missing anything.

I have a trip of my own to Banjermasin, a town in the south of Borneo where the Japs are said to be making wooden luggers and Sugar Dogs. A river runs through the town and some canals and the ships are reported moored everywhere up against the banks.

It is a fine day to fly and we go down over the middle of Borneo, piloting with maps on our knees. On our right we have as a landmark Mount Kinabalu rising in solitary extravagance to twelve thousand, immense, snow on the top of it, a giant above the level green below. I can't tell from the map which is Bt Batabulan, or Bt Djang, or Bt Oekeng, but it doesn't matter. We will fly seven hundred miles and then follow a river.

Borneo is big. It is hard to believe what is below us. Dyaks with blowguns. Rhinos. People out of Somerset Maugham. Japs. The first big river appears running southwest. Perhaps the Mahakam. A little later a second one running south, the Barito. It is lined with little villages, and curves and twists through the flat land ahead as far as we can see.

I go right down on the greasy-looking water and fly the curves of the river. There are a few people out in boats. At last we sight Banjermasin, and beyond it, bright as steel in the sun, the Java Sea. The intervalometer is set on single, we have plenty of bombs, and I plan to take my time. There isn't likely to be a fighter base around here. It is a gold mine. The waterways inside the town are lined with new Sugar Dogs. They are moored end to end and covered with palm fronds and are all apparently waiting on engines or some other vital thing. The canals are just wide enough for a 24 to fly down at ten feet, and we make one circuit merely strafing. Of course Cunningham throws a few friendly bursts at people in skiffs and has to be told off, and while I am busy being indignant we hit the top of a palm tree with an outboard prop, shearing off the foliage as neatly as you could do it with hedge clippers. Then we come across the canals and bomb. This part is hard because of the trees lining the water which hide the ships until the last second. Nevertheless my seaman's eye is in. I hit three solidly with no ricochet and the bombs go off inside the hulls. I blow parts off several more. The water is too shallow for them to sink but they settle nicely down a few feet for the "before and after" photos that Zalewski is taking.

Afterward we go for the ships still up on the stocks. I scatter the incendiaries over them and over the yards, and since the guns are loaded with incendiary rounds every third, we get fires going that rapidly become spectacular. The smoke mounts to a couple of thousand feet and when we head south there are more than a dozen columns. From several miles I can see the big oily patches where the bombs—that missed—tore up the canals. There has not been a single sign of opposition and the only people we have seen were the ones in the skiffs.

I add up conservatively what I think we have destroyed. Three Sugar Dogs in the water, at least seven on the ways, half a dozen damaged. It makes quite a contact report and we get back a Z signal which means well done.

We come out over Laoet and up through Macassar Straits. We are elated. I play the old hand and let Flournoy, one of the new ensigns, fly the ship from the left seat, since he wants to. I am very indulgent when it wanders around on him a little and he confuses direction on the flux-gate compass. It *is* backwards from a gyro after all. All I can think of is that I have made my mark.

Below Samarinda, Spurlock spots two rafts. They are loaded with Japanese who have left the Celebes and are trying to get across the Straits, and these have only about five more miles to go.

I have never done this sort of thing before, shooting starving naked men on rafts, and I wish we hadn't seen these.

We go down to look and I circle them very slowly with the flaps part-way down. Some of them are so apathetic that after one glance they don't even watch us any more. Their rafts are awash and most of the men have on nothing but G-strings around their waists. I am still debating what to do when Zalewski settles it for me.

"Boss, you can kick my ass around the block. I left the goddam lens cap on the K-20."

The intercom crackles with recrimination. "Throw him out."

"Put him on one of those rafts."

"The pride of Hamtramck with his head up and locked as usual."

"I sure am sorry, Mr. Iverson."

I am too disappointed to speak. No pictures and thus no proof. We circle some more, plunged in our gloom. Only Cunningham has his mind on business.

"When we give it to these kids," he says, "maybe Ski can think to take a picture of that." When Cunningham's blood lust begins to show itself again, I make up my mind. I peel off and head up the coast.

"Screw it," I say in feigned disgust. "If you guys can't do any better than that, I don't want pictures of a lot of guys jumping off a raft." There is a stunned silence on the intercom. I have unfairly blamed them all but it gets me off the hook. They will surely tell the story of sissy-boy Iverson back at the base and it is even possible I will get in trouble if the Swede hears about it. But nothing like the trouble I will be in with myself if I massacre fifty helpless people.

Flournoy and the other ensign, Benjamin, pretend it's all right with them but I catch them exchanging grins. To hell with them. Who shall judge the judges? Maybe Cunningham, as he calls after a few minutes to tell me in his most sincere way that he is glad to find a human being still alive out here. It's hard not to remember him at other times and places—at Okino Daito Shima bravely turning his twin fifties on the workers at the phosphate plant, all skipping away like minnows before the rush of the barracuda— or at Chichi the day we caught the two whaleboats with soldiers in them going across Futami Ko. The soldiers were wearing full packs and by the fourth picture most of them had drowned anyway, but not fast enough for Cunningham, who was firing so hard and long he couldn't hear Ashton swearing at him. That is until all the heads were gone.

As for these ensigns who grin, both have been out only a couple of months and already Benjamin has a pair of wings pinned to our raft off the beach so they will become green from the salt water. That pegs him. He is the kind who will award himself a D.F.C. and a couple of Air Medals to wear on his thirty-day leave at home, and perhaps the Purple Heart and a limp. I have seen him before. I recall one of our squadron heroes just after we came back from North Africa. We were on the same train to Chicago and he was soon in so deep telling the grave civilian passengers about lost buddies and hairy times, an illegal D.F.C. delicately half-hidden behind a lapel of his greens, it was impossible not to get involved myself and accept drinks and back him up with lies. It is an infinitesimal part of war's great tragedy that it provides so many serious and sacred moments for the world's fakers and bores.

Perhaps I have avoided doing my duty and my job, and those naked skeletons down there will someday kill Americans on the beaches of Japan. Perhaps it was cowardice of a kind. Then I too should have gone into submarines and kept away from pressures on my ears. Or to Hollywood, the home of congenitally weak tympani. I've had enough tests to show how weak mine are. For example whenever I hear an 1830 Pratt and Whitney suddenly quit, at midnight in the rain, twenty feet off the deck, I have a convulsion.

While we have been gone, a P-51 from the island has splashed a Zeke less than a hundred yards off the beach. No one knows what it was doing here, as it is impossible for a Zeke to fly here from anywhere held by the Japs and fly back again. This leads to the supposition that the pilot wanted to land and surrender. This privilege was twice denied him, once by the P-51 and again by the party of Seabees who went out in a boat to the islet where the Zeke's pilot had managed to swim, and beat him half to death with oars, because as they said, he tried to resist. They also stripped him stark naked for souvenirs.

Monty Herbert is furious because it is the one and only chance he has ever had to get a live Jap pilot and these fools may have spoiled it for him. The Jap is in very bad shape. Roger and Beppo were less concerned about the pilot. They were first to reach the Zeke, which remained awash after landing in the sea, and went right to work on it with machetes and tin shears and screw drivers. Beppo hooked the turn-and-bank indicator, a copy of ours in every detail except for the Jap symbols for right and left on it, and Roger has assorted things, among them a very tricky seat-belt buckle and shoulder-harness fastener, which seems better than ours. The Zeke has a large 1130 painted across the tail, and this, Roger says, was exactly the time of day when it was knocked down.

In the evening I go to see Ashton and tell him my troubles. Troubles with my wife, with a camera, with a conscience. When I tell him about Corinne it comes over me in such shock waves that I burst out crying. I begin to sound like Frank Ainsworth, hating the goddam war only because he is in it. But there just is no clarity about all these things, however much you may be devoted to it. I have never thought plainly and clearly about "the community taking up arms" and the trouble and expense of qualifying a so-called superior member of it to bear those arms in a highly specialized way, and his obligations upon being so qualified. I ask Ashton if I owe the community my wife *and* my life, and he says balls, I don't owe anybody a ding-dong thing any more.

I sit for a long time with my eyes closed and my head resting

against the center pole of the tent and listen to Ashton and Bartlett working on a radio serial, something called "Buck . . . Nigger!
. . . and his *Horse!* . . . Whiteman!" Buck's grandfather, Huck, is
one hundred and seventeen years old and a former slave who
remembers the day as a little boy he saw General MacArthur ride
by on a black horse called Stovelid.

Outside the moon is up. Once in a while from out of the southwest comes the drone of engines, a distant wavering beat, coming
on forever, and forever. In the sound time and space seem infinite
and the effort of these man-made noises to devour them hopeless.

CHAPTER EIGHT

Crying aloud with a smile,
"Tennoh Heika Banzai,"
I shall never forget the cry.

"O'MACMORIARITY jammed an unlit fag in his broken-nosed, freckled face, and rasped sneeringly. 'Whatsa mattah, dago, too much macaroni last night?' 'Jeez,' Toricelli grunted. 'Jeez Cris s'heavy. Goddam canteen's heavy.' O'Macmoriarity laughed jeeringly. 'Why the shid don't you make the Yid carry it, dago? The kikes is awready sway-backed, knock-kneed, and pot-bellied from luggin' them stones up the pyramids.'"

Ashton looks up from what he is reading. "Great," says Bartlett. "Go on."

"'Here, sheeny, carry dis,' grunted Toricelli leeringly. Little Maurice Mikvah smiled searingly through smashed and bleeding lips. The thought of the filthy Irishman's huge, freckled, broken-nosed fists pounding into his mouth, when he had told the goys he would no longer carry all three packs, all three rifles, all three helmets, *and* the hundred forty-seven pound mortar, was almost pleasant. There was victory in pain, he had told Ruth, and she had understood. Well, someday he wouldn't, not even one canteen for the blaspheming goys. It was like when he had nearly died of rickets and scarlet fever and diphtheria, and had been run over by the streetcar and gone blind in his right eye working on his father's accounts all night when he was nine. Somehow he had won. 'Erin go schmuck!' Ruth would say.

"Father Kindly Killarney came peeringly along the support trench."

"Pat O'Brien?" Bartlett asks.

"Who else? 'Naow buoys, be off with you and it's carryin' yer own canteens ye'll be after doin' Timothy O'Macmoriarity and Antonello Toricelli'—make that Toriselli when Father says it, it's a nice little touch—'sure, and the Jewish lad has enough with the three packs and rifles and all.'

" 'Father, I'm afraid to die.'

" 'Naow buoys, t'is not the fear o' death you'll be consarnin' yourselves with, but the fear that the likes o' you will be left alive among the dacent paple o' the airth!' Father Kindly Killarney was often first over the top . . ."

Ashton stops and we all listen. A truck is coming, rattling over the rough road, dust swirling in brown pillars behind it. The people in it are yelling like Indians. It is Frank Ainsworth and his crew who have been to Leyte in the Fat Cat. When the truck is near they begin leaping out over the palings before it can even stop. Monty Herbert is with them, looking very aerial with a set of earphones around his neck and a Marc Mitscher cap.

We all know what it means. We see it in the way that Ashton and Bartlett rush for the truck. We see it in the carefully feigned looks of superior amusement we exchange with each other. We feel it in the awareness of our sudden exclusion. Replacements. They are finally here.

The word is there are four crews flying over from Samar. Monty Herbert has their names and everyone crowds around him to just see a name, as if that will make it irrevocable. "Galbraith?" Ashton says going into his weary-old-slave routine. "Yes, yes, Lawd! Galbraith! I seen dat name! I done seen it written on a golden plate! It done come to me on the heabenly Fox Schedule signed by the heabenly Flag Secretary." He totters around in the road with his hands splayed weakly out in front of him and his eyes rolling. "Dey done hear me topside, boys, de big exec upstairs done hear me, in his wisdom, Lawd, Lawd!" He and Bartlett embrace and dance around.

Even Ainsworth is animated. He slaps people on the back and says over and over, "Well, I'm up. Pull in the ladder."

"Milk, lettuce, hamburgers!"

"Mom's pie!"

"Where there ain't no more night take-offs, lads!"

I finally get a chance to speak to Herbert. "What do they say about a few more, Monty?" These four replacement crews take it down to Tuckerman, and after him come Yokum and Roger and I. Monty looks at me reassuringly through the racket.

"Not more than a couple of weeks, Ivy. One of them said there are so many crews sitting at Kaneohe they don't know what to do with them."

"I got a few ideas."

"Well, it won't be long."

Yoke, Roger and I go back and sit in our chairs and listen to the happy consternation spreading through the camp. We hear whoops of laughter up and down the street, something we haven't heard in a long time.

"Hey, Kirby!" Bartlett calls into the operations shack. "Piss on the fire and call the dog, you're on your way!"

A roaring party gets under way at once in Ashton's tent. The ones who are relieved now give everything away. Homemade chairs and wardrobes, drop-tank boats, pistols, rifles, everything except liquor, which flows in a torrent we haven't seen since England. Whisky erupts from everywhere, there is no more of the grudging trickle, even from people like Ainsworth. He sheds everything except a carbine which he intends to smuggle home. To get it by the authorities at Pearl, he has been practicing walking with the carbine stuck down the leg of his pants.

The new crews arrive in camp and the fit is redoubled. Beppo still hopes that he is going to make it as Ainsworth's copilot and starts to take his pistol apart. He tests all the secret places where he can hide the parts and a chronometer from a nav kit he has filched. If he goes, so will Neely, Cox, Hammond, Foy and Mara, all San Diego recruits. The dumbest thing that Yoke and Roger and I did in our lives was check out as P.P.C.'s. We are months senior to any of them.

The squadron divides itself into gleaners and shedders. Bartlett presents his pistol belt to one of the new guys, none of whom seem to have pistols. "Take this old hog leg and treat it right. It's saved my life many a time going to the head." The ensign grins without understanding. "Some of the flies can take a forty in the chest and still keep coming," Bartlett tells him. "Like one of those Moros around here back in ninety-eight. You better rig shoulder sponsons, quadruple thirty-eights at least, and remember most of the flies here like to make high side passes. But just don't forget it's the pass from below that will kill you." He flinches significantly.

Ashton gets quite stoned. He puts an arm around me and I see tears in his eyes. "Ivy, this is a bad thing, leaving you behind."

"Well, it won't be long."

"In any case, in *any* case! By God, I'll get things moving. I know a prick who has been sitting on his hands in the Hedron at Quonset since forty-two. We are on the wrong list. My God. You see the same ten per cent of the guys where ever you go. You see them in Iceland. Then you see them in Dunkeswell. Then you see them in Building Seventeen in Norfolk. Then you see them on Tinian. The same goddam ten per cent on the wrong list."

"You might call my wife if you have a chance. Ask her what the hell gives."

"Listen! I'll find out what that Morgan le Fay is up to! And I'll have her wagging her tail for you! Listen, your scowl will be the *weather* from now on! She'll be lucky to warm her hands on your occasional smile."

"Well, don't be too rough."

"I mean it! Every word! Lay back and sink the iron in them. Like you'd handle a tuna. Whip them with braided nylon, gaff the bitches, hit 'em with the boat hook. Screaming reels, the story of my married life!" Ashton downs his drink and snickers. "But . . . attention! That's the battle cry when I get home. I can't

be having a kid every time I pass through town. Last time . . .
it was that week at Dam Neck gunnery school . . . *el cheato
grande! El cielito cheato grande.*"

He spots Kirby Stevens who is making a prodigious effort to
go unregular, clumping around with drinks and (although still
saying " 'ere you be, guv'nor,") taking everyone's address. He has
appointed himself a committee of one to arrange an annual re-
union at the *El Cortiz* in Dago for after the war. He also promises
to pursue the chimera of medals for us when he gets back.
"Kirby," Ashton says to me, "is the kind of guy who has a lot of
fun on New Year's Eve. That's when everybody I hate has a
wonderful time. He's the kind of guy who has to piss up against
your car when he gets drunk. You know what I mean? But I
forgive him. Kirby, I *forgive* you! I'm going to forgive you and
go back to California—and live in a giant malted for the rest of
my life." He goes to Kirby and together they reel about the tent
with their arms around each other. "And say, Kirby, if you're
ever down in Mombasa during the next war . . . there's a little
bar down near the waterfront . . . the Zanzibar, get it? You just
go in and ask Mamma Zambesi for the crazy whiteman that plays
piano for her. You'll know me all right by the dirty yachting cap
with four white feathers sticking up through the top."

I feel dismayed by the approaching dissolution of the squadron.
It will be horrible to have an outfit without Ashton and Bartlett.
We will lose all our beliefs. I will also miss Frank Ainsworth's
profane but practical sympathy, and Lord knows, I may even miss
Kirby Stevens saying stern and naval things around the premises.

"There's a terrific place way the hell out on West Sixty-third,"
Neely says to Beppo, who is also from Chicago. "A fag gypsy
comes over to your table and plays for you. He puts the end of
his fiddle against your neck so you can feel the vibrations."

"What are you supposed to do, come?" Yokum says. He is taking
it all rather badly. "You guys aren't going home. Not before me."

"No, it's nice," Neely says ignoring him. "I got a good babe for
any of you who ever come by there. She can dance like a son of
a bitch."

"Sure. A swell dancer, personality plus, drink anything . . . you'll hardly notice the oak tree growing out of the middle of her head."

"Yokum's jealous," Roger says. "Just get him a date with the fag gypsy if you want to make him happy. He goes for white dumpling hands."

When one of the new P.P.C.'s tells Yokum that they were all delayed by getting white instrument cards, Yokum almost collapses. "Jesus, we never even had to pass a Kahn test. Well, prop your card up there on the windshield and bore right in to those big hairy cus. No need to worry any more, it says right on the card you can fly instruments."

I have a couple of drinks but I don't feel a part of the blithe mood and I have to fly tomorrow. Still I want to spend as much time as possible with my friends before they go home; they will probably be gone by the time I get back from the patrol. So I stall about taking a shower and about eating. Ainsworth drinks harder than I have ever seen him and the others aren't far behind. He wants to fire his carbine through the tent roof the way he did at Tinian New Year's Eve, and there are the beginnings of an indoor Rugby game which traditionally would wind up being played on broken glass, when the Captain comes in, followed by Monty Herbert.

Ironhead has just come in from a flight and he looks tired but he smiles around the tent and only Herbert's face presages the shock they are about to deliver.

"Hold it! Hold it!" Herbert says making braking motions in the air with his hands. Ironhead bangs his ball cap on his thigh as though knocking water out of it and looks at the floor.

"Oh no!" somebody says starting the trend. "Oh, my achin' back, no!"

"I'm afraid so," Ironhead says looking at us now. "It's bad news all around. Bill Dougherty got jumped down near Singapore. He either ditched or just went in, we don't know which. We can't raise him." There is a moan of disbelief but Ironhead nods vehemently. Someone drops a glass. The faces turn briefly from Ironhead. It is Ainsworth. He has let the glass fall from his hand in a caricature of incredulity and stands there with the hand still cupped around an imaginary glass. He begins to swear softly. Herbert makes a gesture of entreaty to the room. Plainly that is not all. Ironhead looks appraisingly at us from under his scarred brows. A patch of the thick gray hair on the front of his head slides forward the way a horse's skin moves. He is not setting us up, he is above that. He is genuinely reluctant to tell us the rest.

"Before he sent the fighter contact, he sent something else. He said there were two cruisers and seven destroyers coming out of the Straits. The Air Wing doesn't believe the sighting. But just the same they aren't going to ignore it. If it checks out, and knowing Bill, I'm betting it will, it means there's been a force in there all this time that we didn't know about and that they are probably making a break for home, for the Inland Sea. What it means to you guys only time will tell. I'll clue you this much. Everybody is on stand-by . . ." There is a roar of indignation. ". . . everybody except . . . *except* the four new crews. I'm sorry. It may mean nothing at all except a day's delay for you. But that's the way it is."

He is gone. Herbert stays behind as though it is somehow up to him to regulate the confusion. Everyone crowds around him, swearing. "I don't know, you heard it all," Herbert says.

From the corner where he has gone to sit down, come the profane vows of Frank Ainsworth. "They can take those fuckin' cruisers and insert them by the numbers. I ain't goin' down there. Not me. I swear to Jesus that the whole fuckin' Navy can't get me down there." He gets up and advances on Herbert. "You think I'm kiddin'? Think it. You can all fuck yourselves, because I ain't goin'. Frig it." As if satisfied, he turns away from Herbert and pours himself a drink.

"Why not the four new crews?" somebody asks.

"They fly the regular searches," Herbert says. "They figure if the ships are there and start for home we'll have to have people on them all the way. We'll need everybody till some subs or something can get in there."

"You think those were cruisers?"

"My personal opinion?"

"Yeah."

"No." There is a murmur of confirmation. It is built entirely on wishful thinking. None of us know anything. "Wait now. Not cruisers. Battleships."

"What!"

"The hermaphrodites. The *Ise* and the *Hayuga*. They're around somewhere. They haven't been spotted for a long time. It could be."

"Jesus, carriers!"

"Well, they're half carriers. They've never operated."

"Why the hell do they want to start now?" There is laughter. The new people are accepting the idea. But not me, and I wasn't even going home. We stand around and look up at the ceiling of the tent, as though we have just discovered some valuable and exquisite chandelier hanging there. When Herbert leaves I go out with him. Behind me in the tent I hear someone say, "When you see six white blackbirds flying formation upside down and singing 'Sky Anchors Away'—in Chinese—you'll know you are being replaced. Don't believe it until then." Someone smashes a glass.

Herbert is going over to see a P.P.C. in 420 who heard things on VHF this afternoon while down in the sector adjacent to Dougherty's. The P.P.C.'s name is Scott, and he is sitting tired and dirty in his tent, reading some mail that has come for him while he was out. He has laid a dozen photos of a girl out on his cot like a solitaire game. The pictures seem to me to be all the same except in each the sky is a different shade. In all the pictures the not too pretty girl is standing alone and looking up at the sky with an arcane smile on her lips. Scott leans over them tenderly.

"How to drive yourself nuts," he says apologetically.

"Very pretty," Herbert says. "I wonder, the Captain would like to get more details of what you heard down there. He figures maybe there's a chance that Dougherty ditched."

Scott shrugs and lights a cigarette. His hands are dirty and shake. He has been flying fourteen hours. "I didn't hear much.

Like I told him, I heard some noises and I didn't think anything
about it, that's how big an impression it made. I don't even
know if it was Dougherty." Scott scratches his scalp with the
fingers of both hands like a perplexed Stan Laurel. It is a thing I
have seen Ahab Norton do and there is a lot of Ahab reflected
over here. Green wings, Natal boots, the fancy carved cow-horn
grips on Scott's thirty-eight, hanging on the chair.

We wait for him to elaborate. "It was on channel B," he says.
"There was some talking going on. It could have been from anywhere with the skip distance you get. I was screwing around,
changing channels because they tell us to try to raise that dumbo
sub that lies in there and when I heard the talk I figured it might
be her. Anyway, right in the middle a voice came in strong but
garbled. I couldn't understand a word. It sounded like somebody
excited, like a dame on the telephone . . ."

"When was that?"

"Oh, about one thirty, two o'clock."

"But you didn't see anything?"

"Not down there. Up in the east corner of the sector there was
a smoke column. It was way the hell and gone to the southeast.
But he wouldn't have been up there. Or maybe he would." Scott
grins. Dougherty's wanderings are a legend.

"No, he wasn't up there," Herbert says. "What was the smoke,
could you tell?"

"Too far. It was ten pairs of shoes over there and I wasn't
going over and look. The end of that sector is already eleven
hundred and seventy miles from here. You can't stretch it any
further." Scott shrugs again. "That's it," he says.

Herbert nods. "Well thanks, Scott, sorry to bother you."

Scott leans toward the pictures. "Not at all. Sorry about
Dougherty. He had quite a record, I guess. Oh, I'll tell you this.
Right at the end the voice sounded griped. Just an impression I
had. I still couldn't catch a word of what it said."

Herbert looks at me as though he has just confirmed something
in his mind. I know what he is thinking. He is thinking it must
have been Dougherty and that he probably died down there
feeling angry about something unrelated to dying. He smiles at

me. "Probably someone didn't transfer fuel right to suit him and he was giving them hell."

On the way back to our side of the camp we meet the Captain coming along the road, the brown talcum puffing up from his shoes like little bomb bursts.

"What did he say?"

"Nothing more. Just what you heard." Ironhead nods, the energy seeming to leave him. We stand listening in the twilight, looking unconsciously out toward the south.

"The traditional pose," Ironhead says softly. "Face the quadrant where hope is slowly dying and study the sky . . . which never told anyone a God damned thing. You know I just got the all-time Norton touch. He wanted to commiserate with me so he told me what a shame it was. He said he would have traded any three of his guys to have Dougherty in his outfit." Ironhead hisses in disgust. "The shame being who's going to sink ships for me now, huh? My God! You lose a lot of race horses in a fire but it only becomes a tragedy to people like that if War Admiral is in the barn."

Ironhead shakes his head quickly as though there is a bee around his ear. His scarred face works to keep back what he is feeling—tears, indignation. Dougherty was his pet, but not for the reasons that might have endeared him to Joe Norton.

"What do you want to do, Captain?" Monty says at last.

Ironhead looks at him and then at me. "I want to stand here and swear," he says slowly. "I want to yell every filthy blasphemous thing I can think of. I want to get Dougherty's dirty pig of a wife by the hair and kill her . . . cram her villainy back into her. Take away her stupid, indolent, sand crab life . . . the one she told Bill not to interrupt by coming home. That's what I want to do. But there she sits in her Mercury convertible, maybe right now, waiting for the boot kids to get out of radio school . . . she had an angora monkey hanging on an elastic under the mirror. You could see it there jumping up and down. I always figured she had it there to remind her of Skindome, the poor bald son of a bitch who was always in her way."

He begins to walk back through the thick dust toward the

camp. Once he kicks savagely at the dust with one foot. "Why in the hell doesn't it rain and lay this stuff?" We shake our heads and walk almost as if we were wading to show that the problem of the dust is to us also a very serious thing.

At the operations hut Stevens is trying to get out a new pain sheet. Ironhead glances at what he is doing and tells him he might as well wait. Engelson is holding a meeting in half an hour at which time word will be available as to what Wing wants. Dougherty is now four hours overdue and there isn't the slightest chance of his coming back even with his dexterity. The dumbo sub is looking for him but if he went down in the Straits, it's unlikely they'll find him—the Japs would have scooped him up. Besides that it's a risky place for the sub to spend much time in.

Evening chow takes on the atmosphere of a girl's boarding school after the discovery that someone has had a baby in a closet. We are titillated. shocked, surprised, outraged. The conversation is mostly the filing of lengthy disclaimers as to how little can be expected from each of us when Engelson gets out the Big Game Board. Only Mara is unreservedly pleased with the prospect of events.

"Now," he says malevolently, sitting down beside me uninvited. "Now we're going to see Tod Hale on the Scrub in a barrel of trouble. Now at last, dear God, they're going to take away Tod's baby oil and Pablum and make him eat hardtack with weevils in it. Just like a big grown-up mannikins. Ah, but who will kick that field goal if Tod sulks?" Mara skids the tray away from him so that watery string-bean juice slops out of it, wipes his mouth on his sleeve and belches. "Yes, yes," he says looking around the table. "Who will kick that big field goal?"

"It's too early," I say to him. "Don't fire it all away before you know what you're talking about."

"Not I said the pig, not I said the duck . . . the thing for you Tods to do is hit Engelson with something so stupid that no one else would listen to it . . . say a six-plane raid on that fleet down there at low level at noon. Emphasize the advantages . . . strategic surprise, for one . . . that will offset the suicidal aspects of it. Ironhead can lead, Navy crosses pinned to saddle blankets in advance for the ceremonies at Arlington, and . . ."

"You honestly think Ironhead is stupid?"

"I didn't say *he* was stupid, I was going to say that Engelson, under the theory of historical inevitabilism will suggest something even zanier if you don't get in there first with something relatively reasonable, like a noon raid on battleships with twenty-fours at low level. It's inevitable." Mara spreads his dirty hands out like someone feeling for rain and grins.

"Ironhead would stop him, at least as far as we're concerned."

"Ironhead? A nice, affable, sincere Teddy bear. He's merely in the wrong herring class."

"The wrong what?" I am letting Mara frighten me. I have seen him so often, disheveled and dirty in his broken bed, pouring out his cloudy and fallacious theories, scraping away with that well-resined bow on everybody's nerves, a fat, omniscient, foul-mouthed beggar in a filthy cave, and part of me has always listened. He has managed to make me more aware of weakness and guilt than anyone before, forced on me a sort of unholy catharsis to which I have, willingly or not, in part submitted. I feel the same compulsion to read a bad novel that I do to hear the partial truths and distortions of truths that come out of Mara. Like it or not, I have to know what happens next.

Mara's edgy sarcasm glides into what for him must be warm amusement. "It's strict ecology in the Navy, Iverson. If you don't know that you are a blind man. If you were a herring in the North Sea and were in the age class of nineteen-four, for example, you could expect an unusual survival rate. You would dominate not only the older but the younger age groups all the way up to nineteen-eighteen. The Navy is the same. They develop dominant age groups like herring. They live in the same biotic community. Something in Ironhead's organism . . . his pals' too . . . just flaked out. Maybe it was the water temperature that year. And now his gang is bracketed by dominant age groups above and below. The bigger herrings are eating them up."

"Bull. Ironhead's weaknesses are his own. One of them is trying to get his crews home alive. Thank God."

"No bull. Allnavs. Promotion boards. Ironhead's whole class damn near is headed for extinction. Engelson's hardly drops a name on the way up. Norton's falters only slightly."

"So?"

"The war of the herrings. The real war. The problem isn't to draw your sword and wave it for the *South Dakota* to steam out of Ulithi, followed by a task force ten times the size of the Imperial Navy. The problem is getting to the point where the lead is offered to you instead of to another herring. *They* have to kill *you* to get that chance."

"*They* can try. *They* won't make anyone I know go in low-level on a battleship."

"Wait and see. Unless you are absolutely chrome yellow, like Brady, they can make you do anything."

Mara squashes a cigarette and looks cheerfully around the mess hall. He seems to be counting the victims around him in the room. His lips flick back to show his dirty teeth. "There are ways, subtle herring methods you aren't even aware of, kid. Happy landings, Tod," he says as he leaves.

At seven the P.P.C.'s who are sober gather in the Wing Quonset. The senior ones sit at the table in the middle of the room and the rest of us line up against the rear wall like kids at dancing school. Someone says "right dress" but there are only a couple of minor guffaws and no embellishments. Engelson comes in on cue like a distracted symphony conductor, nodding his head in time to his walk and making vague signals that are undoubtedly to be interpreted—now that everyone has stood up—as meaning no one need stand. He stands behind a recognition projector and allows one hand to rest on it as though the heart of the matter is shortly to come out of that black box. Behind him the red lines of the Big Game Board gleam faintly like the strands of a bloody spider web.

He motions to the last man in the line against the wall. "Cut that light!" There are several seconds of darkness followed by a click and a black silhouette on the screen behind Engelson.

"CA *Nachii*-class," Engelson intones. We stare at the usual meaningless bumps and configurations along the rackish-looking hull. There is another click "Battleship. Made in Japan. Converted into a half-ass carrier. The hermaphrodite twins, *Ise, Hayuga.* Now give me the lights, please." Engelson is quiet, enjoying the consternation he knows he has stirred in every one of us. "Which is it?" he says finally. "We don't know. The man who sent us that contact thought what he saw were cruisers. It is *unlikely* that there are any *Nachii*-class cruisers in Singapore. Everyone known to be in existence is accounted for . . . sunk or at home. On the other hand no one has sighted either of the hermaphrodites for a long time. A year ago they were in the Inland Sea. Since then . . ." Engelson knifes a pudgy hand through the air.

"Whatever, they are big ships and must be pretty much in disorder after all this time. The Japs let things go . . . like the French. I don't mean they keep pigs and chickens on the decks and grow vegetables in the sponsons, but I'll bet they have cannibalized them to death, that the crews are scratch crews, and that there isn't an aircraft on either of them. I figure they just got steam back in them and they're shaking down for a day or two before they run for it."

Engelson sounds so reasonable. The feeling of threat that is always there in that room, the climate of ultimatum, seem dim. I have never heard the Swede speak that way before. His tone is syncretic, appeasing. I expected Marshal Ney exhorting the Old Guard. Our epic is at hand, men.

"We're going to watch them. Morning, noon and night. And get some pictures." Engelson leans forward and taps on the table with his knuckles.

"Here it comes," someone whispers.

"I'll tell you this . . . the man who brings back good, detailed pictures is going to get himself a Navy Cross." He raps harder on the table now, punctuating every word with a beat on the wood. He is like a partridge beginning to drum. It is a real call of the blood now. "And I personally guarantee that Navy Cross," he says several times. He straightens and hitches his pants, looking at us critically with his head tipped to one side. There is complete and utter silence in the room except for the trickle of water somewhere overhead. The sound is almost an embarrassment, like someone's stomach rumbling in church.

From some receptacle in the wall, Engelson illuminates the Big Game Board. It is all brisk business from here on in. Two planes in section to arrive at dawn, two more to arrive at dusk. Both squadrons subdivided to form five strike groups of six aircraft, the groups to rotate on stand-by around the clock. P.P.C.'s not yet having flown five patrols will not be included except in an emergency. If the force is moving and there appears to be nothing around to deal with it, we will attack it, presumably low level and at night, Black Cat style. After all, Engelson tells us matter-of-factly, a PBY sank a heavy cruiser that way at Rabaul.

From time to time the Swede punches the air. It is as though he actually feels the six aircraft as an extension of his fist, as though he is testing the power and muscle behind the blow he is about to give. But at the end he is calm. It seems that by hard work we have gained certain historical rights that we must now be careful not to sacrifice by anything heedless or stupid. Mara has pegged it pretty well.

We begin to play a sort of demoralized musical chairs waiting for the pain sheet. Although it is almost midnight everyone hangs around to monitor Kirby Stevens as he makes it up, and he is of course careful to see that everything is rigidly impartial and we all follow our normal rotation. There is some bitching from the San Diego faction, who seem to have caught nearly all the later trips. They argue that in a few days the Japs will be very tired of us, and that when they stop the music someone is going to lose his seat and his behind will be attached to it. I am with Ashton as a copilot, scheduled for midnight tomorrow. I calculate the risks of this and compare them with those I might acquire by bitching. I have more than five patrols in and could perhaps go as a P.P.C. But when? Go now and get it over with. Bartlett is going with us.

In the morning we will have five hours stand-by. There aren't enough crews to be nautical about it and have four-hour watches.

In the middle of all this Frank Ainsworth comes in and starts inserting things by the numbers again. He is still drunk and wasn't at the meeting in the Quonset. When he sees his name on the sheet for noon tomorrow he explodes. Tuckerman, who is scheduled to accompany him, tries to calm him, but that sort of boyish resignation in the face of absolutism is the very thing that Ainsworth isn't going to be reconciled to.

"Hell, Frank," Tuck says, "we go down there now, we get it over with. No tellin' after a week or so what you're goin' to find. The Japs'll be gettin' awful tired of us by then. Now they ain't ready."

"No, of course not! Skindome just naturally fell out of the sky, didn't he? You think they won't be ready? You're tellin' me we're going to surprise them? Your ass is suckin' straight wind, brother!"

"Dougherty was alone. We'll be able to watch out for each other. You and me ain't crazy, Frank, we'll get into clouds and . . ."

"Captain, I think this is one dirty trick on a lot of us," Ainsworth says to Ironhead who has shaved and bathed and come over to see how things are getting on. The Captain steps behind Kirby and holds the corner of the drooping pain sheet, now in its final stages in Kirby's typewriter. There are little tremors in the paper as he reads it. Ainsworth stands there like a maddened and perplexed bull until Ironhead straightens up and looks at him sympathetically.

"I agree. And I'm sorry as hell."

"Seventy-four trips," Ainsworth says. "I did my bit. I flew all the stinkers they ever asked me to. I flew those bastards out of Reykjavik, and I flew those bastards out of Dunkeswell and I been flyin' every bastard out of here that comes along. Sure I been bitchin', but who hasn't? And I been lucky . . . like some of you guys. We get through the whole goddam thing . . . we get relieved about ten years late . . . and just as we are waving goodbye the hook comes out. Some glory-happy pogue, who don't fly a lick himself, comes up with one more great idea." His voice goes up and tears well in his eyes. "Because I'm tellin' you that a bunch of guys right here in this shack right now are goin' to get it! You know it as well as I do. You can feel it. You're goin' to get killed . . . you hear me? . . . killed! Don't that word mean anything to you? And for what? Nothin'. Absolutely fuckall nothin'! Because those ships don't mean a thing to you, or to me, or to the Navy or to America. They ain't ever goin' to hurt anyone and it's just a matter of time until a carrier air strike knocks them off. And that nut knows it. Well, I said I wouldn't go and everybody snickered and said that's just old Frank sayin' he won't go, but when they blow the whistle the stupid bastard'll slide down the brass pole with all the other morons. Well, I'm telling you now . . . I'm telling you, Captain, in front of everybody here, and I mean it. I quit!" Ainsworth is crying full tilt. Nobody goes near him.

"All right, Frank. Nobody's going to hold it against you." Ironhead says softly.

"I'm no Brady. I don't fake and carry on. I never missed a trip. I just had enough, that's all. Not enough . . . just too goddam much!" He is out of the hut and we can hear him sobbing and cursing as he goes down the road. Tuckerman goes after him but nobody is close enough to Frank Ainsworth to do much for him at a moment like this.

"When was he due?" Ironhead says to Kirby.

"Tomorrow noon. Four twenty has it tonight and we have it tomorrow. The next day we rotate and we'll take the night trip. That is if you have no objection." It is funny to hear Stevens' voice still modulate respectfully for direct intercourse with the Captain.

"Well, put me in there," Ironhead says poking the schedule with his finger. "In his place."

"You just flew today. Frank's just scared, Captain. He'll be all right."

"Everybody's scared. Frank has done all he can. Otherwise he wouldn't say what he just said."

"Yes, sir, but if we all feel that way . . ."

"We don't. And you don't know how he feels. Neither do I.

He's not dicking off, Kirby. You can give his crew to Yokum. My God, he's been around a lot longer than those birds over in 420. Put Yokum in there for Frank's second time around and in all his stand-bys and I'll take the trip tomorrow. I want to go anyway."

"Okay, Captain." Kirby manages to get incomprehension in his voice.

"Who's going first from over there?" Ironhead says, nodding his head in the direction of 420.

"Three guesses."

"I only need one. When the Swede nailed that gold piece to the mast I saw Ahab's eyes glitter."

At one o'clock a two-plane section from 420 led by Captain Ahab is on its way. The other airplane is flown by an ex-airline pilot named Gorilla Joe Donohoe who is forty-two years old. He has gone with Ahab before and is always an indication of Ahab's intentions. Gorilla Joe flies the weather like no one else can and saves a lot of gas and time, and when they get down there he will probably hover around waiting for Ahab to get his pictures, and then bring him home again. There is no doubt that if Cap Ahab gets home at all he will have pictures.

At twenty to eight the first contact comes from Norton. Two battleships and seven destroyers. They are in the Main Straits midway between Batam and Singapore, lying at anchor with steam up. The amplification reveals that they are the hermaphrodites and that there are only six cans in the escort, but these have way on. In the middle of this comes the Z signal meaning attacked by fighters. A few minutes later come the details. Ahab is under attack by five Oscars and they have shot out number one engine which has frozen with the prop blade in high pitch—that is, flat against the air and therefore a terrible hindrance because of the drag. Ahab is going to try to come home eleven hundred-odd miles with it like that.

The morning goes by with the forwarding of all technical help in the lightening of a B-24 airplane, including details of how to hack through the mounts of the radar installation and drop

it out. Ahab reports calmly toward noon that the radar has just
been consigned to the sea, along with just about everything else
that is removable. The PBM misses the rendezvous the first time,
catches up with Ahab when he is already past Balabac and as
he contemptuously announces "can swim home from here." Fifteen hours and fifty minutes from the time he took off, Ahab
arrives home.

Being Ahab, he only just makes it, of course. As he lands and
brakes to a stop, the inboard engine on the same side as the frozen
one dies for want of gas, the prop twitching in little spasms. The
nose-up attitude of the airplane landing has kept the last few
pints of gas from running to it. And last few pints it is. The Plane
Captain has been juggling it almost by the quart from engine to
engine. There are less than thirty usable gallons left in the airplane and one engine burns that up in less than an hour at
normal cruise.

The airplane is riddled and hacked to pieces, some of the
damage self-inflicted in the effort to lighten ship, but there are
far more holes, rips, rends, and gashes in this 24 than I have ever
seen before. Miraculously no one got hit, although judging from
some of the angles the hits took, it seems impossible. Like the
sword trick with the girl in the trunk.

It is apparent what Ahab has done by the pictures he took—
made a low-level pass at a battleship in a B-24. He has surprised
them to the extent that he got away with it. The pictures are
undeniably good, if terrifying to sane men. They show Japs
cringing on the decks of the giant ship and actually deserting
some of the sponsons, and in a dramatic accident one picture
catches the black shadow of the 24 crossing the deck like a huge
flattened eagle.

The evening of Ahab's return is the start of the most nerve-
racking time in squadron history. It doesn't mean a thing that
Ahab himself was unimpressed and pronounces the flak thin and
inaccurate, nor does it help to know that in his opinion the
Oscars were not aggressive. They merely watched him until
he tried for the picture, he says disdainfully. Then three of

them started a series of inept, unco-ordinated runs, which wouldn't have bothered him if he hadn't had a prop frozen flat.

Frank Ainsworth appears at the noon briefing, pale but himself again, and departs an hour later with Tuckerman for the sundown check. The contact comes at six twenty. Enemy fighters sixty miles northeast of the reported position of the force. Eight minutes go by. Tuck sends the two-letter signal which means they are attacked. At six forty Ainsworth says he is badly damaged. He is starting home. He has lost Tuckerman somewhere. At six forty-five Ainsworth changes his mind. He is going to head for Rangoon, which is just as far but has more favorable winds to recommend it. Passing to the west of Kuantan one hour later, he sends his last message. He estimates Rangoon at zero two one zero, an awfully late estimate. There are no more transmissions, not even to acknowledge calls from the base.

Our turn! My stomach knots again so painfully that I cannot walk erect. I can't find the bottle of paregoric so I go to the dispensary, walking bent over at the waist. On the way I decide that if Doc Parker is there I will let him—if he will—take me off the list. I tell myself righteously that I will not pull a Brady, but that I am in fact in terrible agony and that it is no disgrace to tell him the truth. I try not to feel relieved. But I am—vastly—until I arrive at the dispensary tent and find Tom Parker isn't there! Jericho gives me a shot glass of paregoric and in less than ten seconds the pain is gone and I am standing straight again.

Tuckerman arrives home as we are being briefed. He says Ainsworth took him into some big hairy cus when they sighted the fighters and he lost him due to the awful turbulence, which Tuck says, scared him more than the fighters. Five Oscars and a Jack made reasonably determined passes at him for ten minutes or so, as he ducked in and out of the clouds looking for Ainsworth. He talked to Ainsworth on VHF the entire time and was surprised when he said he was cutting for Rangoon because up till then he didn't know he was in any real difficulty. They just couldn't get together, Tuck says. The clouds hid the land and there were no reference points. They didn't see the ships.

"Gentlemen," Monty Herbert says. "Many are called but few are chosen. You heard Tuck, it shouldn't be too bad." He smiles at us then looks grave. He doesn't know how to handle it. He wants to tell us that if Ainsworth hadn't spooked, everything would have been all right, but it's hard for a noncombatant to express this eleven hundred and seventy-nine miles from the scene.

"Of course not," Ashton says. "Ask the warden. He's seen it lots of times."

"How about Frank?" I say. "Has he landed yet?"

"No word, but he's not estimating Rangoon for another hour and a half." Herbert's pipe gurgles as he passes some eight-by-ten photos around. They are Ahab's of the fighters and they show the Oscars all at considerable distances, and the one Jack which made no passes at all. The Jack is one of their late models, stubby and compact and with a very powerful engine.

"Probably their wing exec," Ashton says looking at the picture of the Jack. "Just up controlling traffic."

"Joe Norton said they were educated and not eager, and as long as you mind your business they probably won't do very much. And that is all you are asked to do. The Wing merely wants you to verify the presence of the BB's . . . or the lack of them. Don't do anything hairy." Herbert pulls down an enlargement of the Singapore area on the roller. The position of the ships when Ahab saw them last is indicated in a black square. "Here's where they last were, and here . . ." Herbert puts a typewritten sheet inside a code book, showing everyone the action, "is *what* they might be. The escort, that is. It's a list of all the destroyers that we know of left in the Imperial Navy. On the blow-ups you'll see all known AA sketched in. We are pretty sure now that the nine-inch stuff is radar-controlled. Look for it, and if you see a line of it walking up on you, turn away. Donohoe counted eight puffs all in a row."

"What, those funny little men? They can't even make a Chevrolet," Ashton says.

"Their balance is all fucked up too," Bartlett says. "That's why they do so many rolls. They can't stay right-side up."

Herbert's voice changes tone to talk to the copilots, Cox and Mara and Flournoy and me. "There will be two K-20's in each ship," he says, unperturbed by what he calls the interruptions of the Keystone Cops. "If you go in over the harbor, take all the pix you can from nine thousand. The dumbo sub is going to be lying here . . ." He reads out some co-ordinates which are sure to be out past the Anambas Islands someplace and no good to us where we are likely to get wet. "They are supposed to surface on the hour every hour even if there are hostile aircraft around. Remember to caution your gunners . . . this from Commander Engelson . . . caution them to keep their guns pointed at the enemy even if they have a jam." Herbert raises a sheet of paper and reads the rest. "Never try to fix a jam during an attack. A concentrated burst at long range often discourages an enemy from closing in. At two thousand feet an aircraft with a thirty-five-foot span fills half a ring . . . and so on. You know all this better than I do."

"Remember," Bartlett says to Ashton, "to caution your gunners about letting those Oscars cover the lenses on your K-20's and blanking the cameras out."

"Don't you let yours forget the six steps in the two-thirds-of-a-second method." Ashton says.

Herbert gives us a little bow. "Lots of luck," he says. He begins handing out the packets of secrets with that air of custodianship that I always have found annoying. It is his tacit way of indicating that here and now, in the delivery of the packets, the most important segment of the project is being completed.

"One thing more," he says as we start out. "The night fighters are complaining again. They went out after Tuckerman and one of them got lost. They're going to shoot somebody up sooner or later, so make sure your IFF is on."

"Poor Chèr Ami," Ashton says in a lachrymose voice. "They shot him down because his IFF wasn't cooing."

CHAPTER NINE

Now that I am very well ready
For the call of death at any time . . .

W E STAND outside ACI and wait for the truck. The night is moonless and there is only one narrow ellipse of starry sky far down toward the eastern horizon. To the south, where we are going, golden lightning explodes in the huge white cumulus banks. It is far away, soundless, and only the rippling reflection of it can be seen careening back and forth in its endless ferocity. Around me I see the puny red glow of cigarettes arcing rapidly up to lips and down again. The contrast is shattering. I breathe in the cloying, fine, talcum powder dust stirred by our feet and shiver uncontrollably when one of the tubes of my Mae West which has come out of its holder strokes my throat. Dust, fear, the cured-ham smell of someone's breath, the occasional geyser of coffee mixed with bile in the back of my throat—it is all too familiar.

The truck comes, groaning in the blackness, dust drifting ahead of its dim lights. It looks submerged, as though it is crawling along the bottom of the sea. We toss in our stuff, climb the shaky sideboards, and squat on our heels in the bed. Somebody yells and the truck lurches off. Flournoy is beside me. He is down on one knee like a football player waiting for the enemy's rush. I noticed he sat by me in the mess and again at the briefing I am the kind of person that new copilots attach themselves to, perhaps because I generate no awe. I don't know Flournoy, he has only been around a couple of months and we have flown together only that once, but he strikes me as another talkative suckling like Arnold, except that Flournoy is more articulate. I caught part of a bull session one night. Flournoy was telling some other new boy about the "agitation" he felt the first time (that afternoon) he saw hostile land. When he saw it rising from the sea, Flournoy said, and felt himself at the absolute rim of America's advancing might, he experienced an exhilaration that he would never forget. I'm sure other people are humbly aware of these things, and I don't care if they have ecstasies like that, but I don't want to hear about them.

I go over the airplane briefly with a flashlight while Ashton is having a final confab with Bartlett. Flournoy tags along and peers closely at the oleos, or the nose wheel doors or the turbos during each short illumination. Bud Hartstene is sitting on a cot under the wing where he has spent the night to be sure we have nothing stolen before this hot-sector trip.

"Well, how is she?"

"Both clocks are running."

"How many engines are there?"

"Beats the shit outta me, Colonel. I ain't the regular crew chief."

While I am making my adjustments to pedals and seat, Flournoy taps my arm and then holds out his hand to me. At first I don't get it, but then I see by his deadly serious face that he wants to shake. Perhaps for luck. I haven't seen solemnities for a long time. Not since the rituals of Tim Brady. But if the moment is brimming with mystical forces, I am not the one to dissipate them. I shake.

We have no bombs and it is cool and we get off more easily than usual, but we are heavy enough and can only climb in little wallowing spurts. When we reach some little scattered clouds at eight hundred feet we begin bouncing loggily in and out of the wisps, and for a while the airplane refuses to climb at all each time it encounters the least disturbance in the air. As we turn,

I get a glimpse of Bartlett's lights crawling down the runway. As he gets off they stab down at the ground and snuff out. Another lucky night, as Joe Louis used to say.

"Boy oh boy, are we heavy," Flournoy says to me. "It's worse than being in P-boats. It used to take half the night to get to cruising altitude." I was in P-boats but for some reason I feel like stressing my inexperience in the world of airplanes.

"How high was that?"

"Nine hundred feet."

"At least if you came back down you could land and float."

He nods and smiles to show that he is, at the moment, just as conscious of this advantage as I am. We settle down, climbing out on 235 degrees. The heading will take us between Balabac and Balambangan and give us a landfall at Little Natoena where we will join up with Bartlett for the run in. We will fly together to Berakit, the northeast tip of the big island, Bintan, southeast of Singapore, and make our approach along its northern coast. If we do not sight the ships, we will cross the Straits and fly up the estuary of Johore, turn east again and come down over Katong, photograph Keppel Harbor, cross the Main Straits and fly back the way we came in. All of this at nine thousand feet. This is supposed to afford the best look with the least danger, but no one, possibly excepting Flournoy, believes that we will do anything like this complicated ACI officer's dream trip, and before we do anything we have six hours to fly over the South China Sea.

Ashton tilts his chair back, pulls his cap over his eyes and says his usual "Wake me just before the battle, mother," but tonight he only pretends to sleep. I see his eyes shine under the cap every time there is a jolt or a spatter of rain. We go through some pretty rough cus and the rate-of-climb needle does the usual horrible tricks, but the lightning display is now far off to the east and we won't have to fly through it. Ashton and I have been very jumpy about this ever since the night we hit the freak cold front up near Sakishima Retto. We went in at six thousand in the pitch dark, and the next moment we were going up at four thousand feet a minute with the power nearly off, pitching like mad. A few minutes later the draft reversed and we dropped like a stone, four thousand feet a minute down with forty-five inches on the engines. Everything movable was glued to the overhead, including liquid coffee. Outside the hail beat on the skin, louder, as they say, than a goat shitting on a kettledrum. It stripped most of the paint off the nose section. We came out under a roll cloud just feet off the water, and there we stayed because it was the only place the airplane was controllable. In the lashing winds the waves seemed to rear higher than our wing tips. It was the worst night I ever put in, and far worse than the times we flew through typhoons. The next night one of the San Diego crews was lost up there, presumably in the front.

Tonight we bounce just enough to keep it nervous and after a bit Ashton gives up. He lights a cigarette, stretches, and whistles for coffee. We drink it black, cup after cup. The aircraft bounces, climbs a little, bounces, yaws, jolts, quivers in long spasms. The lights on the Honeywell auto pilot blink and flash—like an untended switchboard where frantic calls are coming in that nobody answers. Once in a while a patch of turbulence makes us both grab the wheel and reach to disengage the auto pilot.

"Some day the old Nickel Plate and China Sea will have a new roadbed," Ashton says after a jarring ride through a cloud we didn't see.

"I hope to God I'm retired."

"You and forty thousand other ex-Naval aviators will be laying track."

"Never."

"A gandy dancer," Ashton says. "That's the job to have. Play the concertina, eat a little garlic and cheese, and . . . dance the gandy."

"I'd rather pump one of those little wagons along the track."

"The commanders will grab those. But maybe you and I could run a Ferris wheel. That's clean, dignified, and still slightly aerial."

"No thanks," I say thinking about my Good Humor truck. I have made my confession to Ashton before. He knows how I feel about flying—this sort of flying. Going up on a sunny morning to wring out an SNJ for an hour, or shooting a few landings (on a sunny morning) in a Twin Beech is something else again. "I've told you," I say to him loudly so that Flournoy will hear, "if I had any guts I wouldn't be here. I'd settle it, like Brady."

Ashton turns around in his seat but his eyes stay on the instrument panel. "No, you wouldn't. You can't and neither can I. We worry about what they'll say at the Kiwanis ten years from now. Well, I can tell you . . . nothing. No one will give a goddam in *one* year that Tim Brady the football hero turned saffron. They won't even believe it if you tell them." In the soft glow from the dials I can see the smile of disgusted pity on his face. It is for us, not anyone else.

"Well," I say. "It's coming closer every night. The night with the JU's, the night we couldn't get into Dunkeswell and were going to jump out, that night we went to Iwo with Four twenty, the night at Sakishima, the . . ." Ashton waves a hand depreciatively.

"Na! You can't put it over. And neither can I . . . and neither could poor old Frank. He had to have people like him after all. But if I was going to quit I wouldn't do it half-ass like Frank. I'd quit."

"What do you mean?"

"I mean quit . . . not let your reflexes carry you along afterwards. All that getting separated in the clouds and heading for Rangoon."

"You think he had that on his mind?"

"Sure . . . but it's so stupid. Put your ass on the line fifty, sixty, a hundred times . . . then head for Rangoon. Defend your life like a madman for two years and then *give* it away. Sure, Frank told *them*. He just couldn't convince himself that it wouldn't make any difference to anybody . . . except for about five minutes right at the moment."

"It would bother you afterwards. Don't kid me."

"Na, I'm gifted. I can tell war stories."

We fly in and out of clouds in the darkness. The lightning still ripples in great yellow welts to the east of us but we are going to disappoint it tonight. After a couple of hours we begin to pick up speed. The load is slowly lessening, and if we could see the wings we could actually notice how they lose their V shape and come back down horizontal again as the weight eases. Spurlock appears, his blond cowlick standing up straighter than ever. He wants to transfer gas from the bomb bays. I turn on the booster pumps for him and he stands there for a minute checking things. He nods at Ashton who has slumped back under his cap again.

"Is he hiding again, Mr. Iverson?"

"He's unconscious from fear."

Ashton waves a hand feebly. "For God's sake, hurry up with that gas so we can smoke." He sits up. "You know I really miss Brady. He used to keep it instruments inside here with his smoking so you could never see a thing outside. It was marvelous." It is true. Brady smoked two packs a trip.

After a long time Spurlock is finished. We light cigarettes greedily and watch our smoke, thin and poisonous-looking in the eerie fluorescent lighting, as it curls around the handles and switches and dials, like incense from some joss rites. Inside me the familiar tug of war has long been going on, but tonight I don't fight back with scientific exercises. I feed every little spike-footed demon that comes along. I pray, quite formally, and align myself rigidly with every spiritual force and divine deputy I can think of. Hail Mary. Our Father. Blessed Jesus. I pray informally too, the way I imagine my father does, with vague man-to-man appeals to treat me square and get me through. I find I am thinking of my father when I pray and not God, and the picture I have is of someone standing in a plowed field—my father, a hundred years ago, with a beard—crumbling a handful of dry earth in a gnarled hand while he shouts familiarly up at the rumbling heavens, "Lord, you know we need rain! And Granny's got the backache again, and one of the mules has colic . . ." I am walking with the wind and I go all the way, leaving decent intervals between each pay-off of the blackmail. I cross my fingers three times on each hand, rub my wedding ring and rap my knuckles surreptitiously on the only wood I can find—my pencil. I remember Frank Ainsworth's pet voodoo, how he always wore the same dirty flying suit. But as he always said it didn't remove the possibility of death, only of someone saying afterward, "Say, did you hear about Frank? First time he *didn't* wear that dirty combo he got knocked off!" Two four six eight, who do we propitiate!

Andretta calls on the intercom. He is operating the radar counter-measure gear which happens to be installed on our airplane, and has picked up something. His voice is calm and comforting with its Bronx accent. It puts New York on the team. It sort of ranges big dirty city resourcefulness and tough guys behind us.

"There's one station awready. It's . . . ah . . . maybe a hunnert and twenny miles at about one seventy-five true. They ain't found us yet!"

"They will," Ashton says. "It's probably Kuching."

"Yeah," Andretta says cynically. "That's a crock of shit about how the Japs don't have decent radar. I remember the day up there around Formosa. There was three of 'em on us and we was seventy miles out."

With counter-measure gear you can see the whole action. You see the sweep of the enemy radar and you see the circling bar of light suddenly interrupted at the moment of discovery, and the searching arm played carefully back and forth across the blip you yourself are making. You can imagine the moan of sirens and the racketing of GQ gongs in the innards of ships and picture stocky-legged men running around ripping the covers off guns—all just for you.

"Yeah, well, they'll never be able to make a Chevrolet . . . or an Ingersoll," Ashton says. "They don't have Yankee know-how and can-do. Somebody pass El Juggo up here, please. I'm beginning to feel too good." We fill the dirty cups with the metallic-tasting coffee and swill it down. My stomach flutters and acid rises in my throat but I pour black coffee on the disturbance and smoke until I am dizzy.

There is faint light now in the east and I have the Natoenas on my radar repeater scope. The islands show as little tufts of white gold on the screen. Cunningham in the bow spots Bartlett a couple of miles off to the left. We turn slightly to close on him. The airplane wakes up. Whitey Nanos gets off his usual feeble imitations of a Jap radio announcer. "Wercome to Singapore, Yankee boy. We rooking flowad to suing you." Cunningham clucks on the intercom like a trotting horse. When Ashton asks if everyone is awake and ready there is a chorus of chirps, lip noises, and untranslatable groans and cries. He has always been satisfied with this response, but he is too lax and pretends to be too debonair. He has played the role of the bored bullfighter in front of them so long that everyone now affects some version of this bravado. We used to practice calling and tracking, and jinking and corkscrewing, for hours synthetically, sitting in chairs while movie enemies rushed at us from screens, but because of the air of exhausted tolerance displayed by Ashton, no one took it seriously. Now when the real business begins, we invariably start badly. There is bedlam on the intercom, guns are not fired at all or fired at the wrong targets, and there is enormous difficulty translating decision into action. There is always a struggle to get a grip on the crew. Once we get going it's all right, but we need time.

The light gains rapidly. The sky to the south is clear and the clouds we have hoped for don't seem to be there. Ashton looks around at the brightening day, screws up his mouth and articulates a dirty word. He puts on an inch more boost and we start catching up with Bartlett.

"What is that thing we send?" he asks me suddenly.

"The Z signal for fighters?"

"What else?"

I tell him the two-letter signal. Flournoy looks more earnest than ever.

"You think they'll be out here?" Flournoy says.

"It won't be long."

"I've never seen a Jap fighter," Flournoy says. "If it's anything

like fighter-affiliation with the gyrenes in Dago, I'm not going
to like it."

"They don't come as close," Ashton says. "You don't see them
on their backs right over you, pushing the goddam stick forward
so they miss you by three feet like those bastards from Ream
Field. On the other hand, they do shoot."

"But they don't make overheads, I hear," Flournoy says.

"They haven't yet. The day they begin will mean the extinction
of the Flying Whale."

We are close to Bartlett now. The man sitting in the waist
hatch in the other ship makes inviting motions at us with his
arm. Ashton flips the switch on the jack box by his seat and
clicks his mike button. He sends a B in code with clicks. There
is an answering crackle. Bart is wide awake. We fly just close
enough so that we don't have to start juggling throttles.

A few minutes later we see the first land, a stretch of rumpled
brown coastline, going out of sight in both directions. Bintan.
As we approach, the brown turns to mottled shades of green.
There is more land to be seen further on around a long headland.
I secure the repeater scope and start with the glasses. The eternal
search. First the entire sky, putting my head in the blister and
looking above and behind and everywhere, clearing the blind
spots behind window frames and obstructions. Then carefully
the water in front. The glasses pull at my eyes. I have done this
so much I have probably weakened my eyes forever.

There is a smear of smoke many miles away, a bit to our right. It
seems detached from the sea, dotting and dashing its way back
over the horizon in intermittent streaks and blanks. I keep searching, coming back to the smoke which doesn't seem to increase or
diminish.

Behind me I hear Flournoy still talking about the marines at
Dago and how you had to open the waist hatches to let them
fly through. It is almost a pleasure when I hand Ashton the
glasses, point, and say, "There they are," because now there is
real consternation on Flournoy's face and not a trace of ecstasy.

Ashton looks for a long time. With the mike button he clicks

out the word "ships." There is a half-minute delay before the
"R" comes back.

"What do you see?" Flournoy says. "Fighters?"

No one answers him. Ashton lowers the glasses and looks with
his naked eyes toward the smoke. "They must be outside. If that's
them."

"Nothing else would put up smoke like that," I say.

At this moment Andretta calls to say we are on the Jap radar.
Ashton calls Bartlett. There is no sense in keeping quiet now.

"They're outside, I guess. What does the syllabus call for now?"
Bart says on VHF. At least we won't have to fly over Singapore.

"Shall we do a fast hundred around them once and get out?"

"Well, if you want to show the white feather."

"It's quite all right with you, you mean? I see that laundry
flying on your masthead. Let's go over there, describe our sensations to the base and haul. They'll probably tell us to remain on
station. When we're sure, I'll send the contact on the ships. We'll
also take care of the contact on fighters."

"Right." Bartlett changes his heading slightly. We slide in close
on his starboard. His waist gunner grins down at us. My teeth
are chattering as I pick up the glasses again and level them on
the smoke.

Now I can see them. Ships and big ones. They are going fast
and there isn't any doubt who they are. There is one big ship and
four smaller. We approach so as to intercept well ahead of them.

Ashton has added boost and rpm's and the engines take on a
keyed-up, anxious sound. In a few minutes we are close enough
to see the formation clearly. The big ship is a battleship-carrier,
one of the hermaphrodites, steaming fast and straight with a
huge disdainful white lip curling at her bow. No one has ever
seen a sight like that and exclamations come from all around on
the intercom. It is obvious they are seriously under way for somewhere.

Andretta has sent the contact and a minute later back comes a
query from Engelson. He wants to know where the other her-

maphrodite is and he wants to know our estimate of "longest possible time on station."

"Fuck the other one!" Ashton says to Flournoy. "Tell him it isn't here." We turn and start down the course of the ships, staying well away. They are steaming north-east and going at least twenty knots, the destroyers hopping about like nervous fleas. The sister battleship may have left earlier. We aren't going to look for her.

Now I see that the big ship has begun making turns. There is already one great creamy S behind her and she seems to be heeling slightly. One of the destroyers has spotted us and comes steaming out to get between us and its huge consort. It has a stack that is almost parallel with the deck, it is so raked.

"Nervous, Zalewski?"

"My ass is biting washers, kid."

"Where the hell are the fighters?"

"It's just a matter of time, buddy."

"If we had twenty miles of wind against us, those goofy cans could outrun us. That one there is up on the step."

"Hey! I just seen a big green ball! Hey! There's another! A yellow one!" I see a burst too. Just as we arrive abeam of the ships, a tandem yellow and red thing explodes ahead. It is low and not at all close to us. Then I realize what is happening. They are firing at us with the main batteries! It is unbelievable! Big guns like that fired at two aircraft. But I can see the smoke jet from somewhere forward on the hermaphrodite and a minute later there are more spectacular fireworks, this time yellow and green, a mile or so ahead of us. "They sure are lousy shots," somebody says jovially.

I keep busy with the glasses, and work them all around, not just on the ships. Suddenly they seem to be full of specks. Behind the ships, rather high over their wakes, there seems to be a swarm of gulls circling for the garbage. Fighters. A whole boodle of them at about five thousand.

I try to do everything at once, tell Bartlett, tell the crew, have Flournoy send the contact, point them out to Ashton. He doesn't see them at first. I take a pencil and try to show him by lining up the pencil. But now I can't find them again and scrabble for the glasses. They seem to be out of focus and the airplane is jiggling too much. I am in a panic. Maybe they are already up and behind us in the sun. But that is impossible. They were a long way from us. I force myself to be systematic. Now, there they are, more to the left and higher. They are not from the hermaphrodite. It is almost certain that they have no aircraft on them and can't launch any. I take the pencil again. "See them? They'll be under that one little puff cloud in about five seconds. Six of them." Ashton sees them. Flournoy is staring past me, his eyes wide, his teeth faintly bared as though in some comic interpretation of discovery.

"Send the goddam contact!" I yell at him. He ducks back into the nav compartment. I call Mara who will direct the evasion tactics when the fighters start to attack. I have one earphone set on VHF and the other on intercom.

"As a matter of fact there are three more," Mara says. "Look at about one o'clock low."

"Hol . . . leee! A whole boodle of them!" Cunningham says from the bow. "There's a stack of them down there on the water, boss. One, two, three, four, five . . ."

Ashton tries to see, raising himself in the seat, but he can't and fly formation. I can't tell which ones Cunningham is talking about. I don't see any new fighters. Perhaps, being Cunningham, he is doubling everything. "Where the hell do you see five, Cunningham?"

"I see nine. Six going from one toward noon and three down there at about one thirty."

"Those are the same ones. Now don't fuck us up!"

"No, sir!"

"Watch the three and keep telling me what they are doing."

"They're sharpening knives and forks."

The colored fireworks have stopped. Perhaps they were to help the fighters locate us in the sun.

Ashton calls to Bartlett, his voice showing strain at last. "Listen, the base says we can finesse trying to find the other BB. They want us to hang on here if we can, and I don't think we can. The syllabus doesn't call for all that competition. How many badmen do you see?"

"At least nine," Cox says quickly, his tone implying that this is only the beginning. There is a pause. We are astern of the ships now, the fighters have crossed in front of us and are climbing on our port. We can go around the ships on the land side toward Singapore and have the fighters coming out of the sun, or we can turn sharply back now and perhaps be high enough to make them chase us from astern for a while.

"We're for hauling ass," Cox now says emphatically.

"I'm your huckleberry," Ashton says promptly. "Haul!"

We bang steeply to port to get around on a northerly heading. As Ashton pulls high on the outside of the turn, I can see the fighters below on our right, only a couple of thousand feet under us and climbing like hell. The black purposeful specks, the metaphoric "angry gnats," have become Japanese airplanes—army Oscars, painted blotchy green and brown, in tight formation for once. All except one guy in the last element. Despite myself I have an instant's reflection about that—the Japs are no different, there is always one guy who won't close up. Old Watanabe had a collision in his nine-plane-formation days at Osaka of the Air and it has spooked him ever since. But I have never seen Japs as determined as this. They usually come around in singles, looking like leisurely hawks, banking, and maneuvering and stunting outside range.

"On with the coal!" Cox says to us as we straighten out heading north. Ashton makes the creeping movement with his right hand that to me is the most characteristic motion in the world. Walking my throttles back home. I push the mixtures up and give him more rpm's. We can't outrun them but we can give them less time to pick on us.

"What are they doing?" Ashton says. He is working now to stay close to Bartlett and can't even look around.

"Three are out of sight underneath us. Six are back a ways, but coming like hell! I don't see the Jack, though."

I can see Standing Room Mara looking out the starboard waist of Bartlett's ship. He should start directing things.

"Come on, Mara, get the lead out!" I say on VHF. I don't look over at him because I am watching the fighters through my blister, but I also have the strange feeling that if I don't watch him Mara will have a clearer and swifter insight into things than if I seem to be hanging on him. It is like looking away when the team has one yard to make on fourth down.

"Okay, I guess we're in business," Mara says calmly. "The ones I see are at five, low, but getting up there. Six of them. And there are three dead astern low. Anyone see any more?" No one does.

The group of six split. Three go ahead, getting out to our starboard beam, still climbing. Slowly they break up into a line astern. They form a queue, one behind the other, and when they get ahead and above they will start their runs. The other three are probably lining up on the other side where they can bracket us.

I feel terribly slow trying to figure anything out. It is as though my mind is moving in a bath of thick oil. The higher pitch of engine noise distracts me and heightens my fear. I feel inept, worthless, and I long to do nothing except rely on the others to get me out of here.

Bartlett's crown turret suddenly fires a burst. The orange balls shoot out and then sag far below the Oscars. "Come on, Gurly, you know better than that," Mara says. "They're two miles away."

"I just remembered we never test-fired the guns," Zalewski says agitatedly on the intercom.

"You can test them on Oscars in about one minute," I say, striving to get a tone of annihilating calm. "Let's see you guys hit something for once in your lives."

The Oscars are ahead of us now and higher. The first one vaults up out of the line. He rocks and skids a little, positioning himself, flashing in the sunlight. Then he is around and coming, dropping and curving, then flat, then curving again the other way as he falls in our quarter. Mara is talking. "At three, at four, at five, coming in level . . . well, come on shoot, for Christ's sake

. . . now turn right . . . right . . . and GO!" Tracers spout from Bartlett's airplane. Overhead Spurlock fires deafeningly, the percussive effect so close to our ears it is actually painful, and the usual rain of things begins. We drop down and follow Bartlett around in a violent bank to the right. The ship shakes with gunfire.

The Jap is shooting too. I can see tracers passing far in front of us and then Bartlett seems to fly right into them. There is a noise like gravel hitting our own hull. I cringe, feeling the sound and the motion as the penultimate sensation of my life.

The giddy rolling of the airplane seems incessant. Mara is talking, calling another Oscar from the other side. His voice drones, it seems almost impassive, faintly stylish. "At eleven starting, at nine, seven, ready . . . turn left . . . GO!" We are corkscrewing, coming out of our seats with the negative g's Ashton is imposing on the Lib as he whips after Bartlett to the left. He has the look of a man driving a heavy truck down a steep grade with no brakes. Dimly I hear Mara and try to imagine the fighters out there on the other side as they turn, pick up speed, and come boring in. A fighter flashes over us, only feet away, throwing a quick shadow across the glass panels in the overhead. As he dives away to the right, the Jap rolls twice, the air around him streaked with tracers, and then drops away on his back.

We are straight and level for a moment. Mara has disappeared from the waist hatch on this side but he is still talking. I look behind on our right. There are two coming. It is obvious Mara isn't talking about them. I grab the mike and shout. "Mara! Ahhhhhh! Heyyyyyy!" Anything to get his attention. He appears again in the hatch, sees the fighters, calls the turn, but we are late. I can feel and hear the hits and I duck toward the floor, catching a quick glimpse of Ashton manhandling the wheel.

"Jesus!" he screams. "These guys aren't kidding!" I have a sudden and overwhelming conviction of disaster. The sight of that fighter, the closest I have ever seen one come—their aggressiveness—the feel of the reeling airplane—above all the lack of confidence I have just seen on Ashton's face—everything combines to tell me it is the end.

Co-ordinated attacks come, one after the other. Tracers fly out like Roman candles, burning out at the end of their arcs. Brass tumbles into the nav compartment. The bag must have broken. The stink of powder smoke, noise, cries, motion, pounding on my head.

We are losing. They are coming faster and we are turning slower. With every pass we are late. Once we start to turn right. "Wait . . . he's not coming," Mara says. "He hung up . . . now he's coming, I think. Okay at five . . ." Bartlett turns without waiting. We have turned and straightened, and when he goes quickly right again, Ashton is surprised. He horses the yoke back and pulls off power with a sickening swallowing sound and we almost hit the other ship. In the next second we have lost a hundred yards. Ashton pounds the pedestal and I hold my thumb on the rpm toggle until the props are in full low. With the other hand I push the throttles up to forty-five inches. Even so we pick up speed again with maddening slowness. Bartlett has on so much extra power we can only creep up on him.

The fighters are coming again, the firing becomes a jam of sound. One of the Oscars knifes between us, lifting a wing delicately and slicing up about ten yards in front of the bow. He is going slow, climbing straight away. For a second he seems to hang there.

"No deflection, right in front of you, Cunningham!" I am screaming like a maniac. But Cunningham is ahead of me. The guns in the Emerson turret move very slightly. It is point blank. At the end of a long burst the Jap levels off, smokes briefly and begins a whipping flutter. A piece flies off. Then he is gone, spinning. I bellow, "You son of a bitch! You son of a bitch! We got you, you son of a bitch!" Flournoy is cheering beside me. I pound him on the leg and he pounds me back on the shoulder. I am insanely exhilarated. "Kill the bastards!" I shout over and over.

We have nearly caught up with Bartlett when I see his airplane jolt, as though it had crossed a slip stream. In the next moment we are flying through dense black smoke. We turn slightly, come out of the smoke and there is Bartlett above us, the smoke pouring from a wing root, thickly black, endless, like dark blood.

I can see the waist gunner in his square window. He isn't shooting, he just seems to be riding along, like a man in a caboose. Above him the crown turret is still revolving unconcernedly. The guns look like the mandibles in the head of a glass beetle.

Ashton has his mike and is yelling at Bartlett. Overhead Spurlock is firing in deafening cycles. I don't see any fighters but there is the thunder above me and the rattle of the links and empties falling down.

Bartlett is turning slowly, the smoke a thick plume behind him. Ashton tells him to let down and get on the water. He does begin to sink but he is already wallowing. One wing goes up thirty degrees as he struggles for control. Ashton saws the throttles with quick, savage motions to stay beside Bartlett without hitting him. The engines surge and die, surge and die. Bartlett is dropping very fast. I can see it from our own dizzily unwinding altimeter. Our airplane is shuddering from the speed. Ashton is telling Bartlett not to go so fast, but now no one answers from the other airplane. It is obviously no longer a controlled descent. We go down together, slanting steeply toward the blue water, and for a moment there is nothing in the world but the overstrained sound of engines, the hideous rushing, the black smoke curling and parting as we rip through it.

Then the fighters are on us again. They come in flat from behind because they can't catch us any other way, and we are going so fast now that when they pass us they seem to be in slow motion. One of them gets in and hangs close under Bartlett's belly. He stays there for a long time, perhaps ten seconds, and jockeys around as he belts the slow-cycle cannon shots into the bomb bays. It is agonizing to see, the sort of horror of watching a python squeeze a goat to death. The horror comes from the time it takes, from our own helplessness, from the inevitability of the result. We can do nothing except scream at Bartlett. Cunningham and Spurlock can't hit the Oscar, he is too close to Bartlett. The Jap knows it. Once he looks back at us. As if to show us how little he cares, he rolls on his back and fires some more. But as he drops away with the roll, somebody hits him. I don't watch him go but I hear Nanos yelling from the tail.

Dead or not it is too late. Bartlett's airplane is beginning to go to pieces. It is burning along the wing as far out as the inboard engine. Hunks of cowling are flying off. Now they are going to start getting out through the waist hatches. Through the gaps in the smoke I can see a couple of figures with chest packs bracing themselves in the square opening. But in the next second something blows inside. The wing comes off at the root and the Lib snaps on its back. For a moment the wing hangs there beside the inverted airplane, the black wheel well sharply defined against the white underside, like an eye. Then the airplane dives into the sea, the wing falling after it, spinning crazily, like a leaf in the wind. A fan of spray rises where it strikes the water flatly, like a paddle.

Ashton is having some kind of a fit. He lets go of the yoke and claws at his clothes as though he wants to get out of them, and out of the airplane too. Tears fly from his face as he struggles. But Spurlock is telling us to turn left, the fighters are coming. I grab the wheel and start around as fast as possible. There are two of them, flat on the ocean and coming in together. They have started from too far out and I am around before they are in range. I push the yoke down hard and head straight for them, going down and down until I am hugging the folds of the sea. We fly at each other head on, and I press lower and lower until it seems I will drag the tail skag in the swells. There is shooting but it is only a minor distraction. Just before we collide the two Oscars split. One goes up and over us and the other goes under us, and hits the water a hundred yards astern. How he got that far I can't understand. I see him as I turn, bobbing there, broken.

I bank this way and that but nothing else comes. Ashton is quiet, his head back, his eyes closed. I climb to five hundred, turning. There is just one fighter, the one who went over us. The others have gone. This one appears outside my window and flies along, turning with us just out of range. Then he does two slow

rolls, the last one just over the water, and goes off in the direction
of Singapore.

I circle the place where Bartlett went in. There is a small slick
but no debris. In the air are still a few striations of black smoke.
When they have vanished in the wind, there will be no trace of
Bill Bartlett and his crew left in the world.

I head north.

It never ends. The crises come like hills you must climb, one
after the other, even after you are exhausted. They come faster
and they compound themselves, and add to themselves like breed-
ing bacteria, until at last, there is a tempo to them and a number
and a final combination with which no one can cope. If you hang
around long enough you will meet yours. Just like you will someday see ten straight passes with the dice.

It began at midnight with an overloaded take-off and too much
gas pulling us down with its weight, and it will end soon with
too little gas to push this shaking, draughty, ruined hulk back
across eleven hundred and seventy-eight miles of China Sea. We
are riddled with holes—in the fuselage, in the starboard engine
nacelles, in the flaps, shredded and drooping on one side, in the
starboard fin, shot away down to the first pintle, in the tubes and
lines and hoses that have squirted the lifeblood of the Flying
Whale all over the place, hydraulic fluid inside, oil outside, in
the tender coils of the command set, scattering bakelite, starring
plexiglas. The holes in number three engine nacelle have caused
it to burn, very briefly, to leak oil very rapidly, and finally to
freeze, beyond any reach of the feathering device, with the blade
frozen flat. The holes in number four engine nacelle have started
a strange phasing in the governor, overspeeding then slowing,
and although its failing health still responds to a jab on the
feathering button, the rising temperature of the oil—which can't
be alleviated because the cowl flaps no longer operate—says it
cannot last very long.

Other holes in other places mean that we have no communica-
tions with the base, nor with the dumbo sub, nor with anyone in

a neighboring sector; that we will have little or no flaps to land
with, possibly two blown tires, probably only the power of two
engines on the same side. All of these holes are our combination,
the speed with which things worsen is our tempo, and the end of
it all is our number, which seems at last to be irrevocably up.

There are of course things to be done if you are intimate with
hydraulic systems and prop governors and know the counter-
strokes that ward off disasters. Spurlock is doing them. But I, I am
a true child of the age and accept the unflagging performance of
machinery without interest. When it fails me I am lost. I can
think only of how we are going to have to drop twenty-five tons
of steel and dural and plexiglas into bottomless water at a speed
of a hundred and twenty miles an hour. With the irresponsible
sounds of the bad engine outside and the wavering, semaphoring
tachs, the lack of any rhythm, even distressed-sounding rhythm,
there is no confidence to be had. I think dully that Standing Room
Mara has finally had his bath and that somewhere far down under
the black water his body and Bartlett's and Cox's are undulating
in the deep currents, in the darkness. Perhaps they are simply
compressed pulp in the corners. Everyone ends there.

Ashton comes back from appraising things in the waist. He
looks at me and shakes his head, his face white and puffy. "I guess
we're screwed." Spurlock smiles wanly at me as I slide out to
take a look. It is as though he wants to apologize for being the
agent for the gloomy sights I am about to view.

It is a shambles aft, the deck slippery with hydraulic fluid, the
skin sieved, pocked, torn. It is impossible to believe that no one
was hit. Hartstene is chopping at the radar mounts with the fire
axe, Andretta and Robinson are jettisoning radio gear, Whitey
Nanos is padding the bulksheads with chutes and blankets.
Zalewski is getting the last gas out of the bomb bay tanks
which we will drop as soon as they are dry. Cunningham is tossing out ammo, links, brass, guns, everything that he can move.
Everyone looks pleased and confident at the way things are going,
despite the sights and sounds. Back here it is like being near a
runaway sawmill.

"Think we'll make it?" Whitey Nanos says. He makes a seasick face and rotates his head in time to the erratic noises coming from the direction of number four.

"The B-24 is a tough baby," I say quoting the title of a pamphlet they once gave us. "You read it, didn't you? Some guy came back from Ploesti on one." We have to yell to be heard.

"I never heard a governor sound like that one."

"There's probably some explanation, like multiple single phasing or something. Only Mr. Dougherty would have recognized it."

Flournoy has taken my seat and I sit at the nav table and try to figure the sensible heading to fly, considering everything. It is only seven thirty, an unspeakable time to think, to act, or to die. There is no point in heading straight for Borneo, we'll hit near Kuching and the Japs will have us. I draw a line. Zero seven eight will put us on the coast a little way below Labuan. The Aussies landed there. I don't know when, I think I heard it.

We stay low and pull off power until we are barely above stalling speed. Then we discuss whether this is the proper technique to extend flight under the circumstances. We want the last possible mile and the last possible moment. We put more power on and get the airplane on the step and not mushing. I compare indicated air speeds and fuel flow in both conditions and try to work out a ratio. I come up with several versions. Flournoy's mathematics seem sounder. On three engines it is better to keep a little speed.

Gradually we become transfixed. We care little about solving fuel equations, little about what's happening to number four, little about doing the scientific things to lighten the ship. We settle into a muddle-through attitude, the enervating result of pressure and fear. Importance has shifted from the long view of careful navigating, die-hard conservation, staying aloft, to the short view —to merely finding land and getting down and out of the air alive. We tighten our shoulder harnesses until they nearly cut us in two.

We approach a long line of towering cumulus clouds that stretch from the southeast to the northwest as far as we can see in both directions. We get close enough to see the bases, low on the water, and they are twisting and writhing with the unmistakable convulsions of a big squall line.

We look up at the tops. In happier circumstances we might have climbed high enough to thread our way through. Now it is out of the question. The clouds pile up higher and higher until they block out everything. It is the front we saw performing earlier on the way down, and we will have to go under it, we have no choice.

I am flying. I let down until I can see the whitecaps plainly. The altimeter says three hundred feet but it is not to be trusted in squall lines. I look at Ashton and he nods. We start down a long gray canyon I have selected between two ranks of ugly giant cus, and although we are still in the clear the airplane begins to jounce. This is always a bad sign. It becomes dark and sheets of rain slant down on both sides. The clouds quickly pocket us in the way they have of doing. They may seem open and spaced from one side but once in you never find the same way out. Now there is no point in seeking it. We twist and turn among the huge masses until at last we must go in. I get a bit lower and head for the lightest part of the line.

The airplane pitches violently, rain lashes on the skin. We turn up the instrument lights and sit there with the good old "patient strain" look that everybody wears inside a cold front. It becomes rougher and lightning flashes. The rain drums. It seems as if the thunder can't become louder but it does. There are a few angry bursts and then the heaviest, most solid rain I have ever heard or seen. We begin to pitch and yaw, the air speed fluttering through an arc of fifty knots.

Suddenly above the clamor there is a new sound, a screaming runaway sound, and a series of hard thuds on my side of the fuselage. I catch one glimpse of an rpm needle far past the red mark on its dial. Number four has shed blades or done something final.

Ashton is trying to feather it but nothing happens when he

pushes the button. He pushes it in and pulls it out over and over again. Nothing. We are sinking fast. The altimeter says two hundred feet but it could be that far off. We are going in, no doubt about it. I put power on but the airplane is yawing. All the power is on one side and it isn't enough. I hold my finger on the alarm bell. Both of us are looking from the instruments to the windshield and back again, trying to see the water when we break out. Down and down and finally there it is, a space of fifty acres clear of rain and cloud. As we sink lower the tiny ruffles on it become waves and finally swells whose white fringed contours are enormous. Ashton takes it.

There are no flaps. I jerk the handle back and forth like a broken pump handle on a well. We drop down lengthwise on the backs of the swells and Ashton pulls the nose up and up as I feed full power on the remaining inboard engine, trying to ease us in. But without flaps it is impossible to get a nose-up attitude without spinning in, and we are going like the devil.

We hit and bounce, rather gently, and hang above a deep trough between two swells. As they roll under us we strike again, this time with an unbelievable impact, considering the gentleness of the first touch.

CHAPTER TEN

Don't sob but cheer me up.
For the peace's sake of the Far East
What e'en my life shouldn't I give.

BEFORE I reach the surface, I have given up and am letting
myself drown.

I have felt in rapid order the surprising shock and the
painful cutting pitch forward against my harness as we struck,
the manhandling of the water as it ripped into the cockpit, the
shouts, the noises like gongs, and then a final deep blubbering,
with the crushing pressure singing higher and higher in my head.

I am in a cage, rotating slowly and going down. I flip the seat
belt buckle open and shrug off the shoulder straps. For a moment
they cling to me and wave about my eyes like ribbons of white
macaroni. Then I am out of the cage and pumping my arms and
legs. But I don't know which way to go. The pressure is changing
and it feels as though I am still going deeper. I scramble frantically, selecting one oblique direction after another.

I let the first water in. It is all fear and pain and my heart
thumping miles away and my stomach cool as ice. There is no
period of tranquillity. I am able to wonder briefly when it will
become bearable to swim softly in the deafness of the water, so
dark and motionless around me, like nighttime blue . . .

There is a new abomination. It is air and it is painful and no
relief. The universe is going to explode. My head hurts as though
it has been ground among big rocks. I cough and gag, and as soon

as I am able, I begin to cry. I try in vain to shield my face from the tiny spat of spray that continually strikes it, but I can't seem to locate my hands. Now I begin to see just in front of my eyes. A gob of bubbly white froth is slopping back and forth on a sea of yellow. I spit into it when it approaches and when it slides away again I work frantically to assemble the saliva and to form my cheeks and tongue to spit again when it comes.

The viscous white froth comes from me. I am lying in the bottom of a life raft, my stomach over the bulwarks, my legs still in the sea. I can feel the rope perimeter around the raft saw-ing into one knee. Somebody is kneading my back, far too strenu-ously, and when I squint over my shoulder I see one of the per-son's forearms and know who it is. Only Spurlock has an arm like that. I turn my head farther and catch a dizzy glimpse of tossed-up storm clouds overhead and tilting gray seas all around. I see the heads of some people. Immediately I am sick again and press my face into the yellow bottom of the raft, feeling the water pulsing through it against my cheek. The rubber lies between me and the sea like some protective fetal membrane, but from some-where the spray pelts me again and again in the same now sensi-tive place and I swear at it sullenly and begin to cry louder in my helpless annoyance.

"He's okay," Spurlock says to someone.

"The dumb bastard didn't inflate his Mae West. Look at it!" Ashton says. "Two black knobs to pull. Too complicated. Loran, radar, astro compass, sure . . . but knobs with strings . . ." Ashton swears unintelligibly amidst the sounds of rushing, tumbling water. Screw him. If that's all he can think about. If that's all two years of . . .

"All right, Mr. Iverson?" Spurlock pats me on the back in-terminably. It is a sign that he is no longer concerned about me but at least he isn't being brusque about dismissing me. At least he is aware of the gravity of the . . .

"He's all right, the plumber! Yeah, you! Next time try the new technique. The knobs are right there where you play pocket pool, Lennie."

I must come to and say something. I nod my head slowly and
then heave myself all the way into the raft and sit up. There is
Ashton, his black hair flat on his head and shiny as a muskrat's.
There is Robinson. He has a mean little face when it is wet. I
am reminded that I have never liked him since he took Nick
Bondar's place in March. New boy! There is Andretta, still head
down over the bulwarks. Robinson is holding him. Andretta's
eyes are open but they wink in a peculiar way as though he is
trying to focus them, and his mouth is open baring his teeth like
a dead gopher's. Ah, and there is mighty Spurlock, squinting
against the spray and peering a bit stupidly around at the swells.

There is another raft fifteen or twenty yards away. Sometimes
it goes out of sight down the back of a swell. There are five
people in it. I take pains to add this all up. Very slowly. Everyone! It is a miracle. I swear hoarsely.

"You'll be a son of a bitch, all right," Ashton says. He still
sounds outraged that I almost left him to handle things all alone.
He points to a place out in the water where a patch of roily suds
is cascading down the sides of a steep swell. "Right about there.
Thank Spur. No one else saw you. Jesus, what a plumber!"

I have a crazy notion that perhaps Spurlock owns me now.
Right of salvage or something. We sit huddled in the raft, ankle
deep in water, and sway and rock and skitter, like the proverbial
three men in the tub. I cough and am sick every two minutes and
Ashton has to help Robinson hold Andretta because if he doesn't
sometimes Andretta falls over sideways and his head sloshes under
water. The eerie part is he doesn't do anything about it.

It begins to rain. The drops are so heavy they hide everything
more than a few feet from the raft. They lash our skin painfully
and drum on our heads. They bound from the gunwales of the
raft and jitter optically in slivers of spray high in the air. They
thrash the sea—and strangely seem to calm it. The raft doesn't
pitch quite so much.

We sit riding the swells, steadying ourselves against the motion, hunching our backs against the rain. This seems enough
work to me, but Spurlock isn't content. He bails, scooping up the

water in a fury and flinging it out from the rubber bailer as though
he were fighting a fire. Once I see him reach out and snag something into the raft that is floating nearby. He claps the soggy
thing on his head. It is Zalewski's ball cap and on the still jauntily
turned-up brim is pinned the rusted trylon-perisphere device from
the New York World's Fair where Ski tells us he pushed a chair
one summer.

The rain eases and we can see a little. We are in one of the
huge black-walled chambers made by the low-flying roll clouds.

In the other raft they have the paddles out and are coming
over to us. We leave our paddles tied to the thwarts, it is useless
to start paddling until it clears a little. When Zalewski sees his
precious cap on Spurlock's head he stands part-way up in his raft
and makes mammy gestures and throws kisses at it. We are all
full of congratulations for one another but thank God it is impossible to start comparing stories. The water is too rough. One
second they are two yards from us and the next twenty. Even
Cunningham can't cope with interference like this.

We seem to be drifting in the belly of a huge rain cloud. I fight
to stop the violent retching. Nothing comes up. There seems also
to be a valve in my chest that is stuck closed and I can't get my
breath. Andretta now lies with his head on Robinson's knee. He
keeps a grip on his middle with both hands, but the water in the
bottom slaps around his buttocks and legs and wafts him to and
fro. It is as though his body no longer has any bones in it.

"Wait a little, Andy," Robinson says every two minutes. "Wait
till we get on shore. Then we can fix you up." Andretta nods,
his eyes closed. He is blue around the mouth and I think something must have crushed him when we hit. Maybe a gun from
the waist. But he is alive and not down there entombed in old
901, and for each of us that is a miracle. The airplane must
have broken at precisely the right places in its anatomy to let us
all out. I suddenly wonder how long I was down there and ask
Ashton. He considers seriously, the water dripping from his nose
and eyebrows.

"Four or five minutes. I don't know. Quite a while. We were

all up swimming around. One raft was out and all of a sudden up comes the other one right in the middle of us. All we had to do was flip it over."

"I come through a big hole in the after station," Robinson says animatedly. "I wasn't in the water thirty seconds."

"Yeah, well, you should have been down there with me, it was really rough," I say paraphrasing the old cliché. "I couldn't tell which way was up. My God."

"I can imagine," Spurlock says sympathetically. He is a true sailor and can't swim without a life jacket.

"We are just screw-lucky," Ashton says. "We hit going like hell, no stalling her in, no flaps, big swells . . . it's too bad Bart couldn't have had some of that luck." Ashton's face suddenly contorts. He bends over and shakes with sobs. It is hard to realize here and now that Bartlett is really gone forever. "That prick Engelson," he says hawking violently.

This stops the talk. The clouds swim over us, alternating the shadows on the sea in different shades of gray and frosted green. They dip and hang in ragged tendrils and dark, sagging pouches above us. The rain stops and begins again, stops and begins. Once when it stops a shaft of filtered sunlight bursts through like a bolt of lightning, but slowly and maddeningly it loses its color, diffuses, flickers out, and the rain falls harder than ever.

We untie our paddles and begin. All morning we make wobbly headway toward the east, steering on the dinky compass from Spurlock's survival kit. At noon we tie the rafts together briefly while we eat a box of dry cereal. We shake the stuff into our mouths passing the box from hand to hand. No one is hungry, but we are all starting to be thirsty just as the rain stops. We have not thought about collecting any of it. However, the land is not far away. We were there by my DR just about the time we encountered the line squall, and I couldn't be very far off since we made a landfall at the island of Soebi Ketjil only an hour and three quarters earlier. Then too we flew east most of the last few minutes, trying to run around the line squall.

But it is four o'clock before we sight land. We paddle harder using a staggered rotation system whereby each man makes five hundred strokes and then passes the paddle to his neighbor. It is like singing "Frère Jacques," where you break in each time when the song is partly over, only not as much fun. The current must be running against us and we seem to get nowhere. After a while there is a frustration in paddling against the senseless tugging of the sea that is akin to that felt in nightmares. It becomes something like that dreadful feeling of being unable in a dream to summon the strength to run or to lift an object that has fallen on someone's chest. As it grows dark it is worse. I have the notion that the sea sucks us backward twice the distance we have achieved with each stroke of the flimsy paddles.

We paddle most of the night. Toward morning the sea becomes very calm and with first light we are close to the shore.

It is a good thing. Our misery seems boundless and all of us, except Spurlock, are behaving like enraged children, swearing and nagging at one another. Spur is a titan and paddles without stopping all during the times that we have given up to argue, and then irritated by our despair taken it up again.

There are palms growing along a strip of low land and around them in every direction stretches a desolate mangrove swamp. Inland a mile away we can see some of the big trees which grew on Morotai. They grow high before branching and have buttressed-looking trunks covered with climbing rattan.

The tide is out. The air coming off the land is heavy and warm and brings with it the stink of humus and mud. We drift along the shore looking for a place to land and Robinson begins telling Andretta, who hasn't asked, that we will soon have him on shore, and Andretta keeps nodding with his eyes closed and thanking him with absurd sincerity. I am aware that Robinson, in prolonged doses at short range, is the kind of person I will come to hate, not quickly or rashly, but with temperate speed, my hatred flowering a little more with each well-resined scrape of his bow across my nerves, until one day I cut him in two and drop him in a sack.

We ease in behind the surf which is crashing on a tiny beach with a steep slope to it, and wait to watch the others try it first.

Flournoy is trying to direct things in time to the sequence of waves, and when he signals, the paddlers stroke and even the two without paddles dig the water with their hands and in they go. They step out on wet sand. But when we try, we lose our wave crest and are sucked back and swamped by a bigger one. We roll around trying to hold the raft and Andretta against the drag of the current. Orders, entreaties, insults fill the air until the others run in to help us. Andretta can't stand and his whole body is easily bent in all the wrong directions like an eel's by the pull of the water. Finally we get under him with our hands locked and carry him up the beach to the crest of sand on top, only a thin slice at the edge of the cluttered, reedy swamp. As we pull the rafts up, two hornbills fly out of the trees with a lot of noise and go off inland.

"Paul Revere and his buddy," Ashton says panting. "Gone to rouse up the Sarawak minutemen." We sit and smoke our only dry cigarettes from a plastic box that Nanos has with him. We promise passionately to pay him back in dried-out soggy ones later on. Ashton and Robinson feel Andretta all over trying to find the place or places where he is injured. Robinson thinks he has located a back injury and they argue briefly and without conviction about it. The truth is no one can diagnose Andretta's troubles short of Tom Parker, about four hundred miles from here. In the meantime Andretta remains the big liability that must be dealt with, no matter how we shy away from it. He must be carried if he can't walk, and he must be left if he can't be carried. He must die or recover instantly to remove himself as a burden upon us. It is obvious he will do neither of these things.

The tide is coming in and we decide to wait for it to flood the swamp and then we can cross it in the rafts, floating, instead of plowing through the mud. While we wait Spurlock takes stock of the supplies with all the aplomb of Robinson Crusoe. He sorts and counts everything out loud, and listening to him you would think we were merely out on a picnic and he was dividing up the hot dogs. We have quite a lot of stuff. There are four of the plastic containers full of chocolate and halizone pills and fish bait and

signal mirrors, Spurlock has an Aussie machete strapped to his
leg, Robinson the aid kit with morphine in it, Hartstene a knife,
most of the people who were aft have odd cans and boxes of
rations which they stuffed in their shirts, and of course there are
the ration bags that are fixed in the rafts. Ashton has two cloth
maps in the knee pocket of his flying suit, and half a pack of wet
Camels. I have most of a pack of Raleighs, soaked through, and
my Zippo. There are no guns, or hats, or canteens, and no jungle
packs.

The sun comes up over the big trees behind us and the land
steams. We take off our Mae Wests and shirts and trousers and
spread them out to dry, and when the sun hits us in the eyes with
its first rays, slanting and gentle, it puts us to sleep like so many
cats in a warm window.

I have a terrible dream in which Standing Room Mara has
locked me in the toilet on a train. The toilet is overflowing, a
revolting brown geyser occasionally spouting from it, and I can
feel Standing Room's hands holding the handle of the door. They
are stronger than mine and anyway the handle of the door keeps
breaking off. I can replace it but it only breaks more quickly the
next time. I am glad when Ashton wakes me.

He has the cloth map of part of Borneo spread on the sand. "I
think it's the wrong one," he says. "See, here, it's only four north
at the end. We're much further up."

"What's the other one you have?"

"Indo-China. Of course I'm saving all my maps to hang in my
den and I don't want to get them dirty so I don't carry them with
me!"

"You did better than I did. I didn't bring a goddam thing."

Ashton makes a dot in the sand several inches above the end
of the cloth map. "Brunei Bay is about there. And Labuan."

"The Aussies are there."

"Do you know that?"

"Well, it seems to me I heard it the other day."

"I think I heard it too, but I can't remember whether they *are*
there or they're *going* to be there . . . Christ, we live in a bubble.

I haven't paid attention to anything since they mentioned relief crews last January." His eyes fill with tears. "That son of a bitch," Ashton says.

"I keep forgetting."

Robinson comes to tell us that Andretta feels better. He doesn't appear to be. His arms and legs seem stiff and he has trouble getting the cigarettes into his mouth that Robinson is feeding him like a devoted nurse.

"Mr. Ashton," Andretta says without conviction, "you guys better shove off and leave me." I wasn't expecting any classic, Scott at the South Pole stuff, but Andretta's accent makes any heroics ludicrous. Besides there is something in his voice that says he is sure we won't leave him. It is far too early in the game to leave anyone and he knows it. But now he can always say he begged us to save ourselves.

It irritates me to hear the round of reassurances his brave suggestion brings. "Don't be silly," I say like the others and try to make up for what I have been thinking by giving Andretta one of my Raleighs, which I have dried out in the sun.

We strike off through the swamp, wading through the shallows and dragging Andretta in a raft. The water is in most places just deep enough to float the raft over the mangrove roots with some bumping and scraping, and just deep enough to wet everyone to the crotch again. The water soon becomes mud. We stumble and splash in the cloying, stinking stuff and every fourth or fifth step we go down into it with a sudden squilch all the way to our hips. When someone does this, he has to raise himself again by means of the raft and this halts progress. While we stand and wait we sink in too. Andretta's head lolls on the gunwale and around him splattered figures churn in the mud and curse. After a couple of hours we reach a slough, get in the rafts and paddle into deep water.

The tide is still running in and chunks of moldering vegetation roll sluggishly along beside us in the humus-stained water. At noon we come to the entrance of a good-sized river. It has a white sandy bottom and here and there a coral reef, giving it a clean look. At its mouth is an ancient fish weir made from gray stakes, most of them broken. We are tired and wet with sweat and we pull to the bank and drag the rafts out. Spurlock opens some coconuts, doing it correctly and dexterously on a stick he has sharpened with the machete, and passes them around.

"Thank God one guy was awake at the Bishop Museum lectures," Ashton says. Andretta drinks some milk from a coconut but throws it up in a minute or two. Robinson studies the vomit like a prospector looking for nuggets.

"No blood," he reports contentedly.

We try to make a fire but there is nothing dry to burn. We open and divide a can of raw bacon anyway. Flournoy persists in trying to light a fire until at last I can't stand the sight of him using up the matches.

"For Christ sake, save a couple of matches, Flournoy!" I say crossly.

"I got plenty more," Spurlock says slapping his plastic canisters.

"Yeah, well we'll probably need every one of them. We got a long way to go, in case you don't know it." This is hardly astonishing information but it is, obviously, the first time anyone has thought about it in terms of distance. It pleases me to see how I have shaken them all up. Nanos even tucks leftover scraps of coconut in his shirt pocket to show how seriously he now regards things.

We lie on the riverbank and nap. My eyelids burn like fire when I close my eyes and I can't fall asleep so I watch the river. To my left it winds into the plushy green of the jungle and where it disappears in the forest it flashes in one spot as bright as quicksilver. In front of me it glides toward the sea a tawny brown. Dead trees and snags go by, nudging the bank, and a huge butterfly skitters across the water toward me and lights on a hummock of grass, its wings beating slowly like two lovely fans. The wings are white on the upper side and bright black and red and orange below.

I fall asleep. When I wake I see Spurlock and Hartstene down

at the water doing something to the rafts. They seem to be washing them or packing them, I can't tell which because the ground
curves. I almost smile. Spur is the man I used to see Sundays at
the lake, sponging the deck of his outboard cruiser and endlessly
coiling and shifting ropes and lines from place to place and cleat
to cleat, with pauses to step back and judge the effect.

Beside me Ashton smacks his lips and yawns noisily. "Arise,
members of the Naval landing forces in northwest Borneo." When
I stretch I feel something strange and rather painful going on
under my flying suit. I zip it down and find I am covered with
red bites in the places where the suit is at all tight. I follow the
bites, like stitches, down to my groin and there I find something
else. At the end of a sinuous trail of slime is a huge leech. I in-
cinerate him with the Zippo, scorching my pubic hair in the
process, and peel him off. He isn't the only thing in the menagerie.
I am full of ticks too. We all strip down and search frantically
for vermin.

Spurlock comes up from the river carrying his dungarees and
underclothes which he has washed.

"Look here a minute," he says to us. We go to where he is
standing by some scrub bushes. "Watch." He waves his hand at
a bush. The bush seems to wave back. I look closely.

"Holy Christ! Leeches! By the gillion!"

"Look at them beckon to you!" The leeches are indeed stretching their bodies from the leaves and groping in the air as though
searching for us.

"Hello, scrub typhus!"

I feel sick thinking about the horror I have been nourishing in
my crotch. We go over each other again carefully and pick off
the ticks. If they don't let go readily, we warm their behinds with
a cigarette. Afterward I hate to sit down again. I stand and wave
my arms as though it will keep the ticks away from me.

Ashton inspects Andretta again. "Feel any better?" Ashton says.
Andretta's eyes seem prone to roll upward in an oddly relaxed
way, but he nods his head and smiles. "Well, we'll have to feed
you. How about some delicious scrambled eggs with ham?"

We open a K ration, give Andretta the canned eggs and divide the other stuff. The little packet of cigarettes inside has for some reason escaped getting wet. It is the first good smoke I've had all day.

Ashton beckons to me to come with him and we go and sit near the water. Flournoy is fiddling with a raft and Ashton calls to him to come over too.

"It's nothing secret," he says squinting at his cigarette. "We have to decide what we are going to do. You guys have at least seen the maps once or twice. So let's make a plan. We could all try the shore, it probably isn't too hard going once we get past this swamp, but we might run into Japs around any corner. They're more likely to be along the coast than inland. This whole corner up here . . . see here, Fourth Division." He spreads the map out. "There's damn near nothing. No towns of any size and we are certainly north of Bintulu. Now this river here could be the Suai . . . or the Niah . . . or the Sibuti . . . or this big one called the Batang. Runs off the map but it starts out north. We could go up the river and try to meet someone on our team. Chinese or Dyaks or whatever. Maybe a doctor. Maybe a coast watcher with a radio. We're either in Sarawak or Brunei and they had a British rajah and you all heard the lecture just like I did and if you remember any of it for God's sake speak up." It is comforting to hear someone making plans using a map.

"I remember waking up once and hearing the man say there were rhinos but no tigers in Borneo," I say.

"He said you couldn't trust the Chinese," Flournoy says.

"I thought he said you could."

"In China, not here. They hate the English and the Dutch more than the Japs."

"That Dutchman in Morotai said all the native people love the Dutch," Ashton says. "The guy who was keeping track of how many mahogany trees we cut down so he could bill the U.S.A. for them."

"That was a different lecture," I say. "That was the one about how the natives are just children. That was the guy who said if you come down in the jungle, just paint your backside green and merge with the plants."

"Well, we're not in Morotai and that's the only thing I am sure of. If we were, the Dutch would already have charged us a landing fee."

We sit and smoke and look at the river. "So what about it?" Ashton says at last.

"You're the boss," I say. Flournoy nods in agreement. He and I are evidently both born leaders.

"Okay. Here's what we're going to do. Flournoy, you and the guys in your raft try the beach. You can go fast without us. You can probably make it up there in one day. Two at the most, if I am right. Watch your step. Maybe it's better to walk at night. That raft is easy to spot, you'll have to decide after you've gone a ways if it's worth holding on to. I'd stay away from everyone . . . except the Australians. You got plenty to eat. If the Aussies aren't on Labuan . . . tough sugar for all of us. If they are, for God's sake tell them about the rest of us." He looks at me. "We'll go up the river. We couldn't carry Andy very far on land without killing him anyway. We can just hope to God we find someone up there who can help us. If you want to, Ivy, you can peel off and take the beach too. The only essential guys for the river trip are Robinson and Spur. Robby is happy to play nurse and Spur can do anything else that's needed.

"I'll stay in the junior varsity shell," I say.

"Fine. Okay let's go. It's after three."

Spurlock has washed out the raft. We put Andretta in and take a minute to divide the rations and say goodbye. We keep the aid kit, the compass, the machete and the knife. I am not sure but I think the other guys are glad to be trying it without us. Cunningham certainly seems cheerier all of a sudden and talks and talks about if "you guys make it and we don't, tell Mother I loved her." Their chances are fifty per cent better than ours and he knows it.

We shake hands with some embarrassment. "What the hell," Whitey Nanos says to each of us in turn. "Maybe a PBM will come along and land right in the river here . . . it's big enough . . . and you'll all be home eating fried horse cock in the morning, long before us."

"Take care of Andy," Cunningham tells Robinson solicitously. "He's my buddy."

"Don't worry," Robinson says fervently. "Andy will get the best care I can give him. He's my buddy too." He is thinking for two now, the little jerk.

"All Andy needs are some APC pills," Ashton says. "He has cat fever." This gets a parting laugh. Cat fever is the Navy's name for any infirmity their doctors fail to identify. "All right," Ashton says. "Tell the coxswains to cast off!"

We climb in the rafts and paddle out into the stream. They turn down and shoot away waving until a clump of mangroves slides between us.

We turn upstream and paddle against the sluggish current for a long time, rounding bend after bend, each time feeling afraid and excited at what we might see, and each time cursing the river for producing nothing. We stay near the bank where the current is less and where we can sometimes be under the shade of the huge trees that line it. It is very hot. For two hours we see nothing. Not a bird, not a crocodile, not a fish jumping.

Then we come to a place where the river has formed a sort of bayou around a mangrove island and there in the middle of the loop, sitting in a high-prowed little boat, are two boys. They are small and look like Filipinos. One of them is wearing a kind of flat turban, like a smashed-down tea cosy, on his head. We wave and shout expansively to show how friendly we, at least, feel about this meeting in the river. They watch us approach and do nothing. They are fishing.

When we are close they simply stare. Their eyes are bright but unexpressive and it is hard to tell if they are surprised or if they even realize what we are. They sit there and the sun shines like gold on their bare backs.

"Hello," Ashton says. Now the boys look at each other with half-anxious smiles. "Japanese?" Ashton says, making twirling motions to indicate a wide circumference around us. Spurlock and I paddle to hold our position. The net picture is slightly ridiculous. "Japanese *here?*" Ashton thinks by emphasizing the key word they will understand him. I stop paddling and pull up the corners of my eyes with my fingers, raising and turning my head in a pantomime of arrogance.

The youngest boy bursts out laughing. Perhaps it is a joke here too. The other boy points up the river. He looks where he is pointing, so whatever he means, it isn't far. They jabber together and then one of them pulls up a rope with a rock anchor on the end and they beckon to us and paddle up the stream.

"What do you think, Ivy?" Ashton says. This threatens to become the stock question.

"Well, we came up here to meet people. At least they aren't Japs."

"I just don't want a poison dart in my ass."

"If we don't go, what then? We can't go back down the river."

"That's right. Let's go then. Any nays?" We all shake our heads. "Okay. When they eat our livers or put our necks on the old block, I don't want to hear any screams from you guys that I was the one who got you into the big tureen."

In a few minutes we see some long-houses, built out on pilings over the water. There are half a dozen of them, different sizes, some with steep chalet roofs and some with pyramidal roofs shaped a little like a Dallas hut. Around the pilings are more of the high-prowed little boats. The boys ahead are shouting and figures appear in front of the long-houses. By the largest I see a man with a collarless white shirt and a calico turban who seems to be giving directions to all the others. He points to a place where we should come and land.

"He looks like a Chinaman," Spurlock says. "Look at the pantaloons." The man is nodding his head at us in little tremors of welcome. His face is old but there is a childish look around his mouth that belies the wrinkles.

"Just to be sure, I'll get out and you pull away a touch and wait," Ashton says.

"Shall we lie to, Captain Decatur?" I say mocking him a bit for his noble conduct.

"Maybe you should get out, Bainbridge!"

"That's okay. Junior officer stays in the boat."

"All right. But don't let them hole the ship." We fend the raft along the pilings to a point where the Chinaman is pointing, a place where a notched tree trunk goes up at an angle to the platform. Behind him is a cluster of people, women with stringy arms and hair in oiled buns, and short men in pajama tops. They peer down at us like bats hanging from the ceiling. The Chinaman bows his head and leers.

"America and Australia," he says a bit unctuously.

"America," Robinson says in a ridiculously proud way.

"America and Australia," the Chinaman repeats emphatically.

"Will you tell us where we are?" Ashton stands up and grabs the notched trunk. The rubber boat starts to slide out from under him. Spurlock paddles and I try to hold on to a slippery piling. Ashton looks like he is treading grapes for a moment and finally he has to sit down. The women up above laugh. They lean far over the edge and titter at us. We try to laugh back but it is very hard to laugh up at anyone. It isn't convincing. It must have been impossible for the Christians to laugh back effectively at Nero.

When we are steady Ashton tries again. "What is this village?" Nothing. He digs out his map and waves it. "Is this Sibuti? Sibuti?"

The Chinaman nods vigorously. "Sungai Sibuti." Ashton begins to climb. There are so many people crowded at the top that there is no room for him to step onto the platform. The Chinaman hisses at the women and complains in a high-pitched voice and they step back just a little. Ashton has to get off the notched pole on his knees and it looks for a moment as though he is going to shake hands with the Chinaman before he is erect. It looks so odd we almost laugh. White humility in a brown land.

The two boys in the boat have come close to us and sit only a few feet away staring. When we stare back they dissemble like children and pretend to be interested in something in their boat. But when I try the brutal grin and pulled eyes of the atrocity posters on them again they do it right back at me. The younger one thumbs his ears and puts his tongue in and out in time to push-button motions of his fingers on his cheeks. There is a lot of hilarious talk all around. God knows what it means. The other boy takes off his tea-cosy hat and pushes his hair up into a sort of pompom. He points at Spurlock, whose cowlick has risen like yeast from his head. We all have another good laugh.

Up on the pier I can see that Ashton is getting no place. There is a great deal of pointing, of confused head-shaking, more pointing in another direction, finally shoulder-settling to show each other they are starting all over. Meanwhile the women have noticed Andretta and are discussing him. Ashton beckons to us and we paddle close in again.

"He's just a parrot. He only knows a couple of English phrases. He doesn't respond to Brunei or Labuan the way I pronounce them but he goes crazy with joy when I say San Francisco, and points over there. I don't know. He understands we have a sick man. Let's land and get Andy out of there and into a house or in the shade. Then we can try some more."

"It would be easier if we go right into the bank with him," Spurlock says. "There's a little landing beach over there."

"All right. I'll meet you over there."

There are palms canting over a sand beach. Behind them is deep shade from some low foliage of a shiny grayish green. Huts and houses show through it as angles or roofs or the white blaze of cut timbers. From the beach we can see a path going into red mud and leading between cleared spaces and houses for a couple of hundred feet. All the houses are on poles.

The people surge down the rickety pier with Ashton in the middle. When they see that Andretta can't walk, some of the men wade in, pick the raft up out of the shallows and carry him ashore in it. We smile and hold up our hands to show we are perplexed as to where to take a sick man. The people look at the Chinaman who finally points up the path and we all start off, the Chinaman first taking short mincing steps and obliging the entire cavalcade to go at his pace. He looks at each house with a studious air of appraisal but shakes his head until at last we come to the most dilapidated of them all. It stands on six-foot stilts near the end of the path in an overgrown garden whose plants have climbed up through the rotting planks of the floor and out through the door and windows. There is water-strewn debris on the porch and in the tops of the bushes all around from floods or tides that must cover the ground here at times.

Inside the house it smells of excreta and there are silver fish scales stuck all over the walls where people have evidently wiped their hands after eating. Spurlock chops down the plant life inside with the machete and we heave the raft up and in and turn it over so Andretta can lie on the bottom. The people stand and watch us like penguins watch explorers in the Antarctic. The first thing I do is to take some bark strips from the walls and plug the numerous holes in the roof, for it is bound to rain soon in this country. I notice that even sitting on the roof I cannot see the river. This seems important because now there are people who know we are here and know what we are, and know where we are—even if we don't exactly.

About six it begins to rain. In a few minutes the pieces of bark serving as plugs pop out and fall into the room. Through the holes come streams of water the size of a garden hose. Robinson makes a bed of the cut plants and we hang the raft over it by its ropes so that Andretta can lie beneath it and stay relatively dry. The rain drives away the people but it brings after it the bugs. Mosquitoes by the thousand. We button and zip everything up tight, roll up our collars and tuck our pant legs inside our socks. But they bite through wherever the wet cloth is stretched tight against the skin. There are also nonflying things crawling around everywhere. We are still in misery when a man comes with a box full of earth and sand. He lifts the box up on the trembling floor and goes off without a meaningful look of any kind. Ashton sniffs the box delicately.

"We do it like cats," he says. "And whoever doesn't bury his nicely is a rotten sport. Listen, I'm going out to talk to Charlie Chan again, and see what he and his Dyak bloodsuckers have on their minds, if I can. You all stay here." He jumps off the porch and follows the disappearing native down the path. While he is gone a shriveled woman arrives. She has sticks and bundles of things—bananas, things like potatoes, something sticky in an iron pot that must be the famous sago. She lights brands and sticks them in cracks around the room, then she builds a fire in the box and cooks. She won't smile or even look at us, but she gets things going nicely, covers the fire a bit with sand, points at it and leaves. We wait for Ashton and when he comes back we take turns fishing in the hot sand with the knife. There is some kind of tough meat buried in there. It is wrapped in leaves and too tough for us to swallow, but the other things taste fine.

Ashton hasn't gleaned anything new except the suspicion that the Chinaman isn't as dense as his bland looks seem to show. Once or twice, he says, he thought the Chinaman understood him perfectly.

Just before the brands start to splutter and go out, an army of sand fleas attack through the floor. They come in such numbers that it is impossible to combat them. It is like swatting at a cloud of dust. They bite us and we thrash around with the brands until they go out and then we simply lie there and curse. In the middle of the night Andretta begins to scream uncontrollably. He is awake but out of his head. He gargles in his throat and his feet bang on the floor. Robinson sits beside him the entire night, talking softly to him and rubbing his arms and legs.

In the morning it rains again. We sit silent and dejected in the hideous leaking hut with the roar of rain on the jungle, dispirited from lack of sleep and the intolerable itch of insect bites. Ashton says we must keep a watch on the river and I go down first and sit under a pier in one of the boats for two hours. I try to think of something sound to suggest when I get back, but it looks to me as if we are waiting for Andretta to die or our morality to disintegrate sufficiently so that we can rationalize leaving him here with the Chinaman and his friends.

When I get back Andretta is worse. He hasn't eaten and is incoherent and in pain. Robinson is indefatigable. He has fought Andy's battles with the ticks and fleas, tried to feed him, cleaned up his mess, sat with him and talked to him the entire time. Yet instead of emerging as a heroic figure, Robinson is becoming merely a nervous fuss-budget. Andy is wet, Andy is hot. The food is too hot for Andy. Save that piece for Andy, it looks softer. I begin to frame savage replies in my mind to whatever Robinson says. But I keep my temper. I know what a job he is doing and I want him to keep on.

Ashton has brought the Chinaman to see Andretta, to emphasize how critical our situation is. But not even by pantomime can we get over the idea of "doctor" or "help" or "Englishman." He remains as obdurately stupid as ever. I can't decide whether it is deliberate or if he is just the inscrutable Oriental and does not feel the urgent need of shot-down Americans with a dying man among them to get home. He doesn't say go up the river and he doesn't say go down. But his villagers have become rather definite about things. It is evident they want us to give them something— the raft and the machete. The men openly begin to finger things. When I go out to cut some sticks, one of them touches the machete and taps his chest. Their grinning brashness becomes open greed in the afternoon. The boys shoulder each other out of the way to walk close to me when I go again for my stint of watching the river. Now their faces seem cruel and almost lifeless in their intentness. They squat beside me and study me and discuss me among themselves without the faintest trace of the shyness they showed yesterday.

When I get back this time Robinson is terribly upset. While he slipped out to go do something in the woods, somebody robbed Andretta. They took his few cigarettes, and tore the dog tags and scapular from his neck with such violence that they cut the skin. And they cut down the raft and took it. The rest of us are wearing everything we own, so there was nothing else to steal.

Ashton and Spurlock are out scouting. I am afraid to go down alone and raise hell but I realize that we have to show the flag. I stride down the path, scowling, to find the Chinaman, but when I am halfway there I hear the sound of airplanes. I run toward the river, the only open place to see anything, and am just in time to see three American PV's pass over at treetop height.

They are from the island and I can see that the rockets are gone from under the wings. I get a glimpse of their white bellies and squat bodies with the vent behind, like a carp, where the two thirties stick out, and their noses bristling with the packaged fifties, and they are gone. In five minutes they will pass the big green headland that we could see yesterday to the north. It may take us five days to get there.

The sight of the airplanes has so geared me to flying again that I visualize the monotony of the trail ahead of me. I'll never be able to do it. None of us will. We will just become cumulatively more frightened of our situation, more restless, more bored with the harassment of insects and with Robinson cooing and clucking to Andretta all night.

Oddly enough the place I most want to get to is the squadron. Not home to Corinne or America. I don't even like to think of my mother who will soon be spending hours on her knees. Those rasping prayers of hers for me are sure to be spiked with malevolence for someone else. I wonder if they have told Corinne I am missing. Perhaps they wait a week or two. It is dreadful to think of all those unnegotiable convictions at home, just waiting on the news. My mother will now have to place me. Heaven Bound or Not? She will have to preside at one more culling, like an archangel with drawn sword, perhaps dispatching horrid demons to seize the garments of her son and drag him offstage to flames and torments, like a Renaissance fresco but not as universal. Not the Blessed and the Condemned. Not even the Baptists and the Others. When The Goodman appears on the wall and speaks and reminds my mother that Carl hasn't sent the money for her teeth . . .

My resolve to find the Chinaman and have a showdown has melted. In a rain forest in Borneo the realities are so different. The popular cause is simply life and the reigning prejudice is death. Words are dust and without them we shall probably all find out what kind of men we are.

Ashton and Spurlock are back and have seen the airplanes and belatedly hung a skivvy shirt on a pole over our hut. I suggest putting our yellow Mae Wests on the roof. They are under Andretta's head. I wait tensely for a nanny objection from Robinson, determined to lay down some basic social precepts about the good of all and the commonwealth, but he doesn't say a thing. I go up and spread them out and sprinkle dye marker around on the thatch.

Andretta is nearly comatose, his eyes dull, his breathing so shallow we can hardly hear it. But Robinson insists he is better and that he is "healing inside." Ashton examines him every two or three hours, not because he thinks he can do anything, but because Andretta seems to like it. Ashton has a real bedside manner as he feels the pulse, kneads the stomach and pinches Andretta's legs in places where he claims he can feel nothing. But I notice he feels and pinpoints the two-inch leech that has fastened to the back of his knee. I burn it with a match and when it lets go I roll it through a crack in the floor.

We talk about borrowing a boat and going up the river in the morning, but it seems unlikely that after the business today we can get one. Ashton says it is useless to try to explore on foot along the river but he thinks we might try it straight inland. Maybe the country opens up when it gets drier. Spurlock has tied the knife to a long stick and goes off to watch the river and try to spear us a fish. At least he has imagination. Ashton sits and contemplates his responsibility in bleak silence, I brood almost methodically, Robinson reads the first-aid book from the kit when there is nothing to do for Andretta.

Spurlock has only been gone for a half hour when he comes trotting up the path again. "I hear a motor . . . a boat. Listen!" He stands below us with a finger cocked. I can't hear anything. "Come down by the water!" Spurlock says starting off. We jump off into the mud and run after him. There is no one in sight on the path or at the main pier and we go out on the end of the rickety structure and stand still, listening again.

From downstream comes the faint but certain putter of a gas engine. Implicit in the sound is the suggestion of great power not in use. It is the sound made by a powerful launch or torpedo boat, with the motor idling.

"You know what they say. Anything with power is Japanese!" Spurlock says.

"Listen!" Ashton cocks his head. The sound of the motor comes in intermittent putts as though the exhaust were being submerged in water every few seconds. "It's under way."

"Why would anyone come up this creek?" I say. My fear speaks, not my logic.

"Because someone told them what they would find," Ashton says. He points to the little beach behind us. The Chinaman and some of the village men are there. One of them is the one who coveted the machete, a gnarled little bastard with muscles popping out of his skin. They are watching us. "Come on," Ashton says.

Trying to appear very casual we walk back to the bank and pick our way down to where the Chinaman is standing. Ashton points downstream and cups his hand to his ear. "Japanese?" A forlorn look comes into the Chinaman's eyes. But it isn't quite the same old incomprehension. It changes to worried concentration when Spurlock moves close to him and plants the stick with the knife lashed to it almost on the Chinaman's toes. Then he smiles suddenly at us and in one second is the grandfather of all Oriental knaves. He spreads his hands, flexing them helplessly like a dying chicken's feet, and scratches the sides of his fingers with his long bony thumbs.

"Is it the Japs?" Spurlock says loudly, leaning close to him. "No one around here has a power boat, do they?" The Chinaman flutters his fingers some more but he has control now. He turns to the other men as though seeking some confirmation from them that he doesn't understand and can't speak.

"You son of a bitch," Ashton says. "I think you're selling us. If I were sure I'd drown you in the river!" We stand and look them all up and down from head to foot as though somewhere we will find an area of truth. I feel reckless and somehow powerfully competent. I tap the gnarled little man on the chest.

"You, you little fucker, you're in on it too!" He looks hurt and mildly annoyed.

"Come on, let's get out of here!" Ashton says. We start for the path and the Chinaman begins to talk. He says more English words in one sentence than he has said since we arrived. "You friend sick. Need doctor. Marudi have doctor. Bintulu have doctor. Tomorrow we find."

Ashton stops and stares back at him. At that moment the boat comes around the bend, two hundred yards downstream. It is a Japanese patrol boat, the kind we have often seen, covered from bow to stern with palm fronds and stalks of cane. There are vines wrapped around the barrel of the gun forward. The boat goes very slowly and it has learned to move like this, a drifting island of plants, because of the American airplanes that pass over it every day by the dozens.

"Someday you bastard . . ." We run, bulling our way up the path like people in a jungle movie. Bruce Cabot in *Terror in Tobango*. We get to the hut and already we are weak-legged and panting. I lean against the poles feeling as if I have just risen from a sickbed. "Now what? What do we do with Andretta? If we lug him we can't make it for sure."

Robinson is above me on the porch. "I'm not gonna leave him." His face has a petulant look like a child's. "If you want to go, go, but I'm not gonna leave Andy."

"Oh for Christ sake, Robinson, we won't leave him!"

"We can carry him a ways and hide him real good," Spurlock says. "Then we can come back and pick him up again."

"There's no choice. Help me get him, you guys." Ashton is already up. He and Robinson hand Andretta down. We each take him by an arm or a leg and trot off down the path heading inland. I have been a little way down it and know it ends soon at a big marshy savannah of coarse cogon grass.

We reach the savannah and start across. Our feet sink into the spongy green ground and it is all resistance, the weight, the clawing grass, the ground that tries to swallow our feet. Soon the trees close in again. A swarm of bugs swirls around our heads moving with us. Two kingfishers make loud and persistent cries above us, flitting just ahead of us through the trees and showing over and over again just how startled they are to see four downed

American airmen carrying a fifth downed American airman, right here in Borneo. "Remind me," Ashton says gasping, "to devote the rest of my life to shooting birds of all kinds."

We stop and rest at the edge of a little meadow of cogon grass. Behind us our tracks show as black breaks in the soft green. "It's like following four million buffalo," I say. "But what the hell can we do?"

"Stay ahead of them until it gets dark," Ashton says. "At least they'll have more trouble doing it with flashlights." I try to imagine the pursuit. All I can think of are shrill whistles, shouts, lights probing wet corners for the criminals who are slithering here and there trying to keep one last angle between their shivering bodies and the law's accounting. How I long for the hue and cry and the dreadful pomp with which Anglo-Saxons harry fugitives! Behind us are small, silent, powerfully built brown men, perhaps even now trotting noiselessly through the jungle with grass stuffed in their helmet covers. I wish Monty Herbert were here to prove conclusively once more that the American fighting man has no equal in the world, and to trace again that fatal flaw of the warrior peoples—their empty spirituality!

We go on for another two hours. Before it is too dark we find a hill with a grove of trees and under the trees thick beds of ferns in which we bury Andretta and Robinson to the ears. We reckon we have come six or seven miles from the village and have been heading northwest most of the time. The coast cannot be far away. Tomorrow we will strike due west until we reach it. Our best chance will be flagging a Dumbo plane from the beach, now, because without the raft we can no longer travel by water and we cannot carry Andretta up and over that big headland. We squat a few yards away and smoke a cigarette and slap at the mosquitoes. A pale wafer of moon is in the west. There are sounds everywhere but we quickly develop an ear for them —birds moving in trees, small animal cries, a roar like a distant waterfall from the insects.

I backtrack a little way and sit down to watch our trail while the others hide in the ferns. I have been there perhaps ten

minutes when Andretta screams. There is no mistaking his voice.
It is the same thing as last night. He screams in shuddering
blasts of sound as though pumped by a bellows. But he stops
abruptly. I fancy I hear Robinson talking softly to him, and let
my head sink back on my forearms. The glandular fear slowly subsides. I long for another smoke but can't strike a match now. A
mosquito whines viciously by my ear. I will let him land and then
smash his guts out . . .

The laugh seems to bubble with good humor. It rises and falls,
stifled and choked and then all at once clear and relaxed. It
comes from behind me, just to the left of the grove of trees.

For a moment I think it is Andretta but the laugh is moving
along the base of the little hill, a controlled titter, like a birdcall
—ho-hee-hee-hee-ho-hee-hee-hee. At the end it suddenly acquires
a human tonality again.

I can't move. I can't even turn my head toward the sound. I
am like a child lying paralyzed in bed after going to the forbidden
horror movie. Bela Lugosi is behind the curtains and I can't even
turn over to face him.

"Yankee, Yankee, oh Yankee!" a voice says distinctly not thirty
feet from me. Then there are yells and men ripping through the
ferns all around, and the glare of a flashlight. I get up and run,
slamming into trees and falling in the creepers, certain that each
time before I can struggle to my feet a body will pin me from
behind and I will feel a knife in my back or a thin loop of wire
around my neck.

I run through the sickening smells and the noisy black world
toward the only thing I can see, the pale moon low in the sky,
seeming to dance just out of reach, flickering as the black bars of
trees pass over its face. I run until I am exhausted and then I
walk. I keep going the whole night toward the west. I can do this,
because when I come out in a clear space, I can see the big
headland to the north in the moonlight and guide myself by it.
When it is first light I lie down to rest but almost immediately
some white ants find me and I go on, not stopping now until I
see a loop of shoreline through the trees and feel the first feeble

sea air moving through the sweet stink of the forest. Just as the sun comes up I stagger out onto a small crescent beach. That is the end. I flop in the sand.

When I wake the sun is high up, baking me in the sand like a suckling pig. My head aches terribly and I have pains in my chest from running so hard. I don't know what the hell to do. If the others got away, possibly they made it over to the coast and we will meet. If they didn't, I can wait here forever for them.

My clothing annoys me. It is tight and wet and abrasive and I take everything off. My flying suit is caked with blood and dirt. I have scratched my face and neck, cut my head open, twisted a knee and rammed thorns and splinters into my hands by the dozen. But my six Raleighs and the Zippo are still there in a knee pocket. I take them out, put them carefully in my shoes, and carry my clothes into the water. It is shallow and warm as soup and stings my cuts like fury. It is so warm I keep right on sweating in the water. After a while I scrub the flying suit with sand, rinse it and spread it on a rock to dry.

I sit on my beach and smoke a Raleigh. Last night already seems ages ago. I am not worried or lonesome, and in fact if I am utterly honest about it, I am relieved to be away from the others and on my own. I refuse to think about them and whether they are dead or captured.

After a while I look myself over for ticks and leeches, put on my clothes and start off north. My knee hurts but the going is easy, at first a series of shallow bays, and then after a while some long points of land which I must climb. I swim across three narrow rivers, holding my Raleighs in my teeth, and stop only long enough to wring out my wool socks after each crossing. My father was right. My feet are the only things that don't hurt.

Sometime around noon I stop long enough to bash in a coconut with rocks. It is not as neat as Spurlock's method but it works. In a spirit of argosy that would have made the Bishop Museum proud of me I eat some snails that I find in the shallows. They have a core of flesh a little like a scallop but are very bloody. I feel very resourceful eating the snails and cracking coconuts and

I am almost beginning to enjoy myself and the exercise of my huge talents. I hardly think about the others, and feel only my own legend growing richer. I am a born castaway, I tell myself dreamily, adroit, tough, clever. Wait until Yokum hears. He'll collapse. Inspired, I make myself a sunshade by plaiting two banana leaves together. It looks like a canoe but fits my head beautifully and even hangs down far enough to shield the upper part of my spine, which as every adventurer in the tropics knows, is to be protected from sunstroke at all costs.

I come to a deep bay. Far to the right I can see a river flowing into it. Halfway across the bay is the wreck of a ship. It is a long swim, but I can rest on the wreck for a while on the way over. Something about it is strangely familiar. I think back to Morotai days, when we used to fly around the north end of Borneo and down the east coast, dropping propaganda leaflets. Sandakan, Jesselton, Bintulu. Suddenly I know the place. That wreck is the famous decoy ship that killed Hank Cowap from 420. It was loaded with dynamite and someone detonated it from the shore just as he flew over it on a bombing run. Hank and his crew lie entombed in the silt right over there beyond the charred ribs of the wreck.

Getting home from here seems inevitable and I am at once excited. Still I can't recall the name of the place, or exactly where it is in relation to Brunei. Never mind, I am filled with sentiment for it and name it Albert Lea Bay. Someday I will come back here and open a little restaurant and bar with a menu that features Colonel Lea Burgers, and has written at the top inside quotation marks, "May we suggest a cocktail?" like my father had when I was in high school.

I am impatient to go but I must be a little wacky from the sun or something, and feel like a drunk trying to sneak into the house without being heard, when I see some people sitting in a proa fishing near the river mouth, and others doing something in a field beyond. I am quite weak and it's a good third of a mile to the wreck, but thank God this is Borneo and not Novaya Zemlya or some horrible place where the water is freezing cold. On the

Murmansk run they say you last about thirty seconds in the water. Then you turn blue. I figure I can stay in this water about an hour before I turn red.

Off with the clothes again. The cigarettes are a problem. I put the butts on the top of my head and anchor them down with a shoelace tied under my chin. With the other lace I tie everything else together so I can tow it as one bundle. I walk out into the water. After a hundred yards I am still only waist deep. It is just as the bottom begins to shelve steeply that I hear the airplane behind me.

It is a Liberator, a blue one, coming right up the shore at a couple of hundred feet. I have no time to run out of the water but I quickly rip my skivvy shirt and my blue-and-white-striped shorts out of the bundle and flap them like a madman. I even yell, and start back for the shore making a wake like a destroyer in my haste.

The airplane dips and turns to avoid the wreck, going out over the bay and then circling back very low. I jump up and down like a jack-in-the-box waving my underwear at it. Now it comes by me very close. I can see the nose emblem. A naked drum majorette. It is *Sioux City Sue*, Ironhead's airplane, and they have seen me. He wiggles the wings and the man in the waist hatch makes a quick fighter's handshake signal as they pass.

They come around again and begin to drop me things. Rations, two canteens, a thermos that unfortunately hits the beach and breaks, throwing coffee all over the sand. I stay in the shallows where the things won't bust so easily, and when I retrieve something I hold it up and rub my stomach to express my joy. Last of all a note comes down fluttering in front of a weighted streamer. "Dumbo estimated at fifteen thirty. Are you okay? Are there any others? We will stay here until they arrive."

I have no idea how long it is until fifteen thirty. When they come around again I shrug my shoulders and hold out my hands with the palms up. I point inland, and shrug some more.

After a long time another note comes down in an empty Coke bottle. "The PBM will be here in twenty minutes. We are low on gas. Don't worry. See you tonight. The Captain." I wave to show them I haven't a care in the world and they go off to the north, wiggling wings to show me everything is going to be great from now on.

I sit and eat and wait for the PBM which in my opinion takes a lot longer than twenty minutes to arrive. I have begun to worry by the time it finally shows up, and then I am afraid that the pilot has confused directions because he seems to be hunting for me on the other side of the bay. But at last he lands and comes ticking slowly in toward me. Once he strikes the bottom and there is a lot of gunning of engines to get off. Finally they have to row in a rubber boat to get me.

Tom Parker is on board and gives me a huge slug of brandy. I lie in a bunk on a fat mattress and he fixes me up with a bandage skullcap and lots of tape to make me look more heroic. We spend two hours sweeping up and down the coast and I go up on the flight deck and try to find the place where I came out of the forest. I am not sure, nothing looks the same. I finally count three rivers and after the third we turn and fly inland but there is nothing to see but the tops of the rain forest and here and there a savannah. No villages and no patrol boat. It can't have been more than five miles inland. The pilot says they will cover the whole beat again with several airplanes tomorrow.

It is two more days before we hear from all the rest of them. Flournoy and his group have been hiding near Brunei and finally make contact with the Australians. They have to wait a day or two to be flown out. They have had no troubles at all except with Cunningham whom they caught stealing extra rations at night.

Ashton and Spurlock make it to Brunei too. On the way, quite by accident, they pick up Robinson. They work their way out onto the point that encloses Brunei Bay. Just across the water is Labuan and there is smoke rising from it in great columns, proving that Australians have at least landed there. At sunset Spurlock spots what they are sure is a patrol of Jap soldiers on a ridge. The soldiers come right down toward them and there is nothing to do but run. The soldiers fire at them with auto rifles, and Spur is killed instantly with seven bullets in him. Ashton is hit in the knee in a very bad way. Only Robinson is untouched. The soldiers are Australians. They thought they were shooting at Japs.

Robinson remains the hero of the day. When we all ran he stayed behind with Andretta. A man jumped on him and Robinson is sure that it was one of the villagers. He stabbed the man with our knife, which luckily he was carrying, and the man ran off. Robinson says he thought he saw one Jap, possibly an officer, searching around with a flashlight. He was hiding only twenty yards away when they found Andretta. They did dreadful things to him, put out his eyes and slit his cheeks and pulled his scalp down over his ears and a lot more, and yet when they left him he was still alive. Robinson gave him all the morphine in the kit, nine Syrettes, and sat with him until he died. Then he dug a grave with the knife and buried him. He said all the prayers he knew but he didn't dare put a cross on the grave for fear the villagers would dig him up, and maybe drag him around behind a carabao the way the Filipinos like to do with dead Japs.

As Robinson was walking along a day later he heard someone call to him. He started to run and then he realized that anyone who knew his name must be a friend. It was Spurlock.

"All I want to do in this world," Robinson says, grinding his jaws and wiping away the tears that roll down his face with his forearm, "is go back there with some napalm. That's all I ever want to do."

Ashton is flown out via Hollandia and I don't see him again. The others get orders to leave, but there are none yet for me. Before they go we have one drunken evening together on my whisky, but it isn't much fun. We miss Spurlock and Ashton too much. Everyone is still down on Cunningham and he doesn't join us.

Spurlock is brought back to the island and we bury him in the new part of the graveyard. The original cemetery was laid out to accommodate the hundred P.O.W.'s the Japs murdered, but since then it has been taking in aviators at such a rate that there is now no room left. Spurlock is the ninety-sixth airman.

Hartstene and Nanos and Zalewski and I hold the flag corners for Spur. At least he is all there and not one of those ham-sized bundles we stick in here so often. Spur looks big and strong inside the poncho, only I wish they hadn't done him up with cord. He will be lying under a correct marker, which isn't always the case after a hundred-octane gasoline fire. And he is under a tree, a nice one resembling an oak, with thick branches twisting up toward the sky. They have stacked his cross with a lot of others against the base of the tree and leaned three shovels on it, but we take his out and Robinson holds it during the ceremony.

Ironhead and I have on our real Navy caps and the whole squadron is turned out. The Army Engineers supply a chaplain, a bugler, and a firing squad who are even dressed in leggings. The three volleys are a bit ragged and Whitey Nanos drops his corner of the flag once. The four of us cry unashamedly.

Afterward I borrow Ironhead's jeep and Hartstene and Zalewski go with me down to the village where we pick a huge bouquet of flowers from the abandoned gardens. We smooth the dirt around the cross and pile flowers and ferns around it—white camellias, cornflowers, and some big pale red things that someone insists are frangipani. I don't know.

Spurlock. The Navy Department regrets to inform you . . . on the eighteenth of May in forty-five . . . When we go through his stuff I learn for the first time that his father is a minister. I wonder if he will take the death of his son with the resignation proper to a man of his calling. I wonder if he will nod humbly toward justice drowsing on her rotten seat. Thy will be done.

I wouldn't. The whole thing is just one big putrid gyp, from beginning to end.

CHAPTER ELEVEN

"Do not plan for my return.
They have burned everything above the ground."

THE SKY is falling! Chicken Little is going home! Ironhead, who has come to see me every morning since I got back, is going to tell the mighty Seventh that Carl Iverson has had enough. They will send me some orders, perhaps inside of four days!

It means one sad thing only. I won't see Yokum and Roger. They are up at Lingayen, with their own crews at last, pursuing the battleship fiasco to its bitter and ridiculous end. The Jap ships have been at sea nearly a week now, running the gantlet of submarines, airplanes, cruisers—and the enthusiastic if pinprick attacks of a Blue Raider or two—without being touched. Very soon they will be in the Inland Sea and that will be that.

The entire thing is a gloomy story of service jealousies that no sane person would believe. The Wing has refused to pass on their sightings to the Army, who have been attempting to hit the ships from high level. The subs remain mute, presumably reluctant to share any kill. 420 has told us practically nothing that would help us, although we have alternated with them in trying to shadow the fleet for eight days and nights. 400 has lost twenty-two men on this job and 420 one man. The odd fellow is a third-class mech in Cap Ahab's band of pistoleros who was killed by flak from a sharpshooting Jap DD when Ahab ventured

too close as the ships were passing Hainan. The single bright note
is that Frank Ainsworth made it! He and his crew have been heard
from passing through Karachi on their way home. Presumably
Beppo has long since quenched his indefatigable Latin ardor in
the arms of his indefatigable Latin *fidanzata*.

The Wing, goaded by Ironhead, has put CAC 13 up for a few
gongs. Ashton will get the Navy Cross, if all goes well, and
Robinson and I each a Silver Star, mine presumably for winning
the sprints at what has become known as the Battle of Bull
Run. (What did you do? I ran!) Spurlock and Andretta will get
posthumous Purple Hearts, of course, and everyone else Bronze
Stars, including the two dead men. It is useless to point out how
silly this is. Robinson should probably have a Congressional and
I should be drummed out of the Navy. Spurlock deserves what
they want to give me. But Spur is dead, I dislike Robinson as
much as ever, and I want a Silver Star as much as anyone. It
is being awarded ostensibly because we stuck with Bartlett
all the way to the finish, anyway, and though I had no choice
about that, there is not such a discrepancy between the way I
can conscientiously tell about that part and the way I can
conscientiously tell about the Battle of Bull Run.

Ironhead tells me it wasn't just accident that he found me.
Our command set died slowly and issued loud if meaningless
sounds for some time after Andretta had decided the output was
through. He was smart enough to screw his key down, and long
dashes of sound on CW made their way to the base, proving
someone was still flying as late as eight o'clock that morning.
Ironhead scoured the Borneo coast from Kuching to Kudat that
whole day but of course we hadn't landed yet. He came back
every day and on the fourth try found me.

There is a short memorial service for Andretta in the Engineers'
chapel, and ironically I go straight from the chaplain's appeals
for peace and mercy in this world to an interview with an Englishman, who has been fetched here from somewhere to try to identify
the village where we were betrayed. He lived in Brunei for
thirty years and knows every inch of what he terms "the avail-

able country." With his good maps and photos it isn't hard to locate the village, and the same morning Engelson sends six of his PV's down to convert the Chinaman to our way of life. They are perhaps the most heavily armed airplanes in the world, with rockets, packaged nose fifties, napalm and bombs, and they annihilate the place. I sort of hope the boy in the tea-cosy hat and his friend were down fishing at the bayou when the airplanes came.

And then it comes, on gray, strangely pigmented paper with a new whorly "CI" embossed in an upper corner. I know intuitively what it is and carry it away to the bushes with me like a nervous pack rat. Each word pulls me apart nerve by nerve. He isn't a floorwalker, he is a boy that used to be in a philosophy class of mine at Madison, and was fond of quoting Montaigne. Handsome, rich, vain, sincere.

Corinne despises herself for letting it happen. He despises himself. They know I despise them. She knows I despise him even more because he has been deferred to work in his father's machine-tool plant. Sometimes, she admits, this bothers her too. She doesn't want to divorce me while I am overseas, that would be too callous and gross a thing to do. But she wants me to know that they have been having an affair since the first of April, that she loves him, that she wants to marry him. The words trail off like vengeful bees leaving their victim. They just seemed to fall into it, neither of them meant to do anything wrong, someone to talk to, her mother is furious, one of those terrible things . . .

At least there isn't a hoary quote about anyone can fire the gun, it takes courage to stay out of uniform and work where you are really needed. At least there is nothing about the surprise baby coming, the proverbial joke about the proverbial Seabee's wife.

Ironhead comes to visit as usual and catches me in my sack. It seems I now spend a tenth of my life in tears, and he is always around to dry them. He thinks of course I am upset about leaving or about the others leaving. He sits on the edge of the cot and pretends to examine my scratches, a daily rite with

him. They wander spectacularly all over my neck and chest in
long dotted lines of coagulated red. I am burned a dirty, dusty
black by the sun, my hair is bleached white and streaked with
old yellow and grows down to the cervical vertebra, I have lost
twenty pounds . . . Ironhead clucks like a kindly old prior.

"You are about the most disreputable-looking Naval officer I
have ever seen," he says. "And I'm going to get you out of here
fast before you demoralize the whole squadron. So buck up. It's
only a matter of two or three days."

"It isn't that. I don't want to go now, Captain. I want to wait
for Yokum and Roger Smith."

"Come again?"

"Look, I was crying because . . . I got bad news. If it's still
possible I'd like to finish my tour and go home with Roger and
Yoke. We've been together from the start, I want to finish
together."

"I know you have," Ironhead says musingly. "I know, I remember when you arrived. McCord called you 'laddy buck.' None
of you liked it."

We stare at the ground and I make a little sniffing noise to
show him I remember too the funny part of it. "Tuck can go.
He's ahead of me anyway," I say.

"Tuck hasn't been through what you just have. Look here, it's
turned your hair practically white, like mine." We smile but
there is another awkward pause. He doesn't want to ask.

"It's my wife, Captain. She's leaving me."

"No!"

I nod. Sniffing once or twice, I tell him about the new guy.

Ironhead sits there a long time. He doesn't curse the frailty
of women, or swear at random as do so many male sympathizers.
He doesn't really commiserate with me. But he talks, very softly,
and tells me a story, *the* story, about himself and about his wife,
the infamous Eileen. He is of course trying to ease my despair,
to banish the imagined tribulations of ridicule in store for me.
But it is more. He is hungry to expose himself and his own pain.

It all comes out—Eileen's first marriage, their little girl, Wendie,
the day Ironhead found Eileen's stud book hidden in the closet

in Wendie's room. He is amused by one thing. What will happen
in the next world when it comes time for dear ones to meet each
other at heaven's threshold and pair off again? Who will get
Eileen? Whoever keeps the celestial register is going to have a
hell of a time with the overlays in Eileen's case.

"She is nobody's darlin' but everybody's." Ironhead says sadly.
He stands up and shakes one leg to get the needles out of it.
"You know if I sit on the head for more than three minutes I
can't get up? My legs are sound asleep. I guess my circulation is
bad. There's one thing, if I'm ever bitten by a snake all I have
to do is go to the head and sit down to cut off the poison."

Outside a truck moans, coming over the bumpy road from the
field in second. Unconsciously we both tilt our heads to listen
to it. It waddles along, flattening the dust drifts with its lumpy
tires and rocking like a top heavy coach. The palings clatter as
it crosses the burnished corduroy of the culvert by the Wing
Quonset, raising a dust cloud that will settle gently on the scum-
laden surfaces of the three washing drums by the mess shack door.
It is the mail truck. We listen and we know it brings nothing for
us, however the brakes may squeal and the horn may blow,
however loud the cheers.

Ironhead claps me on the back and is gone. I get up and blow
my nose and hobble around the tent looking for Roger's whisky.
Perhaps Ironhead has helped. I feel a little harder. Damn her
to hell anyway, I'll fix her. A mean guy like me! I may even cut
off her allotment!

Two evenings later Tuckerman goes home. We have so little
to say. He tells me to take it easy, hear? I tell him to say hello
to Charlene if she is still at the Passion Pit, and finish with the
hackneyed caution about wearing his goggles there, because the
foul exhalations of lust from the Naval aviators who frequent the
pit can cause blindness. Our eyes water. We stand in the dust
and look at everything but each other. Nearby the new guys are
already singing "It's the foam on the neck of the bottle, that's
draggin' me down to my grave." The voices sound so ambitious,
so arrogant, so undepleted. Tuck shakes his head.

"Pretty sad, huh?" He stares at me quickly.

"Pathetic."

"Take care now."

"You too, Tuck." He is gone.

Kirby Stevens' replacement is named Lester and—oh death where is thy sting-a-ling-a-ling?—of course, "Jeeter." Two crews are assigned to temporary duty up on Mindoro and Lester sends me with one of them and Neely with the other. We are given the crews of two of the j.g. replacements who have come out after twenty-five years of training at Olathe and Kearney Mesa and Kaneohe. Unfortunately the j.g.'s go with the crews as copilots. Mine is named Ludwig. He is twenty-one or -two, short and plump, and given to wearing dark glasses even indoors. Naturally he resents my taking over and hides it very badly. He tells me he hopes the crew will "work" for me as hard as they have for him. Jesus! All de crewmen am a weepin', massah's in de copilot chair!

Ludwig has done a three-month tour somewhere in P-boats and claims to have belonged to a squadron that sank several submarines. He is full of sea stories. In two nights I have heard about twenty of them and gained the certain knowledge, by sea-man's intuition, that Ludwig wasn't a participant in any of them.

It is unbearably lonely, there are only half a dozen crews here flying two sectors, and only a skeleton base organization. There isn't even a movie except five miles away at the P-38 diggings. I sit in the evenings with Neely and we watch his copilot, who is really sick, building something called a Sikorsky Grand, an airplane, he tells us, designed in 1913. He has blueprint copies of the original design and is cutting all the pieces to scale. Neely and I find it inexcusable to be so interested in aviation. After a few nights of this we become desperate and even go down to the village of San José where there is no electric light and the eternal bug-picking on the veranda goes on by kerosene lamp.

The flights are easy, only ten hours long and in daylight, and always to the China coast. We leave at first light and are back by two or three. Every fourth day the Fat Cat comes with mail and supplies, none of which interests me much any more. I get a letter from Ashton who is at the Naval Hospital at Corona. He has a mahogany bed—it was once a luxury hotel—and there is a lake with geese and ducks outside his window. Every night he and the other non-ambulatory cases, most of whom are marines, are rolled to the movies on trolleys. "Don't ridicule the brave folks at home who have found time during a swing-shift dance to tack one of your flying tree-houses together," Ashton says. "We don't know what hardship is. Thank your lucky stars you were not at the bombardment of Santa Barbara. You think the shelling of Mindoro was something? Santa Barbara was sheer, unmitigated, sulphurous, implacable hell! Ask anyone.

"I had not yet recovered my self-respect from the Borneo affair, when Robinson and Cunningham came to see me, Cunningham sporting a Pacific Theater ribbon with so many stars that it looked as though it got in the way of a riveting machine. They said that Zalewski and Nanos and Hartstene got into trouble in Honolulu. They were all at the Royal Hawaiian for a week and they got drunk, got in a fight, stole a Coast Guard commander's car, wrecked it over near Eva, fought with the marines, punched an officer and were chucked in the brig. Where they still are, I guess. My God! Didn't they get enough? Robinson presumably had a steak at P. Y. Chong's and went home to play with himself. But what can I say? How about *that* kid? Do you feel as big a yellow belly as I? Bigger? Good. My own feeling was based on precedent—if we were to fight we were too few, and if to die, too many!"

Bigger is right. I haven't once tried to make anyone collapse over that episode!

My first trip is to Swatow and I spend about half of it going and coming through a freak cold front that gives me the shakes that won't quit. It is one of the most violent pieces of weather I have ever been in, the same old chute-the-chutes, up to twelve thousand, pitching and snapping, and down to two hundred again, coffee cups, cigarettes, canteens glued to the overhead. In a harbor I can't identify in the mist and rain, but which I assume

is Swatow, or at least Amoy, I fly around under the ceiling of
scud at three hundred feet. The water is rough from the wind
and there are hundreds of junks sheltering inside. Ludwig the
U-boat killer, who hasn't had much to say in the up and down
drafts, comes to life like a Pennsylvania deer hunter, frantic to
fire at everything. I explain to him that the junks are Chinese and
hence allies of ours.

We root around for something more appropriate and finally
spot a powerboat wallowing across the harbor with water smash-
ing over its bows. This is *of course* the Jap harbormaster, and he
is *of course* unpopular here because he is forever collecting
exorbitant mooring fees in the name of Greater East Asian Co-
prosperity. We go after him.

I miss him with a G.P. from ten feet but the blast nearly flips
the boat over anyway. When he recovers he is turned around
and goes plowing off in the opposite direction. The shooting is
so bad from the bow and crown that even Ludwig razzes the
gunners. I see about two tracers actually connect with the cabin.

I turn but lose the boat in the drizzle. Then I lose myself in
the harbor. I go round and round but not once do I see anything
familiar or pass the same place twice. This is a feeling I have
had so often in flying that I don't even fret about it. I will simply
drone around till the time is up and then climb up and head for
home. It is hard to get lost over the ocean. If you go in the
right direction and what you are looking for is bigger than an
acre, it is far easier to find than a point on land because the
water around it eliminates all false signs and appearances. What
you finally see, after miles of water, has to be what you are looking
for.

But now I spot a Sugar Dog, trying to nose in between two
junks in a long row. It has heard or seen us and is trying to hide.
It will be difficult to hit it without harming the junks but—perhaps because of Ludwig—I am determined to get it. I tell
everyone not to shoot, put down the flaps, and come in from
the stern in a delicate gliding approach. Shades of Tommy Prime,
only I miss. The bomb throws water over the deck but does no

damage. I try again from the beam. This run takes us over fifteen or twenty junks, moored together, at masthead height. We can see the crews on them running around and gesticulating at us. The closer they are to the Sugar Dog, the more excited they are.

I squint through the mist, push the yoke forward and squeeze the pickle—and lob a bomb right into the side of the Sugar Dog, neat as you please. In a minute it rolls on its side and sinks. The crew doesn't even get wet as they scramble over onto the junks.

Ludwig is overwhelmed and the crew is so inspired that when we catch the powerboat again on the way out, they strafe it until it falls apart and sinks. Going through the cold front we hit hail that strips paint off portions of the hull and makes the most frightening noise I have ever heard inside an airplane.

That evening the story of my neat surgery among the junks is recounted and there is a moment's danger that one of the big cowards of the Pacific will start becoming a legend to these simple transfers from the Atlantic Fleet, and even to himself, but luckily the next afternoon Roger stops on his way home from Lingayen and sets everyone straight. He spends the night and tells us all the news, some of which is shocking.

The final total loss on the battleship business is forty-three men. 420 lost two crews in the last days, one of them Herb Millar's, simply because they went too close. There were no more fighters after Singapore.

"Two subs claimed hits," Roger says. "The Army dropped from fifteen thousand through an overcast, so of course they couldn't miss. The cruisers gave them hell, you know those cruisers! Funny thing. Two Ise-class BB's were seen only yesterday tied up at Mitajuri."

"Dummies," I say. "Those ships were sunk, destroyed, bombed to Hades."

"Blasted into oblivion," Roger says. "Consigned to Davy Jones' Locker, man."

So much for Engelson's "project."

Ironhead has gone to Kaneohe and not come back, Roger has heard, and Lester will be given the squadron, which is filling up

with friends of his. They are all terrible liars and wear jackets
with incredible things painted on them and the squadron number
the size of football numerals. They have fancy green nylon flying
suits with zippers every inch. Roger says they will go anywhere,
now that there is no place left to go, and are inventing the most
fantastic stories of sightings and even sinkings. Everyone is out
for extra hops because the word is through that the D.F.C. and
Air Medal are going to be awarded on the debased Army system,
that is, on the number of missions. Perhaps the Eighth Air Force
can earn it that way, but we shouldn't. Kirby will get two or
three D.F.C.'s now, and he never did anything but keep track of
the beer and make out the schedule.

Neely takes a pencil and figures that to date the squadron has
something like 514 D.F.C.'s and 2,570 Air Medals coming. It will
indeed take a riveter to put in all the stars. At the moment there
are only three D.F.C.'s, about five Air Medals, and a couple of
green Commendation Ribbons in the whole squadron. It doesn't
seem like a hell of a lot for the three hundred-odd ships and the
forty airplanes we've destroyed.

I am more morbid. I tally up the dead. Of the 180 flying members of the squadron who made up the crews when I joined a
little over twenty months ago, 119 are dead. Eleven complete
crews plus fragments, among these Ed Werner who was killed by
a bomb on the ground at Morotai, the only man who didn't die
in an airplane.

Roger has a fifth of bourbon with him and we go down and sit
on a big rock by the ocean to kill it and feel very sad. The moonlight shines on the South China Sea as it never did in a Conrad
story, and out there along that golden road is where everybody
will meet some day when they call us in. Even Segrave and he is
down thirty thousand feet at the bottom of the Manila Deep, far
lower than he ever went high in a B-24.

Neely and I spend almost a month on Mindoro. The war is
rapidly moving north and petering out, only the people at Clark
are bagging anything. There are tales of convoys up in the Formosa Straits that are being protected by biplane training planes,

and Jap pilots have been picked up who have less than thirty hours in the air. The Jap radio is no longer careful to keep its Delphic utterances adaptable to the direction of the wind as in the old days and now says only the most startling and irrational things. Women are being trained for the defense of Honshu. Grandfathers are trudging in from the Kuriles to enlist. The Divine Wind program is swamped with applicants.

My last trip is made in sunny cloudless weather and the mountains of Formosa can be seen for a hundred miles, the snow on them lighting the deep blue of the sky above like flood lamps. Near the Pescadores I catch a black dot with the glasses, an airplane, but so far away I can't even tell which way it is going for a long time. After a bit it seems to be approaching us obliquely. It crosses far in front and moves away to our left, and when I think we are behind enough not to be seen easily, I turn after it and push her up to forty-five inches. We pound along and the dot slowly grows in front of us.

I can see now the aircraft is twin-engined. It is not a Betty. Perhaps it is a Frances, in which case we can sneak right up behind it and stick our guns up her behind, for a Frances has no tail guns and poor visibility aft. I hand Ludwig the glasses and he looks and begins to lobby. It is a Betty and one of the new ones with the powerful tail stinger, he says, and I shouldn't get too close. I don't think straight, I listen to him. The Betty has certainly seen us, I reason, and is going like hell and we don't seem to be gaining as much as we were. I am using up my gas at a tremendous rate and by the end of the chase will have little left. The thing to do is fire carefully at long range and slow them up with a few hits. We are just in range.

I give the word to shoot. The bow and crown fire. For a moment the tracers arc by the Jap and nothing happens. Suddenly there is smoke from both his nacelles and he falls off on his right wing. I whoop. He is obviously hit although I don't stop to wonder by what.

In the next second the Jap is flat on the gray green of the sea and pulling away at a speed that must be over three hundred. He zigs left, zags right, and is up, climbing vertically and rolling and then back down at us, bow on. The smoke was merely the pilot shoving it in auto-rich.

It is an Irving, a very fast twin-engined fighter with a good man in it. He had no way of seeing us and we could have come right up behind him. He was merely flying along at his cruising speed which is almost the same as our top. I feel like a fool but I haven't time to worry about it because he is coming for us. I go low but he goes lower and only the bow can fire at him. It is so quick the bow gunner gets off just one short burst. But the Irving's cannon are winking all the way in. Something hits us. He goes under, skimming the water, and when I turn I see him going away toward China. In a moment he is only a speck again. The Jap has hit us once, the shot striking the bombardier's window and blowing the nose wheel tire before going out through the bomb bay door.

I am furious with Ludwig, and then with the people in the refueling area over toward Balintang because they are reading a spare parts list on the VHF channel we are supposed to use to report things like this. Someone is droning, ". . . item twenty-seven, item two seven, carrier arresting hooks, mark nine maud two, repeat carrier arresting hooks . . ." I can't get in. I rave and curse on every channel. Nothing. Beaver Base has the floor and they aren't giving it up. So I chew out Ludwig and tell him he has cost us the first Irving in squadron history.

Of course it is my own fault. But this was no typical Jap canary paralyzed by fear of the cat. I might easily have become just another painted cherry blossom on the side of the Irving, especially if he had seen me first.

When we land everybody sits aft to take the weight off the blown nose wheel tire, but it is no strain. The next morning Neely and I leave Mindoro and fly back to the island. The first people I meet are Whitey Nanos, Hartstene and Zalewski. They are on the gassing detail at the strip, sent back for a month as punishment. It was that or a real nasty General Court, Hartstene says.

Whitey says they came into school a little bit too noisily and teacher sent them out to try it again.

Otherwise it is scarcely the same island. They have cut the road straight through the palm grove with horrible carnage and the tents are all gone. Half a mile from the grove along the road, baking in the sun, are rows of huge Quonsets, each holding about twenty people. 420's part of the camp looks like a housing project at Pacific Beach. They have grass planted outside their huts and handsome signs indicating just about everything. A painted stake with a huge javelin-shaped board nailed to it is planted outside their operations hut. It has the squadron number in gold and the words "Blue Raiders," mysteriously enough in red. The street has a name too. It is modestly called "Murderers' Row."

They have fitted the walls of the photo lab with outside glass panels and 420's exhibit of photography is quite impressive. Norton is of course in almost every non-combat picture. In one he is pointing to a new meatball being painted on his airplane, in another going through that ancient demonstration of something aerial with the hands, in yet another he has poked his head through an enormous flak hole in someone's wing. In each picture he makes a face of evil rapture. Under the pictures are newspaper captions which Ahab has obviously written himself, full of compelling and colorful words that carefully underscore his name and fame. "A pilot of the Navy's renowned 'Blue Raiders' gets a 'well done' from the skipper of this crack outfit, Commander Joe Norton, USN."

My embarrassment with 400 is just as acute. We have become as Hollywood as our neighbors. Besides the green suits and painted leather jackets, we have acquired ball caps from the St. Louis Cards. Captain Lester has personally devised a squadron scrimshaw, a denatured Jap mortar shell with a denatured brass fuse, which is being mass-produced by artisans in the tin-bender rates, one of whom has already lost a finger when the fulminator cap accidentally went off in the toy he was working on. The copper *bourrelet* around the base of the shell is adorned with a

rather heady inscription by Lester for his parvenus. The words
Leyte, Iwo, Luzon, Okinawa, Bornea (and space to add Japan)
are etched in longhand, and the squadron number painted in yellow against the black of the casing. It is a fine trophy, menacing
and polished with its two tones of copper and brass, and its red
and black paint. There are plans for yet a new jacket emblem
and a volume history of the squadron taken from our War Diary.
Passage and Barker are busy all day typing up recommendations
for awards. Down at the field Libs are as rare as Sikorsky
"Grands." There are only three left, Neely's, mine, and the Fat
Cat. Everything is now Privateers.

In the evening of my return I duck Yoke and Roger and walk
down to where the windy old road enters the palm grove. It is
already choked with vegetation, like some bayou long since sev-
ered from the stream, but it is easy to charge my feelings, the
reminders are plentiful. Here, where these yellow file cards are
scattered in the dirt, was operations, where Stevens sat and
daubed his face with ready smiles for the Captain. Here sat the
unspeakable McCord, mortifying his flesh with quick salutes and
nimble bounds to his feet when rank approached. There, next
door, was Monty Herbert's domain. Monty has gone too, but there
he rolled his maps and fiddled with his packets, and from here set
out, with a last pluck at his puffy overseas cap, to go and sit
nervously in the fringes of power. He believed it all and believed
in it all, the bulging ships and roaring airplanes and piled dumps
and long-billed khaki caps on intense seamed faces.

In this corner of earth we sat so many nights to be briefed. I
belched paregoric while Ashton attacked as hard as he could the
deceitful valor that was always around us but never with us.
"Now men, you will seal yourself into this self-disintegrating war-
head and will be fired from the main battery of the *South Dakota*
at zero two hundred hours, arriving in Tokyo at approximately
zero two oh three hours. Remember, that's Zebra time and don't
be late. And while you are with us let me remind you that the
showers to the west of the Wing Quonset are off limits. You are
of course permitted to use the carabao wallow to the east of . . ."

Ashton giving the benediction: "Fight on there every valiant soul, and courage, Engelson comes!"

Bartlett giving the benediction: "They left the peaceful river, the cricket field, the quad. The shaven lawns of Oxford, to seek a bloody sod . . . they left the sands of Texas, the roaches and the crabs, the shaven whores of Z street, to seek a cure for scabs."

Here we stood and trembled waiting for the trucks. Here stood Dougherty. Here once stood Bartlett and Mara and Spurlock and Andretta and a whole lot of guys whose names I hardly knew. They climbed into the truck and never came back. They sang about the Golden Gate in forty-eight but they will not make it that year or any other.

I wander along the road poking in the rubble where the tents once stood. There is a chessman that belonged to Mara. There the rusty hatchet with the broken handle that Beppo used to throw at trees. He said that he could kill a Jap with it if the Jap would oblige him by standing at exactly six and a half feet distance from him, or, if he'd rather, at eleven feet. At those ranges the blade was facing forward as it rotated through the air, and would stick in something.

Where our tent stood there is nothing left but the broken seat of my old chair and a piece of clothesline, white and rotting, still stretched between the trees. I sit down in the chair and let the drops of sweat run down my back and into the towel tucked around my waist. Around me the air seems to sigh with loneliness, and the reek of canvas and creosote and perishing plants comes to hang in folds about me, like the odors of some battered nosegay. I can almost sniff them singly, in layers, the way you might eat a parfait. At the bottom is that old added fragrance we always get when the breeze blows northeast, a sweetly blown corruption said to be the dead Japs they bulldozed in to make the base material for the runway. Or perhaps it is from the hulks in the airplane graveyard this side of the field. There is an odor about a hulk where men have burned that is like no other, not the lush smell of death itself, but a thin, sanitary one, perhaps like the dry and bloodless smell around an electric chair. A hundred of us died down there and were trussed up in ponchos. How many more were burned, drowned, eaten elsewhere, up to a thousand miles from here?

For a moment I am terribly sentimental and want to weep. I love the dead. I love them more than the living because I feel their fellowship, their staunchness, their valor, even their humor, things they can never again lose by being alive. I felt it long ago as a child when my great-grandfather walked with me by the lake in Albert Lea and told me of the dead at Gettysburg. He had a picture of some of them, men from the Third Minnesota, some of them comrades of his from Freeborn County. They seemed sublimely animated, lying there with their knees up and their faces turned discreetly away from one another. It was as though after a regimented death they were insisting on some final privacy. The old man had been there and I wished always that he had marched into the mystery and fascination of that picture and I didn't have to see him now with his ruined face, the drain of his memories so plain upon it, and listen to his efforts to express himself to a small boy disintegrate into a few feeble gestures and a mumble from an angry old man. So long ago . . . I can't remember the names of the boys, Carl.

I took Corinne to Gettysburg and found the exact place of the picture. She was patient about it, but *living* dead were too abstract for her. It's a little silly, Carl, you wouldn't have liked the county men any more then than you do now.

I get up. It is nearly dark. I have the feeling standing here that I am rushing into oblivion along with all of this. Were there really values around me somewhere in this desolation that were epic and will never find expression again? Are they lost? I do not feel lost so much as wasted. I was never needed and so many of the things we were all called on to do and that killed us were unnecessary. Our lives trickled away, the death rate averaged about ten a month, and yet no one I knew could say why those who had died were really required to die, and what purpose their dying had served. Worse, no one seemed able to remember who had died. It was in some ways such a subtle decimation, despite the violent character of all airplane deaths.

And the blood of others I have shed, will I have to think of that when I am old? Perhaps I have killed a hundred men. We were authorized and encouraged to do it, but a rift has been opened in the boundary of human behavior, and behind it we have reveled and rejoiced in the lightless chaos we have found. Men tumbling from a burning ship, a few, how many, a dozen? Men sinking under their packs, twenty and more in a single picture, black dots drowning. Streaks of fire in the sky, billows of it rolling on the ground. It is quicksand as well as chaos, events sink beneath the surface of time quickly and leave so little memory. We seem to have been living in a vacancy beyond the world and many of us have died there, rather stupidly, in dribbles.

I smell the sweetness strongly as I start back along the road and feel a little immoral about wanting the intrusion of it. A necrophile. A neurotic old woman in a garden.

Perhaps this is my emblematic garden, the bouquet of my life.

CHAPTER TWELVE

"Voiceless they have returned, those heroic souls.
May they rest serene at Yasukuni Shrine, I pray."

THERE are three replacement crews at Samar. They have
come out without airplanes and will be fetched in the Fat
Cat. Since they are for Yokum, Roger and me, at least the
officer portion of them, we will fly it over and they will fly it back.
We are finally on our way.

We spend the day checking out, running around the now com-
plex Wing village with sheets of paper on which various chief
petty officers and supply people will admit that they at least
didn't see us steal a parachute.

I haven't seen Swede Engelson since I got back here but that
evening I get a summons. Poor Swede, his industry has betrayed
him. He has nothing left for victory's final savor. Not a taste of
the steel sides he had hoped for, nothing but the stale story of his
destruction of the pedestrian traffic trickling up and down the
coast. He is still about as unpopular as higher officers, infre-
quently seen and not actually leading, can ever become. He has
organized a thing known colloquially as "Engelson's Revenooers,"
a detail that conducts a nightly search for liquor in enlisted men's
quarters. One of the detail always appears in advance to say,
"Anyone got any bottles? Get 'em out by eight fifteen cause we're
coming by. Listen, get mine out too, will you?" The whole thing

was rendered routinely safe the first night of its existence. Added
to this is Cap Ahab. The Swede is now nearly buried under the
tumulus of publicity that Norton has raised up for himself and his
Blue Raiders, despite their dull performance on the ships from
Singapore. Norton is riding high and the drums are beating in
Congress for him to collect that medal they give out.

When I go in to see him, the Swede and a couple of Wing officers are sitting at a table watching a movie that is being pro-
jected on a screen at the end of the room. The sound is deafening,
it leaps and rasps and crackles from a speaker under the table.
I recognize the film, *"The Amazing Mrs. Holliday,"* starring
Deanna Durbin, a picture not yet shown at the camp.

"Travis, shut it off," Swede says. The whirr of the projector
ceases, the sounds blurt into the bass and die, the lights come on.
On the table is a turkey with a carving knife stuck in its breast.
The Swede sees me looking at the turkey. "It's my birthday," he
says. "I decided to celebrate. I got that from a reefer in the harbor. The movie too." He turns in his chair to face me more
squarely, more man to man. "Iverson, you've been out here with
me a long time, a hell of a long time, and you've done your job
and I just wanted to take this opportunity of telling you this and
wishing you the best of luck. You are going to get the Silver Star,
I can tell you that the papers left here a few days ago and I'm
just sorry I can't pin it on you. But you'll get it from the skipper
at your next base. What are you going to put in for?" He smiles
indulgently as though it will be the most natural thing if I ask to
be retired.

"I don't know, sir. The West Coast if I can get it."

"Good. I'm sure you will. And now . . ." He stands up and
offers me his hand. ". . . all the best and a good trip home. Anything you need?"

Something occurs to me. "Commander, there are three men
from our old crew back here. I guess there in the Acorn. They are
being punished for raising hell . . ."

"Hartstene . . . Nanos . . . somebody else."

"Yes, sir, Zalewski. I just wondered if they have to stay . . . if they couldn't have another chance, now, with me. I mean, go home at the same time."

Engelson looks over at one of the officers who is cleaning his nails with a table knife. "How about that, Jock? As I recall they were to stay on probation for a month."

The officer nods several times, slowly turning his head toward us as he nods. "We can let 'em go," he says as though he is freeing sparrows from a cage.

"You'll have to get up the orders fast. Iverson here is leaving tomorrow."

"I'll give 'em temporary orders and shoot the permanent ones along later," the officer says, nodding his way back to his nails.

We shake hands again. As I leave, Engelson calls to Travis.

"Travis, start her up." The lights go out, the projector whirrs, the voices come back from the edge of doom. I am careful not to slam the door. There may be a dozen ping-pong balls on a table somewhere around.

We say goodbye. There is almost no one to say it to. Neely and Foy are the only people left among even the new boys. Flournoy doesn't count and Brady is careful not to be around. Tom Parker has gone to Samar to a conference and we will probably see him there.

In the afternoon Yoke, Roger and I leave. Since there are thirty men coming back in the Fat Cat, we take no crew. Hartstene acts as Plane Captain, assisted by Zalewski and Whitey Nanos. All three have been busted to seaman second. Two Wing officers are going along en route to Tacloban and that restricts us to mild flat-hatting. I fly and we buzz Iloilo and Bantayan islands because there is supposed to be a Jap radio on one of them that calls to American aircraft to land and pick up passengers and I can pretend I am looking for it. No one calls to us, however, and we make it to Tacloban in two and a half hours. We have planned it so that we spend the night at Leyte instead of Samar, because of the good O Club. Samar is only fifteen minutes in the morning and we can hop over there early to catch the NATS plane.

The O Club is vastly improved. The sign that used to say "East of Tokyo Officers' Club" in simple white letters, is now an ornate thing in gold, with painted palms on a green board enclosed in a fancy spliced rope frame. There is a foyer made of palm fronds and Marsden mat outside where you can scrape the mud off your shoes. Inside, every wall is decorated with extravagant murals of ships and submarines and airplanes, all dealing out furious punishment to the enemy. The bar is twice as long, there are pool tables now, and even a piano.

"You should have been here when I got here, it was really rough," someone says to us as Yoke, Roger and I sit down at the bar. A hand drops heavily on my shoulder. It is McCord. He has on natty shorts with knee stockings like the British Navy, and a freshly pressed short-sleeved shirt. In the shorts his behind looks bigger than ever. "Where are you squirrel hunters bound? Don't tell me you're finally on the way?" McCord is *trying* to be friendly and we *are* going home. We give him big hellos and shake hands all around. What the hell!

"Well, well, so you finally made it!" McCord keeps saying as though he had always considered it particularly unlikely in the case of us three. "What's the news? I heard about Skindome getting it."

"Bartlett too," I say.

"Oh no, Bart bought it too?"

I tell him about it briefly. McCord interrupts from time to time to call instructions to the bartender. This proves he is running the O Club.

"Old Ashton, huh? I guess he can't make *el cheato grande* now for a while."

"Not with a cast up to his crotch."

McCord seems suddenly to have a little trouble remembering the names of old squadron mates. He hesitates as though momentarily stumped. "How's ah . . . what's his name . . . Ironhead? And old . . . you know . . . Frank?" He is trying manfully, for the sake of comradeship, to recall one or two of the more vivid happenings of the "old days," when a commander enters. McCord waves to him, slaps me on the back and tells us to make ourselves at home—and shoves. "Hi, Tom," we hear him say to the commander. McCord settles himself, legs stretched out, fingers entwined on his stomach, at a table stuffed with rank. There is even a captain sitting there.

"Let's see now, where are you guys . . . Little America?" Roger says wrinkling his brow in mock concentration.

"*Who* are you guys?" I say.

"That captain . . . what's his name. . . . Meathead?"

We roll for a drink, the long way, and Roger loses. The bar is filling up fast. Two Army pilots sit next to us and borrow the dice cup, and some officers from the ships in the harbor, their cap braid corroded bright green, stand behind us and bawl orders for drinks to the mess steward bartender.

Yokum looks at their hats and shakes his head. "They must tow those things behind the boat on a string," he says. When Roger tries to pay for our drinks the steward says he will have to get a book with tickets, they don't take cash.

"How do I get one?"

"See Mr. McCord, right over there," the steward says. One of the Army pilots pushes a book of tickets over. "Take what you want out of there. You can pay me the money." He is a captain with a D.F.C. and a bunch of Air Medals and the European ribbon on his shirt. We look automatically at his wings almost before we look at his face.

"Thanks," Smith says. "Knowing McCord you can probably only get tickets every other Tuesday between eleven and eleven oh five or something."

"Don't bitch," the other one says. "You got it by the ying-yang over here." He is a lieutenant, tall, with red hair and a big bony face.

"You should see our place," the captain says.

"Where is that?" Roger is counting out three dollars worth of twenty-five cent tickets.

"Little garden spot called Dagupan," the red-headed one says. "It's gouli-gouli, I'll clue you."

"What are you flying?" I say trying not to sound like a mystic aerial knight.

"Jugs. They got us skip-bombing whorehouses up in Baguio. You break ground, snatch the stilts, drop the load, extend the stilts, spread her on the sand. Time, fourteen minutes and thirty seconds. I've flown a hundred and eighty sorties since we came out three and a half weeks ago." He looks at the captain. "How many D.F.C.'s is that, Branning?"

"I left my bead counter at the base," the captain says dolefully. "Just to think that we could still be sitting drinking those cognacs that won't quit and making le promenade with the cute things."

"Belgian cognac," the lieutenant says winking at me. "Bring them the sugar tonight and they give you the cognac in the morning. You hold it in your mouth and age it."

"Belgian babes. If you bring anything to them in the evening you get it long before morning," the captain says. Yokum begins to look disgusted. It's the same old self-projection game.

"Four hundred and seventy-two miles at about two sixty true," Roger is saying to the redhead who has asked him where *we* are. "No cognac, no dames, just guys pissing in a well." The redhead doesn't get it and nobody explains it to him.

McCord comes back. He stands with one hand on my shoulder and one on the captain's and says to him, "You associate with this riffraff?" He nods at us but smiles to show that we are old friends. Nobody says anything. McCord tries running with the ball again. "You see those murals? Are they jazzy or not? I had to go to Sydney for ten days to get just the right paint." He kisses his finger tips ecstatically. "I met a little girl whose husband was in New Guinea. She hadn't seen him for three years." The Army guys look interested.

"I hear the women are hairy," Roger says. "I hear they have armpits like ether cones. Knock you flat with one whiff."

"This friend of mine has a PT-boat down there running some kind of tests," McCord says concentrating on the Army pilots. "We took about eight dames out on it. Everyone was loaded. This guy went charging around Sydney harbor at about forty-five. The limit is five, I think. Dames were crumped out all over the place. One of them even drove the boat a while. We had to dress them up in foul weather gear to get them back on shore." McCord shakes his head as though he can't believe it ever happened. The captain shakes his head, too, wistfully.

"Sounds like a Brussels orgy, huh Chick?"

"Say Ivy, remember that day we borrowed the jeep at Clark and drove down to Manila?" Roger says. "*That* was fun." He looks earnestly at the captain. "It's about ten pairs of shoes down there, you know. And bumpy? I'll clue you. Yoke here wanted to go dance at the biggest dance hall in the world, or something. We heard it was, anyway. We stopped in San Fernando and bought three eggs for a buck each. The dance hall was burned out. Dewey Boulevard looked like a junk yard. We didn't see one dame. We fried the eggs by the road and drove home. Seventy-five miles each way. Laugh, I thought I'd split. What a time!" Roger shakes his head just the way McCord did.

"Say McCord, are you too cheap to buy another dice cup?" one of the ship's officers behind us says. He has a hook nose and an autocratic voice with a New England accent.

"One of your buddies," Yokum says to Roger. "You can talk East Hyannis Sandwich Port talk with him."

"Captain," McCord says pointing his finger in a friendly but admonishing way at the officer, who is a loot com, "I could go aboard your ship right now and find one dice cup . . . that I know of . . . in the ward room, that belongs to us."

All the officers surrounding the loot com laugh. He smiles and stares at McCord enigmatically. "Would you like to bet on that?" They all look around at each other and laugh some more. McCord looks at his watch and then at the clock over the bar.

"That I can't go down there right now and find one dice cup that belongs up here?" His voice rises all the way to the end of the sentence. "Sure, I'll bet. Providing the ship is here. I can even describe the cup. It's red . . ."

"You didn't say anything about the ship being here," a j.g. says.

"Well, hell, obviously I can't swim to it. Where is it?"

"You'd have to go up to Yonabaru and dive in about twenty fathoms," the hook-nosed loot com says. "We got kamied on Tuesday."

"Jesus, you're kidding!" McCord says looking relieved and solicitous at the same time. "Did you lose a lot of people?"

"Remember Wilson, my exec? He got blown off. And two men. That's all. We were lucky, the fellow hit us wrong."

"Wilson, I sure do, Christ sake, what a shame!" McCord is all sympathy. "I remember how he said he never obeyed the directive to change the eagle on his hat . . . when the navy found out an eagle facing left was a sign of cowardice. Wilson always said he wanted them to know that's exactly what he was, a yellow son of a bitch."

The loot com looks at us. "When are you guys going to get that CAP down cold and stop these guys?"

"We don't have anything to do with that," I say. "We're land-based."

"Patrol planes?"

"Yeah, PB4Y's."

"Well, you can't help us, I guess. But you can stop hindering us. I remember at Okinawa we damn near shot one of your jokers down. Came barging right into the refueling area. Everybody cut loose . . . it's a wonder they didn't splash him."

Roger and I automatically look at Yokum. His face is reddening. We are all nettled by the remarks but traditionally Yokum makes the first rejoinder.

"His name was John Honey," Yokum says, "and he was a real joker and deserved to get shot down, chasing a Betty through the refueling area like that just to keep it from sinking something. Someone was reading a spare parts list on the emergency channel so joker Honey couldn't explain he didn't mean any harm." Yoke borrows segments of several stories in his extremity. It is legal because it is a cinch no airedale ever got straight answers from the seagoers.

"Baloney," the j.g. says looking very stern. "This guy came over above the clouds, no IFF, never answered a recognition signal, nothing, right up to the tankers. There was no Jap involved in it."

"One of our guys damn near blew up one of your plumbers the other day," Roger says conversationally. "A sub. A little matter of being a mere eighty miles out of the sanctuary and not knowing the morning greeting."

"That was Jake Harding in *Yellowfin*," the loot com says to his friends, as though we don't exist. "I talked to him. He wanted to find that pilot and lynch him. They apparently flashed every signal in the book at him and Jake told me they were more than ten miles inside the sanctuary." Now he looks at Roger. "You aren't going to say the navigation officer on an S-boat makes that kind of a mistake."

"No, he must have been right because the airplane guys are always wrong," Yokum says getting really angry. "Only they aren't. The guy who dropped on that sub can DR as well as read and write, and he had a fix on Daito Jima less than fifteen minutes earlier. And I'll tell you something else. That same guy had sunk thirty-five ships and never missed before. That was his first flub."

"He shouldn't have dropped on any sub up there, even if it had a meat ball on the conning tower," the loot com says.

"What did they do, take his flight pay away for a day or two?" one of the other ship's officers says.

"He's dead right now," Yokum says. "Is that enough for you?"

"I hear you guys only fly every third day, and get two off," the stern j.g. says to Roger.

"That's right. We do." The j.g. raises his hands upward as though in despair.

"My God, all that and money too. Mother should have told me."

"You should have checked the post office. They have the ungarbled word," Roger says trying to keep it fairly friendly. But Yokum doesn't want it that way.

"You guys kill me," he says, "with that flight pay gripe. 'Why don't they pay us? We been out seventeen years and stood two million watches and sailed through nine typhoons and been to East Jesus and back five hundred and fifty times.' But the question is, how many guys did you lose on every one of those deals, all rolled into one? I admit, the kamies have changed that recently, but until now? The answer is that until now you haven't lost doodley squat. There's a little extra dimension in there, it's called up and down, and when you're up and something happens, you have to get down. And that is what the pay is for. In a nutshell."

The j.g. jeers. "Oh come on! Sky anchors aweigh! You haven't been up to Okinawa recently, friend."

"I said until now. We lose twenty per cent before we ever see the Japs. Or the Germans." Yokum bangs his glass for the steward to come. I have never seen him so agitated.

"I had it explained to me," the captain says in a sort of umpire's tone. "The extra pay is to attract the best kind of guys. Everybody can't do it, not that we're supermen, but maybe eyes stop you or you just aren't the type or something." Yokum leans away from the bar so obviously disgusted by the naïve complexion his new ally is casting on the conversation, I think for a moment there will be a fight.

"Never have so many been so snowed by so few," the j.g. says holding up his glass.

"Three cheers for the Flying Trojans," the hook-nosed loot com says genially raising his glass too. "I hear they recruit them in groups and give them stirring group names . . . the Flying Badgers or Woodchucks or something like that."

"That's the only way to recruit morons," Yoke says, "with some stuhhing gwoop name. We can't all be on the Harvard sailing team and win a lieutenant commander's letter. What do you call yourselves, the Ivy League Yacht Club Boys?"

"We're a pretty effete bunch, all right," the loot com says. "John here went to Lehigh. Cohane, where did you go, Illinois? I went to Colby and Wilson went to a junior college in Kansas that no one has ever heard of."

"Who went to Colby?" Roger says. "I went to Bates."

"Did you really? Well, I expect I'm a little older than you. I expect you wouldn't know the friends I had at Bates. What class were you?"

"I would have been forty-one."

"Well, you see I was thirty-six at Colby." They are smiling now indulgently at each other.

"Let's not play that game," the j.g. says. "Cohane, I'll roll you to see who pays for a drink . . . and one for the airedales too."

"We'll roll too," Yokum says still bristling. "How's the book holding up, Fatfag?" Roger has six tickets left.

"I got another," the red-headed lieutenant says feeling in his shirt pocket. "We're fat. We'll get in too." We roll endlessly, a game involving up to three rolls per person to decide anything. In an hour we are all fairly drunk. We haven't waited to see who lost before ordering the next round. The conversation goes over into something obscure where each of us mysteriously becomes a senator.

"The senator from Illinois has the floor," someone shouts, and the one called Cohane says something which, under the circumstances at that moment, seems terribly funny. When he is through he gives "the floor" to the senator from Massachusetts. Roger enacts his last night at home. He is with his girl in a car and each time he starts to unbuckle his belt his wrist is seized in a grip of steel (his own) and forced onto the bar. "Hold me, just hold me," he moans. "Don't spoil it now." We laugh like lunatics. "If you can just get it out," Roger says frowning seriously, "you know she'll fall on it like a Notre Dame end recovering a fumble. But when they know all the breaks and holds . . ."

There are two Army nurses sitting nearby with two commanders. We lean back occasionally to look at their legs. The nurses look a little old and bulky and the tendons around their ankles show through their stockings. Still, one of them isn't bad and they both look pretty knowing. Men lurch up to them with drinks in their hands and are eventually crowded out by other men—all except one who has squatted by the chair of the good-looking one and thrown an arm across her lap. He looks up at her seriously and every now and then she laughs and rubs his blond crew cut with her glass while she takes a good look around. The two commanders are talking animatedly to each other. One talks and the other takes his cigar out of his mouth and stares at the sodden end of it while he listens, and then they reverse the process.

We are listening to the senator from Pennsylvania and in the middle of it Roger nudges me. Yokum is sitting on the arm of the good-looking nurse's chair. There are unmistakable telltale signs that he is making some kind of hit. A few minutes later they leave. The nurse doesn't even say good night to her commander but she rubs the blond crew cut once more on the way out.

"She's telling him to be a good boy," Roger says. "I know. That's where I always am, sitting on the floor and people telling me to be good when I haven't a chance to do anything bad."

About midnight I go to the transient hut and feel my way down the row of sacks until I find an empty. The sheets are swept back and rumpled and someone has just gotten out of the bed so I lie on top of them, drunk but fastidious. My ears ring and I haven't had anything to eat and I am depressed by the long hours of masculine barroom diversions. After a while I scuff off my shoes and go to sleep.

Sometime later I hear a loud voice. "Now hear this. All officers and men of the Y-41 report to the dispensary on the double. They found leg make-up on the captain's ears again." It is Roger, hopelessly drunk. There are curses and yells from every corner of the room. "All right, all right, if you want the awful-awful. You know what happened to the mate . . . the pogey-bait mate." He is stumbling around looking for a place to lie down.

"There's always one wherever you go," someone says in the dark. "Ulithi, Maug-Maug . . . *Jeesus!*"

"It's probably the same one," another voice says. "Are you a skinny bastard on Reedholm's staff?"

"The mate got his head caught in a porthole," Roger says coming closer. "I know where Maug-Maug is . . . where is *Jeesus?* All right, let's get those people moving forward there . . ." He trips and falls heavily against a bed.

"I hope to God you broke your neck," someone says fervently.

"Rog, are you okay?" I say. "Come down further. There's probably an empty sack here somewhere."

"Rog, are you okay?" a voice says mockingly. "My God, who would care?"

"You know that gash hound Yokum is misbehaving, Ivy?" Roger says floundering toward me.

"Go to bed!"

"Knock it, for the love of Christ!"

"Well, he *is*," Roger says aggrievedly. He seems to have found an empty bed. He grunts and his shoes thud on the floor. There are groans and more curses after each thud. At last the room is quiet again except for snores. I can't sleep. I think about Yokum and what he is undoubtedly doing. In retrospect the nurse seems prettier than she was. Her rather bony face and angular shape melt into attractive curves in my imagination. I try to picture myself going over to her and saying something calculated to get me somewhere with her—on an island where there must be ten thousand men. It makes me tense and my mind fills with fantasies about the nurse and about Corinne. It is strange, at the moment the nurse seems almost as desirable as Corinne. A trick of the libido. I hug the pillow and try to pretend it is Corinne's lap. Just to get the hell out of this all-male society, to live among the fragrances and softness of women, away from leather shaving kits and rumpled jockey shorts and sweaty smells. I go into a reverie where Corinne and I are way off somewhere on a sunny hill, hidden in tall grass, where it is impossible for a man to be within a mile of us. After a while to get more distance I change it to a boat . . . we will rent a boat and go cruising. Corinne will never be fully clothed at any time and I will slip in and out of a green nylon flying suit, and the boat will never rock, nor will the wind ever blow hard. The images become striking, vivid . . . but there will *be* no Corinne. I roll in vexation, the pillow falls on the floor. God damn Roger.

In the morning Roger is sick and doesn't want to get up to eat. I prod him at intervals until at last he sits up. "Where's Yoke?"

He looks up and down the rows of beds. All the people have gone.

"Come on, we have to get over to Samar or someone will get sore."

"Still shacked up," Roger says smacking his lips experimentally. "What an operator. What a horrible night. If I open my mouth real fast it'll crack like a pistol. You going to eat?"

"Sure."

"Okay, wait a sec until I get some water on me." He finds a used towel on one of the beds and goes to the shower. I hear him snorting and gargling, running water over his head. "Now for a nice mess of fried Goodyear heels," Roger says blotting the water on his neck with the dirty towel.

Yokum arrives in the middle of breakfast. He makes the most of it, strolling casually along with his tray and pretending he doesn't see us. He even says hello to a couple of people who greet him first. Sort of table hopping at the Pump Room. He has an annoying ability to center himself in the arena and to draw attention and greetings from people, who might know me just as well, but would never say the spontaneous things to me that they say to Yokum. He makes other people say hello first. He seems important without trying to look important. Even walking along now with his tray and that droopy gait of his and his mouth open, he gives the impression that he is somehow outstripping everyone around him.

"Well, he got in," Roger says in tones of motherly disgust. "That insipid smile tells the story." Yokum comes up, gives a startled little grimace when he sees us, and still saying something to somebody over his shoulder, slides into a chair. He frowns as if totally perplexed.

"Where the hell you *been?*" he says. "We've been down at the strip ready to go since seven."

"Uh huh," Roger says sawing a piece of Spam. "Sure you have."

"Ready to roll, but one big sow belly always holds up the task force."

Yokum begins to eat his Spam with relish, dusting it interminably with salt and pepper, playing the well-balanced fellow, sip-ping and chewing and wiping his mouth, until Roger can't stand any more.

"Okay, lover, describe the evening."

Yokum sips, wipes, sips. "Well, there's nothing to tell. After you guys disappeared I sort of wandered around . . ."

"Tell us just one thing . . . did you or didn't you?" Roger is almost desperate.

Yoke raises his knife. "Tut, tut! All the gentlemen are honorable, and all the ladies virtuous. I thought you learned that at the trade school, Smythe."

I am curiously indifferent to Yokum's accomplishment and really no longer jealous of his windfall. My mood has altered completely. I can remember the same transition taking place almost daily when I worked part of a winter in Chicago. I would ride the I.C.C. in the morning with nothing but disinterest in the hordes of white-faced women sitting or standing in the train, stupefied by the motion they seemed, the very same women who were infinitely attractive and for whom I yearned on the way home from work only the night before.

We catch a ride down the dusty hill, change from the truck into a yellow jeep and start hunting for the Fat Cat. It is a job to find it. There are hundreds of aircraft in the revetments, parked along the strip itself and even on roads that are not part of the Tacloban field. In the air there is a swarm, landing and taking off in both directions in what seems a precariously meshed procedure. We watch some Corsairs landing to the south at the same time that two R4D's are taking off to the north. The Corsairs make double S-turns on the approach to weave between the R4D's. Once on the ground they roll with their tails in the air to get clear in a hurry. Along the water, wrecked airplanes lie in distorted heaps where they have been pushed or scraped, their tattered skins peeling upward from the carcasses, cables like raw tendons sprouting through the rents. There are a couple of ours in that billion-dollar junkyard.

Hartstene, Nanos and Zalewski are already there, lying in the shade under the wing. There are also three officers who want a lift to Samar. They are new-looking and self-conscious and appear to be already dubious about the airplane with its shabby paint and "puttied up" turrets. They have hats with shiny metal eagles on them and camera cases over their shoulders.

Hartstene gets up from the ground and comes over to us. "Did you check it?" Yokum says negligently.

"I counted some rivets. There are four engines. I didn't think we ought to kick the tires today. They might bust." Hartstene grins. Yoke ducks under to climb in, making rallying motions with his hands. I climb up last. It is Yokum's take-off and Roger's landing. The last they will make in 400. I sit in the waist with Whitey Nanos and while we are waiting we make up comfortable seats and back rests out of the parachutes that are piled everywhere to accommodate the thirty returning people.

Yoke is in a hurry. He taxis like a madman, runs the engines up two at a time while rolling, doesn't bother with the turbos. It is a reaction to flying the Fat Cat. It is stripped of everything and so light that everyone feels completely safe in her.

As we wait for the tower, one of the officers comes aft and squats beside me. "The skipper sent me back here. He said it might not fly with everyone up front."

"It'll fly," I say. "Grab a chute and make yourself comfortable." I point at one hanging from a bungee cord above his head. At that moment Yoke barrels out on the runway and still turning applies full power. There is enough centrifugal force to sling the officer flat on the deck. He starts to get up, grinning at me. But there seems to be a rather unusual oscillation. He can't get up. The airplane bows and bobs on the nose wheel and swings back and forth. We are going quite fast.

Without warning the motion becomes violent. We tilt backward and forward in seesawing arcs. For a moment I think the controls are locked but I can see the rudder fin on my side moving freely. The officer is smiling in a bewildered way, trying to steady himself with his hands. Then there is a wrench and a terrific crack and we are plowing through parked airplanes. Behind my back I feel the bulkhead twisting. There is a vicious snap and the tail

section tilts, goes high in the air and falls back again. We are free
from the rest of the airplane. I scramble toward the dusty light,
dive into it, fall a long way down landing on my shoulder. I take
off on all fours as the blast I have subconsciously anticipated goes
off behind me.

It is not a big fire as fires in airplanes go. There were only seven
hundred gallons in her. But it is enough to burn the airplane up
with a little left over to trickle through the sand and give it that
magic effect that the sand is dancing.

Eight of the nine people that were in the Fat Cat walk out of
her after she has stopped sliding and bouncing. Five come out
through orange flame as though through a door. People come
running and grab these five and roll them on the ground and
throw sand on them to put out the fires in their clothing. All of
the rescuers get painful burns themselves because there is a roving
quality about a fire feeding on gas and oil, and the flames seem
to attach themselves to your hands.

We climb—even the five who are burned black and whose flesh
hangs in strips—into the bed of a truck that has beaten the am-
bulances to the scene, and head for the Army hospital. The rest
of Leyte seems unmoved by the accident, planes continue to land
and take off in both directions, some of them flying through the
pillar of black smoke that has drifted out over the downwind leg.

I look around me in the cruelly bouncing truck. I can't tell who
is who among all these hideous cadavers except for Whitey Nanos
and the officer who was aft with us. We have only burns on our
hands and necks and some cuts and bruises. The others look like
blobs of scorched gingerbread with here and there a patch of
white underwear clinging by a seam or the collar of a flying suit
with the zipper hanging down like a chain. It is strange that when
they speak their voices sound as normal as ever.

At last I see. Yokum is missing. That one there is Roger. I know
him when he smiles at me. His "longhorn" mustache is burned
away. I try to tuck the blanket around him but he winces with
pain. The actual sear of the fire he does not feel in such deep
shock, but the slightest touch

There is no question in the minds of the Army doctors. Everyone's future can be mathematically computed. It depends entirely on the square inches of surface area that have been burned, and of course the degree, which here is irrelevant. All the burns except those like mine, which are the result of touching others, are of no particular degree except fatal. Hartstene is burned the worst. He will die this afternoon around five o'clock. Zalewski and the two officers will follow him at certain intervals. Roger will last . . . until early tomorrow morning.

Tom Parker flies over from Samar. He finds that Roger has a broken arm and a concussion, but there is no point in bothering him about that. "The problem is in keeping the liquid in," Tom says. "The serum runs out through the damaged tissue." He talks about paraffin coats and other "war techniques," none of which he says are really effective.

I sit beside Roger who is in the end bed in the row of figures. They are all bandaged beyond recognition and connected to glucose and plasma rigs. All are under deep sedation. There is a nurse for each and Roger's nurse turns out to be Yokum's friend of last night. It is obvious she doesn't know who we are or what has happened to Yoke and I don't tell her.

Roger wakes in the late afternoon. His face is covered with cloth but the tiny part I can see is as full of expression as ever. He can see me and he makes a little flopping motion with one arm, shaking his tubes, and tries to look down his chest to see what's happened to him. He shakes his head and swears softly, Roger's usual protest when things take an improvident turn. The bandages extend several inches in front of his face.

"What did you do to your nose?" Roger says.

"Just cut it a little bit."

"I'm glad you got out."

"We were lucky in the waist. It broke off."

"Yoke didn't make it. I know he didn't."

"No, he didn't get out."

"I was surprised. I would have bet he would be . . . he would have got out of anything."

"Me too."

"He'd collapse if he knew he was the only one . . ." Roger chuckles through his bandages. The nurse leans over him making tiny adjustments to things here and there.

"You must keep quiet. Save your strength. You'll be on your way home soon," she says in her nurse's voice. Roger is looking out through his tunnel at her.

"My God," Roger says. "It is, isn't it?"

"Yeah, it is," I say. The nurse pretends she is not confused.

"It is," she says. "Now please don't talk."

Roger is silent for a few minutes. Then he says, "The gear caved in. I guess it was an oleo. I can't think what else it could have been." Silence for a moment. "So near and yet so far," Roger says with a sigh of disgust. I don't know whether he is aware that he is uttering something significant, or if he is thinking about Yoke, or if it is just a cliché. He falls asleep.

Hartstene dies at twenty to six without waking up. Zalewski goes an hour later with a tearful Whitey Nanos telling him to the end that he'll be out pitching softball before he knows it. The officers die too. They bring me a cot and I lie beside Roger. My burns are now painful and my shoulder hurts. Tom Parker gives me some pills that ease the pain and make me doze. The nurse tells me each time I come to that Roger isn't suffering. It finally becomes a standard thing. I start up every few minutes and bend over to make sure Roger is breathing; she rises and bends beside me. "At least he isn't suffering," she says.

"Thank God for that," I say.

When I am awake I try to remember if I made the usual propitiations to God and nature before the take-off. I decide I did not. But God is indifferent anyway. I laugh silently thinking that all we ever asked of God is a safe take-off every third day. Heaven is only the place where there are no more engine failures and no more fires.

Down the room they are taking somebody away. One of the middle beds. Roger is awake and shakes his tubes gently. The nurse comes quickly over. She seems thinner and darker and terribly strange to me now, standing there over Roger.

"Do you have pain? I gave you some more sedation only a little while ago. You should go right back to sleep."

"Where is the doctor?" Rogers says thickly.

"He was just here. Everything is all right."

Roger makes a slight tip with his head. "Did someone die?"

"Of course not. Why do you think that?"

"That bed they're moving." The nurse shows her confusion now with a frantic batting of her eyes. Perhaps Roger can't see her. I make pushing motions at her with my hands.

"They took one of the boys to another room, that's all," the nurse says.

"They disconnected the hoses," Roger says. It sounds as if he almost giggles. "You could have told me he was still in the bed, I can't see down so far, but I can see the hoses. I'd have believed you if I couldn't see the hoses." He sleeps again. Tom Parker comes and goes but there is nothing to be done.

At two o'clock we are alone in the room, the nurse, Roger and I. The others have been removed. I am quite dopey and fight against falling asleep, but I seem to glide in and out, along the edge of a huge boiling black cloud. Yokum is flying us somewhere and I keep telling him to keep the wing tip out of the cloud and he keeps telling me not to attract the attention of the nurse. I can see her. She seems to be sitting at the end of a short alley and I can look from her to the cloud and back, from the radiant daylight above the big black cloud to the disk of orange light behind her head, and I giggle and check from time to time to see that she is still there with her head down and looking at whatever it is she is looking at. And while we ride the edge of the cloud and feel the tiny jars as we flick through tendrils of it, I wait patiently for an emotion to emerge, for the thing that governs this lonely and inexplicable flight along the cloud bank. I think of Corinne but the passion for her has become a ghost. I try to feel something, anything, loyalty to the squadron, to Ironhead, to Ashton, to feel the flight harmonized with some effort or duty involving them, but there is none. Memory is necessary and I cannot summon it. The only thing I can remember is that Roger Smith is around somewhere and may be dying.

I voice a string of obscenities, verbalizing irritation in the only way we know, trying to treat this slithering, illusive, dramatic nonsense with the disrespect and derision it deserves. Clouds, for the love of God! Now don't romance me! For one second I halt it, the disguises drop away. There is the nurse and by God she is reading and here in this room I know so well . . . in a moment I will have it, it is all rushing back into my head. I swear, lashing at the perplexities in my head, seeing them reeling backward, knowing I am gaining. God damn Tom Parker, to do this to me.

The nurse is bending over Roger. She is feeling him here and there with her hand, being careful not to muss the sheet that is turned back in neat folds on his chest. I struggle up from the cot. I know I must lean close. We both lean close, our mouths open, our eyes fixed on each other.

The slight noise that Roger makes dying is almost lost in the clamor of an airplane taking off.

THE AUTHOR

As somebody said, I was born in New Jersey and came to this country two years later. I grew up in Southern California in the twenties and thirties. In 1925 the dirigible *Shenandoah* flew over our house at five hundred feet. There was a big earthquake the same year. That was about it for the twenties. In the thirties I went to military school and spent a couple of years at Princeton. There I was, back in New Jersey. I went down to 90 Church Street in New York City and joined the navy. It was 1939 and I had wanted to become a pilot ever since seeing Errol Flynn and David Niven in *The Dawn Patrol*.

When our war started, I was sent to fly patrol-boats and hunt U-boats, down around Trinidad and British Guiana. There were dozens of them but we were too slow to get to them in time. We attacked twenty-six in the early part of 1942, claimed them all as sunk, and found out later that we had actually gotten one!

During 1943 I flew a very fast twin-engine land-based bomber called the Ventura. It was a scary year. A lot of people got killed flying that plane and I was happy at the end of the year to go to operational training in the *Liberator*. I flew them for the rest of the war, about twenty months in North Africa first, and then in the Pacific. *Goodbye to Some* is the story of the time spent out there. I was pretty senior but it is harder to write from anything like an eminence—you lose the leverage on so many things you want to say—so I wrote the book from the perspective of a younger junior pilot. I flew eighty plus operational missions all together. After the war I flew commercially for ten more years, some of them with American Airlines.

I wanted to live in Europe and for about five years I did, in Austria and Switzerland, mostly because I had become addicted to skiing. I wandered around, went to India, to East Africa, where I almost stayed, and to the Soviet Union where I didn't come close to it. My kids didn't like it in Europe so we came back and settled in Colorado.

At age forty I went back to school, to Berkeley, to Michigan, and to Colorado, assembling a bachelor's degree in Russian and studies of the Soviet Union.

I have lived in or near Aspen for more than thirty years, and though I ski very little I have everything else that I like in these mountains. For fifteen years I played trumpet in a local jazz band—traditional jazz and Dixieland. The best of times, until one band member Made It Big in New York, a second was killed in a car wreck, and a third moved to L.A. and got married. Those of us left behind could never decide which of these fates was the most tragic. Playing was the most fun I ever had and I wished I had started earlier. My chops were pretty low range and I was several years older than anyone else in the band but I had some times, and some sweetheart gigs.

I have translated some German things and am translating the works of a popular German writer into English. I am also a sometime-speaker of Spanish and am the "official" interpreter for the small town police department where I am an officer, also sometime. I do these things in lieu of crossword puzzles or playing Yahtzi.

I am married to a lady twenty years my junior but she is an awfully good sport about it. We have lots of kids between us. I have thirteen grandchildren.

GORDON FORBES
1989